CURSED
BY THE
SHADOWS

VERONICA HOPKINS

Copyright © 2025 by Veronica Vincenti

All Rights Reserved

ISBN: 979-8-218-77605-3

No part of this publication may be reproduced, distributed, or transmitted in any form or by any means, including photocopying, recording, or other electronic or mechanical methods, without the prior written permission of the publisher, except as permitted by U.S. copyright law.

The story, all names, characters, and incidents portrayed in this production are fictitious. No identification with actual persons (living or deceased), places, buildings, and products is intended or should be inferred.

Cover art by Veronica Vincenti

PROLOGUE

I shouldn't have been here. I told myself that over and over, every whispered warning scratching at the back of my mind. But I couldn't stop, couldn't turn back. Something was pulling me forward, something I couldn't name but felt deep in my chest, clawing at the edges of my resolve. It wasn't just curiosity—it was something deeper, darker. A need. A truth waiting just out of reach.

I had been warned about places like this, about stepping into the unknown with nothing but hope and defiance. Stories whispered by trembling voices spoke of forces that didn't forgive, that didn't forget. Forces that watched, waiting for a single misstep to draw blood. Forces that thrived on fear. But warnings had never stopped me before. They wouldn't stop me now.

As the first snowflakes began to fall, my journey through the labyrinth of my own mind was set in motion. I would soon face the shadows of the past, each step drawing me closer to the truth. Some relics are not meant to be unearthed, and some stories are better left untold. Yet, in the face of darkness, there is always a glimmer of light, a beacon of hope that guides one through even the most treacherous nights.

This was wrong. All of it. And yet, as the whispers clawed at the edges of my thoughts, pulling me deeper into the encroaching blackness, I knew I couldn't turn back. The truth was here, waiting, buried in the shadows. Whatever had brought me here—whatever had pulled me away from safety—it wouldn't let me go until I had found it.

I didn't know what I was searching for. But I knew I couldn't leave without it.

Welcome to Rockport, where the past never truly dies, and the future is forever shaped by the shadows of yesterday.

CHAPTER I

Echoes in the Shadows

I had always felt a strange connection to my grandmother's old house, though I haven't been here in many years. Every story and photograph painted vivid images in my mind, making the place feel oddly familiar. One stormy night, I found myself standing in front of the house, but I couldn't remember how I got there in the first place. The surroundings seemed familiar, yet unrecognizable. The once bright and welcoming house was now enveloped in a thick fog, and the air was heavy with an eerie silence. I hesitated but felt compelled to step inside. As I crossed the threshold, the door creaked and closed behind me with a resounding thud.

The interior was dimly lit, shadows flickering in the corners of the rooms as if they had a life of their own. I felt a chill run down my spine, and my hand instinctively reached for the necklace I wore—a silver chain with a glowing ruby pendant. I felt a warming yet very unsettling feeling in the hand holding the pendant, and it was almost like it was burning through my skin.

As I wandered through the house, the shadows seemed to follow my every move. I heard whispers, barely audible at first, growing louder with each step I took. The voices were insistent, demanding.

Give us the necklace they hissed. *It belongs to us.*

Fear gripped my heart, but I clutched the pendant tightly, refusing to let go. The rooms became a maze, each turn leading me deeper into the house that seemed to stretch endlessly. Familiar objects appeared, yet their placement was wrong, adding to the unsettling feeling of the space. The shadows grew closer, their dark presence becoming more tangible.

Shadows danced around me, whispering my name in voices that sent shivers down my spine. I tried to run, but my feet felt as though they were sinking into the ground. The shadows grew closer, and one particularly large figure emerged, its eyes glowing with a malevolent light.

Iris it hissed, *You cannot escape us.*

I tried to find an exit, but every door led me back to the same room. The whispers turned into screams, echoing through the halls. The shadows reached out, their cold fingers brushing against my skin.

I woke with a start, my heart pounding in my chest. The room was cold, and I realized I was clutching the pendant tightly in my hand. Shaking off the fear, I tried to convince myself it was just a dream. The shadows, the whispers, the endless maze—they had all been figments of my imagination, remnants of a nightmare.

But as I looked around the room, I couldn't shake the feeling that something was off. The eerie silence still hung in the air, and the fog outside the window remained dense and impenetrable. Despite the unease, I took a deep breath and decided to explore further, hoping to find some clarity or an explanation for what I had just experienced.

"It was just a dream," I whispered, my body shaking uncontrollably. "It was just a dream, you're okay, Iris, you're okay…"

As I sat up in bed, sweat trickling down my forehead, I couldn't shake the thoughts of the nightmare and its increasing recurrence over the past few weeks. Each night, the dream grew more vivid, more demanding, as if the house and its shadows were calling to me, trying to draw me back into their grasp. The pendant's faint glow was a constant reminder of the sinister presence that lurked just beyond my awareness. I felt a strange connection to it, an inexplicable bond that defied logic and reason.

I tried to calm down as I felt myself gasping for air and the dryness building up in my throat. I decided to go to the kitchen and get an ice-cold glass of water. Every step I took was cautious, the floorboards creaking softly under my weight. The pendant, now seemingly ordinary, continued to glow faintly, guiding me through the dimly lit corridors. The necklace had this eerie yet familiar feeling attached to it, and it held secrets I could no longer ignore.

"Why did I have to go to that shop in the first place?" I said to myself.

Memories of the night I bought the necklace began flooding back, bringing with them a wave of unease that I wished I could forget. The feeling it evoked was one of regret and dread, and I often found myself wishing that I had never stepped into that shop. Yet, despite my aversion, there was something about the necklace that held me captive, an inexplicable connection that I couldn't quite grasp.

I had always been drawn to antique shops, the allure of old trinkets and forgotten memories pulling me in. One overcast afternoon, while wandering through the narrow streets of this small town, I stumbled upon a quaint little shop I hadn't noticed before. The sign above the door read "Whispering Antiquities." Curiosity piqued, I stepped inside.

The shop was dimly lit, the air thick with the scent of aged paper and varnish. Shelves lined with relics from bygone eras surrounded me, each item whispering its own story. But it was a necklace that caught my eye. Delicately crafted, with an intricate silver chain and a pendant that housed a deep red ruby, almost the color of blood. The necklace seemed to shimmer in the low light.

"Ah, I see you've found our most mysterious piece," came a voice from behind me. I turned to see an elderly shopkeeper with piercing blue eyes that seemed to see right through me.

"It's beautiful," I murmured, reaching out to touch the pendant.

The shopkeeper nodded slowly. "It is, and it comes with a story—a dark one. They say whoever wears this necklace is plagued by vivid nightmares. Some believe the ruby holds the memories of its previous owners, both their dreams and their darkest fears."

I hesitated for a moment, but the allure of the necklace was too strong. Ignoring the shopkeeper's warning, I decided to buy it.

That night, as I lay in bed with the necklace around my neck, I felt an unexplainable chill. The room seemed darker; the air heavier. I closed my eyes, and soon, sleep took me. The dreams began almost immediately. At first, I would find myself in a vast, desolate landscape, the sky an ominous shade of red, and then my grandmother's house would appear, hidden in the thick clouds of fog that start to form every time I get closer to the main entrance. The rest is history.

As the days turned into weeks, the line between reality and the dream world began to blur. The shadows crept into my waking hours, their whispers echoing in my mind. The same questions repeatedly roam in my head: why does this keep happening to me? What did I do to deserve it? Will the nightmares ever stop? I knew that I had to confront the darkness, to face the malevolent force that sought to claim the pendant—and perhaps my very soul. I just couldn't do it.

The next day, I awoke with hopeful expectations for the future, only to find out how misguided I had been. It was a bitterly cold winter morning in Rockport, a town nestled in the far northeastern corner of the county, in the state of Massachusetts. My feelings towards this place were conflicted; there was a charm in its picturesque setting, with quaint downtown shops, delectable local seafood offered by charming little restaurants, and sandy beaches that reflected its coastal nature. Many would deem it the perfect retreat for relaxation. Yet, for me, this small fishing village held nothing but the bleakness of what I had lost. I longed for the perpetual warmth of my previous home, the companionship of my friends, and most of all, my father—or at least, the memory of him.

Three years ago, my mother decided we should move to Rockport, her hometown, after my father's passing. Her excitement was palpable; she wanted me to experience the place where she had grown up, a town I barely remembered, as the last time I visited, I was merely five years old. The impression of never returning lingered until now.

"You're going to love it here!" she exclaimed with enthusiasm.

"I'm sure I will, Mom," I replied, attempting to dispel thoughts of everything I was leaving behind.

"Honey, it's for the best. You know neither of us could've stayed in that house after what happened," she said, her voice trailing off into a whisper as she uttered the last words.

What happened... I wasn't entirely sure I wanted to stay there anymore. The remainder of the ride to our new home was spent in silence, my thoughts consumed by past events. Memories of my friends often surfaced, yet I tried to stay positive for my mother's sake. If she was happy, then perhaps I could be too. Still, I struggled to refer to this place as home.

I finally decided to get out of bed, still shaken by the nightmares that haunted me the night before. Pushing them aside, I got ready for the day. After graduating from school, I moved into this little yet charming apartment just a few minutes from downtown. Today, I had a long shift at the café, and even though I wasn't looking forward to it, the thought of meeting my friends afterward kept me going—they were my lifeline.

Dressed simply, I chose plain dark jeans, a white t-shirt with lace on the sleeves, my signature Converse, and, of course, the necklace I couldn't seem to take off. I loved wearing white as it contrasted with my dark brown hair. As I stepped outside, the crisp winter air greeted me, and I made my way through the quiet streets of Rockport. The town was slowly waking up, and despite my inner turmoil, I couldn't help but notice the serene beauty that surrounded me.

The morning rush was in full swing, the cozy chaos of The Velvet Brew humming with the sound of espresso machines and the low murmur of conversations. The café's name glinted proudly on the sign outside, catching the morning light as customers filtered in and out with steaming cups in hand. I threw myself into the rhythm of it all—the clinking of mugs, the swirl of milk in lattes, the familiar shuffle of feet across the tile floor. It was a comfort, in a way, letting the routine drown out the darker corners of my mind.

But no matter how hard I tried to focus, my thoughts kept slipping away, drifting back to the pendant resting against my chest and the dreams that had shaken me to my core. They clung to me like shadows, refusing to fade. I had to figure it out—whatever "it" was. I just wasn't sure if I could. The question lingered, heavy and sharp: Was I ready for the answers I might find?

A tap on my shoulder jolted me back to reality, pulling me out of the swirling shadows in my head. Tessa stood there, her auburn hair cascading over her shoulders, her smile bright but laced with concern. She was my favorite person to work with—her presence was like a warm ray of sunshine breaking through the cloudy haze of my thoughts.

"I've been trying to get your attention for *five* minutes," Tessa said, crossing her arms with mock frustration. "What's going on in that little mind of yours? You were in your own world."

I blinked, shaking my head to clear the lingering fog. "Hey, Tessa. Sorry about that. I haven't been sleeping well."

Her playful demeanor shifted as she leaned closer, her voice lowering with worry. "Are you okay? You look awful. Seriously, have you seen the bags under your eyes? Do you need to, like, see a doctor or something?"

I couldn't help but smile at her bluntness—classic Tessa. "I'm fine. Just tired, that's all. I'll feel better as soon as the shift is over."

She didn't look convinced. Her amber eyes softened, tinged with sadness as she studied me. "You know I can cover for you, right? It's no problem."

"It's okay, Tessa," I said quickly, determined to deflect her concern. "Don't worry too much. I'll survive."

She frowned but nodded reluctantly. "Just don't overwork yourself, alright?"

"Promise," I said, forcing a smile. The truth was, I wasn't sure if I *would* be fine, but Tessa didn't need to know that. The last thing I wanted was for her to think I was losing my grip on reality.

Tessa was an energetic whirlwind, her presence a burst of sunshine on even the gloomiest days. Her long, auburn hair cascaded in waves, framing a face that seemed to perpetually wear a cheerful expression. She had the kind of warmth that drew people in, making them feel instantly at ease. Her laughter, a melodic sound, could often be heard ringing through the café, spreading joy to everyone around her.

Beyond her vibrant exterior, Tessa possessed a depth of empathy that was rare to find. She had an uncanny ability to sense when something was wrong and never hesitated to offer a listening ear or comforting word. It was this trait that made her not just a coworker, but a true friend. She had been there for me countless times, her support unwavering, her loyalty unfaltering.

Even now, as I battled my own demons, Tessa remained a beacon of light. Her genuine concern for my well-being was evident in every word, every glance. And though I was determined to shield her from the darkness that plagued me, I couldn't deny the solace her presence brought.

With Tessa's encouragement echoing in my mind, I pushed through the remainder of my shift. The café buzzed with the usual rhythm of clinking cups and murmured conversations, but today it felt heavier, like I was trudging through quicksand. Every smile I gave customers felt forced, and every interaction left me drained, as though the weight of the necklace and the nightmares had sapped all my energy.

As the hours dragged on, I couldn't shake the feeling that something was... off. The shadows in the café seemed darker, deeper, like they were holding something just out of sight. The ache in my temples grew sharper, my movements slower, and even the comforting hum of the espresso machine felt unnerving.

I forced myself to continue working, wiping down tables and rearranging chairs, yet the sensation of being watched lingered. Each time I looked up, I half-expected to see a shadowy figure lurking just out of sight. My mind raced, and I found it increasingly difficult to concentrate.

As I reached for a dishcloth, my hand brushed against the pendant hanging around my neck, the cool metal sending a shiver down my spine. The connection between the pendant and my unease grew stronger with every passing moment. Was it possible that the object held some malevolent power, or was my mind playing tricks on me?

In the midst of my internal turmoil, a customer approached the counter, snapping me back to reality. I mustered a smile and took their order, my voice steady despite the turmoil within. But the questions remained, haunting me as I moved through the motions of my shift. What was the source of this unease, and why did it feel so intimately tied to the pendant?

I paused briefly, then excused myself from Tessa and walked towards the bathroom. As I navigated through the crowded room, my mind wandered, distracted by thoughts of our previous conversation. Suddenly, my face hit something hard, causing me to fall to the ground. Dazed and bewildered, I looked up to see a hand that was lazily hanging over me. The realization of the impact began to sink in as pain shot through my forehead. Onlookers gasped and murmured, and I could feel their eyes on me as I tried to regain my composure.

I took the stranger's hand and stood to thank him. As I looked at him, my heart froze. He was very tall, with light skin that had a hint of warmth, almost like a subtle glow under the dim lights of the café. His dark hair was neatly styled, framing a face that was both striking and stern. What caught me most were his eyes; they were a paradox, appearing as warm as coffee yet cold at the same time, reflecting a depth that seemed to hold countless secrets. His features were chiseled, with high cheekbones and a strong jawline, exuding an air of quiet strength and an enigmatic aura that made it difficult to look away.

"Thank you," I attempted to say, but my words came out hesitantly.

He held my gaze, "No problem," he murmured, his eyes seeming to delve deep into my very essence, as though he was searching for secrets buried within. Slowly, his gaze drifted downward to my collarbone, where the pendant hung. The sense that the necklace was throbbing, almost alive, intensified with every passing second. A frown creased his brow, adding a layer of mystery to his already enigmatic presence.

"Just be more careful next time," he said, his voice firm yet laced with a curious undertone. With that, he walked away, leaving me standing in a mix of embarrassment and inexplicable attraction. There was something about him, an energy that drew me in, a sense of danger that I couldn't ignore, yet I felt powerless to walk away.

I made it to the bathroom, looked at myself in the mirror, and understood why Tessa would be worried. My reflection stared back with a tired, worn-out expression. I observed dark bags under my eyes, starkly highlighting the toll that sleepless nights had taken on me. It was clear that the lack of sleep over the past few weeks, ever since the nightmares began, was affecting me significantly. The vivid and unsettling dreams haunted my nights, leaving me restless and drained by morning.

My skin looked pale, and there was a noticeable slump in my posture, as if the weight of those haunting visions pressed down on me even in wakefulness.

But one thought troubled me—it wasn't the necklace. The man's stern, smooth voice echoed in my ears, reverberating through my mind like a relentless drumbeat, trapping me in a trance I couldn't escape. His words were like a dark spell, weaving through the corridors of my consciousness, growing louder with each passing moment. It was as if his icy gaze had pierced right through me, leaving an imprint that refused to fade. My surroundings blurred into obscurity, overshadowed by the overpowering weight of his presence. Every beat of my heart mirrored the intensity of his lingering voice, creating an unending symphony of dread that kept me captive within my own thoughts.

"I'm losing my mind," I said to my reflection. "Get a grip, Iris. You just met him and don't even know his name!" But why did he seem so familiar?

Tell me, Iris, the voice murmured, weaving its way through the shadows of my mind. It wasn't loud—it didn't need to be. Each word dripped with menace, like venom sliding off a blade. *Do you truly wish to know who he is? The truth, Iris. He scared you, didn't he? That chill running down your spine, that ache of dread in your chest.* The voice lingered for a moment, heavy and suffocating. *If you value your life, stay away from him. Some doors are better left unopened.*

The sound of the voice echoed deep within, cold and sharp, slicing through my thoughts. My eyes widened in pure terror. For a fleeting moment, I clung to the notion that my mind might be unraveling, deceiving me with illusions. But the truth stared back at me—my reflection in the mirror, pale and haunted, the beads of sweat trickling down my forehead, and the eerie, pulsing glow emanating from the necklace around my neck. They told a tale far more chilling than my imagination could conjure.

I took a deep breath and summoned every ounce of courage I had left, staring into the mirror and bracing myself for the unknown.

"What do you want from me?" I felt on the brink of madness. "I don't know who you are or why you torment me, but please, just leave me alone!"

Suddenly, a chilling laugh echoed throughout the room, bouncing off the walls with eerie resonance.

"Silly girl, you will never escape us. You will never escape me." The voice seemed to linger for a moment, then vanished into silence, leaving only the haunting sound of laughter reverberating through the bathroom's cold tiles and echoing in the empty spaces.

Though I had survived another day, the unease lingered, whispering that the real challenges were yet to come.

CHAPTER II

The Pendant's Weight

After the incident in the bathroom, my mind was filled with thoughts of the unsettling voice that had mocked me earlier and images of the enigmatic man I had encountered. My shift eventually concluded, albeit feeling endless, and I proceeded to the counter to finish for the day, hanging up my apron as I approached the café door.

As I was about to leave, Tessa hurriedly came from behind the counter to catch up with me.

"Hey, Iris!" she called out urgently. "Go home and get some rest, okay? You'll need your energy for tomorrow!" Despite her attempt at optimism, there was a palpable sense of concern behind her kind words. I turned around and smiled, trying to reassure her so she wouldn't worry anymore.

"I will, Tess, thanks," I said, sounding more fatigued than convincing. "I have to run some errands, but I'll be here bright and early tomorrow."

As I stepped out into the cold night air, the weight of the pendant around my neck felt heavier than ever. Each step echoed the turmoil within me, a mixture of fear and determination. I knew that retreating into the safety of my apartment wasn't an option that would bring me peace. Answers lay somewhere beyond the shadows, and I needed to confront them head-on.

The shadows in the corners of the café seemed darker, and every creak of the floorboards felt amplified in the quiet that followed the closing rush. I couldn't help but glance over my shoulder, the weight of an unseen presence pressing on my mind.

Out of the corner of my eye, I thought I saw someone staring at me. I quickly turned, but no one was there. Am I experiencing a hallucination? My heart pounded in my chest as I tried to refocus on the task at hand, but the unease gnawed at me. The café's familiar surroundings suddenly felt alien, the faces of regular customers blending into a blur.

Lost in my thoughts, I was jolted back by my phone ringing. The sound pierced through the silence of the room, making me jump. As I reached for my phone, a notification appeared on the screen, casting a small glow in the dim light. Panic set in as I read the message.

"Shit! I forgot I was meeting them!" I slightly shouted, noticing I was late, reprimanding myself for not remembering. I unlocked my phone to see a text from Jayce.

Iris, where the hell are you?

Luna and I are so worried about you

We'll wait for you...just please text me back

I felt guilty for not noticing the text and began responding quickly while walking through the empty streets and alleyways near the café. The cool evening air hinted at the approaching night, and the distant hum of traffic was the only sound breaking the silence.

Guys! I'm so sorry! I'm on my way now.

I got caught up at work.

With urgency fueling my movements, I started speedwalking through the poorly lit streets. My heartbeat quickened with every step, the pendant's weight a constant reminder of the secrets I needed to uncover. The cool air nipped at my skin as I navigated through the labyrinth of alleys and lanes, avoiding people and keeping to the shadows.

As I hurried across the street, I could see Jayce and Luna's concerned faces through the bakeshop's window. Their expressions softened slightly as they noticed me approaching. I pushed open the door, the warmth of the shop contrasting sharply with the cool night air outside. The familiar scent of freshly baked goods was a brief comfort.

"I'm so sorry for being late," I said, sliding into the chair beside them. "It's been a crazy evening."

Jayce's eyes narrowed as he took in my disheveled appearance. "What happened to you?"

I took a deep breath and recounted the events of the past hour, the weight of the pendant heavy against my chest. Luna listened intently, her brow furrowed with concern. When I didn't respond, Jayce was the first to speak.

"May I assume that you did not sleep again?" he inquired with a firm tone, clearly confident in the accuracy of his observation, irrespective of any explanation I might give them.

Luna glanced between Jayce and me, then placed her hand on his. He seemed to calm down as she turned to me.

"We're just worried about you, hon," she said softly, smiling. "We don't know what's going on, but we see you're not sleeping well."

"She's right," Jayce added, looking into my eyes. "Sorry if I sounded harsh. We love you. You seem tired and rarely leave your house. We miss you, Iris, and want to help."

My heart fluttered with happiness at their words. How fortunate I was to have such steadfast companions in my life.

The loneliness that had once enshrouded me when I first moved here, with only my mother for company, had dissipated like morning mist after meeting Jayce and Luna on a desolate beach.

It was a day that seemed pulled from the pages of a novel. The sky wore a somber gray coat, with clouds drifting languidly overhead. I had wandered to the beach, seeking solace in the waves that crashed rhythmically against the shore. The emptiness of the landscape mirrored the void within me.

I first spotted Jayce standing near the water's edge, his tall and athletic frame silhouetted against the ocean. His dark hair tousled by the wind, he exuded an air of quiet strength and determination. His piercing green eyes scanned the horizon with a contemplative intensity, hinting at a depth of thought and an unwavering resolve.

Beside him stood Luna, petite and graceful, with a cascade of auburn curls that danced in the breeze. Her bright blue eyes sparkled with warmth and curiosity, a stark contrast to Jayce's solemn demeanor. Luna's gentle smile and the way she seemed to radiate kindness immediately drew me in, her presence like a beacon of hope in my solitary existence. They were deep in conversation, their connection palpable even from a distance. As I approached, Luna's eyes met mine, and she beckoned me with an inviting wave. The moment felt surreal, as though fate had orchestrated our meeting. We exchanged introductions, and it wasn't long before their genuine warmth and easy laughter dissolved the barriers of my loneliness.

Jayce, with his pragmatic and protective nature, always seemed to have a plan, a solution for every challenge. He was the rock, the anchor that steadied our little trio amidst life's tempests. Luna, on the other hand, was the heart and soul, and her empathetic disposition and boundless optimism were constant sources of comfort and joy.

Together, they had become my lifeline, their unwavering support and love filling the emptiness that had once consumed me. We've been together ever since. Now, as I sat in the cozy bakeshop with them, their concern for my well-being touched me deeply.

"I love you," I said, my eyes filling with tears. "I'm sorry, I've been so stressed."

They exchanged a concerned glance. Luna approached and embraced me in a warm hug, which I returned.

"I didn't know work was so tough for you! I'll sort them out!" Jayce joked, making us all chuckle. He leaned back in his chair with a mischievous grin, clearly enjoying his role as the group jester.

"It's not too bad, really. Tessa keeps me company since you two aren't always around doing God knows what," I joked, wiggling my eyebrows at them. Luna pretended to be offended, gasping dramatically as Jayce laughed at her reaction. "Oh, come on, love birds! You know I'm just kidding," I added with a wink.

Jayce shook his head, still chuckling, "You better watch out, or she'll make you pay for that one." Luna crossed her arms and put on a mock stern face, "Indeed, I might just have to teach you a lesson about teasing your friends."

We all burst out laughing, and the camaraderie and light-hearted banter made the evening feel even more delightful. Moments like these reminded us of the strong bond we shared. Luna curled up beside me, seemingly content with the lively atmosphere.

The conversation kept us up all night. We talked about everything, from funny moments to random stuff that happened during the week. It was one of those nights where you lose track of time because you're having such a good time sharing stories and laughing together. I refrained from discussing any issues related to my sleep disturbances or the necklace. It became apparent to me that the pendant had felt unusually light and silent earlier today, following the conversation with the internal voices, shortly after my interaction with the individual I refer to as the mystery man. My thoughts were interrupted by Luna speaking loudly to Jayce.

"I'm not watching that, Jayce. And I doubt Iris wants to see... that either," Luna said with a dramatic roll of her eyes. Jayce looked puzzled and a bit taken aback by Luna's reaction.

"Come on, babe. You used to love horror movies! And I'm sure Iris would be up for it. Right, Iris?" Jayce said, hoping to light up his eyes.

I was amused by the interaction and thought about joining in on the fun. Suddenly, an idea sparked in my mind, and I cleared my throat loudly enough to catch their attention. Both Jayce and Luna turned to look at me, their faces curious. I grinned, feeling a surge of excitement. I glanced between them before speaking.

"How about we watch something else?" I suggested, trying to steer the conversation away from horror movies. The reason? It was pretty obvious.

Jayce raised an eyebrow, clearly intrigued by my sudden interest. "Got any suggestions, Iris?"

I thought for a moment before replying. "How about a mystery or a thriller instead? Something that keeps us on the edge of our seats without scaring us to death."

Luna nodded eagerly. "That sounds perfect! I could definitely use a good mystery to distract my mind."

Jayce chuckled, leaning back in his chair. "Alright, mystery it is. But remember, Iris, you owe us one horror night soon."

Luna whipped her head around to face Jayce, annoyance flickering in her eyes.

"She owes you a horror night. Don't even think about dragging me into that again—count me out!" Luna declared, punctuating each of the last three words with exaggerated emphasis. Her glare left no room for debate.

Jayce held up his hands in mock surrender. "Alright, alright! Relax! Jeez. So, tomorrow work for movie night?" he asked, glancing between us with a hopeful grin.

"Works for me," I replied with a shrug. "My shift ends early anyway, so I'll just meet you guys at the theater after work." I shot a glance at Luna, who still looked a little miffed.

After a moment's pause, she sighed dramatically. "Yeah, fine. It's good with me, too," she said, her annoyance softening.

"Then it's a plan!" Jayce declared, his excitement bubbling over. Turning to Luna, he added with a playful smirk, "Pick you up tomorrow?"

She rolled her eyes, but a smile broke through. "You're my only ride, dummy," she said, her voice laced with affection. The lingering tension vanished as Jayce leaned in to give her a quick peck on the lips.

"Ugh, gross!" I groaned, feigning disgust and pretending to gag. "You know, I might need to get myself a boyfriend just to survive these hangouts."

The three of us laughed, and for a moment, everything felt light and uncomplicated—just the way it should be.

Luna suddenly turned to me, a mischievous glint in her eyes. "Speaking of boyfriends," she said, dragging out the last syllable with a teasing smile. "Who was that guy with you before you walked into the bakery? You didn't even say goodbye—so rude!" She let out a laugh, but it faltered when she caught the confusion plastered across my face.

"Who are you talking about?" I asked, genuinely perplexed. "I came alone."

Now it was Luna's turn to look bewildered. Jayce stepped in, glancing at her with an eyebrow raised. "Babe, are you sure you saw someone? I didn't notice anyone earlier."

"No, no, I'm sure. I swear I saw a tall guy right next to you. He was... handsome," Luna insisted, her expression shifting from certainty to mild unease. "And he didn't take his eyes off you."

Her words sent a ripple of fear through me. Someone had been following me, and it wasn't my mind playing tricks on me. Why me? Why now? The necklace—it had to be the reason. What other explanation was there for someone to shadow me during what was already the worst week of my life?

"Well, that's... odd," I managed, my voice shakier than I'd intended. "It's funny you say that because something really weird happened at work today." My attempt at humor fell flat; even I could hear the underlying terror in my tone. Slowly, I recounted the unsettling encounter with the mysterious man at the café and the uneasy feeling that had lingered long after I'd left.

By the time I finished, the air between us felt heavier—like whatever had happened to me wasn't just strange. It was something much worse. Something none of us could ignore.

I felt a strong sense of familiarity towards that man. When I saw him, I felt like I knew him from somewhere, and it made me feel curious and interested. Although I did not understand why, his presence was highly compelling. There was something about the way he looked and moved that grabbed my attention and made me want to learn more about him.

However, I did not want to see him again.

"First the nightmares, and now I'm being followed? None of this makes any sense!" I burst out, frustration bubbling over as I paced the room.

"What nightmares?" Jayce asked, his tone suddenly serious, the concern etched into his face impossible to miss. "Is that why you haven't been sleeping?"

I froze. I hadn't meant to let that slip—my sleepless nights and haunted dreams were the last things I wanted them to worry about. But as their expectant gazes locked onto me, I realized I couldn't keep this to myself any longer. They were my best friends. If anyone deserved to know, it was them.

With a heavy sigh, I turned to Jayce. "It started when I bought this necklace." I reached for the pendant hanging around my neck and held it up to the light. Its beauty was captivating, almost otherworldly—a beauty so intense, it felt like it carried the promise of my undoing.

Luna's eyes widened in recognition; her voice tinged with disbelief. "The one you bought a few weeks ago? From that little shop downtown?"

Her question hung in the air, and for a moment, I wondered if they would believe what I was about to tell them— or if I even believed it myself.

"Yes, that one," I confirmed, my mind drifting back to the day I purchased it. The shop had been quaint and filled with curiosities, and the pendant had caught my eye immediately. I had felt an inexplicable pull towards it, a compulsion to make it mine.

"Since then, my dreams have been filled with strange, unsettling images," I continued. "I keep seeing my grandmother's house surrounded by fog, and I'm always being hunted by someone…or something. And now, it feels like those dreams are spilling into reality. I keep seeing the same man everywhere, and I can't shake the feeling that they're watching me."

Luna's expression was frozen in disbelief, her wide eyes searching mine for any hint that I might be joking. Jayce looked equally unsettled; his brows knit tightly together, his fingers nervously fidgeting with the hem of his sleeve. Neither of them said a word for a moment, letting the weight of my confession hang in the air.

"I… I don't even know what to say," Luna finally stammered, her voice quieter than usual. "That's—terrifying."

Jayce nodded, his gaze locking onto me with a mixture of concern and resolve. "Why didn't you tell us sooner?" he asked, his voice steady but tinged with frustration. "I mean, this isn't something you should go through alone. You're clearly scared, Iris."

I sighed, running a hand through my hair as the tension in my chest grew. "I didn't want you to worry," I admitted. "But now… I don't know what's happening. Every time I think about it, it just—it doesn't make sense. And that necklace… it feels like it's pulling me into something I don't understand."

Luna stepped closer, her hand hesitating before resting lightly on my arm. Her eyes softened, though the unease didn't disappear entirely. "Maybe we can figure it out," she said, her voice steadier now. "Together. You don't have to deal with this on your own."

Jayce chimed in, his tone firm. "She's right. If there's something weird going on with this necklace, we'll help you find answers. Whatever it is, we'll face it together."

Their words brought a flicker of relief, but the knot in my stomach didn't ease completely. Deep down, I had a feeling that this was only the beginning—and that whatever I was about to face would be far beyond anything we could imagine.

As the three of us sat at that small table, the silence between us felt charged, like we were on the edge of something much bigger than ourselves. The clock ticked on, but none of us moved. We were waiting—for what, I wasn't sure. For answers? For danger?

I just knew one thing. Whatever was coming, I wasn't ready for it. But I wouldn't be facing it alone. Not anymore.

A voice broke our trance. We looked up to see Mrs. Thompson, the bakery owner. She was a woman in her early sixties, with silver-streaked auburn hair neatly pulled back into a bun. Her eyes, a warm shade of hazel, held a depth of wisdom and kindness accumulated over years of tending to her bakery and the people who frequented it. She wore a simple dress, adorned with a flour-dusted apron, hinting at the day's baking endeavors. Despite the long hours she put into her craft, there was an unyielding grace in her movements and a genuine smile that could soothe even the most troubled soul.

"Hey, kids," Mrs. Thompson called out gently, her warm smile spreading across her face. "I'm not trying to rush you, but we're about to close."

We all blinked, startled by how much time had passed. It felt like we'd been rooted to our spots the whole night, the hours slipping by unnoticed.

I turned to her, a sheepish smile on my face. "Sorry, Mrs. Thompson. We were just catching up and lost track of time. We'll head out soon."

Jayce quickly chimed in, his usual charm on full display. "Yeah, don't worry, we're sorry for bothering you so much. But hey, you know we're hooked on those croissants of yours—I seriously can't get enough!"

Mrs. Thompson chuckled, her sweet demeanor never wavering. "You kids know I love having you here. Don't go making me feel old now, you hear?" She was about to walk away when something seemed to flicker across her mind. Her expression brightened as she turned back toward us. "Oh! I almost forgot—do you kids know about the new arrival?"

The three of us exchanged puzzled glances, curiosity lighting up Luna's eyes. "There's someone new in Rockport?" she asked, leaning forward like Mrs. Thompson was about to spill the juiciest gossip.

"Who in their right mind would move here of all places?" Jayce quipped, his words punctuated by a quiet laugh.

His amusement was cut short as Luna swatted the back of his head with a dramatic roll of her eyes. "Show some respect," she said, shooting him a glare before turning to me as if looking for backup.

I shrugged and offered a small smile. "You know I don't mind, Luna. Don't be so hard on him." Then, with curiosity tugging at my voice, I asked, "So, Mrs. Thompson, who's the new arrival?"

She glanced around the room like she was afraid someone might overhear, then leaned in slightly, her voice dropping to a conspiratorial whisper. "Well, it seems someone's moved into the old mansion on the hill. A young man. He showed up a few weeks ago, and it's all anyone in town can talk about. I can't for the life of me figure out why anyone—especially someone his age—would want to live there."

The words sent a shiver through me. The mansion on the hill had been abandoned for decades. It loomed over the town like a ghost of its former grandeur, its cracked windows and overgrown grounds the stuff of local legends. And now someone was living there?

"Have you seen him?" I asked, my curiosity flaring like a spark to dry kindling.

Mrs. Thompson shook her head. "Not yet. But I've heard plenty." Her voice dropped even lower, as if the walls had ears. "Rumor has it he's very handsome—about your age, I'd guess—but there's something... strange about him. People say he has this old-world air, like he doesn't quite belong. Polite, sure, but distant. Keeps to himself."

The room fell silent as her words hung in the air, heavy with unspoken intrigue. I could feel the tension crackling between the three of us like static electricity. The mansion. The strange new tenant. It was almost too perfectly eerie, like something out of the kinds of stories I'd been trying so hard to escape lately.

And yet, a part of me—the part that never seemed to learn—felt drawn to it. Maybe it was just morbid curiosity. Maybe it was something more.

"Well… I think it's time for us to head out. I've got work in the morning," I said, my voice heavy with exhaustion. My body felt like it was begging for sleep, and I silently hoped tonight would be the night I'd finally get some rest. Just once.

Luna blinked, snapping out of her thoughts. "Oh, yeah, you're right. We should get going, too—it's late," she agreed, glancing at Jayce. He gave her a small nod, his usual energy dimmed by the hour. "See you tomorrow then?" Luna asked, her gaze shifting to me.

I mustered a tired smile, trying to inject some enthusiasm into my reply. "Of course! It's movie night—I wouldn't miss it," I said, hoping to reassure her.

She stepped closer, wrapping me in a warm hug that felt like a silent promise of support. Jayce followed suit, his embrace quick but comforting. As we exchanged goodbyes, I couldn't help but feel a flicker of gratitude for them. No matter how chaotic my life seemed, they were always there, grounding me in the moments that mattered.

As I walked away, the weight of the day pressed down on me, but their presence lingered—a reminder that even in the darkest times, I wasn't alone. Tomorrow was another day, and for now, that was enough. The old mansion loomed in my mind, its shadow stretching far beyond the hill it perched on. Something about this new arrival didn't sit right, but I wasn't sure if it was intrigue or dread tightening its grip around me. Whatever it was, I had a feeling this wasn't the last I'd hear of him.

CHAPTER III

The Stranger

That night, sleep came reluctantly, like a wary visitor unsure of its welcome. But when it finally claimed me, it wasn't the restless, nightmare-ridden sleep I'd grown used to. Instead, I found myself standing on the edge of a forest, shrouded in thick mist that clung to the ground like a living thing. The air was cool, carrying the faint scent of damp earth and fallen leaves, and the only light came from the silver glow of a crescent moon peeking through the tangled canopy above. Despite the darkness, the scene wasn't menacing—it felt ancient, hushed, like the forest itself was holding its breath.

As I took a cautious step forward, the stillness of the place seemed to deepen, each sound muffled as though the world had been wrapped in velvet. And then I saw him. He stood just beyond the reach of the moonlight, his figure partially obscured by the haze. His presence was magnetic, drawing my gaze despite the shadows that veiled him. There was no menace in his presence this time, no shadow of fear creeping up my spine. Instead, he seemed... calm. Almost peaceful.

He didn't move, didn't speak, but there was something about him—something unearthly and captivating. The dim light caught the sharp angles of his jaw and the faint glint in his eyes, making him look both impossibly beautiful and entirely unreachable. He seemed as much a part of the forest as the towering trees and the mist that swirled around his feet, as though he belonged to this place in a way I never could.

As I stepped closer, I noticed the way the light caught in his eyes, making them seem impossibly deep, like they held secrets older than time itself. He was mesmerizing, just as I remembered. His dark hair was perfectly styled, each strand in place, catching the faint silver of moonlight. His tall, lean frame carried an effortless grace, an air of casual confidence that seemed untouched by the forest surroundings—the mist swirling at his feet, the shadows stretching across the trees. There was something about the way he moved, unhurried and unbothered, that made it impossible for him to look away from—as though he didn't simply exist in this place but commanded it.

Then out of nowhere, he turned around. He didn't speak, but his gaze met mine, and in that moment, it felt as though the weight of the world had lifted from my shoulders. The tension that had gripped me for days melted away, replaced by a strange, inexplicable sense of comfort.

His expression flickered with surprise, his brows knitting together in confusion moments later. It caught me off guard. Why did he seem so startled? This was my dream, after all—or at least I thought it was.

He began to move toward me, each step deliberate and unhurried, the forest around us holding its breath. He stopped just inches away, close enough for me to make out every detail of his face. For the first time, I truly saw him—I appreciated him even more. The sharp lines of his features softened in the shadows, casting him in a light that felt... different. At the café, he had been severe and intimidating, but now he looked vulnerable, like a secret hidden in plain sight.

He didn't speak. He didn't need to. Slowly, he extended his hand toward me, his movements cautious, as if afraid to disrupt the fragile stillness between us. Against all logic, my own hand rose to meet his, my fingers brushing against his palm. The warmth of his touch washed over me, steady and grounding, and suddenly the suffocating weight I'd been carrying melted away.

For the first time in what felt like forever, I wasn't consumed by fear. I wasn't questioning everything. In that moment, I felt safe. And yet, as I stood there in the quiet dark, I couldn't shake the thought—why did he feel so familiar? Why, in this fleeting, impossible dream, did he feel like someone I should've known all along?

The forest seemed to transform around us, its shadows deepening and the muted tones of the night growing more vivid, almost alive. The air thrummed with an unspoken energy, a low hum that sent a shiver down my spine—not of fear, but of anticipation. It felt as though the entire world had paused, waiting for something to break the stillness, some unseen force to set it all in motion. But the moment stretched on, unbroken. We stood there, tethered by the fragile thread of that fleeting touch, suspended in a silence that felt charged with meaning I couldn't begin to understand.

His gaze flickered from my eyes to where our hands touched, then back again. My breath caught, my heart skipping like it couldn't decide whether to race or stop altogether. His eyes were magnetic—compelling in a way that made it impossible to look away. His eyes were unlike anything I had ever seen—deep, piercing blue, flecked with subtle shades of gold that seemed to shimmer, even in the dim light. They were captivating, drawing me in like the pull of a tide, beautiful in a way that felt almost otherworldly.

Then he spoke, his voice soft, almost hesitant, pulling me out of the daze I hadn't realized I was in.

"H-How did you...?" he murmured, his words barely audible, as though he wasn't entirely sure he should be speaking at all.

I searched his face, trying to make sense of the emotions flitting across it, but his expression was unreadable—confusion shadowed his features, and yet, there was something else I couldn't quite place. The air between us felt charged, heavy with questions that neither of us seemed ready to ask.

Then, as suddenly as he had appeared, the mist thickened, swallowing him whole. The forest seemed to exhale, and the sounds of rustling leaves and distant whispers returned, breaking the spell. I was alone again, the weight of his presence lingering like the memory of a touch that had never happened.

When I woke, the memory of the dream lingered like a whisper, soft and elusive. The dream clung to me like the mist from that forest, its details vivid and unsettlingly real. The image of him standing in the shadows refused to fade, and I couldn't decide if his presence had been a comfort or a warning. All I knew was that it wouldn't be the last time I saw him—not in my dreams, and perhaps, not even in reality.

I stared at the ceiling, my heart still steady from the calm I'd felt in that forest. It didn't make sense—none of it did. But for the first time in weeks, I didn't feel like I was drowning.

As the morning light began filtering through the curtains, the world outside felt distant—irrelevant even. I sat up slowly, still clutching its weight, the vividness refusing to fade. The shadows of the forest, the chill in the air, and *him*—everything was so real it sent a shiver down my spine.

I rubbed my eyes and swung my legs over the edge of the bed, my feet brushing against the cold floor. The pendant around my neck felt heavier than ever, like it carried the echoes of the dream. His presence was unmistakable, and as much as I tried to shake the thought of him, it clung to me like an uninvited guest.

The day began like any other, but I couldn't ignore the way everything felt slightly... off. The hum of the coffee machine in the kitchen, the chatter of pedestrians outside my window, the distant sound of a car passing—all seemed quieter, dulled somehow, as if the dream had left me standing in two worlds at once.

I pushed the thoughts to the back of my mind and forced myself to focus. It was still early, but I decided to get ready for work, hoping the familiar routine would help me clear my head. The extra time felt necessary—I needed a moment to pull myself together. A hot shower sounded like the perfect solution. As the steaming water cascaded over me, I leaned against the tiles, letting the heat soothe the tension in my muscles. But no matter how hard I tried, I couldn't shake him from my mind. Every time I closed my eyes, his face appeared, sharp and vivid. The images of the misty forest and his piercing eyes haunted me. They weren't frightening, but their mystery gnawed at me like an itch I couldn't scratch. Who was he? Why did his presence feel both comforting and strange, like an answer to a question I didn't even know I was asking? Was he connected to the necklace? The question lingered, heavy and unanswered, as I tried to wash away the unease. Those sharp features, those piercing blue eyes—they wouldn't leave me. It was as though he was etched into my memory, demanding to be remembered.

With a deep sigh, I turned off the water and stepped out, a towel wrapped snugly around me, the weight in my chest hadn't eased. The bathroom mirror fogged up, but I avoided looking at it, afraid of what I might see staring back. I dried off quickly, hoping that routine could anchor me. I was just reaching for my hairbrush when the shrill sound of my phone ringing pierced the silence. I froze, my heart skipping a beat as I glanced toward the bedside table.

I hurried over and picked it up, glancing at the screen. Tessa's name flashed across it. A frown formed on my face.

"Why is she calling me this early? She's not even supposed to be at work yet," I muttered, suspicion threading into my voice. Swiping to answer, I brought the phone to my ear.

"Hello?" I said, a little hesitantly.

"Thank God you're awake!" Tessa's voice came through the speaker, sharp and panicked, her usual cheerfulness replaced by outright alarm. "It's a disaster, a complete disaster!"

Her panic hit me like a cold wave. "Tessa, slow down. Breathe. What's going on? Are you at work?" I asked, gripping the phone tighter.

"The café!" she cried. "It's upside down—it looks like a hurricane tore through it, and none of us even noticed! Everything's—everything's ruined!" Her voice cracked, on the verge of tears.

"What?!" The word came out louder than I intended, my own concern rapidly climbing as her words sank in. "What do you mean? What happened?"

My pulse quickened as her desperation bled through the phone. Whatever had happened at the café, it wasn't just bad— it sounded catastrophic. Ignoring the chill that crept over me, I rushed to grab my clothes, the necklace brushing against my skin as if reminding me of the weight it carried. Something about this didn't feel right, but I didn't have time to dwell on it. Tessa needed me, and I had to be there.

I moved as fast as my frantic hands would allow, rifling through my clothes without thought. The black AC/DC t-shirt I grabbed was soft with wear, the logo faded from countless washes, but it would do. The first pair of jeans I found was slightly crumpled, but that didn't matter now. I shoved my feet into my black Converse, the laces fraying at the ends, and tied them with a speed that betrayed my urgency. Pulling my hair into a hasty ponytail, loose strands slipping free to frame my face, I snatched up my phone and keys before bolting out the door.

The cool morning air hit me like a sharp slap, sending a shiver up my spine as I sprinted down the street. My breath came in uneven bursts, the pendant bouncing against my chest with every hurried step. The faint hum of distant traffic played in the background, blending with the rhythmic pounding of my feet against the pavement.

As I rounded the corner, the café came into view, its front windows bathed in the soft golden light of the early morning. Tessa stood near the entrance, her silhouette framed by the glass, pacing with frantic movements that spoke volumes about her panic. I slowed just enough to catch my breath before pushing open the door, the familiar warmth of freshly baked goods wrapping around me like a brief moment of reprieve.

Tessa turned sharply to face me, her eyes wild and rimmed with worry. "Iris!" she cried, rushing toward me. "It's worse than I thought! You have to see this."

I followed her deeper into the café, my sneakers squeaking faintly against the polished floor. As I stepped inside, the full scope of the damage came into view. Tables were overturned, chairs scattered as though a storm had ripped through the space. Flour dusted the counters, mixing with the shattered glass from a broken display case, and the air felt heavy—charged, almost.

Tessa turned as I entered, her face pale with worry. "Iris, thank God you're here," she said, her voice shaky. "It—it was like this when I got here. I don't know what happened."

"What the hell happened here?" I whispered, the weight of the pendant pressing harder against my chest, as if it too could feel the tension in the room. My mind raced with possibilities, none of them good, and I couldn't shake the feeling that this wasn't just a random disaster—it was something more.

Tessa's voice broke through my thoughts, shaky and uncertain. "I don't know... I showed up for my shift, and it was like this. Iris, you don't think—"

My eyes darted around the wreckage, my heart sinking further with every broken detail. "Did anyone else see this? Did you call the police?" I asked, my voice low but urgent.

I swallowed hard, the unease twisting in my gut. This didn't feel random. The pendant pressed coldly against my skin as though it were reminding me of its presence, but I shoved the thought aside. This couldn't be connected... could it?

My thoughts were interrupted by the sound of footsteps outside. Both of us turned sharply toward the door, the tension in the air growing thicker by the second. For a fleeting moment, I thought I saw a figure lingering just beyond the edge of sunlight streaming in through the windows, but when I blinked, the space was empty. The bright daylight outside somehow made the unease even sharper, as though whatever had passed by didn't belong in the warmth of day.

"I think we should call someone," Tessa said, her voice breaking slightly.

"Yeah," I murmured, my own voice distant. But even as I spoke, my mind was elsewhere, chasing after a nagging feeling that this was just the beginning. Something was happening, and I wasn't sure I wanted to know what it was. But I had a sinking suspicion that I wouldn't have a choice.

I turned to Tessa, attempting to mask the unease clawing at my chest with a forced air of composure. "Call the manager," I said, my voice steady despite the turmoil brewing inside me. "Tell him we'll have to close for today. I'll call the police."

Tessa gave me a quick, determined nod before darting toward the kitchen, her fingers already tapping furiously at her phone as she prepared to call Mr. Ramsey, the café's manager and proud owner.

Mr. Ramsey was a man of contrasts. On one hand, he was known for his sweet and caring nature, his warm smile making every customer feel like they were stepping into their own home. Yet beneath that kindness was a strict and fiercely protective man—a businessman who viewed the café not just as a job, but as a legacy. He had inherited it from his grandfather, a man he spoke of with reverence, always careful to honor his memory. The café was more than brick and mortar to him; it was a piece of history, built on tradition and hard work.

And now, that legacy was in chaos. I could only imagine the storm of emotions Mr. Ramsey would feel when Tessa delivered the news. He had poured his heart into the place, ensuring that every croissant and cup of coffee reflected his grandfather's vision of quality and community.

As I dialed the police, my mind couldn't help but wander to what Mr. Ramsey would say—or do—when he arrived to see the café in ruins. For all his sweetness, he was not a man who tolerated negligence or disrespect toward the place he called home. I could picture him now, his sharp hazel eyes narrowing as he assessed the damage, his jaw tightening as he prepared to take control of the situation.

The phone rang in my ear, snapping me out of my thoughts. I refocused, gripping the pendant around my neck as though it could anchor me. Whoever—or whatever—was responsible for this mess, I knew one thing for certain: this was just the beginning. And Mr. Ramsey wasn't the kind of man to let the fight end without answers.

The café was buzzing with an uncomfortable energy when Mr. Ramsey arrived, his sharp figure cutting through the tension like a knife. He stepped through the door with brisk precision, his presence commanding the room before he even spoke. Dressed in his usual pressed shirt and neatly polished shoes, he carried the air of a man who knew how to take control. His silver-streaked hair and strong features bore the weight of a man deeply tied to his legacy – The Velvet Brew – his pride and responsibility since inheriting it from his grandfather.

I stood near the counter with Tessa, recounting everything to the police officer who was jotting down notes in his little pad. My hands were clenched at my sides, the pendant heavy against my chest, as I tried to focus on the details. Across the room, Mr. Ramsey surveyed the damage with sharp, calculating eyes, his expression a careful balance of disappointment and resolve.

"Officer," he spoke, his tone steady but firm as he approached, "will this investigation interfere with business operations? My staff tells me we'll need to close today, but I won't let this place stay shut a moment longer than necessary."

The officer gave him a curt nod, glancing at Tessa and me. "That's correct, Mr. Ramsey. We'll need to assess the scene thoroughly before you reopen. It appears there's significant vandalism here, but we'll know more after reviewing the footage."

Mr. Ramsey's jaw tightened, his fingers brushing against the collar of his shirt as though grounding himself. "I see," he said evenly. "Well, I trust you'll get to the bottom of it quickly. This café isn't just a business; it's a cornerstone of this community."

I exchanged a glance with Tessa, who was pale and biting her lip to keep her composure. I didn't blame her—seeing Mr. Ramsey so resolute was equal parts reassuring and daunting. He cared deeply for the café and wouldn't rest until everything was back in order, but his expectations were clear, and we knew the weight of meeting them.

Once the officer finished questioning us, Mr. Ramsey turned his attention to Tessa and me. His expression softened slightly, though the lines of worry remained etched into his face. "Are you two alright? This must've been a shock."

"I'm fine," Tessa replied, her voice small but steady. "It was just... unexpected."

Mr. Ramsey nodded, then turned to me, his gaze steady. "And you, Iris?"

I swallowed, the pendant pressing coldly against my skin, as though it was reminding me of its presence. "I'm okay," I said, hoping my voice didn't betray the lingering unease. "I just want to make sure we figure out what happened."

"Good," Mr. Ramsey replied, his tone firm but not unkind. "We'll need to handle this together. The café may be out of commission for the day, but that doesn't mean we stop working."

Tessa and I nodded in unison, knowing that this wasn't just a cleanup—it was a fight to preserve something bigger than all of us. As the officers began their investigation, I caught Mr. Ramsey's gaze lingering on the shattered display case, his fingers curling into a loose fist.

Something about the sight made my stomach churn. The damage was physical, but the weight in the air—it felt like something more. And as I stood there, trying to shake the feeling, I couldn't help but wonder if this was just the beginning of the storm brewing around me. Whatever was happening, I had a sinking feeling that the answers wouldn't come easily—or without a cost.

The café was still filled with a tense silence as the police officers wrapped up their initial investigation. One of them approached Mr. Ramsey, who was standing near the counter, his stern expression betraying a simmering frustration.

"We'll review the surveillance footage and analyze the scene further," the officer said, his voice professional yet reassuring. "If there's anything unusual or identifiable, we'll be in touch. For now, you can focus on cleaning up and securing the café."

Mr. Ramsey nodded, his arms crossed tightly over his chest. "I'll be expecting updates. This place means a lot to me and this community. Please don't let this fall through the cracks."

The officer gave him a firm nod in return before turning to Tessa and me. "Thank you both for your statements. It might be helpful if you keep an eye out for anything unusual, even outside the café. We'll be in touch soon."

Tessa offered a weak smile and nodded quickly, her nervous energy still palpable. I echoed her response, keeping my expression composed even as my thoughts churned. The officers thanked us once more before gathering their equipment and heading for the door, their voices fading as they stepped into the daylight.

As the sound of their departing footsteps drifted away, the café seemed eerily quiet. Mr. Ramsey let out a deep sigh, rubbing his temples. "Alright," he said, his tone calm but firm. "This isn't the end. We're going to fix this, and I won't let anything jeopardize this place. You both can head home for now—I'll start organizing the cleanup."

Tessa hesitated, glancing at me before addressing him. "Are you sure? I can stay and help."

"I appreciate the offer," Mr. Ramsey replied with a small, genuine smile, the softer side of him breaking through. "But you've done enough for now. Go home, get some rest. We'll regroup tomorrow."

His words felt like an order more than a suggestion, and both Tessa and I nodded, sensing it was best not to argue. As we stepped out into the bright daylight, the tension clinging to us eased just slightly, though the unease in my chest refused to fade.

As I stepped out of the café, I decided to text Luna and Jayce to tell them something happened at work and I'd be headed home for the day to get some rest. I reached for my phone, unlocking it and scrolling until I found Luna's contact.

Hey, I'm going home from work, something happened

They let us go home early. I'm gonna get some rest

Then you guys can come to my apartment to go to the movies.

Not even a minute had passed when I got a reply from her.

Hey babes! No worries, go to sleep.

We'll see you later to get ready.

You need to spill the tea on what happened!

A smile crept on my face as I stared at her text. She was always about gossip, even though this wasn't a good one.

Okay! See you later.

I'll tell Jayce, see you later, hon.

By the time the conversation ended, and I headed home, the streets seemed brighter than usual, the midday sun casting sharp glints off storefront windows and painting the pavement with a gentle heat. People moved in steady streams around me, a blur of chatter and footsteps, but I barely noticed them. The necklace around my neck pulsed faintly, a sensation that was becoming too familiar.

I adjusted the strap of my bag over my shoulder and kept walking, weaving through the crowd with my head down, trying to ignore the strange weight pressing against me. And then, just as I passed a busy corner, I felt it—a shift in the air, subtle but unmistakable. It wasn't threatening, but it was enough to make my breath catch and send a chill down my spine.

For a moment, the world seemed just a beat out of sync, like the shadows around me stretched a little too long, the warmth of the sun faltering against my skin. My steps slowed instinctively, my heart thudding louder in my chest. Whatever it was—whoever it was—I could feel it lingering. Close enough to stir the smallest ripple in the ordinary chaos of the city. And yet, as I glanced over my shoulder, there was nothing. Only the endless crowd and the hum of midday life moving on without me.

Whatever had brushed against my awareness, it wasn't gone—it was waiting. And deep down, I knew I wouldn't be able to ignore it for long.

On the way home, I ducked into the small convenience store just around the corner. I'd left in such a rush this morning that I hadn't even grabbed breakfast, and by now, my stomach was making its dissatisfaction known. I wasn't in the mood for anything fancy or a big meal—I was too drained for that. But as I wandered down the aisles, my eyes landed on my usual favorite: a turkey and cheese sandwich with crisp lettuce and bright red tomato tucked neatly between two slices of golden bread. My stomach growled loudly in anticipation, spurring me forward to grab the sandwich and a bottle of orange juice before heading to the register.

When I approached the counter, I found Ian slouched behind it, his head buried in his phone, tapping at the screen like the store wasn't his responsibility. He didn't even glance up as I set my items down. "Welcome," he mumbled, the monotone delivery making it clear he was reading off a mental script. "Did you find everything okay?"

I raised an eyebrow and crossed my arms. "I don't know how you still get paid," I said, my voice dripping with sarcasm. "The enthusiasm is truly inspiring. Honestly, the customer service here is just... impeccable."

Ian's eyes flicked up from his phone briefly, and I caught the flash of irritation before he sighed heavily. "Iris, just go away," he groaned, his exasperation palpable.

I leaned on the counter, tilting my head with a smirk. "You know you can't kick me out, Ian. You should be thanking your lucky stars that you're even working here." He looked ready to retort, but I didn't give him the chance. "The only reason you're still here is because your mom owns this place, and..." I paused dramatically, watching his jaw tighten. "She loves me."

Ian glared at me, his expression a perfect mix of anger and frustration. "Don't you have anything better to do than ruin my day?" he snapped.

Before I could reply, a sharp slap landed on Ian's arm, making him wince and turn in surprise. "Ian!" Mrs. Davis scolded, her voice firm but not unkind. "Don't be disrespectful! Iris is our most beloved customer, and you know it."

Ian looked at his mother in disbelief before shooting me a glare. I met his stare with wide puppy-dog eyes and an overly sweet smile, leaning into the moment. He groaned loudly before muttering, "Whatever," and immediately buried himself back in his phone.

"Hi, Mrs. Davis," I said cheerfully, turning my attention to the woman standing behind the counter.

"Oh, honey, you know you can call me Mandy," she said with a warm smile, the kind that could make anyone feel instantly at ease.

Mrs. Davis was one of those people who exuded kindness. Her warm brown eyes always sparkled with a mix of humor and genuine care, and the crinkles at the corners of her eyes showed how often she smiled. As the owner of the convenience store—and Ian's mother—she managed to keep the place running with a balance of efficiency and charm. She'd been best friends with my mom growing up, and somehow, even after all these years, it was like my mom had never truly left Rockport. Mandy was the kind of person who made you feel at home, no matter where you came from.

She reached out to pat my hand as I handed her my money, her smile never wavering. "You make sure you eat properly, sweetheart. No skipping meals, alright?"

"Yes, ma'am," I said with a grin, tucking my sandwich and orange juice under my arm. Behind her, Ian rolled his eyes so hard I thought they might get stuck. I didn't care. As I stepped out into the sunlight, I felt lighter, even if just by a little. Some people made the world feel heavier, but Mrs. Davis wasn't one of them.

I dropped my apartment keys onto the dining table, the metallic clink echoing through the quiet room. The soft afternoon light filtered through the blinds, painting uneven streaks across the walls. It was only midday, but I already felt the weight of exhaustion pressing down on me, heavy and unrelenting.

I sat at the kitchen table, unwrapping my sandwich and taking a bite. The familiar flavors of turkey and cheese melted together, but even the satisfying crunch of lettuce couldn't distract me. My thoughts drifted back to the café, to Mr. Ramsey standing amidst the chaos, his jaw set tight, his sharp eyes scanning the damage. If the mess had been overwhelming for Tessa and me, I couldn't imagine what it felt like for him—watching the legacy he'd inherited crumble, if only temporarily. The image stuck with me, lingering like the faint pulse of the pendant against my chest.

Finishing the sandwich, I tossed the wrapper into the bin and shuffled toward the bedroom, each step dragging with the weight of fatigue. The room welcomed me like a quiet retreat, my sanctuary after a day that felt heavier than it should've. I pulled on a pair of soft pajamas, tucking myself beneath the covers and sinking into the mattress. Lying on my back, I stared at the ceiling, one arm stretched above my head, the other brushing against the necklace. My fingers absentmindedly traced the smooth edges of the ruby, its deep red glint catching the soft glow of daylight seeping through the curtains.

The pendant's presence was calming, grounding even, but it held secrets I couldn't begin to untangle. And yet, as my eyelids grew heavier, the urge to question it faded. My thoughts blurred, slipping away bit by bit, until sleep finally tugged me under.

The dream crept in slowly, like the edges of my consciousness dissolving into mist. The forest was back, its shadows deep and sprawling, the air humming with that same indescribable energy. The ruby glinted faintly against my chest, a soft pulse that seemed to sync with the rhythm of my heartbeat. It was familiar, and yet, it unsettled me every time I found myself here.

Then I saw *him.*

He stepped out from the veil of fog like a fragment pulled from my waking thoughts. His movements were measured, deliberate, yet his expression betrayed something I hadn't seen before—a flicker of disbelief that darted across his face when his eyes landed on me. For a moment, I froze, my breath catching in my throat as his gaze searched mine.

"You," he said, the word sharp but layered with confusion.

I swallowed hard, my fingers brushing against the pendant as if it could anchor me here. "Me," I replied, my voice distant, barely audible over the hum of the forest.

His blue eyes narrowed slightly, not in suspicion, but in something deeper—something like incredulity. "How?" he asked, his tone low but strained, as though he didn't expect an answer. "How is this possible?"

I blinked, the weight of the pendant pressing harder against my chest. "You don't know?" I asked, though the question sounded foolish the moment it left my lips. Of course, he didn't know. If he had answers, we wouldn't be standing here in mutual bewilderment.

He shook his head slowly, his dark hair shifting with the motion. "No," he admitted, his voice trailing off like he was trying to work through the pieces in his mind. "I don't understand this."

The forest around us felt alive, the mist curling closer as though it had its own purpose—its own secrets. I wanted to move, to step toward him and demand answers, but the confusion etched into his face kept me rooted where I stood.

"Have you been here before?" I asked hesitantly, unsure of how else to make sense of this.

His lips pressed into a thin line before he responded. "Only when you're here." The honesty in his words hung heavily between us, each syllable steeped in the same unspoken question I couldn't bring myself to ask. I hadn't noticed before, but every word was smooth and measured, yet the distinct twist in his accent made simple phrases feel almost exotic to me.

"This place—it's not real, is it?" he asked suddenly, as though testing the thought out loud.

I wanted to answer him. I wanted to say something, *anything*, that could help us understand why he kept showing up in my dreams, why this forest pulled us both into its shadows. But the truth was, I didn't have answers. The only thing I knew was the feeling in my chest, the weight that told me this wasn't an accident.

He seemed to sense my silence, his gaze flicking to the pendant, the ruby gleaming faintly in the murky light, before returning to my face. His jaw tightened slightly as he stepped back into the mist. "I should've known," he murmured. "I'll see you again," he said quietly, though it felt less like a promise and more like a certainty. "I don't know how... but I will."

He turned his back to me, the mist curling around his figure as he began to walk away, his movements deliberate and unhurried. A sharp sense of urgency clawed at my chest, pulling the words out of me before I could think them through.

"Wait!" I shouted, my voice cutting through the eerie quiet of the forest.

He stopped. His shoulders stiffened just slightly, enough to let me know he'd heard me, but he didn't turn fully. Instead, he tilted his head, glancing back at me with a sharp gaze that sent a shiver down my spine. Those blue eyes studied me for a moment, their depth both unyielding and unreadable.

"What's your name?" I asked the question tumbling out in a rush, my voice steadier than I expected.

For a heartbeat, he didn't move. A flicker of amusement crossed his face, subtle but impossible to miss. Then, the corners of his mouth curved into a small, enigmatic smirk, the kind that made me feel as though I'd asked something far more significant than I intended, one that felt equal parts teasing and cautious, like he wasn't sure whether to answer. But when he did, his words settled between us like they carried something heavier.

"Felix," he said simply, his voice smooth and deliberate. The name hung in the air, echoing faintly. Then, without another word, he turned away again, and before I could respond, the fog swallowed him whole, leaving me alone once again. And as the dream began to dissolve, pulling me back into reality, I couldn't shake the feeling that Felix had left behind more questions than answers—questions that wouldn't stop chasing me, even after I woke.

CHAPTER IV
Reel Revelations

It was already afternoon when my phone buzzed on the nightstand, pulling me from the haze I'd been stuck in all day. A text from Luna lit up the screen:

We're outside. Jayce made me drive again.

Get moving, we're not waiting forever.

I sighed, running a hand over my face as I sat up. I'd been in bed since morning, turning the dream over and over in my head, trying to hold onto every fleeting detail before they slipped away. Felix's face lingered in the shadows of my subconscious, his words replaying like a half-remembered song. I hadn't told anyone about it, and I wasn't planning to—it felt too strange, too personal. And honestly, I didn't even know where to start.

Sliding out of bed, I grabbed a hoodie off the back of my chair and pulled it on, not caring that it didn't match my jeans. My hair was a mess, but I tied it back in a loose ponytail and called it good enough. Grabbing my keys from the table, I texted Luna back.

Door's open, come up.

It didn't take long before the sound of their footsteps echoed in the hallway, followed by the familiar creak of my apartment door. Luna strolled in first, her energy filling the space like she owned it. Her curly hair was tied up in a high bun, and she was already wearing her favorite leather jacket—a sure sign she'd decided tonight was an *event*. She had an incredibly sweet demeanor, but there was also this undeniable diva flair to her that made her absolutely hilarious. Jayce followed behind her, his usual stoic expression intact, though the sight of his sneakers tracking in dirt had me glaring at him.

"Shoes off," I said, pointing to the mat by the door. "Seriously, Jayce, are you raised in a barn?"

He rolled his eyes but kicked off his sneakers, muttering something under his breath about my "obsessive cleaning habits." Luna plopped down on my couch, stretching her legs across the cushions like she hadn't a care in the world.

"You're not even ready?" she asked, glancing at me with mock horror. "Iris, what have you been doing all day?"

"Nothing," I said quickly, brushing past her into the kitchen. "I wasn't exactly feeling productive."

Luna raised an eyebrow, clearly unconvinced. "Sure. Well, you'd better start feeling productive, because we've got a movie to catch. Thriller, remember? I'm risking my emotional stability for you two."

"It's a thriller, not a horror movie, remember?" Jayce pointed out as he leaned against the wall. "You'll be fine. Maybe."

Luna shot him a glare, but I could see the corners of her mouth twitching. Typical banter between them, and normally, I'd jump in—but my mind wasn't quite there. As I rummaged through the fridge for a bottle of water, I couldn't help but think about this morning. About the café, the mess, and Mr. Ramsey's steely resolve as he faced the disaster.

"You okay?" Luna's voice cut through my thoughts, soft and a little concerned.

I straightened up and turned to face them, forcing a smile. "Yeah, I'm fine. Just... tired. The café was a mess this morning. Like, *really* bad. Mr. Ramsey's going to have a hard time cleaning it all up."

"What happened?" Jayce asked, his brows furrowing slightly.

"I don't know," I admitted, leaning against the counter. "It was like a hurricane hit the place overnight. Tessa and I just... walked into chaos. It was overwhelming."

Luna tilted her head, watching me carefully. "You didn't mention this earlier."

I exhaled, trying to tamp down the wave of frustration rising within me. "I did," I said flatly, the annoyance slipping into my voice despite my best efforts. "Luna, I texted you earlier. You just weren't paying attention." I sighed, "Anyway, they called the police and everything, so hopefully they'll figure it out."

The words came out casual enough, but I felt the weight of my lie settle over me. I'd left out so much—the pendant, the strange tension in the air, the creeping sense that there was more to it than met the eye. And, of course, the dream. But that was something I wasn't ready to explain, not yet.

"Well, Mr. Ramsey's tough," Jayce said finally. "He'll handle it."

"Yeah," I agreed softly, though the knot in my chest didn't ease.

Luna stood and clapped her hands together, breaking the moment. "Alright, enough doom and gloom. Let's go. I'm ready to get scared out of my mind."

"Speak for yourself," Jayce muttered as he grabbed his jacket. "I'm ready to enjoy you two freaking out while I stay calm."

I laughed, grabbing my bag and heading for the door with them. Maybe tonight would help me clear my head—or at least give me something else to think about. Because whatever was happening, whatever was hiding in the edges of my reality, wasn't going away. I just had to hope it would wait until I was ready to face it.

The air was cool and crisp as we stepped out of my apartment, the gentle night breeze carrying with it the hum of downtown life. The streets glowed under the soft light of the lampposts, and strings of bulbs draped across buildings added a warm, festive shimmer to the cityscape. For the first time in weeks, I felt... weightless. The laughter bouncing between Luna, Jayce, and me felt effortless, the kind that made my worries fade like shadows retreating into the dark.

Jayce was in rare form tonight, rattling off jokes he'd apparently picked up earlier. Some were ridiculous, others borderline clever, but Luna and I couldn't stop laughing, and his grin only widened with each giggle he managed to pull out of us. For a moment, I let myself sink into the ease of it all—the carefree bubble of friendship that felt like an escape from everything lingering under the surface.

But even amidst the joy, the thought of Felix tugged at the edges of my mind, refusing to be dismissed. The nightmares had stopped, which was a relief. And yet, their absence left behind a growing void filled with questions. Why did Felix keep appearing in my dreams? Why did he seem so familiar, yet so elusive? And why—despite the strangeness of it all—did his presence make me feel calm in ways I couldn't explain?

The swirl of questions was beginning to grow louder when Jayce nudged me back to reality. "Iris," he said, leaning in slightly as we crossed the street, waving one hand in front of my face. "Hello? Are you lost in your thoughts again?"

"Huh?" I blinked, glancing at him. He was smirking, and Luna was watching me with raised brows.

"We've been talking for like ten minutes," Jayce teased, nudging my shoulder. "Earth to Iris. You gonna join us anytime soon?"

"Sorry," I said, brushing it off as casually as I could. "Guess I spaced out."

"Spaced out, huh?" Luna chimed in, eyeing me with that mischievous look that always spelled trouble. She crossed her arms, a teasing smile tugging at her lips. "Or is there a *boy* you're thinking about?"

I froze for half a step, my cheeks warming under her gaze. "What? No!" I said, maybe a little too quickly.

Jayce snorted, clearly enjoying this far more than he should. "Oh, there's definitely a boy. Look at her—she's practically glowing."

"I am not glowing," I snapped, shooting him a glare. "You're ridiculous."

Luna leaned in closer, her grin widening. "So, who is it? Come on, you can tell us. Is it someone new? Someone mysterious?"

Jayce jumped in before I could reply, throwing his hands dramatically into the air. "I bet it's that guy from the coffee shop last week. The one who smiled at her for like three seconds. She's been haunted by his charm ever since."

"Stop." I groaned, covering my face with my hands and picking up my pace to escape their relentless teasing. "There's no boy. You're both imagining things."

"Right," Luna said, clearly unconvinced. She hurried to catch up, her voice dripping with playful suspicion. "Then why were you practically spacing out the whole time we were talking? You've got secrets, Iris. I can tell."

I rolled my eyes, determined to keep Felix out of this conversation. "If I have secrets, they're definitely not about boys. You can stop now." I shot them a glare. "Besides," I added, with a pointed look, "you already know a pretty huge secret." My fingers brushed against the necklace, its familiar weight grounding me as I watched their playful expressions shift, just slightly, at the reminder of what they already knew.

As the theater came into view, its glowing marquee lighting up the street, Luna hooked her arm through mine. "Fine, we'll drop it—for now. But I'm watching you," she said with a wink. "You can't hide from me forever."

"We'll see," I replied lightly, forcing a laugh as we headed inside. The mystery of Felix was still there, nestled in the corners of my thoughts. But tonight, I wasn't going to let it take over. For now, all I wanted was to lose myself in the world of thrillers and jump scares, leaving the questions—if only briefly—behind.

As Luna headed toward the snack counter, she glanced back, casually calling over her shoulder, "Tell me what you want—I'm paying." Her tone was light, almost teasing, but I knew her well enough to catch the underlying meaning. This was her way of apologizing, and I couldn't help but smile to myself. Luna had a knack for saying sorry without actually saying it.

Jayce and I found a small table by the wall and sank into the chairs while we waited for her. The hum of the theater lobby buzzed around us—conversations blending with the distant beeping of registers and the low rustle of popcorn bags.

"Hey," Jayce said, his voice quieter than usual. I turned to look at him, and he met my gaze with an expression I didn't see on him often—one filled with something like guilt. "I'm sorry…" he started, his words trailing off as he scratched the back of his neck. "We weren't trying to upset you, you know. I mean, Luna and I… we know what you're dealing with isn't easy."

He paused, running a hand through his hair, clearly searching for the right words. "We just wanted to lighten the mood," he continued, the shame in his voice softening into sincerity. "To make you laugh, even for a little while. So you wouldn't have to think about the nightmares or the necklace. We weren't trying to make it worse."

I felt my chest tighten at his words, the weight of their meaning settling over me. My frustration from earlier melted away, replaced by a swell of gratitude. "Jayce, it's okay," I said softly, a small smile tugging at my lips. "If anything, I should be apologizing for overreacting."

He let out a quiet chuckle, his shoulders relaxing slightly. "You didn't overreact," he said with a sigh. "I just… I want you to know we're always here for you. We're going to help you through this, no matter what. We'll face it together, alright?"

His words hit me like a warm hug, and I nodded, my smile growing. "Alright," I replied, the tension in my chest easing.

Before either of us could say more, Luna reappeared, balancing a tray stacked with snacks. She slid it onto the table with a dramatic flourish, grinning as she started divvying everything up. "Large popcorn, large Coke, and gummy worms for Jayce," she said, placing the items in front of him with exaggerated precision. Then she turned to me, her eyes sparkling mischievously. "And for Iris... medium popcorn, peach iced tea, and mini pretzels." She set them down in front of me, drawing out her words like she was announcing a grand prize.

I met her gaze, holding it for a moment before breaking into a wide smile. "Apology accepted," I said, my tone playful but sincere.

Luna's eyes widened slightly before a huge grin lit up her face. "Thank you, thank you!" she exclaimed, her voice bubbling with relief. "I wasn't thinking—I'm so sorry."

"It's okay, really," I reassured her. "Just maybe ease up on the whole 'Iris is secretly thinking about a boy' thing next time, yeah?"

Jayce snickered into his soda, and Luna raised her hands in mock surrender. "Fine, fine. I'll behave... for now."

With the air between us lightened and the tension from earlier fading into the background, we grabbed our snacks and headed toward the theater. The smell of buttered popcorn filled the hallway, and the excitement of the crowd buzzed around us as we found our seats. As the lights dimmed and the screen flickered to life, I let myself relax, sinking into the moment. For now, it was just us, the movie, and the thrill of escaping reality—even if only for a little while.

The movie had been better than expected—not mind-blowing, but solid enough to keep us talking about it as we spilled out into the cool night air. Luna was already in full post-movie-analysis mode, her voice louder than necessary as she flailed her arms like she was trying to reenact the whole thing. Jayce ducked dramatically out of her range, pretending to shield himself from her animated gestures.

"That twist was insane!" Luna practically yelled, her curly hair bouncing with every over-the-top movement. "I *knew* the brother was the villain the whole time! They made it way too obvious!"

Jayce smirked, shoving his hands into his jacket pockets. "Uh-huh. Sure, detective. You're just mad it wasn't the dad, like you said halfway through."

Luna gasped, turning on him with mock betrayal. "Excuse me? I literally called it an hour into the movie!"

"And you also called three other people the villain, so forgive me if I'm a little skeptical," Jayce teased, sidestepping just as Luna swatted at his arm.

I laughed, the banter between them pulling me out of my own head. The pendant felt heavier beneath my hoodie, its faint pulse a constant reminder that my world was about a thousand times weirder than theirs. But for a few minutes, their bickering was grounding—normal.

"Okay, but can we talk about how the protagonist just *knew* how to fight at the end?" I said, cutting in before Luna could escalate. "Like, where did that come from?"

"Plot convenience," Jayce said immediately, shrugging. "The writers didn't know how to wrap it up, so... martial arts montage."

Luna groaned, throwing her head back dramatically. "Ugh, why do you always ruin everything with logic?"

"It's a gift," Jayce replied with a grin.

As the glow of the theater faded into the distance, the buzz of the movie still hung between us. But there was something else there, too—a heaviness that I couldn't quite shake. The pendant pressed lightly against my chest, hidden beneath my hoodie, its faint warmth grounding me. I'd tried to push the forest and its secrets to the back of my mind, but the connection was always there, lingering just out of reach.

"You've been quiet," Jayce said, his voice cutting through my thoughts. "Something on your mind?"

I blinked, forcing myself back into the present. "Nah, I'm good," I said quickly, keeping my tone light. "Just tired, I guess."

Jayce didn't look convinced, but Luna jumped in before he could press further.

"She's probably just mad the movie didn't explain how the brother pulled off framing his dad," Luna said, linking her arm through mine. "Classic Iris. Always overthinking."

I rolled my eyes, grateful for the distraction. "Sure, let's go with that."

Luna grinned, tugging me forward as we neared the diner on the corner. The familiar neon lights washed over us, casting a warm glow on the cracked sidewalk. Inside, Luna wasted no time ordering milkshakes for all of us—chocolate for her, vanilla for Jayce, and peach for me.

We settled into a booth near the window, the hum of conversations blending with the clatter of dishes. Jayce and Luna dove into their usual banter, Luna's dramatic recaps paired with Jayce's dry commentary. I leaned back, sipping my milkshake as I watched them. For the first time in a while, I felt something close to normal. The pendant's faint pulse was still there, a quiet reminder of the chaos waiting for me, but for now, I let myself sink into the moment.

Jayce and Luna walked beside me, and the quiet hum of the city was our only soundtrack as we made our way back to my apartment. The clock had already ticked past midnight, and the chilly Friday night air seemed to bite sharper with every gust of wind. I pulled my hoodie tighter around me, grateful that tomorrow didn't involve alarms or rushing out the door.

When we finally reached the main entrance to my building, Luna stopped and turned toward me, her curls catching the faint glow of the streetlight. "Promise me you'll get some sleep tonight," she said, her voice soft but firm, her pleading look impossible to ignore. "And if anything happens—if you even *think* something's wrong—call us, okay?"

Her words brought a lump to my throat. They'd been so understanding, so there for me since I'd told them about the nightmares and my suspicions about the necklace. I didn't know how I'd gotten so lucky to have them, standing by my side through something they couldn't fully understand but refused to walk away from.

Jayce nodded, his tone warm but serious. "She's right, Iris. Anything happens, you call us. We'll be here in no time. Promise."

I smiled, the sincerity in their voices wrapping around me like a second layer of warmth. "Thank you," I said quietly. "Let's hope it doesn't come to that. You guys should get home—it's late, and freezing."

Luna didn't hesitate, wrapping me in a hug that held a mix of reassurance and urgency. "Goodnight, hon," she murmured against my shoulder. "I'll call you tomorrow."

Jayce leaned in for a side hug, his shoulder steady under my head as I rested there briefly. "See you later, Iris. Take care, alright?" His voice was quieter than usual, but it carried the same grounded strength he always seemed to exude.

As he stepped back, he caught Luna's hand, their fingers entwining as they both gave me a small wave. I watched them stroll into the night, their silhouettes fading into the glow of distant streetlights, leaving me standing alone at the threshold of the building.

I sighed as I stepped inside, the warmth of the lobby a stark contrast to the sharp night air. Even as I climbed the stairs to my apartment, the weight of their words stuck with me—alongside the unspoken reality of what lay ahead. I didn't know what the coming days would bring, but Luna and Jayce had made one thing clear: I wasn't facing it alone.

CHAPTER V

Family Secrets

When I opened my eyes, I expected to feel the same weight dragging me down—the exhaustion of sleepless nights, the lingering haze from restless dreams. But this time was different. My eyelids were heavy, sure, but not from fatigue. It was the kind of heaviness that came after a good night's sleep, when your body finally decides to rest the way it's supposed to. As I sat up and stretched my arms high over my head, I felt something I hadn't felt in weeks: relief. For once, I didn't feel completely drained.

And yet, as I took a deep breath and let the morning light filter in through the curtains, an ache settled in my chest. A quiet sadness. Because last night, for the first time, there were no dreams. No forest. No Felix. The void left behind felt almost worse than the restless nights—like something important was missing.

My fingers brushed against the necklace resting lightly against my skin, its weight softer now, almost unfamiliar. That scared me. The dreams had made it feel so significant, so heavy with meaning. Now, it was just… a necklace. And maybe that's all it ever was. Maybe the dreams weren't real, and I'd been chasing shadows all along.

Today was Saturday, and Saturdays meant visiting my mom. It had become our tradition ever since I moved out—something that felt normal, even comforting, in a time when my life seemed anything but. After high school, I'd made the decision to live on my own. Not because I didn't love her, but because I wanted to give us both room to breathe. Losing my dad had changed everything, especially for her. In Rockport, a small town where everybody knows everybody, even getting by could feel like a struggle. She worked tirelessly to keep us afloat, but I could see the toll it took on her.

Taking the café job was my way of helping. Saving up enough to move into my own place felt like the least I could do— to give her space, to not feel like a burden. And now, every weekend, I made sure to visit her, share what I could, and remind her she wasn't alone.

The walk to my mom's house was familiar and comfortable in a way that only small-town streets can be. The sidewalk was cracked in places, weeds peeking through, but it felt like home—steady and unchanging. Rockport had a quiet charm, the kind of place where time seemed to move slower, though not always in a good way. I could count on two hands the landmarks that mattered: the café where I worked, the park with its tired old swings, the corner store run by Mrs. Miller, who never forgot anyone's name.

When I reached the house, I saw her sitting on the porch, a book balanced on her lap and a mug of tea in her hand. She always made tea in the mornings. She said it calmed her nerves, though I knew better—it was her little ritual, her way of grounding herself when life felt uncertain.

"Morning, Iris!" she called, her face lighting up as she spotted me walking up the path. She closed the book and set it aside, holding the mug with both hands like it was the only thing keeping her warm.

"Morning, Mom," I said, stepping onto the porch. The air smelled faintly of flowers from the garden she tended religiously, even on bad days. I hugged her tightly, feeling the comfort of her presence settle over me.

Inside, the house welcomed me with its usual warmth—the faint scent of cinnamon lingering from the pastries Mom always bought, the mismatched furniture that had been here for years, and the memories that lined every wall. My dad's presence was everywhere, even after all these years—the framed photographs of him holding me as a baby, laughing at the beach, or leaning over a table with one of his signature chess moves. I lingered in front of one photo, tracing its edges lightly with my finger. In it, my mom had her arm wrapped around him, squinting against the sun, and my younger self was perched on his shoulders, grinning like I'd conquered the world.

Mom placed a plate of pastries on the table, her movements careful as always, her eyes flicking to me briefly. "You've been quiet lately," she said, her tone soft but edged with concern. She set out mugs for tea, the steam curling up into the air between us. "Is everything okay?"

I hesitated, the weight of the pendant pressing lightly against my chest. I hadn't told her about the necklace, the dreams—not about Felix or the forest or the strange connection I couldn't explain. She already had so much to worry about; I didn't want to add to it.

I paused, my fingers brushing the edge of the mug she'd slid toward me. "I've just been busy," I said finally, forcing a smile. "Work's picking up."

Her knowing look told me she wasn't fully convinced, but she let it go. She'd never been the type to push—not after everything we'd been through. She'd always said I reminded her of my dad in that way. Quiet, thoughtful, carrying more than I ever let on.

"You work too much," she teased lightly, sitting across from me. "But I know it's not just work, Iris."

I didn't answer, not directly. Some things were easier to avoid—like the dreams I hadn't told her about, the weight that pressed on me every time I woke up. She worried enough without me adding to it.

She glanced at me, her expression soft but searching. "You know you can tell me anything, right?"

"I know." And I meant it. But this? This wasn't something I could explain, not yet.

As the afternoon passed, we talked about little things—the garden, how Mrs. Miller's niece was coming to visit, and what new books she wanted to order from the library. But there was an underlying tension, one I couldn't fully explain or shake. Her gaze flicked to me every so often, as though she was searching for something I wasn't saying. I thought of the necklace, tucked beneath my shirt, its smooth ruby surface pressing lightly against my chest.

I grabbed both mugs, hers and mine, from the table, intending to take them to the sink. But as I stood, the necklace slipped out from beneath my shirt, its ruby glinting faintly in the kitchen light. My mom's reaction was instant—her eyes widened, and her face went pale, a mixture of shock and fear clouding her expression.

"Mom?" I asked, stopping in my tracks. "What's wrong?"

She didn't answer. Her gaze was fixed on the pendant, her lips slightly parted like she wanted to say something but couldn't. The silence dragged on until she finally blinked, her wide eyes snapping to meet mine.

"W-where…" she started, her voice trembling. "Where did you find that necklace?"

Her tone sent a chill down my spine. I clutched the mugs tighter, trying to make sense of her sudden change. "I bought it," I said slowly, the words sounding almost foreign. "From an antique shop. A few weeks ago. Why?"

Her gaze dropped again, as though she couldn't bear to look at me. "You… bought it?" Her voice rose slightly, tinged with disbelief. "How is that possible?" she murmured, more to herself than to me.

My chest tightened as fear started to creep in. Did she know something about the necklace? Something she hadn't told me? Carefully, I placed the mugs back on the table, the sound of ceramic against wood seeming louder than usual. I stepped closer, my movements cautious, until I was only a few inches away from her.

"Mom?" I said softly, trying to keep my voice steady. When she didn't look up, I tried again, this time louder, more insistent. "Mom!"

Her head snapped up, her disbelief etched clearly into her features. I could feel my frustration building, the weight of unanswered questions pressing harder against me.

"Is there something you're not telling me?" I asked, my tone firm, almost demanding.

She shook her head, but it wasn't denial—it was disbelief, tangled with something deeper, something she wasn't ready to admit. And as the seconds ticked by, her silence became harder to bear.

"Mom," I repeated, my frustration inching closer to the surface. "You're clearly upset about this necklace. Just… tell me why." My voice wavered slightly, but I was determined to get an answer.

She shook her head again, her hands clutching the edge of the table like it was the only thing keeping her grounded. "It's nothing," she said, her voice quieter now, almost fragile. "It just… surprised me."

I frowned, unable to shake the feeling that there was something deeper beneath her words—something she wasn't ready to share. "Surprised you how?" I pressed, leaning closer. "Mom, this isn't just a random piece of jewelry, is it?"

She glanced down, avoiding my gaze as she spoke. "I don't know what you mean," she said, though her tone betrayed her. "It's… it's just unusual. That's all."

Her answers felt hollow, each one carefully chosen to avoid saying what she really meant. And as much as I wanted to keep pushing, the sadness in her eyes stopped me. It wasn't that she didn't want to tell me—it was that she couldn't. Not yet.

The tension lingered as I helped her tidy the kitchen, neither of us willing to breach the silence. I kept my movements slow, deliberate, watching her out of the corner of my eye as she rearranged the mugs and plates on the counter. Her hands moved mechanically, her gaze distant, like her mind was somewhere else entirely.

When it was time to leave, she gave me a hug, holding me tightly as though she was afraid to let go. "Take care, Iris," she said softly, her voice still tinged with that same disbelief from earlier. "And…be careful who you trust."

Her words sent a shiver through me. They were meant to be reassuring, but they felt more like a warning. I wanted to ask her more, to force her to say what she was hiding, but the look in her eyes stopped me again. Whatever she knew, she wasn't ready to share it. Not yet.

The streets were quiet as I made my way back to my apartment, the fading sunlight casting long shadows across the cracked pavement. My fingers brushed against the necklace beneath my shirt, its faint weight pressing against my skin like a reminder of the unanswered questions lingering between me and my mom.

Why had she reacted that way? What had she seen—or remembered—that made her so afraid? The words she'd said seemed simple enough, but the tremble in her voice had said more than she intended. She knew something. Something important. And I wasn't going to let her avoidance stop me from finding out the truth.

The pendant pulsed faintly as I climbed the stairs to my apartment, the rhythm matching the steady beat of my heart. It wasn't just a necklace—not anymore. It was a thread, pulling me toward something bigger than I could see, something my mom had tried to bury.

But secrets like hers didn't stay buried forever. And as much as it scared me, I was determined to unravel them.

I decided to stop by the café before heading home, mostly out of habit but partly because I couldn't shake the restless feeling that lingered from my visit with Mom. The necklace was still tucked beneath my shirt, its faint weight pressing against my skin as I pushed the door open. The familiar jingle of the bell overhead welcomed me, and for a moment, everything felt normal.

But that feeling didn't last. Instead, I froze in the doorway, my eyes darting around the room in disbelief. Everything looked… fine. No sign of the chaos from just a few days ago—the shattered glass, the overturned furniture, the scattered flour that had painted the floor in white streaks. It was like nothing had ever happened. The counters gleamed, the shelves were fully stocked, and the smell of fresh coffee mingled with the faint sweetness of pastries. My heart sank, unease creeping in. How had they fixed it so quickly?

Tessa was behind the counter, her dark curls tied up in a messy bun, humming softly as she wiped down the espresso machine. She looked up as I walked in, flashing me her usual grin. "Hey, Iris! What's up?"

I hesitated, glancing around again before making my way to the counter. "Tessa," I said slowly, "is it just me, or is everything… back to normal?"

Her brow furrowed slightly, but the smile didn't fade. "Yeah, isn't it great? The repair crew worked overtime to get everything cleaned up. Mr. Ramsey made it happen, though. He's… a determined guy."

At that moment, I spotted Mr. Ramsey near the back room. His head was bent low, and his hand lingered longer than necessary on the doorframe. For someone who'd orchestrated the café's swift return to normalcy, he didn't seem particularly relaxed. His shoulders were hunched, and his eyes darted back and forth, as though scanning for something—or someone.

"Is it just me, or has Mr. Ramsey been acting strange lately?" I asked, leaning in slightly as I glanced in his direction.

Tessa paused, setting the cloth aside and resting her hands on her hips. "Mr. Ramsey? Hmm. Now that you mention it... maybe a little? He's been quieter than usual, but honestly, after what happened, I don't blame him. That kind of damage would stress anyone out."

She meant it casually, but her words didn't sit right with me. Mr. Ramsey hadn't just been quiet—he'd been calculating, almost wary. His focus on that back room during the cleanup had stuck in my mind, and his current behavior only added to the feeling that something wasn't right.

Tessa's voice cut through the quiet hum of the office, sharp and tinged with unease. "The cops called him. The video footage wasn't useful," she said, her words quick, clipped, as if she were afraid to linger too long on the subject. Her gaze flicked toward our boss, hesitant, like she was searching for an anchor and not finding it. "Apparently, when they checked the footage from the cameras, thirty minutes were... missing."

I froze, the weight of her words settling uncomfortably in the pit of my stomach. "Missing?" I echoed, my voice strained with disbelief. My eyes locked onto hers, searching for clarity. There was no way the footage could just vanish—things like that didn't happen without a reason.

Tessa shifted awkwardly, her hand brushing across the edge of her desk as though she needed something to hold on to. "I mean, like... the cameras stopped working or something," she muttered, her shoulders rising in a shrug that did little to mask the tension in her stance. She was trying to keep it casual, but her eyes betrayed her. They darted toward mine, wide and unsettled, carrying the shadow of fear she couldn't quite hide.

I felt the air shift, heavy with questions I wasn't sure I wanted answers to. Something wasn't adding up, and judging by the way Tessa's voice faltered, she knew it too. My pulse quickened. Thirty minutes gone? That wasn't just a malfunction—that was deliberate. It had to be.

Before I could say more, a flicker of movement caught my eye. I turned toward the corner near the windows and froze again. Felix was sitting there, one leg crossed over the other, his attention fixed on the book in his hands. He didn't glance up, didn't seem to notice me, but his presence was unmistakable.

My pulse quickened as I stared at him, the edges of the café blurring slightly as my thoughts raced. This wasn't the Felix from the forest—this was real. Tangible. Here, in the café, as if it were the most normal thing in the world.

Tessa followed my gaze, her voice breaking through the haze. "Oh, that guy? He's been here for hours. Just reading, sipping tea. Pretty quiet. Why? Do you know him?"

I quickly shook my head, forcing myself to look away. "No," I lied. "He just looks... familiar."

"Hmm." Tessa shrugged, picking up her clothes again. "Well, he's nice enough. Hardly said a word, though."

I found a seat near the counter, far enough from Felix to keep my distance but close enough that I couldn't help glancing his way. The café buzzed quietly around us, customers chatting, orders being called, the hum of the espresso machine blending into the background. But I couldn't shake the tension knotting in my chest.

What was Felix doing here? He hadn't looked at me once, hadn't acknowledged my presence at all. And yet, it felt impossible to ignore him, as though the connection from the forest had spilled over into the real world, tethering us even when we weren't speaking.

The necklace pressed harder against my skin, its warmth pulling me back to the questions I didn't have answers for. My mom's reaction. Mr. Ramsey's strange behavior. And now Felix, sitting in the café as if he belonged here.

Whatever was happening, it was growing harder to separate the normal from the strange. And I had a feeling that Felix wouldn't stay silent for long.

I stayed seated near the counter for what felt like an eternity, though it was probably only a few minutes. My focus kept pulling back to Felix, even as I tried to distract myself by scrolling through my phone or sipping the too-sweet caramel latte Tessa had convinced me to try. He didn't glance up from his book once, not even when a group of high school kids spilled through the door, their laughter cutting sharply through the calm buzz of the café.

He looked so... normal. Ordinary. Like any other customer who'd decided to spend a lazy afternoon reading, completely unaware of how much of my life he'd managed to upend in such a short amount of time. It was almost funny, except it wasn't. The longer I sat there, the more the questions in my head began to stack up, each one louder than the last.

Why was he here? Why now? And why wasn't he acknowledging me?

I let out a quiet breath, my fingers brushing the edge of the mug as I considered my options. I could leave, pretend I hadn't seen him, and let the mystery continue to twist itself into knots in my mind. Or I could do what I'd been avoiding since I walked through the door.

I chose the latter.

Picking up my mug, I made my way across the room, each step feeling heavier than the last. Felix didn't look up as I stopped by his table, his eyes still fixed on the book in his hands. The light from the window fell across his face, casting faint shadows over his sharp features. The book itself was thick, worn at the edges, and I caught a glimpse of the title as I stood there awkwardly. *The Picture of Dorian Gray*. Of course.

"Hey," I said, my voice quieter than I intended. When he didn't respond, I cleared my throat and tried again. "Hey, Felix."

This time, he looked up, his expression unreadable as his sharp blue eyes met mine. But instead of the familiarity I'd been expecting—or hoping for—there was nothing. No flicker of recognition, no acknowledgment. Just polite confusion.

"Sorry, have we met?" he asked, his accent crisp and undeniably English, the kind of voice you'd expect to hear on a BBC drama.

I blinked, my brain scrambling to process the words. "What?"

"You said my name," he continued, closing the book carefully, as though he had all the time in the world. "But I don't believe we've been introduced."

Was he messing with me? Was this some kind of game? My fingers tightened around the mug, its warmth grounding me as I tried to find something—anything—to say.

"I... I thought I recognized you," I said finally, the words tumbling out in a rush. "Sorry. My mistake."

Felix tilted his head slightly, studying me with a faint curiosity. "Happens all the time," he said lightly, the corners of his mouth twitching into what could have been a smile. "I must have one of those faces."

His tone was calm and even polite, but there was something about the way he spoke that put me on edge. Like he was trying too hard to seem unaffected, like he knew exactly who I was but wanted me to doubt myself.

I stood there for a moment longer, feeling like the ground had shifted beneath me. Then, realizing I'd overstayed whatever welcome he was willing to offer, I nodded quickly. "Right. Sorry to bother you."

"Not at all," Felix said, his voice as smooth as ever. He picked up his tea, taking a measured sip before adding, "Enjoy your afternoon."

I walked away without another word, my heart pounding in my chest. When I reached my table, I sat down heavily, the mug in my hands trembling slightly. Tessa glanced over from the counter, raising an eyebrow as though to ask, *What was that all about?*

I shook my head, my lips pressed into a tight line. Whatever game Felix was playing, I wasn't sure I was ready for it. But one thing was certain—he wasn't just another customer, no matter how much he pretended otherwise.

And I wasn't done trying to figure him out.

My chest tightened as I replayed our previous interaction in my head—the way he'd looked at me, his polite but distant dismissal. He'd treated me like I was nothing more than a stranger, like he hadn't been a recurring figure in my dreams for days. The thought made my stomach twist uncomfortably. What if I was wrong? What if Felix wasn't connected to any of this, and I was just grasping at threads that didn't exist? What if he really *didn't* know me?

Even as the doubts crept in, my eyes kept drifting to him, as though pulled by an invisible thread. He hadn't moved much, his attention still fixed on the book in his hands, his expression calm, composed. But the pendant felt heavier against my chest, its faint pulse urging me forward. It was maddening—the conflict between my fear of rejection and the inexplicable pull to try again.

I swallowed hard, wrapping my fingers more tightly around the mug. No matter how much I wanted answers, the lingering sting of his earlier words kept me rooted in place. I couldn't bring myself to confront him again—not yet.

But deep down, I knew I couldn't leave it alone. His presence wasn't just a coincidence. The dreams, the pendant, the strange pull I felt when I looked at him—it all meant something. Even if I couldn't figure out what that something was, it refused to let me go.

No. I wasn't going to let him brush me off, not like that. I didn't care how indifferent he tried to seem—Felix was part of this, whether he liked it or not. And I wasn't leaving until I got answers.

Straightening my shoulders, I picked up my mug, the confidence swelling inside me like a flood, ready to overflow. There wasn't going to be a "next time." This was the time. With each step I took toward his table, my determination solidified. He could act distant, dismissive, whatever he wanted—but I wasn't letting him get away that easily. Not this time.

I stopped just beside his table, the sunlight streaming through the window catching the edges of his sharp features. Clearing my throat, I tried to steady my voice. "Felix."

"Can I help you?" he asked politely, tilting his head slightly. His English accent was undeniable, each word crisp and deliberate, like he'd just stepped out of a London bookstore.

"We've... met," I said hesitantly, the weight of the pendant pressing harder against my skin. "Not like this, but... before."

Felix tilted his head further, his lips pulling into something that wasn't quite a smile. It didn't reach his eyes, didn't soften the coldness in his gaze. "I don't think so," he replied, his voice smooth, almost dismissive. "You must be mistaken."

"But I'm not," I pressed, the words spilling out faster now, my hands tightening into fists at my sides. "I know it sounds insane, but—you've been in my dreams. The forest, the mist... you were there. And now—now you're here."

Felix leaned back in his chair, the subtle movement making him seem taller and more imposing. He crossed his arms loosely, his gaze never leaving mine. "Dreams have a way of playing tricks on us," he said calmly, his voice devoid of emotion. "They're not real. Whatever you think you saw, it's just your imagination."

The pendant pulsed faintly against my chest, its warmth growing stronger, more insistent. My throat tightened as his words sank in, cold and dismissive, like stones dropping into a deep, dark well. He wasn't denying it outright, but he wasn't acknowledging it either. His detachment only made the air between us feel heavier, charged with something I couldn't name.

"Who are you?" I asked finally, my voice quieter now but steady. "Why do I feel like—like I know you?"

For a moment, Felix didn't answer. His fingers brushed the edge of his book, his movements deliberate, calculated. When he looked back at me, his expression was carefully controlled, like someone who knew exactly what to say to make someone doubt themselves.

"I'm just Felix," he said simply. "Nothing more, nothing less."

The pendant pulsed faintly against my skin, as if rejecting his words. But he was already turning his attention back to his book, effectively ending the conversation. For a moment, I stood there, caught between the pull to walk away and the urge to demand answers.

But Felix didn't look at me again. And as much as his detachment felt like rejection, I couldn't shake the feeling that this wasn't over—that there was more to him, and to the dreams, than he was letting on. I left the café knowing one thing for certain: Felix wasn't just a stranger. He was a question I didn't yet know how to ask—and a mystery I couldn't escape.

CHAPTER VI

The Key

The door to the café closed behind me with a jingle, the cool afternoon air hitting my face like a slap. My hands clenched into fists as I walked down the sidewalk, my chest tight with anger and confusion. The nerve of him—acting like he didn't know me, like I was just some random stranger. My mind was spinning, trying to piece together his cold indifference with the Felix I'd seen in the forest.

"He could've at least acknowledged it," I muttered under my breath, my words sharp and clipped. "I mean, how hard is it to say, 'Yeah, you're not crazy, we've met before,' instead of acting like I'm making it all up?"

I kicked at a stray pebble, the motion doing nothing to release the knot of frustration tightening in my stomach. "Rude," I hissed, the word carried away by a sudden gust of wind. "That's what he is. Rude and—"

My words cut off abruptly as a sharp, cold sensation crawled up the back of my neck, like icy fingers brushing against my skin. I froze mid-step, the world around me dimming as a low, faint whisper curled into the edges of my consciousness.

Stay away from him.

The words slithered through my mind like smoke, dark and invasive, sending a chill down my spine. I stumbled slightly, clutching the strap of my bag as I looked around wildly. But the street was empty—just cracked pavement and rows of quiet storefronts. And yet, the whispers didn't stop.

"You again," I muttered under my breath, my voice shaking despite the defiance lacing it. "What do you want?

The voices curled tighter, their weight pressing against my thoughts like a storm building on the horizon.

He can't help you. He won't.

The voices were layered, overlapping in a way that gave me a headache. They weren't loud, but they were heavy, each word sinking into me like claws. My knees wobbled as I leaned against the nearest lamppost, the pendant burning faintly against my chest.

The laughter that followed was low, guttural, and filled with a kind of malice that made my skin crawl. *We told him. We warned him. And he listened.*

My heart hammered in my chest, the pendant pulsing faintly beneath my shirt. The whispers were stronger now, cutting through my thoughts like jagged glass. I clenched my jaw, trying to push them back, to keep my mind from spiraling. "What are you?" I said through gritted teeth. "What do you want from me?"

The necklace, they hissed, their voices twisting together like threads of smoke. *It belongs to us.*

I shoved the apartment door closed behind me, the sound echoing in the quiet space as frustration poured out of me.

My bag landed with a heavy thud on the couch, but it wasn't enough to ease the fury building inside me. I started pacing, each step sharp and purposeful as my mind raced. I had to talk to Felix. No—I *needed* to talk to him. None of this made sense—him brushing me off, the voices warning me to stay away, the invisible thread trying to keep us apart.

How could I reach him? I hadn't even dreamed about the forest last time. What if it didn't happen again? My hand closed around the necklace, the ruby pressing into my palm as I clutched it tightly, hoping—*praying*—that it would pull me back to him. The pendant warmed against my skin, but it wasn't enough to quiet the storm in my chest.

Dinner didn't even cross my mind that night. I couldn't think about food, not when every thought was consumed by lingering questions—about my mom, the voices, Felix. The weight of it all pressed down on me, suffocating and relentless. I yanked off my clothes, kicking my Converse across the room as I grabbed my nightgown. Even though the air in the apartment was cold, sweat clung to my skin, my body burning with the fire of frustration.

I tried lying down in bed, pulling the blankets tight around me, but sleep refused to come. My thoughts wouldn't stop, each one twisting tighter until I had to escape. I got up and sank onto the couch, grabbing the remote and flipping through channels. The glow of the TV cast faint shadows across the room as I landed on *10 Things I Hate About You*. I'd seen it so many times I could recite the lines without thinking. It was enough to dull the edge of my thoughts, at least for a little while.

As the movie went on, my breathing slowed, the tension in my muscles easing as exhaustion began to pull at me. My eyelids grew heavier with every scene until, finally, I let myself drift into sleep. The voices, Felix, the forest—they waited for me, just beyond the surface of the dreams I couldn't escape.

The forest returned to me that night—dark, endless, and alive with the faint hum of the pendant's pulsing glow. The mist curled tightly around the trees, thick and suffocating, as if it wanted to keep me out. But I pushed forward, my steps slow but deliberate, the warm light of the necklace guiding me through the shadows.

Felix was waiting for me. He stood in the clearing, his silhouette sharp against the hazy backdrop. He wasn't moving, his arms crossed loosely over his chest, his gaze fixed on the pendant as it glowed against my skin. There was something colder about him tonight—more distant, more guarded.

"It's you," I said, my voice sounding distant, even to my own ears.

His eyes widened briefly when he saw me in my nightgown, the reaction quick but unmistakable. It was gone just as fast, his face smoothing into calm neutrality as though it had never happened. But I noticed. I couldn't help but notice, and the warmth of a blush crept across my cheeks before I could stop it. I swallowed hard, forcing myself to push the moment aside, to keep my own expression steady and serious. Whatever flicker had passed between us, I wasn't about to let it show. Not now.

He tilted his head slightly, his expression carefully blank. "I told you—dreams aren't real," he said evenly, but his words felt wrong, like they didn't quite fit the moment.

"But you're here," I insisted, the pendant feeling impossibly heavy against my skin. "You always are."

Felix didn't answer. He just stood there, watching me, the silence between us stretching like a thread pulled taut. The forest swirled faintly around us, the mist creeping closer, wrapping us in its veil.

"And you're back," he said finally, his voice cutting through the stillness like glass. His accent was stronger here, its clipped precision giving every word weight.

"I didn't have a choice," I replied, my own voice steadier than I'd expected. "And I think you know that."

Felix raised an eyebrow, his lips pulling into a faint, humorless smile. "Do I?"

The glow of the pendant pulsed harder as I took a hesitant step forward, and for a fleeting moment, I thought I saw something flicker across his face—an emotion too quick to name. Then it was gone, replaced by that familiar, calm neutrality.

"You're here," I insisted, the words tumbling out before I could think them through. There was more weight to them than I intended, more frustration, more desperation.

"I am," Felix replied, his voice smooth, but there was a careful edge to it. His accent seemed sharper in the stillness of the forest, each syllable clipped and deliberate.

My hands tightened into fists at my sides, the memory of his behavior at the café still fresh in my mind. "You pretended not to know me," I said, the accusation tumbling out before I could stop myself. "Like we're strangers, like none of this is real."

His gaze didn't waver. "Did I?"

"Yes," I said firmly, stepping closer. The mist seemed to part around me, drawn by the heat radiating from the pendant. "You looked me in the eye and lied. Like I'm imagining things."

Felix sighed softly, tilting his head just enough to make me feel small under his scrutiny. "And what would you have preferred? That I acknowledge you in the middle of a café? Tell everyone we've been meeting in a dream-filled forest?"

"I would've preferred the truth," I snapped, the words cutting through the quiet. "I'm sick of half-answers, of warnings, of whispers in my head. I need to know what's going on, Felix. Why are we here? What does that even mean?" I demanded, my voice breaking through the mist. "The forest, the pendant, you—it's all connected. And you're part of it. So stop acting like I'm imagining things!"

His gaze flicked down to the necklace, the ruby glinting faintly in the dim light. "You're asking questions you're not ready to hear the answers to," he said, his voice lower now, more careful.

"I'll decide what I'm ready for," I shot back, clutching the pendant tightly. "All I know is that this—whatever this is—it's real. And you know more than you're telling me."

Felix sighed, his shoulders relaxing slightly as he dropped his arms to his sides. "What you're looking for... It's not as simple as you think," he said, his tone softer now.

I stepped closer, the pendant flaring brighter as the distance between us narrowed. "Then tell me," I said, the words sharper, more desperate. "Why are you here? Why are we connected? What are you hiding?"

Felix didn't respond immediately. His fingers twitched at his sides, his jaw tightening as though he was weighing his options. Finally, he took a step forward, the distance between us shrinking as the glow of the pendant reflected in his eyes.

"The pendant," he said quietly, almost a whisper. "It ties us to this place. To each other. But it's not just a connection—it's a key."

"A key?" I echoed, my voice trembling. "To what?"

"To something better left locked away," he said, his tone dark, the edge of warning unmistakable.

The weight of his words pressed against me, heavier than the pendant resting on my chest. But the way he looked at me then—like he wanted to say more but couldn't—only made my frustration deepen. "Why?" I asked, my voice softer now, but no less insistent. "Why can't you just tell me?"

Felix didn't answer immediately. His gaze flicked briefly to the pendant before returning to me, the tension in his posture giving away more than his carefully measured expression. "Sometimes," he said finally, "answers aren't what we want them to be."

The pendant pulsed harder, its warmth spreading through my chest like a beacon. "Stop talking in circles," I said firmly, my voice steadier now.

Felix's expression darkened, his jaw tightening as though he was holding something back. "You've heard the voices," he said, his tone low. "Haven't you?"

The question sent a shiver through me, but I nodded slowly. "Yes."

"And did they tell you to stay away from me?" he continued, his eyes narrowing slightly. "To keep your distance?"

My stomach twisted as his words sank in, their weight pressing against me. "They said you couldn't help me," I admitted.

Felix laughed quietly, the sound hollow and bitter. "And you believed them?"

"I don't know what to believe," I said, my voice trembling despite my efforts to stay calm. "But they told you to stay away from me, didn't they? And you listened."

The endless back-and-forth had pushed me past my breaking point. Anger burned through me, sharp and unrelenting, as the frustration bubbled over. My steps quickened, closing the distance between us with more force than I intended. Felix's eyes flickered with a hint of surprise as he instinctively took a step back, his calm composure slipping just enough to show he hadn't expected me to confront him like this. But I didn't care. I was done holding back. I couldn't take it anymore.

"I've heard enough warnings, enough whispers. I want the truth," I said firmly.

Felix hesitated, his expression shifting just slightly. For a moment, I saw something different—a flicker of vulnerability, of conflict. "The truth doesn't just answer questions," he said. "It changes everything. And I don't know if you're ready for that."

The pendant pulsed harder, its warmth spreading through me like a quiet defiance, as though it was urging me to push further. "Ready or not," I said, squaring my shoulders, "I deserve to know. The voices—whatever they are—don't want me near you. Don't you think that means something?"

His gaze hardened again, the vulnerability slipping away as quickly as it had come. "It means you should listen to them," he said, his voice sharp now, his words cutting like frost.

"No," I said firmly, my anger flaring again. "It means they're afraid. And if they're afraid, there's a reason."

Felix took another step back, his hand brushing against the nearest tree as if steadying himself. "You don't understand," he said quietly, his voice almost hollow. "What they can do. What they'll do if you keep pushing."

"Then explain it to me," I said, the demand hanging in the air between us. "Tell me what I'm up against."

I stared at him, the warmth of the pendant battling the chill that had settled over me. "Who are they?" I asked, my voice barely a whisper. "And why do they care so much about this necklace? About us?"

For a long moment, there was only silence, the mist curling tighter around us like it was listening, waiting. When Felix finally spoke, his voice was cold, detached. "They'll take everything from you. Your memories. Your choices. The parts of you that make you... you. And they'll use them against you." He said, ignoring my questions.

His words hit me like a tidal wave, leaving me breathless. But even then, I couldn't back down. "Then help me stop them," I said, stepping closer again. "If you know so much, help me."

Felix didn't move. "It's not that simple."

"Then make it simple," I said, the plea cutting through my anger. "I can't do this alone."

Felix's gaze lingered on mine, his expression unreadable. The pendant burned against my skin, its pulse steady, insistent. "I can't promise you anything," he said finally, his voice softer now. "But if you insist on going down this path... don't expect me to save you."

"I don't need saving," I replied, my voice firm. "I need answers."

Felix's expression softened, just barely, as he shook his head. "You didn't do anything. And that's the problem." He whispered, more to himself than to me.

The mist thickened again, swallowing the clearing, and Felix's figure began to blur. I took a step forward, reaching out, but the forest pulled me back. The last thing I saw was the faint glint of his eyes before the darkness consumed me, leaving only the glow of the pendant to guide me.

The warmth of the pendant faded as the darkness closed in, pulling me deeper into the dream. The forest dissolved around me, its mist curling away like smoke, and I found myself standing in front of my grandmother's house. The sight of it sent a shiver down my spine. It was exactly as I remembered—small, weathered, with ivy creeping up the sides and the faint glow of the porch light flickering in the night. But the air felt wrong, heavy and oppressive, like the house itself was holding its breath.

I stepped forward, the crunch of gravel beneath my feet echoing louder than it should have. The pendant pulsed faintly against my chest, its warmth barely noticeable now, as though it was struggling to keep me grounded. The door creaked open before I could reach it, the sound cutting through the silence like a warning.

Inside, the house was dark, the shadows stretching long and deep across the worn wooden floors. The faint scent of lavender lingered in the air, a memory of my grandmother's favorite candles, but it was overpowered by something else—something sharp and metallic, like the smell of rusted iron. My heart pounded as I stepped inside, the pendant's pulse quickening slightly, as though it knew what was coming.

The whispers started almost immediately, curling around me like smoke, low and guttural, their words indistinct but heavy with malice. I froze in the center of the living room, my eyes darting to the corners where the shadows seemed to move, shifting and twisting like they were alive. The pendant burned hotter now, its pulse steady and insistent, but it wasn't enough to drown out the voices.

The necklace belongs to us.

Their voices overlapped, each one layered with a different tone, a different threat. I clutched the pendant tightly, its warmth grounding me as I tried to keep my fear from spiraling out of control. "It's mine," I said, my voice trembling but firm. "You can't have it."

The figures moved closer, their shadows stretching toward me like claws. *You don't understand,* they hissed, their voices cutting through me like ice. *It's not yours to keep.*

He will only betray you.

The words cut through the haze, sharp and clear, and I turned toward the sound instinctively. The shadows in the corner deepened, pulling together until they formed a shape—a figure, tall and indistinct, its edges flickering like a flame. My breath caught as more figures emerged, their forms twisting and shifting, their presence filling the room with an unbearable weight.

Felix cannot be trusted.

Their voices overlapped, each one layered with a different tone, a different threat. I clutched the pendant tightly, its warmth grounding me as I tried to keep my fear from spiraling out of control. "You don't know that," I said, my voice trembling but firm. "You don't know him."

The figures moved closer, their shadows stretching toward me like claws. *We know more than you think,* they hissed, their voices cutting through me like ice. *He hides the truth. He hides it from you.*

The walls of the living room seemed to shift, the familiar wallpaper peeling away to reveal something darker, something older. The floor beneath me creaked and groaned, the wood splintering as though it couldn't bear the weight of the entities pressing down on it. The pendant burned hotter, its pulse quickening as the shadows closed in.

"You're lying," I said, forcing the words out even as my voice shook. "I don't believe you."

The figures laughed, the sound low and guttural, filled with a kind of malice that made my skin crawl. *You will,* they said, their voices twisting together like smoke. *When the time comes, you will.*

"You can't scare me," I said, with resolve. "I'm not giving it up."

The figures' laughter rang out, low and chilling, crawling under my skin with its cold, cruel edge. *You don't have a choice,* they said, their voices twisting together like smoke. *It will consume you.*

The pendant flared suddenly, its light cutting through the darkness like a blade. The entities recoiled, their forms flickering and twisting as though the glow was burning them. But their voices didn't stop.

He will destroy you, they hissed, their tone sharper now, more insistent. *You think he's your answer, but he is your undoing.*

My stomach twisted as their words sank in, the memory of Felix's guarded expression flashing through my mind. "You're trying to turn me against him," I said, my voice louder now, more defiant. "Why? What are you so afraid of?"

The figures moved closer again, their shadows stretching toward me like claws. *He is not what you think he is,* they said, their voices overlapping, heavy with malice. *And when the truth comes to light, it will break you.*

The pendant flared brighter, its pulse steady and insistent, and the entities faltered, their forms flickering like flames caught in the wind. But their presence didn't fade, their voices still pressing against me, suffocating and relentless.

You are unaware of the burden you carry, they stated, their voices merging with a tone of grave seriousness. *It is destined to bring destruction to both you and him.*

Felix couldn't be trusted. He would betray me. He would destroy me. And yet, I couldn't bring myself to believe them—not entirely. Because if they were trying so hard to turn me away from him, maybe—just maybe—he was more important to all of this than I'd realized.

CHAPTER VII

Hello Stranger

I jolted upright in bed, my breath coming in sharp, ragged gasps as the remnants of the nightmare clung to me. My chest ached, the weight of the pendant pressing against my skin as if it were trying to anchor me. The darkness in my room felt suffocating, too similar to the shadows from my dream, and for a moment, I wasn't sure if I was fully awake or still trapped in that warped version of my grandmother's house.

The cold sweat clinging to my skin made me shiver, and I reached up to push damp strands of hair from my face. The air in my room felt heavy, wrong somehow, like the dream had followed me, refusing to let me go. I glanced at the clock on the nightstand, its glowing numbers cutting through the darkness. It wasn't even 4 a.m. The world outside was silent, but inside, my thoughts were anything but calm.

I pressed my fingers against the pendant, the ruby cold now, its faint weight no longer comforting. "Felix," I whispered to the empty room, the name slipping out before I could stop it.

The memory of Felix in the forest—his guarded expression, his cryptic warnings—swirled around me, pulling me further into confusion. He'd said the pendant was a key, a connection to something better left locked away. But he hadn't told me what that something was, only that it could change everything. And the way he'd looked at me, like he wanted to say more but couldn't—it was impossible to ignore.

Pacing across the room, I replayed the entities' warnings in my mind, each word cutting deeper than I wanted to admit. They were trying to turn me against him; I was sure of it. But why? What were they so afraid of? And why was Felix tied to all of this, to the pendant, to me?

I stopped by the window, staring out at the quiet street below. The world looked so normal—calm and still, like none of this chaos could touch it. But it felt fragile, like a thin layer of glass separating me from something darker, something waiting to break through.

"I need answers," I said to the night, my voice steady despite the uncertainty clawing at my chest. The pendant pulsed again, almost as if it agreed. Felix might not want to give me the truth, but I wasn't going to let him keep me in the dark. Whatever this connection between us was, it meant something. And I intended to find out what.

I couldn't close my eyes after the nightmare. Every time I even tried, the darkness seemed to creep back in, bringing those whispers with it. Sleep wasn't an option—not after that. Before I realized it, the morning light had started creeping through the blinds, soft and golden, but offering little comfort.

With a heavy sigh, I pushed myself up from the couch, my body protesting with every movement. My muscles felt stiff and sore, like I'd run a marathon in my sleep. Every step was a reminder of just how restless the night had been.

I shuffled into the kitchen, dragging my feet across the cool floor, and reached for the coffee maker. The familiar hum of it brewing filled the silence, grounding me slightly. The rich smell of caffeine was the only thing that felt real, the only thing I could count on to get me through the day ahead. I wrapped my hands around the counter, waiting for the first drop to pour, trying to shake off the lingering weight of the night. Coffee wasn't a cure, but it was a start. I needed something to keep me going, even if it was just enough to keep the memories at bay—for now.

The piercing ring of my phone cut through the silence, jolting me out of my restless pacing. I glanced at the screen, the glow of Jayce's name staring back at me. My stomach tightened slightly, the tension from the nightmare lingering despite the daylight streaming through the windows. It had been hours since I woke up, but the heaviness of the dream hadn't faded. I could still feel the icy whispers of the entities wrapping around me like smoke, their warnings replaying in my mind.

Jayce had been one of the few people I'd confided in about the necklace and the nightmares. He didn't judge, didn't call me crazy, and even if he didn't completely understand, he tried. Right now, that was all I needed.

"Hey," I said, trying to keep my voice steady as I pressed the phone to my ear.

"Hey, Iris!" Jayce's voice was bright, familiar, almost comforting in its casual energy. "I was thinking—Luna's tied up with some family stuff today, so I'm free. Want to hang out? Thought we could grab food or something, unless you've got plans."

His easy tone was enough to pull me out of my spiraling thoughts for a moment, but the weight of the pendant against my chest brought everything rushing back. My mind was still racing with fragments of the nightmare, and I couldn't shake the feeling that the answers were just out of reach, slipping through my fingers every time I tried to grasp them. I needed help. And Jayce was the only person I could turn to right now.

"Jayce," I said, my voice a little sharper than I intended. I paused, taking a deep breath and trying to soften the edge. "Actually, yeah. I could really use your help with something."

"Help?" he echoed, his tone shifting slightly, curiosity mixing with concern. "What's going on?"

I hesitated, biting my lip as I stared out at the quiet street below. The pendant pulsed faintly against my chest, its warmth steady but offering little comfort. "It's... the necklace," I admitted, my voice lowering slightly. "Something happened last night, and I don't think I can figure it out on my own."

Jayce didn't respond immediately, and for a moment, I worried I'd scared him off. But when he spoke, his voice was steady, calm, and as reassuring as ever. "Okay. Where do you want to meet?"

Relief washed over me, and I leaned against the windowsill, clutching the phone tighter. "The park," I said, my voice soft but firm. "The one near the mansion on the hill."

"Got it," he replied. "I'll meet you there in twenty."

As the call ended, I set the phone down, my fingers still gripping the pendant tightly. For all the warnings and all the uncertainty clawing at me, one thing was clear: I couldn't face this alone. And while Jayce didn't know everything—didn't know about Felix—he knew enough. He'd help me figure this out, no matter how strange or impossible it all seemed.

I drained the last sip of coffee and set the mug in the sink, the warmth lingering in my chest as I turned to get ready. The chill of the morning seeped into the room, making the air feel sharp and biting. Pulling open my closet, I grabbed a plain t-shirt and black skinny jeans, pairing them with my favorite Nirvana hoodie—the one that was soft and broken in, like a second skin.

This time, I swapped out my usual Converse for a pair of combat boots, the thick soles and worn leather adding a bit of edge to my otherwise simple look. I ran a hand through my hair, deciding to leave it down, the loose waves brushing against my shoulders. My makeup was quick and minimal—just enough to keep me from looking as exhausted as I felt. There was no time to waste. Not today.

The walk to the park was longer than it felt. Maybe it was the crisp air brushing against my skin, or maybe it was the way my mind raced with fragments of the nightmare and the weight of the pendant against my chest. Either way, by the time I reached the familiar stone pathway leading through the trees, I was barely aware of my surroundings. The mansion on the hill loomed in the distance, its sharp silhouette cutting against the bright sky like something out of another time. It always felt like it didn't belong there, standing too still, too perfect, watching over everything below.

I spotted Jayce sitting on a bench near the fountain. He was leaning forward, his elbows on his knees and his phone in his hands. His dark curls caught the sunlight as he glanced up at me, the easy grin that followed doing little to mask the concern flickering in his eyes.

"Hey, you made it," he said, standing and shoving his phone into his pocket. His smile was genuine, but it wavered when he took a closer look at me. "You look... I don't know, like you haven't slept."

"Yeah, well," I started, managing a weak smile, "sleep isn't exactly my thing lately."

Jayce frowned, his eyebrows pulling together. "More nightmares?"

I nodded, hugging the strap of my bag tightly over my shoulder as I moved closer. The pendant pulsed faintly, as if responding to the mention of the nightmares. "Yeah," I admitted, my voice quieter now. "Worse this time."

He stepped back slightly, gesturing to the bench. "Sit," he said, his tone softer. "Tell me what happened."

I sank onto the bench next to him, the cool stone beneath me grounding as I fidgeted with the hem of my sweater. For a moment, I debated whether I should tell him everything—or at least, as much as I could without mentioning Felix. I didn't want to keep secrets, but Felix's existence felt like something too fragile to share. Not yet.

"It was different this time," I began, my voice unsteady. "It started at my grandmother's house again. The same dark, warped version from before." I paused, staring down at the ground. "But the entities... they weren't just vague this time. They said something about the necklace."

Jayce's jaw tightened slightly, his gaze fixed on me. "What did they say?"

"They said it'll destroy me," I replied, my voice trembling despite my effort to stay calm. "And they—they said it isn't mine. That it belongs to them."

Jayce let out a low breath, running a hand through his hair. "And you believe them?"

"No," I said quickly, clutching the pendant through my sweater. It's faint warmth pushed back against the cold in my chest. "I mean, I don't think I do. They're trying to scare me, to make me doubt everything. But... I don't know. It's hard not to wonder."

Jayce nodded slowly, leaning back against the bench. "They've been messing with your head for weeks. Honestly, I'd be worried if you *didn't* wonder." He glanced at the mansion on the hill, his expression thoughtful. "The necklace is still glowing, right? Doing its weird... pulsing thing?"

I hesitated, then pulled the pendant out from under my sweater. It caught the sunlight, the ruby glinting faintly. The pulsing wasn't as strong as it had been in the dream, but it was still there, a steady rhythm beneath my fingers. "Yeah," I said softly. "It hasn't stopped since it started."

Jayce's brow furrowed as he studied the necklace, his eyes narrowing slightly. "And you're sure it's connected to the nightmares?"

"I'm sure," I replied, my grip tightening around the pendant. "I don't know how, but it is. And I feel like... like I'm running out of time to figure it out."

He straightened, meeting my gaze. "What do you need from me?"

His question caught me off guard—not because I didn't expect him to offer, but because I hadn't let myself think about what help would even look like. For weeks, I'd been trying to navigate this on my own, spiraling deeper into confusion and fear. Asking for help was harder than I thought it would be.

"I need..." I started, my voice faltering. I looked down at the pendant, its faint pulse steady against my palm. "I need someone to keep me grounded. To help me figure out what's real and what's not. And I need to know I'm not completely losing my mind."

Jayce's expression softened, and he reached out, placing a hand on my shoulder. "Iris, you're not losing your mind," he said firmly. "And you're not in this alone. Whatever's going on with that necklace, we'll figure it out. Together."

His words settled over me like a blanket, offering warmth and comfort in a way I hadn't realized I needed. I managed a small smile, the knot in my chest loosening just slightly. "Thanks, Jayce."

"Anytime," he said, leaning back against the bench with a grin. "But you're buying me coffee after this. Deal?"

"Deal," I said, a quiet laugh slipping out. It didn't fix everything, but it was a start. And right now, that was enough.

The conversation with Jayce helped, even if only a little. Talking it out, hearing someone else say the words "we'll figure it out," felt like a lifeline. But as we started to leave the park, I couldn't shake the feeling that the answers weren't as far away as they seemed. I adjusted the strap of my bag over my shoulder, the pendant pressing against my chest, its faint pulse an ever-present reminder of the weight I was carrying.

Jayce walked ahead, his hands shoved into his jacket pockets as the path curved toward the exit. The mansion on the hill loomed behind us, its jagged silhouette making its presence known, unnaturally motionless, unnervingly flawless—like a monument to something long forgotten, yet still watching, still waiting, as if it remembered every secret the world tried to bury.

That's when I spotted him. Felix.

He was standing near the park's edge, just inside the shadow of the mansion's towering iron gates. His posture was casual, with one hand in his pocket, and he leaned against the post like he had all the time in the world. But his gaze locked onto mine the moment I noticed him, and just like that, the pulse of the pendant quickened against my chest.

For a second, I thought maybe he'd followed me, but then something clicked. The mansion. He wasn't just passing by—he lived there. It wasn't hard to imagine him belonging in a place like that, with its sharp edges and secrets carved into every brick.

"Iris?" Jayce's voice pulled me out of my thoughts. He'd stopped walking and turned to look at me, a confused expression crossing his face. "You coming?"

I hesitated, glancing between Jayce and Felix. Felix hadn't moved, but the faintest smirk tugged at the corner of his lips as he caught my hesitation. The logical part of me wanted to ignore him, to keep walking and let whatever this was go. But something about him—about the mansion, the necklace, everything—kept me rooted in place.

"Wait here," I said quickly, my voice firm but not unkind. "I need to do something. Just… wait for me. I'll be back."

Jayce frowned, his confusion deepening, but he nodded. "Okay. Don't take too long."

I adjusted the strap of my bag over my shoulder and headed toward Felix, my steps cautious but deliberate. When I was close enough to see him clearly, he straightened, the smirk on his face softening into something unreadable.

"Wasn't expecting to see you here," Felix said, his voice calm and casual, as though we were just old friends running into each other. "Should I assume you were looking for me?"

His tone was playful, but there was a sharpness to it, like he was testing me. "Actually, I wasn't," I replied evenly, crossing my arms. "But apparently, you live here."

Felix raised an eyebrow, glancing over his shoulder at the mansion. "Guilty. I moved in a few weeks ago. Not that the locals have been particularly welcoming, though. A place like that doesn't exactly scream 'warm vibes.'"

I glanced at the mansion again, its cold, imposing figure making the hair on the back of my neck stand on end. "Makes sense," I said, keeping my tone neutral. "It fits you."

Felix chuckled softly, but his attention shifted past me, toward Jayce, who was waiting by the fountain in the distance. "Your boyfriend?" he asked, his voice light but laced with something else—a hint of curiosity, maybe even jealousy.

I scoffed, shaking my head. "No. He's a friend. Not that it's any of your business."

"Touchy," Felix replied, his smirk returning. "Just curious. You've got that 'I'm not interested in explaining' energy."

I rolled my eyes, resisting the urge to fire back. Instead, I stepped closer, my grip tightening on the necklace through my sweater. "Why are you here, Felix?" I asked, keeping my voice steady. "Why this mansion, this park?"

His smirk faded slightly, replaced with that guarded expression I was starting to recognize. "Why not?" he countered. "A place like this has history. Secrets. Felt like the right fit."

There was more to it—of course there was—but I wasn't about to let him pull me into circles. "Fine," I said, turning to leave. "Enjoy your secrets."

"Wait," Felix called out, and I stopped, glancing back over my shoulder. He was studying me, his blue eyes sharp and searching. "You never told me your name."

I hesitated, the pendant pulsing faintly against my chest. He didn't know. He had seen me in the dreams and talked to me, but he didn't know who I was outside of them. Part of me wanted to keep it that way, but the other part—the curious, reckless part—didn't see the harm.

"Iris," I said simply.

Felix's smirk returned, softer this time. "Iris," he repeated, the name rolling off his tongue like it had been waiting there. "Good to know."

I didn't wait for him to say more. Without another word, I turned and walked back toward Jayce, my thoughts swirling as I tried to make sense of everything.

Jayce was still sitting by the fountain, his elbows resting on his knees as he stared down at his phone, idly scrolling through something. His head snapped up the moment he heard my footsteps, his expression shifting to one of curiosity as I approached.

"You good?" he asked, straightening and tucking his phone into his jacket pocket. "What was that all about?"

I hesitated, my thoughts still swirling from the encounter with Felix. His playful smirk, the hint of jealousy in his voice—it all felt strangely out of place, like a puzzle piece that didn't quite fit. And yet, something about him seemed tied to everything: the mansion, the necklace, the nightmares. I wasn't ready to explain it, not entirely.

"Nothing," I said quickly, forcing a small smile as I adjusted the strap of my bag over my shoulder. "Just... thought I recognized someone."

Jayce raised an eyebrow, his lips twitching like he was holding back a grin. "Right. Sure. Someone you recognized just *had* to stop you in the middle of a park. Totally normal."

I shot him a look, but he just smirked, falling into step beside me as we headed down the path toward the park's exit. "You're really good at avoiding the question, you know," he added with a teasing edge. "Super smooth."

"I'm not avoiding anything," I replied, crossing my arms defensively. "I told you, it's nothing."

"Uh-huh," Jayce said, his tone playful now. "So, this 'nothing'—did it have a name? Or were they one of those mysterious 'I'd-rather-not-say' types?"

I rolled my eyes, trying to fight the flush creeping into my cheeks. "You're impossible."

"And yet, you still hang out with me," he quipped, his grin widening.

Despite everything, his lightheartedness eased the tension in my chest just slightly. The path ahead was still uncertain, and the answers felt farther away than ever. But at least I wasn't facing it alone.

Jayce sighed, running a hand through his hair as we reached the sidewalk. The world outside the park felt brighter, noisier, and more normal than it should have—like a sharp contrast to everything that had happened inside. "Alright," he said finally, his tone shifting back to something steadier. "So, what's the plan? How do we crack this thing?"

I shook my head, staring down at the pavement as we walked. "I don't know yet," I admitted, my voice quieter now. "But I think we need to figure it out step by step."

Jayce nodded slowly, his gaze thoughtful. "Alright. Any starting points in mind?"

"I'm not sure," I said, clutching the pendant through my sweater. Its pulsing rhythm was steady, persistent, as though it was trying to remind me of something I hadn't figured out yet. "It's all tangled up in something bigger, I know that much. I just need time to sort it out."

Jayce raised an eyebrow, smirking slightly. "Okay. So, we're starting with cryptic statements? Could we at least try for a solid lead?"

"Jayce," I groaned, shaking my head, "you're not helping."

"I'm just saying," he teased, bumping my shoulder lightly. "I'm all for the mystery vibe, but you gotta let me in on the plan. You *do* have a plan, right?"

"I'm working on it," I muttered, though a faint smile tugged at the corner of my lips, even though I tried not to.

"Good," he said, his tone softening slightly. "Because whatever it is, you're not doing it alone. We'll figure it out, even if we have to wing it."

His words were enough to make the knot in my chest loosen, just a little. The path ahead was still foggy, full of questions I didn't have answers to. But with Jayce by my side, it didn't feel quite as overwhelming.

The coffee shop was small and cozy, tucked away on the corner of a quiet street. The smell of freshly brewed espresso hit me the moment I walked in, and for the first time all day, I felt the tension ease slightly from my shoulders. Jayce was already standing at the counter, chatting with the barista like they were old friends. Typical Jayce—charming his way through the world one grin at a time.

I stepped up beside him, fumbling with my wallet. "You're not getting anything fancy," I teased, pulling out a few bills. "You said I owe you coffee, not a five-course meal."

Jayce smirked, leaning casually against the counter. "What, no whipped cream? No caramel drizzle? You wound me."

"Keep it simple," I shot back, shaking my head. "I'm not made of money."

After ordering, we grabbed a corner table near the window. Jayce leaned back in his chair, sipping his coffee and watching me carefully as I stirred sugar into mine. The playful edge to his grin had faded, replaced with something quieter. "So," he said finally, breaking the silence, "you gonna tell me what's been going on? Besides the nightmares, I mean."

I hesitated, my fingers tightening around the mug. Jayce wasn't pushy—he never was—but his patience made it harder to avoid the subject. "I talked to my mom yesterday," I admitted, my voice quieter than I intended. "It... didn't go the way I thought it would."

Jayce frowned, leaning forward slightly. "What happened?"

"She saw the necklace," I said, glancing down at it as it rested against my chest. "And she... she froze. Like she couldn't believe it was real. I tried asking her about it, but she wouldn't say anything. She just changed the subject every time I brought it up."

Jayce's jaw tightened slightly, his gaze flickering to the necklace. "She didn't say *anything*? Not even why it freaked her out?"

"No," I said, frustration creeping into my voice. "It's like she wasn't just avoiding me—she was avoiding *it*. She wouldn't even look at it for more than a second."

Jayce shook his head, leaning back in his chair. "That's... weird, even for your mom."

"I know," I said, guilt twisting in my stomach. "And I couldn't push her. She looked so shaken, like just talking about it would break something inside her."

Jayce studied me for a moment before taking another sip of coffee. "Okay, so that's another mystery to add to the pile. Great. This thing keeps getting weirder."

I sighed, swirling the last bit of coffee in my mug. "We need Luna," I said finally, setting it down with a quiet clink. "She might know where to start."

Jayce raised an eyebrow, his grin returning. "You're saying we need the brainiac in on this? You finally admit we're in over our heads?"

"I'm saying she's good at figuring things out," I replied, rolling my eyes. "She might know how to make sense of this, or at least give us a direction."

"Fair," Jayce said, leaning back again. "So, when are we looping her in?"

"Tonight," I said quickly. "She's supposed to be free later, so we can meet somewhere quiet. No distractions, no interruptions."

Jayce nodded, his grin fading slightly. "Alright. Just promise me you're gonna be careful with this. Luna's great and all, but... this necklace? It's not just some puzzle. You've already got people trying to mess with your head."

"I know," I said, my voice steady. "But I can't ignore it. If I don't figure it out, it's just going to keep getting worse."

Jayce studied me for a moment before nodding. "Okay. Let's do it. But if this turns into a ghost-hunting expedition or something, I'm out."

I laughed, the sound lighter than I'd expected. "Deal. No ghost-hunting. Just answers."

The café door chimed softly as we stepped outside. The air was crisp, carrying the faint scent of rain that hadn't yet fallen. I hugged my arms around myself, the day's exhaustion settling heavily on my shoulders. Jayce walked beside me, his hands tucked into his jacket pockets as he glanced down at his phone.

"So," he said, tilting the screen toward me, "I texted Luna. She said she's on her way and should be here any second. Figured we could use her brainpower to piece this whole mess together."

I nodded, grateful but nervous. "Good. The sooner we figure this out, the better."

Jayce smirked, nudging me playfully with his elbow. "Don't worry, she's already invested. You've had her hooked ever since you told her about those nightmares."

I rolled my eyes, but a small smile crept onto my face. Jayce wasn't wrong. Luna loved puzzles, and if there was anyone who might actually make sense of everything, it was her. Still, the thought of rehashing the details made my stomach twist.

As if on cue, a familiar voice called out, "You guys better not have started without me."

I turned to see Luna striding toward us, her dark hair swept into a messy bun, a notebook tucked under her arm. She had the kind of presence that demanded attention—not because she was loud, but because she carried herself with a quiet confidence that made people stop and listen.

"You didn't order me coffee, did you?" Luna teased, her eyebrow arching as she stopped in front of us. Without missing a beat, she leaned in, rising onto her toes to plant a quick, playful kiss on Jayce's lips. The gesture was casual, effortless, but it carried that spark of familiarity—the kind that made you feel like you were intruding on a moment meant just for them. Jayce grinned, his hand brushing lightly against her arm as if to say, *I knew you'd show up.*

"Relax," Jayce replied, holding up his hands. "We didn't even know what mood you'd be in—black coffee? Chai latte? Double espresso with a side of sass?"

Luna rolled her eyes but smirked. "Right. Because my personality is a roulette wheel, anyway, what's the deal? You dragged me out here without much context."

Her attention shifted to me, her sharp gaze softening slightly. "Alright, Iris. Catch me up. Jayce said your mom reacted to the necklace? What exactly happened?

I recounted everything—the pulse of the pendant against my chest, my mom's strange reaction when she saw it, and the lingering tension that had followed me ever since. Luna listened intently, her expression a mix of curiosity and concern. She didn't interrupt, but I could see the wheels turning in her mind, her notebook poised in her lap as if she was mentally taking notes.

"So, let me get this straight," Luna said when I finished. "You've got a necklace that pulses like it's alive, nightmares that seem tied to it, and your mom acted like she'd seen a ghost when she noticed it?"

"Pretty much," I said, biting the inside of my cheek.

"And don't forget the park," Jayce added, smirking. "She had a little run-in with a mysterious guy who may or may not be connected to all of this."

Luna's eyes narrowed slightly, her curiosity sharpening. "Mysterious guy?"

"It's not important," I said quickly, shooting Jayce a glare. "He's just... someone who lives near the park. I don't even know if he's connected."

"Uh-huh," Luna said, clearly unconvinced but not pushing the subject. She tapped her fingers against her notebook, her eyes distant as she thought. "Okay. First things first, we need to figure out what this pendant is. If it's glowing, pulsing, and giving you nightmares, it's not just a random piece of jewelry."

Jayce nodded, his earlier joking demeanor giving way to something more serious. "Agreed. Any ideas where to start?"

"There's a library near my place," Luna said thoughtfully. "They've got a section on local history and folklore. Maybe there's something there about this kind of thing—objects with... effects."

"That sounds like a good place to start," I said, relief mixing with apprehension. Finally, a concrete plan, but the weight of the unknown loomed large. "Thanks, Luna."

She waved me off, a small smile tugging at her lips. "Don't thank me yet. We've still got a lot of digging to do."

CHAPTER VIII

The Diary

As we started walking, the conversation shifted into planning mode. Luna flipped open her notebook, jotting down quick notes as she spoke. "We'll need to look for anything that mentions glowing objects, curses, or connections to dreams. If there's a pattern, we'll find it."

Jayce glanced over her shoulder, his brow furrowing. "You think it's cursed?"

Luna shrugged, her pen pausing mid-sentence. "I don't know. But if it's tied to nightmares and your mom's reaction, it's not exactly harmless, is it?"

I stayed quiet, my fingers brushing against the pendant through my sweater. The idea of it being cursed felt... wrong, somehow. It wasn't just the nightmares or the pulsing—it was the way it felt, like it was alive in some strange, unexplainable way. But I didn't know how to put that into words.

"We'll figure it out," Luna said, her voice cutting through my thoughts. "Whatever this thing is, it's not going to stay a mystery forever."

Jayce grinned, nudging her playfully. "Look at you, all determined. You're really leaning into the whole 'detective' vibe, huh?"

Luna rolled her eyes, but her smirk returned. "Someone has to keep you two on track. Otherwise, you'd just sit around making jokes while Iris spirals."

"Hey," Jayce protested, holding up his hands. "I'm here for moral support. And snacks. Don't underestimate the power of snacks."

Much to my own surpirse, I laughed—a small, genuine sound that felt like a relief after the weight of the day. For the first time in hours, the knot in my chest loosened just slightly.

The three of us walked through the quiet streets, the evening settling into a peaceful rhythm around us. Streetlights flickered on one by one, casting soft pools of light that stretched across the pavement. Luna led the way, her notebook clutched tightly in her hands as her determined stride set the pace. Jayce walked beside me, his hands buried in his jacket pockets, stealing occasional glances at my face as though he was gauging how I was holding up.

"You know," Jayce started, his voice cutting through the silence, "this whole library thing feels very old-school detective. Next thing you know, we'll be solving mysteries with magnifying glasses and trench coats."

Luna turned slightly, her brow arching as she shot him an unimpressed look. "Well, maybe you could focus on being useful instead of cracking jokes. Or is that too much to ask?"

Jayce smirked, nudging me lightly. "See? This is why I'm here for moral support. She's relentless."

I couldn't help but laugh—a quiet sound that felt more like a reflex than anything else. But it was nice. For a moment, it lightened the weight pressing against my chest.

The library was tucked into a narrow building near the edge of Luna's neighborhood. It wasn't grand or intimidating, but there was something about the quiet hum of its fluorescent lights and the endless rows of books that felt welcoming. We stepped inside, greeted by the faint smell of old pages and the low hum of the air conditioning.

"Alright," Luna said, her tone brisk as she led us toward the back of the library. "The local history and folklore section is over here. Let's not waste time."

Jayce leaned closer to me as we followed her. "Always nice to see Luna in her element," he whispered with a grin.

Luna must have heard him because she shot him a look over her shoulder. "If you're not going to help, feel free to leave."

"I'm just saying you're impressive," Jayce replied, holding up his hands defensively. "No need to bite my head off."

I shook my head at the two of them, a small smile tugging at my lips. Even with the strange tension in my chest, their banter felt like a reminder that I wasn't alone.

We split up to comb through the shelves, each of us scanning book spines for anything that might hint at answers. My hands trembled slightly as I reached for titles—*Myths and Legends of the Region, Old Families and Their Secrets, History of Unusual Objects*. Each one felt like it could hold something, but I wasn't sure what I was looking for.

Jayce was the first to break the silence. "Found something that mentions necklaces. Think it's relevant?"

Luna appeared beside him in seconds, her eyes narrowing as she took the book from his hands. "We'll see," she said, flipping through the pages with practiced ease. Her gaze sharpened when she stopped on a passage. "There's a section about objects that are said to 'carry energy.' It's not specific, but it mentions connections to dreams, memory, and emotion."

"That's... creepy," Jayce muttered, leaning closer to peer over her shoulder.

I stepped beside them, my chest tightening as I scanned the words. Energy. Dreams. Emotion. It all sounded too familiar, too close to what I'd been experiencing. My fingers brushed against the pendant through my sweater, its faint pulse grounding me as I tried to process the information.

Luna tapped her pen against the page. "This isn't much, but it's a start. We'll need to dig deeper, maybe cross-reference with something else."

Jayce leaned back, his arms folding across his chest. "So, what? We stick to books, or do we actually try talking to someone? Like an expert or historian or whatever?"

"We'll do both," Luna replied decisively. "But first, let's see if we can find more here."

As we combed through the shelves, Luna's sharp eyes spotted something unusual—a gap behind one of the older books, just large enough to hide something. She reached for it, her fingers brushing against a cold, leather-bound object. When she pulled it free, Jayce and I immediately moved closer out of curiosity.

"What is that?" Jayce asked, his voice hushed as though he didn't want to disturb the library's quiet.

"It's a diary," Luna replied, her fingers tracing the worn edges of the cover. Strange symbols decorated the front, almost faint with age but still discernible. "And judging by its condition, it's been here for a long time."

She opened it carefully, revealing pages filled with handwritten text. The ink was faded but legible, the language archaic yet eerily familiar. Luna skimmed the first few pages, her brow furrowing as her eyes darted across the words.

"It's about objects," she said, glancing up at us. "Someone's research—stories of artifacts that carry energy, that... affect people."

Jayce leaned closer, peering over her shoulder. "Artifacts like necklaces?"

"Exactly," Luna replied, her tone steady but laced with intrigue. "And there's more. Whoever wrote this seemed to think these objects were connected to specific families. It mentions warnings and... consequences."

A chill ran down my spine as I touched the pendant beneath my sweater. "Do you think this could be connected to my necklace?"

Luna nodded slowly. "It's possible. But we'll have to read through it to know for sure."

The three of us huddled around a small, circular table in the quietest corner of the library, the diary resting between us like a sleeping beast. Its leather cover was cracked with age, the strange symbols etched into it almost glowing under the dim light. It felt heavier than it should have—as though it carried more than just words.

Luna opened the diary slowly, her movements careful, almost reverent. The first few pages were filled with flowing script, the handwriting meticulous but archaic. The ink had faded, and parts of the text were smudged, but the meaning was still clear enough to send chills down my spine.

"This is... really old," Luna murmured, her fingers brushing over the page. "The language—it's ancient, but familiar. There's a mix of Latin and something else I can't quite place. Whatever this is, it goes back centuries."

Jayce leaned closer, his brow furrowed. "What does it say? Anything useful?"

Luna's eyes scanned the page, her lips moving slightly as she read to herself. Finally, she spoke, her voice barely above a whisper. "Like I said, it's talking about objects—artifacts that were created using... dark magic."

I felt a shiver run down my spine, the pendant pulsing faintly against my chest. "Dark magic?"

Luna nodded, her expression grim. "This diary—it's not just a collection of folklore. It's someone's account, their research. They were trying to document these artifacts, how they were made, and what they were used for. And your necklace— it matches one of the descriptions."

I felt my stomach drop. "What does it say about the necklace?"

Luna flipped through the pages, her fingers skimming over the text until she found the section she was looking for. "Here. It mentions a pendant—small, glowing, with a steady pulse. The writer refers to it as... a key."

"A key to what?" Jayce asked, leaning in, his voice hushed now.

Luna shook her head. "It doesn't say. At least, not yet. But it does mention something else. Something... unsettling." She glanced at me, her expression cautious. "It requires a sacrifice."

The air seemed to grow colder around us, the words hanging heavy in the silence that followed. I reached for the pendant beneath my sweater, its warmth contrasting sharply with the chill spreading through me. "What kind of sacrifice?"

"I don't know," Luna admitted, her voice barely audible. "The text is vague. It just says that the key's true purpose can only be unlocked with... blood."

Jayce let out a low whistle, his attempt at levity falling flat against the weight of Luna's words. "That's... wow. Okay. This is officially way beyond the 'creepy dreams and glowing jewelry' stage."

I stared at the diary, my mind racing. The words blurred together as a thousand questions fought for dominance in my head. *Who created this necklace? Why was it tied to me? And what would the key unlock?*

"There's more," Luna said, breaking the silence. She pointed to a passage farther down the page. "The writer talks about consequences. They believed that these artifacts—especially the ones tied to blood sacrifices—were cursed. Anyone who possessed them would be... haunted."

"Haunted," I repeated, the word tasting bitter on my tongue. "Like the nightmares."

"Exactly," Luna said, her eyes meeting mine. "But it's not just nightmares. The writer mentions shadows, voices, and the feeling of being watched. They believed the artifacts were... alive, in a way. Like they had their own will, their own purpose."

Jayce looked between us, his expression a mix of disbelief and concern. "Okay, so let me get this straight. This necklace is ancient, tied to dark magic, requires a sacrifice, and might be... alive?"

"Alive isn't the right word," Luna said, though she didn't sound entirely convinced herself. "But yes, that's the gist of it."

I leaned back in my chair, my fingers clutching the pendant tightly. It felt so small, so innocuous, but the weight of its meaning was suffocating. "Why me?" I whispered, more to myself than anyone else.

"We'll figure it out," Luna said firmly, her determination cutting through the fear that threatened to swallow me whole. "This diary is just the beginning. There's more here—we just need time to piece it together."

Jayce placed a hand on my shoulder, his grip steady and reassuring. "She's right. We'll figure it out. Whatever this thing is, we're not letting it mess with you anymore than it already has."

I nodded, swallowing the lump in my throat. The pendant pulsed faintly against my chest, a reminder of its presence, its power. The answers felt closer than ever, but so did the danger. Whatever this key unlocked, I knew one thing for certain: it wasn't meant to be opened lightly.

I turned my head back to Luna, a nervous laugh slipping out as I tried to mask the unease bubbling in my chest. "You know," I said, letting my tone take on a teasing edge, "for someone who's completely freaked out by horror movies, you sure have a thing for dark and creepy stuff."

Luna glanced up from the diary, her lips curling into a faint smile. "I hate watching them," she said with a quiet chuckle, "but there's something different about reading it all. Mysteries don't scare me—they intrigue me." She tapped her fingers on the diary's cover for emphasis, her expression light but focused. For a moment, it felt like she had pulled me just slightly out of the shadows swirling around us.

Jayce, who had been surprisingly quiet for the last few minutes, leaned back in his chair and crossed his arms with a smirk. "Well, I hate to break it to you, but I think we've officially crossed over into horror movie territory. Creepy necklaces, haunted diaries, sacrifices—what's next? A haunted mansion?"

Luna didn't look up from the diary, but I could see the corner of her mouth twitch as if she was trying not to smile. "Don't give the universe any ideas, Jayce. We're already knee-deep in weird."

I looked out the library's window, and the darkness outside pressed up against the glass like it was waiting for us. The pendant beneath my sweater pulsed faintly, its rhythm steady but insistent, as if reminding me it was still there. Still waiting.

"I think we've gotten everything we can from the diary for now," Luna said suddenly, snapping the cover shut and startling me out of my thoughts. "But we can't stop here. This thing," she motioned toward the pendant, "is connected to something bigger. We need more than just cryptic warnings and old stories."

"Like what?" I asked, my voice quieter than I intended.

"Answers," Luna replied firmly. "Real, tangible answers. The diary mentioned objects tied to families, curses, and sacrifices. Maybe that means there's a history to track down—something local we're missing."

Jayce raised an eyebrow. "You're saying we take the field trip route? Start poking around places that might tie into this?"

"Exactly," Luna said, standing and tucking the diary under her arm. "But not just anywhere. The mansion on the hill—that's where we need to go."

My heart sank, and I felt the blood drain from my face. "The mansion? Why?"

"Because," Luna said, meeting my gaze, "it's the only place that makes sense. The diary talks about artifacts being tied to people and locations. If there's a connection, that's where we'll find it."

"And if there isn't?" Jayce asked, his tone light but edged with unease.

"Then we move on to the next lead," Luna said simply. "But we have to start somewhere."

"So," Luna said finally, breaking the silence. Her voice was calm, steady, the tone of someone who'd already mapped out their next move. "We know someone lives there now. What's the plan? Knock on the door and politely ask for a tour of their ancient, possibly cursed mansion?"

Jayce snorted, his smirk cutting through the tension like a blade. "Yeah, that'll go over well. 'Hi, we're just here to poke around your house because of a weird necklace and a haunted diary.' Totally normal. I'm sure he'll invite us in for tea and cookies."

I tightened my grip on the strap of my bag, shifting uncomfortably under their scrutiny. "We can't just... show up like that. It's not realistic."

"Okay," Luna said suddenly, "the mansion is off the table for now. But that doesn't mean we're out of options."

Jayce rocked his chair forward with a thud, raising an eyebrow at her. "Care to enlighten us? Because right now, all I'm seeing is a lot of dusty books and zero leads."

Luna didn't look up from the diary, her fingers tapping lightly on the page. "There's more here. This writer—whoever they were—they were obsessed with the connection between these artifacts and families. If we can trace the mansion's history, we might be able to figure out how it ties into all of this."

"And how exactly do we do that?" Jayce asked, his tone teetering between genuine curiosity and exasperation. "It's not like we can just Google 'creepy mansion family tree.'"

Luna's lips curved into a faint smile, her gaze still fixed on the diary. "We don't need Google. We've got this." She gestured to the stack of books she had pulled earlier—histories of the town, local records, even folklore collections. "If the mansion has a history, it's in here somewhere. We just have to dig for it."

I stayed quiet, my fingers brushing against the pendant through my sweater. My thoughts were a tangled mess, circling back to Felix and his cryptic presence at the park. The more I thought about him, the more his words gnawed at me—the way he had looked at me, like he knew exactly what was going on but wasn't going to say a word.

Jayce must have noticed my distraction because he let out a low whistle and leaned his elbow on the table, his gaze fixed on me. "You know," he started, his tone casual but laced with something sharper, "it's funny how you're so against going to the mansion when you were perfectly fine chatting it up with its mysterious resident earlier."

My stomach dropped, and I shot him a glare. "Not this again."

"Oh, absolutely this again," Jayce said, his smirk growing. "You were talking to someone at the park, weren't you? And let me guess—he just *happens* to live in the mansion."

Luna looked up sharply, her eyes narrowing. "Wait— what is he talking about?"

I sighed, realizing there was no way out of this. "Yes, someone lives there. His name's Felix. I ran into him at the park earlier."

"And you didn't think to mention this?" Luna asked, her tone sharp but not angry—more like she was trying to piece together a puzzle.

"It didn't seem relevant," I said defensively. "I don't even know him."

"Well, time to read then," Luna said, with a hint of irritation in her voice.

The conversation faded into silence, the weight of our task settling over us like a heavy fog. With a quiet determination, we turned our attention to the piles of books spread out in front of us, each one a potential gateway to the answers we so desperately needed. Pages turned, pens scratched against paper, and the soft rustle of shifting tomes filled the space. We clung to the hope that somewhere in this sea of words, we'd uncover even the tiniest scrap of information—some detail, no matter how small, that could guide us through the dark and tangled web we'd found ourselves in. The library around us felt timeless, like it was holding its breath, waiting for us to unlock its secrets.

The conversation at the park kept replaying in my mind—his sharp gaze, his cryptic tone, the way he'd seemed like he was holding something back. But I couldn't tell them about that. Not yet. The more Luna and Jayce probed for answers, the more I felt the walls closing in around me.

"Hey, Iris," Jayce said suddenly, snapping me out of my thoughts. "You good? You've been quiet."

"I'm fine," I said quickly, forcing a small smile. "Just... thinking."

"Yeah," he said, eyeing me skeptically. "You've been doing a lot of that lately. It's almost like you know something you're not telling us."

My stomach dropped, panic bubbling up in my chest, but I kept my expression neutral. "I don't know anything more than you do," I lied, hoping it sounded convincing. "I'm just as in the dark as you are."

Jayce studied me for a moment longer before shrugging and turning back to Luna. "Alright, detective. What's next?"

Luna didn't seem to notice the brief exchange; she was too focused on jotting something down in her notebook. "Next, we hit the archives. If there's a connection between the mansion and the necklace, that's where we'll find it. We just have to be thorough."

The rest of the evening passed in a haze of quiet murmurs and the soft sound of pages turning. We combed through history books and town records, piecing together fragments of the mansion's past. But it was slow going, each lead feeling more like a dead end than a breakthrough.

By the time we finally packed up, the library was nearly empty, its usual hum of activity replaced with an eerie silence. I clutched the pendant tightly as we walked outside, the cool night air biting at my skin. The mansion loomed in the distance, its dark windows glowing faintly in the moonlight like watchful eyes.

"We'll figure this out," Luna said, her voice quiet but firm. "It's just a matter of time."

"Yeah," Jayce added, his smirk softer now. "No ancient mystery's gonna beat us."

I managed a small smile, but the weight of their words felt heavier than it should have. Time wasn't something we had in abundance—and I wasn't sure how long I could keep Felix out of the picture.

As the library's closing announcement echoed softly through the aisles, we packed up our scattered notes and closed the heavy tomes, their worn covers shutting with soft thuds. The air between us was quiet but charged, each of us lost in the gravity of everything we'd uncovered—or hadn't.

"Alright," Luna said, tucking the diary securely under her arm. Her tone was calm but decisive, her gaze flicking to me and then Jayce. "We'll regroup tomorrow. Same time?"

"Sure," Jayce said, stifling a yawn as he pushed himself up from the floor. "You know I can't stay away from dusty books and dramatic mysteries for long."

Luna rolled her eyes but didn't bother replying, her focus already elsewhere. She turned to me, her expression softening slightly. "Take care of yourself, okay? The nightmares... just don't let this get to you more than it already has."

"I'll be fine," I said quickly, forcing a small smile. "Promise."

Jayce shot me a skeptical glance as he shoved his hands into his jacket pockets. "You sure? You've been looking a little... you know, haunted."

"Thanks for the vote of confidence," I muttered, shaking my head.

"I'm serious," he said, his smirk faltering for just a moment. "If things get worse, you let us know. We're in this with you, alright?"

I nodded, the warmth of their concern settling over me like a soft blanket. "I will."

With that, we parted ways, Luna heading toward her bike and Jayce disappearing down the street with a lazy wave. I lingered for a moment, letting the night air wash over me before turning and starting the walk back home.

As I neared my apartment, the familiar glow of the diner caught my eye, its neon sign buzzing softly in the night. My stomach growled before I even realized it, the sound cutting through the quiet like a reminder I couldn't shake. I placed a hand over my stomach, as if that could somehow quiet the hunger. The sign felt brighter than usual, almost like it was calling out to me, tempting me with the promise of warm food and a break from the eerie stillness that had been following me all day. It was magnetic in a way—an anchor in the middle of everything unknown.

By the time I stepped into the diner, the cool night air clinging to me, the place was quiet, almost deserted. The neon sign outside buzzed faintly, casting an uneven glow across the cracked asphalt of the parking lot. Inside, the hum of fluorescent lights and the comforting scent of coffee and fried food wrapped around me like a blanket. The quiet felt soothing, a stark contrast to the chaos of my thoughts and the persistent pulse of the pendant beneath my sweater.

Sliding into a booth near the back, I grabbed the menu from its holder, the laminated edges worn and curling slightly. The crackle of vinyl beneath me was oddly grounding, a reminder of the normalcy I was trying to cling to despite the weight pressing down on me. Living alone had its moments of quiet solace, but tonight the silence had felt suffocating—like I was teetering on the edge of something I couldn't see yet. This place, with its comforting hum and mundane rituals, felt like a lifeline.

The waitress—a tired-looking woman in her forties with kind eyes—approached to take my order, her pen poised over a faded notepad. "Grilled cheese and a bowl of tomato soup," I said softly, handing her the menu. She nodded with a practiced smile before disappearing behind the counter.

I let my gaze wander, taking in the faint stains on the tiled floor and the flickering lights of the jukebox in the corner. As much as I tried to ground myself in the diner's ordinary rhythm, my mind kept circling back to everything we'd uncovered at the library—the diary, the mansion, the threads tying it all together. And then there was Felix, his sharp gaze and cryptic words lingering at the edges of my thoughts like shadows I couldn't shake.

CHAPTER IX
Uninvited Guest

The sound of the front door opening barely registered until I felt a presence near me. I glanced up sharply, my heartbeat stuttering when I saw him. Felix. His dark hair was tousled, his sharp features softened by the dim light of the diner, but his expression held that same air of mystery—like he was playing a game only he knew the rules to.

He didn't say a word as he slid into the booth across from me, his movements as casual as if he'd been invited. I stared at him, startled, a mix of annoyance and unease bubbling up in my chest.

"For someone who lives alone," he said, his voice smooth and measured, "you seem to gravitate toward places like this."

I frowned, narrowing my eyes. "And for someone who clearly enjoys being cryptic, you have a habit of showing up unannounced." I said, irritation bubbling up in my voice. "How do you know I live alone anyways?

Felix smirked, the corner of his mouth lifting in amusement. "Would you prefer I announce myself? Perhaps send a carrier pigeon?" He said, completely dismissing the question.

I let out a frustrated sigh, leaning back against the booth. "What do you want?"

"To talk," he said simply, leaning back as well and resting his arms casually on the table. "You seem interesting."

I blinked, caught off guard. His demeanor was... different. Less cold, less guarded. The sharp edges of his personality felt blunted tonight, replaced by something quieter, almost curious.

"Interesting," I repeated flatly. "Is that why you keep showing up? It's because I'm interesting?"

Felix shrugged, his gaze steady on mine. "That's part of it. The other part is that." He nodded toward the pendant beneath my sweater, his expression shifting slightly—softer, but still carrying a weight I couldn't quite place.

I swallowed hard, my fingers brushing against the cool metal of the pendant, its faint pulse thrumming in sync with the tension between us. "It keeps pulling us together," I said, my voice low but steady. "Why?"

Felix leaned back slightly, his eyes never leaving mine, the faint trace of a smirk playing on his lips. "Because it's tied to both of us," he said, his tone calm but laced with something unspoken. "You know that already."

"But what does it want?" I pressed, the knot in my chest tightening. "Why does it feel like it's... alive?"

Felix tilted his head, the smirk deepening into something quieter, almost thoughtful. "Because it is—just not in the way you think. It's not about wanting. It's about purpose. The connection isn't random, Iris. It chose us."

The weight of his words hung heavy in the air between us, and the pulse of the pendant seemed to echo the truth of what he'd said. It wasn't just the dreams. It wasn't just coincidence. The bond between us was woven into the very fabric of whatever the pendant was—and somehow, that felt even more terrifying than the nightmares themselves.

"Last night, after you… left," I began softly, my voice wavering slightly. I couldn't quite meet Felix's eyes, the weight of my words making me feel exposed. When I finally looked up, his expression was unreadable, his brow furrowing slightly as though he didn't fully grasp what I meant. "I was pulled into another nightmare," I continued. "They stopped after I met you—sort of—but they came back. Worse than ever."

Something shifted in his expression, and then, a flicker of understanding came to his mind as the meaning behind "left" clicked into place. He knew I wasn't talking about a casual departure. I was talking about the way we were forcefully separated in the dream, as if something—or someone—had torn us apart. "I guess it's safe to say they don't like how much I talk," he said, his voice edged with irritation.

I crossed my arms, holding his gaze with a seriousness that felt heavier than the air between us. "They're afraid. Of us—of *you*," I said, my voice steady despite the knot twisting in my chest. It was the only explanation that made sense. Last night, the shadows in my dream had seemed desperate, more than ever before. "Or maybe it's what you might have to say," I added, my words pointed.

Felix tilted his head slightly, the faint smirk on his lips returning like it never really left. "They better be afraid," he said, his tone light but his words cutting like glass. "They need me. I don't need them."

I frowned, trying to parse the meaning behind his words. What did he mean, they need him? Who were *they?* Questions piled up in my mind like a stack of unread books, but I already knew he wouldn't answer. He wasn't the type to explain things without playing games first.

Before I could press further, the waitress returned with my order, sliding the plate and bowl in front of me with practiced ease. I thanked her quietly, but her attention had already shifted to Felix. Her eyebrows raised slightly, a playful smile curving her lips as she looked him over.

"And can I get you something, young man?" she asked, her voice pitched higher than necessary, a sugary sweetness dripping from her words.

Felix's lips curved into a charming smile—a smile so unlike the guarded ones I'd seen before that it threw me off balance. "Just a cup of tea will do, love. Thank you," he said, his accent suddenly thicker, smoother, like melted honey. The waitress practically beamed, fussing with her hair as she sauntered away. The nerve.

I turned back to my food with an exaggerated look of disgust, grabbing my spoon and stirring the tomato soup a little too aggressively. Felix's attention shifted back to me, his dark eyes glittering with amusement. "Who eats tomato soup with a sandwich?" he asked, his smirk deepening. "Humans amaze me sometimes."

"At least I actually eat food and don't settle for 'a cup of tea, love,'" I shot back, mimicking his accent as I took a bite of my grilled cheese. The fact that he said "humans" didn't even register—it just slid right past me, like water off a glass.

His smirk turned into a wide smile, and then he started laughing—a real, full-bodied laugh that caught me completely off guard. It was warm and alive, nothing like the cold, careful demeanor he usually carried. His eyes crinkled at the corners, and for a moment, he looked less like the mysterious figure tied to my nightmares and more like... well, a person. It was disarming in a way I hadn't expected.

His laughter slowed, and he leaned back in the booth, his grin lingering. "Somebody sounds jealous," he teased, his voice laced with mock innocence.

I froze, my eyes widening in horror. "Jealous? Of course not. I barely know you," I snapped, my voice rising just enough to betray how flustered I was. *This guy is insane.*

Felix chuckled again, clearly enjoying himself. "Jealous, right. I'm not the one flirting with women who could be their mother," I added quickly, my thoughts slipping out of my mouth before I could stop them.

He laughed even harder at that, the sound rich and infectious despite my irritation. "Who said she's older?" he asked, his tone nonchalant, like he hadn't just dropped another confusing comment into the mix.

I nearly choked on my soup, coughing as I stared at him in disbelief. "What?!"

"Nothing," he said smoothly, still smiling as if he hadn't just upended the conversation. Before I could push for an explanation, the waitress returned with his tea, setting it down in front of him with an almost reverent care. "Thank you… Alice," he said, glancing at her name tag before looking back at her with that same charming smile.

Alice blushed, her grin widening as she gave him a small, almost theatrical bow before walking away. It was ridiculous— she was treating him like some kind of royalty. Unbelievable.

I shook my head and returned to my food, trying to ignore the way Felix's presence seemed to fill every inch of the booth. Even when he was irritating me, even when his words left me with more questions than answers, there was something about him I couldn't shake. Something that made me feel, despite everything, a little less alone.

The warmth of the diner, the steady hum of its fluorescent lights, and the low murmur of conversation around us faded into the background as Felix's presence seemed to take over the booth. I found myself stealing glances at him, trying to make sense of the way he could shift from infuriatingly cryptic to surprisingly charming in the blink of an eye. And somehow, despite everything, the sharp edges of his personality didn't seem so daunting anymore.

"Alright, tell me," Felix said suddenly, his voice cutting through my train of thought. "What's so fascinating about grilled cheese and tomato soup? You can't seriously think that's gourmet."

I rolled my eyes, setting my spoon down with a huff. "It's comforting. Not everything has to be gourmet to be good."

He smirked, leaning forward slightly, his elbow resting on the table. "Comforting. That's adorable. You sound like someone who writes poetry about warm bread."

"Bread doesn't need poetry," I shot back. "It's already perfect on its own."

Felix chuckled, shaking his head, his dark hair catching the faint light above us. "You're full of surprises, Iris."

"And you're full of judgment," I countered, lifting my sandwich and taking a deliberate bite. The smug look on his face only grew as he watched me.

"Well, forgive me for being curious about your culinary choices," he said, his tone light and teasing. "You are, after all, still a mystery to me."

His words sent a subtle shiver down my spine, not because of their playful edge, but because of the deeper truth they carried. We were tied together by something far bigger than either of us, and yet, sitting in this diner felt strangely... normal, like we were two regular people figuring each other out.

As I reached for my soup, Felix picked up his cup of tea, swirling the dark liquid with an air of exaggerated elegance. "And here we have a human tradition," he said, his voice adopting an overly serious tone, "pairing melted cheese with tomato broth, claiming it's comfort. Fascinating."

I stifled a laugh, shaking my head at his theatrics. "You're ridiculous."

"I prefer to think of myself as observant," he replied, taking a careful sip of his tea. His gaze flicked to me again, soft but calculating. "Observing you has been... interesting."

I raised an eyebrow, narrowing my eyes slightly. "Are you studying me or something?"

"Maybe," he said, his smirk widening into something almost genuine. "You're much more fun to figure out than most people."

Without meaning to, I felt a smile tug at the corners of my lips. He wasn't trying to hide his curiosity—not tonight, anyway—and somehow, that made his presence feel less intimidating. Maybe even comforting in its own strange way.

The waitress reappeared with a pot of tea, refilling Felix's cup and flashing him another radiant smile. I watched her out of the corner of my eye, barely holding back a snort as Felix thanked her with the same charming warmth that had been catching me off guard all evening.

"Do you flirt with everyone, or am I just lucky?" I asked sarcastically, leaning back in my seat with an exaggerated sigh.

Felix grinned, setting his cup down and meeting my gaze head-on. "Lucky, obviously."

"Wow," I said, rolling my eyes but unable to suppress the faint blush rising to my cheeks. "You're even worse than I thought."

He laughed softly, the sound rich and warm, and for a moment, it felt like there was no distance between us at all. His guarded demeanor, his cryptic remarks—it was all peeling away, revealing someone... real.

"Am I really that bad?" he teased, his voice dropping just slightly, like he was letting me in on a secret.

I shrugged, trying to play off the way my chest tightened at his tone. "You're not the worst, I guess."

Felix leaned forward, resting his chin on his hand as he studied me. "You're honest. I like that."

"I'm not as complicated as you think." I shot back, keeping my tone light. His eyes locked on mine for what it felt like forever.

"Maybe," he said, his smirk softening into a smile—one that felt almost vulnerable. "Or maybe I'm just more myself when I'm with you."

The words hung between us, unexpected and unguarded. I stared at him, my heart racing, unsure how to respond. But then, Felix picked up his tea again, the smirk returning as he took a sip. He didn't push for a reply, didn't pressure me into breaking the moment's quiet.

As I finished the last bite of my grilled cheese, the tension in my chest eased, replaced by a warmth I hadn't expected. Felix's presence wasn't just tolerable anymore—it was grounding, in a strange way. The connection between us, whatever the pendant had forged, felt less like a burden and more like... something I wanted to explore.

"So," Felix said, breaking the silence, "Tomorrow. What's the plan?"

I frowned slightly. "What do you mean?"

"You're looking for answers," he said simply. "You've been searching. At the library... even in your dreams. You think I don't know?"

His gaze sharpened, but there was no malice in it—just understanding. It startled me, the way he could see through me so easily. "I don't have a plan," I admitted quietly.

"Maybe you should," Felix said, his voice softer now. "And maybe you should include me in it."

His words were bold and direct, but they didn't feel forced. Somehow, I found myself nodding, the faint pulse of the pendant steady against my skin, as if it agreed. Maybe it did.

Maybe the connection was meant to bring us together, not just in dreams but here, in the waking world.

"What happened to the whole 'if you keep going down this path, I'm not saving you' crap?" I shot at him, raising an eyebrow as my lips curled into a mocking smirk. The tone of my voice was sharp enough to cut through the diner's soft background hum, but I had no intention of letting my actual emotions show. Felix was always playing games, twisting words, and weaving mystery like it was his second nature. Well, two could play at that game.

Felix leaned back in the booth, his dark eyes glinting with the faintest hint of amusement. "I changed my mind," he replied smoothly, wrapping both hands around his teacup like it was some kind of anchor. "I'm not exactly in the habit of rescuing people from themselves, but... I guess I'm making an exception."

"So what? You think I need saving?" I countered, crossing my arms and leaning forward slightly, daring him to take the bait. My heart was beating faster than I wanted it to, the pulse of the pendant against my chest syncing perfectly with the tension that crackled between us.

"You don't," Felix said, his smirk softening into something quieter, his voice dropping slightly. "But that doesn't mean they won't try to make you believe otherwise."

The shift in his tone threw me off, the weight of his words settling over me like a blanket I couldn't quite shake. I blinked, feeling the fight drain out of me for a moment. "And what about you? Are you here to make me believe otherwise? "Felix's smirk returned, but there was no malice behind it, just something playful—something that felt like it was meant for me, and me alone.

"Is this entertainment for you?" I said, completely angry now.

Felix's smirk softened into something quieter, his voice dropping slightly. "Not quite. But I won't pretend I'm not invested."

I blinked, the weight of his words settling over me. "Invested in what?"

"In you," he said simply, his gaze steady on mine. "You keep pulling me back, whether you realize it or not."

His words struck deeper than I expected, and I didn't know how to respond. The connection between us, forged by the pendant and solidified by the dreams, felt less like a choice and more like inevitability. And despite my irritation, I couldn't deny how his presence steadied me, even when it left me full of questions I wasn't ready to ask.

"You're ridiculous," I said finally, leaning back in my seat and reaching for the soup bowl again. "You say everything like it's some kind of prophecy. Do you have normal conversations, or is this just your personality?"

Felix laughed softly, his gaze fixed on me in a way that made my stomach flip. "I'm having a perfectly normal conversation now, aren't I?"

"If this is normal," I said, stirring my soup with a pointed look, "then I don't want to know what dramatic looks like."

"Oh, dramatic, looks like me waiting for you to figure out all the answers while you insist I'm just here to bother you," he teased, his smirk widening.

I froze for a second, the spoon still in my hand, before narrowing my eyes at him. "You're lucky I haven't thrown you out of this booth yet. You don't seem all that helpful."

Felix leaned forward, resting his chin on his hand as he studied me with that infuriating smirk. "And yet, here I am. Seems like I left quite an impression."

My cheeks burned, and I hated that he could see the blush rising to my face. "An impression, sure," I said quickly, trying to regain the upper hand. "Like the kind a thorn leaves when you step on it."

His laugh was louder this time, warm and rich, and it echoed faintly through the diner. For a moment, I forgot about the tension, the pendant, the questions—everything except the sound of his laugh and the way it made him seem lighter, more human. "You're good at this," he said, shaking his head slightly. "I might have underestimated you."

"And you're bad at this," I shot back. "It's like you're trying to be mysterious on purpose."

"Only because it's fun," Felix said, his smirk softening into a real smile—one that caught me completely off guard. "And because you haven't asked the right questions yet."

I stared at him, my heartbeat quickening, the warmth of the diner suddenly feeling suffocating. "What's the right question?" I asked, my voice quieter now.

Felix shrugged, his gaze dipping to the pendant around my neck before returning to meet my eyes. "That's for you to figure out."

"And you're just going to sit here and drink tea while I do?" I asked, raising an eyebrow.

He leaned back, his grin wide and unapologetic. "Exactly."

Against my better judgement, I felt a smile tugging at the corners of my lips. Felix had a way of frustrating me, of making me feel like I was constantly chasing answers, but tonight, that frustration felt different. It felt... alive, like a spark igniting something I hadn't let myself think about.

We sat in silence for a moment, the space between us crackling with something unsaid. Whatever had pulled him into my life, whether it was the pendant or something else entirely, I wasn't ready to let it push him away—not yet.

I pushed my plate to the side and raised my hand, signaling the waitress for the check. The exhaustion that had been creeping up all evening was finally catching up to me, weighing down every movement like I'd been pulling a cart uphill for hours. Felix, on the other hand, seemed completely unfazed, his gaze steady as he rested his chin on his hand, like the night could stretch on forever if he wanted it to.

The waitress arrived with the check, her usual cheerful smile in place as I handed her my card. When she returned, I left a tip, grabbed my hoodie, and stood, ready to head home and collapse into bed. Felix stood, too, sliding out of the booth with practiced ease and falling into step beside me as we left the diner.

We stepped out into the cold night air, the breeze sharper now, biting at my cheeks and tugging at the hem of my sweater. The streetlights cast long shadows across the pavement, their glow reflecting faintly on Felix's face as he turned to look at me, his expression softer than I expected.

"Leaving already?" he said, his lips curling into a small smile that didn't quite reach his eyes. There was something in his tone—something sad, like he didn't want me to go. That sadness tugged at me, catching me off guard. I was starting to like this version of him, the Felix who let his walls down just enough to seem... real.

"Yeah," I said, yawning as I pulled my hoodie tighter around myself. "It's late, and tomorrow's going to be busy. Work, research..." I hesitated before adding, "probably more nightmares."

Felix's gaze shifted, his hands clasping together in front of him. "Not if I'm there," he said quickly, his voice edged with something fierce, almost protective.

His words caught me off guard, sending a sharp jolt of warmth through my chest that made my stomach twist. My cheeks flushed, and I turned my face away, focusing instead on the cracked pavement beneath my boots. "Um, okay... it's time for me to go. That diary isn't going to read itself tomorrow," I said, trying to shake off the strange feeling curling in my gut.

At the mention of the diary, Felix's head shot up, his dark eyes sharpening with sudden resolve. "Diary, you said?" His voice was steady, but there was something in his gaze— something I couldn't quite decipher, like he'd just pieced together a puzzle I hadn't even noticed yet.

"Yeah," I said cautiously, watching him closely. "My friends and I found this diary in the library... it has information about artifacts created with... dark magic," I whispered, the last part, my voice barely audible, afraid someone might overhear and think I was insane.

Felix's reaction startled me. Excitement flickered in his eyes, a spark I hadn't seen before—like he'd finally found what he'd been searching for all along. "I'm going with you tomorrow," he said, the statement final, leaving no room for discussion.

"What? No!" I snapped, my voice louder than I intended. The sudden outburst made him flinch, his expression shifting to something questioning, almost wounded. I took a deep breath, forcing myself to calm down. "My friends don't know about you. They know about the nightmares, the voices—that's it."

"You told them about the nightmares and the voices, but not me?" His voice was quieter now, tinged with something that sounded almost... hurt.

"I think that's enough information for them right now," I said quickly, sighing. "They already think I'm barely keeping it together after what I've told them. Imagine if I said, 'Oh, by the way, there's this guy I keep seeing in my dreams, and we're weirdly connected by this necklace.'" I paused, throwing my arms up for emphasis. "Besides, Jayce has already been teasing me since he saw us talking at the park. I don't need more of that."

Felix's smirk returned instantly, his demeanor shifting back to its playful edge as he leaned a little closer. "Oh, your 'not-boyfriend,'" he said, clearly relishing the tease. "Well, since I'm your little secret for now, you can come to my place once you're done."

I froze, the words hitting me like a bucket of cold water. Turning to face him, I narrowed my eyes, completely thrown by the suggestion. "What did you just say?" I asked, my voice too sharp, a hand flying to my mouth as I realized how loud I'd been.

Felix stepped closer, just enough for me to hear his steady breathing over the wind. He stopped a few inches from me, his smirk soft but unyielding. "You heard what I said," he murmured, his voice carrying a quiet confidence that made my pulse race. His gaze flicked to the pendant hanging beneath my sweater before returning to meet my eyes, locking me in place.

"I... I have to go," I stammered, my cheeks burning red as I took a step back, my thoughts scrambling for an exit. "I'll see you around."

"See you tomorrow, Iris," Felix said, his voice trailing after me as I turned and hurried toward my apartment, my heart hammering against my ribs.

CHAPTER X

Carrow

The next day, I woke up after a deep sleep. The sunlight streamed through the sheer curtains of the window, painting the room in soft, golden hues. The once heavy quiet of the apartment seemed lighter now, warmed by the morning light. My alarm went off, I blinked against the brightness, the haze of sleep slowly fading as reality settled in. The day ahead loomed large in my mind—work, the diary, research with Luna and Jayce—and the strange, persistent pulse of the pendant against my chest.

I stretched, groaning softly as I swung my legs over the side of the bed. The apartment was still chilly from the night before, and I pulled on a sweatshirt as I made my way to the kitchen. The usual rhythm of my mornings grounded me— coffee brewing in the corner, the faint hum of the refrigerator, the scent of toasted bread filling the air. But even with the comforting familiarity, my thoughts kept circling back to the necklace, to Felix's cryptic presence, and to the moments that lingered long after he'd said goodbye.

Last night was free of nightmares, which I was grateful for, but also free of the forest dream, which made me almost sad.

The necklace was still there, resting against my skin, its weight as steady as ever. As I wrapped my fingers around the smooth metal, I felt the faint pulse again—the one that seemed to sync with my heartbeat. The pull of it felt stronger in the daylight, more insistent.

The thought came unbidden: *What if I take it off?* The question lingered in the air, daring me. It hadn't even crossed my mind before now, but suddenly it felt important. Necessary, even.

Bracing myself, I wrapped my hand around the chain, the delicate links pressing into my palm. I lifted it slightly, the pendant catching the dim light, and slid my fingers toward the clasp at the back of my neck. My breath caught as I hesitated, a strange unease settling in my chest.

"Just take it off," I muttered under my breath, trying to ignore the way my hands were trembling. My fingers found the clasp, fumbling with it for a moment. But as I tried to unhook it, something stopped me—a resistance, like the chain wasn't just tangled but fused together somehow.

My pulse quickened. I tried again, pulling more firmly this time. The clasp wouldn't budge. It was as if the necklace had welded itself shut, defying any attempt to remove it. Panic began to bubble under the surface as I tugged harder, my breathing growing uneven. "What the hell?" I whispered, yanking at the chain with both hands now.

The necklace stayed in place, unmoving, unyielding. The pendant seemed to pulse against my skin, its rhythm stronger, more insistent than before. A wave of dizziness washed over me, forcing me to let go. I sat there, frozen, my hands trembling in my lap as the realization hit me.

I couldn't take it off.

I leaned back against the headboard, my heart racing, the pulse of the pendant seeming to echo through my entire body. The room felt colder now, the shadows on the walls stretching longer, darker. The air itself felt heavier, like the necklace wasn't just a piece of jewelry anymore—it was something alive, something that had made its home in me.

My fingers instinctively found the pendant again, clutching it tightly as if holding onto it would keep the nightmares away. But in the back of my mind, I knew the truth.

The necklace didn't just belong to me.

I belonged to it.

The day was a blur of clinking coffee mugs, hurried orders, and the steady rhythm of footsteps darting back and forth behind the counter. Despite the hustle, my mind wasn't really here. It was somewhere else—on the necklace, on what had happened this morning, and most of all, on the afternoon ahead. I couldn't wait to tell Luna and Jayce about the bizarre resistance I'd felt when trying to take it off. There had to be some kind of explanation, and I was desperate to find it.

Finally, after what felt like an eternity, my shift ended. I practically sprinted to hang up my apron and punch out, my fingers fumbling with the buttons as I fixed my shirt and let my hair fall loose from its messy bun. The pendant slipped forward, its smooth, cold surface resting over the fabric of my long-sleeved shirt. I traced my finger along its edges absentmindedly as I walked toward Tessa to say my goodbyes.

But just as I rounded the corner, I nearly collided with Mr. Ramsey. Lately, he has been lingering around the café more than usual. I figured it had something to do with the vandalism from a few weeks back—he was protective of this place, sometimes maybe a little too much.

"Sorry, Mr. Ramsey—I didn't see you there," I said quickly, apologizing with a small smile. My voice was polite and practiced, just like always, but something about his expression stopped me cold.

At first, his face was neutral, but then his eyes fell on the pendant dangling over my shirt. His features twisted into something unreadable, his gaze distant—like he wasn't even seeing me anymore, but something far beyond. When he spoke, his voice was barely audible, and the word sent a chill down my spine.

"Carrow," he whispered, the name slipping from his lips like it weighed him down.

I froze, confusion and unease swirling together in my chest. "Mr. Ramsey? Are you okay?" I asked carefully, my words shaking slightly as I studied his far-off expression. His eyes seemed glazed over, lost somewhere I couldn't follow.

Then, as if waking from a trance, he blinked rapidly, his focus snapping back to me. He smiled nervously, shifting his stance like he was trying to shake off whatever had just happened. "Iris, sorry—I didn't mean to startle you," he said, his voice noticeably forced. "Did you need anything?"

"No, just apologizing for bumping into you," I replied, forcing a smile that didn't quite reach my eyes. "I was heading out for the day."

He straightened, clearing his throat and nodding briskly. "Of course. Have a good rest of your day." Without another word, he brushed past me, his pace quick as he disappeared into his office.

I stood there for a moment, rooted in place, the faint echo of his whisper looping in my head. *Carrow.* He thought I hadn't heard him, but I had—and now I couldn't stop hearing it. What did he mean by that?

By the time I reached Tessa, I still hadn't pieced together what had just happened. She looked up from where she was wiping down the counter, her eyebrows furrowed as she glanced between me and the door to Mr. Ramsey's office.

"What the hell was that?" she asked bluntly, her confusion mirroring my own.

"I don't even know," I muttered, shaking my head. But the truth was, his words lingered—like they were begging to be unpacked. "I'm heading out, though. See you tomorrow?"

Tessa gave me a small smile, leaning in for a quick hug before pulling away. "Of course. Get some rest, okay?"

The library wasn't far, but I felt like I was running the entire way. The streets blurred past me as my thoughts kept circling back to Mr. Ramsey, his gaze, the name he'd whispered like it carried some kind of weight. Carrow. It was impossible not to wonder—could he somehow be connected to all this? To the necklace, to Felix, to the mounting questions I had no answers for?

Luna and Jayce would know what to do—or at least, they'd try. They always had my back, even when the pieces didn't seem to fit. But as I thought about the day ahead, one thing became clear: I wasn't walking into the library with a clean slate. I was walking in with more questions than ever, and the answers weren't going to come easily.

The library's front doors loomed ahead, their glass panes shimmering in the afternoon sunlight. It was one of those buildings that felt bigger on the inside, like it had secrets tucked away in every corner—and lately, I couldn't shake the feeling that its secrets were starting to notice me. My steps faltered for half a second before I pushed the door open, the faint smell of old paper and wood polish wrapping around me as I stepped inside.

Luna and Jayce were already waiting for me at our usual spot: a round table tucked into an alcove near the shelves marked *Mythology & Folklore*. Luna was hunched over her laptop, her dark hair spilling over her face as she furiously typed something, while Jayce was leaning back in his chair, flipping through an old book with the kind of lazy confidence only he could pull off.

"You're late," Jayce said without looking up, the corners of his mouth quirking into a grin. "Let me guess—coffee shop chaos?"

"Something like that," I muttered, sliding into the seat across from him. The pendant brushed against the edge of the table as I sat down, and I quickly tucked it back under my shirt, hoping neither of them had noticed. "Got caught up, but I'm here now. And I have... a lot to tell you."

Luna finally glanced up, her sharp green eyes narrowing as she studied me. "You look like you've seen a ghost. What happened?"

I hesitated, my fingers brushing against the edge of the table. Where did I even start? With the necklace refusing to come off this morning? With Mr. Ramsey and the cryptic word he'd whispered—*Carrow*—like it was something he recognized? The weight of it all pressed down on me, and for a moment, I wasn't sure I could say any of it out loud.

"Iris," Luna prompted, her tone softening. "Whatever it is, you can tell us."

Taking a deep breath, I let the words spill out. "This morning, I tried to take off the necklace... and I couldn't. It's like it's stuck, like it doesn't want to come off." I paused, glancing between them, their reactions unreadable. "And then, at work, Mr. Ramsey saw it and—he said something. He said... Carrow."

Jayce's book snapped shut, his easy grin vanishing. "Carrow?" he repeated, his voice unusually serious. "What the hell does that mean?"

"I don't know," I admitted, frustration creeping into my voice. "He acted like he didn't even realize he said it—just brushed it off and walked away. But it's been stuck in my head ever since. What if he knows something? What if he knows what this necklace actually is?"

Luna leaned back in her chair, her gaze thoughtful. "Carrow," she said slowly, as if tasting the word. "It sounds... old. Like a name or a place."

"Or both," Jayce added, his brow furrowing. "You think Ramsey's involved in this? He's just the guy who runs a coffee shop."

"So was the library ghost last week," Luna said dryly, her fingers drumming against the edge of the table. "We should start with the diary—maybe it mentions the word somewhere."

Luna pulled the old, weathered diary from her bag, its leather cover cracked and faded. We'd found it during one of our late-night hunts through the library's restricted section, tucked between books that hadn't been checked out in decades. It was full of cryptic notes about artifacts, rituals, and what the author called "the balance"—whatever that meant.

"Where did we leave off?" Luna murmured, flipping carefully through the fragile pages. The handwriting was jagged and uneven, the ink smudged in places like the writer had been in a hurry.

"Here," Jayce said, leaning over her shoulder and pointing to a section near the bottom of one page. "Something about 'bindings' and 'seals.' It sounds... prison-y."

Luna's eyes narrowed as she read the passage aloud. "'Artifacts forged to bind what should never be set free. Sealed in the shadow of the divide, where the keeper stands eternal.'" She looked up at me, her expression grim. "Sound familiar?"

"'Divide' sounds like another word for separation, maybe another realm," Jayce said, crossing his arms. "And 'keeper'... who's that supposed to be?"

A shiver ran down my spine as I thought of Ramsey's distant, hollow expression. "What if Ramsey knows about the 'keeper'? What if *he's* the keeper?"

"That's a stretch," Luna said, though there was a flicker of doubt in her voice. "But it's not impossible. If the necklace is connected to this... realm, and Carrow is its name, then he might know more than he's letting on."

The pendant seemed to pulse faintly against my skin, as if agreeing with her. I swallowed hard, my fingers brushing against it through my shirt. "We need to figure this out. Whatever's happening with this necklace, it's not normal—and if Ramsey's involved, I need to know why."

The library was colder than usual, the air heavy and still, as though the building itself had caught wind of the weight we carried inside. Shadows curled in the corners of the alcove where we sat, barely pierced by the dull glow of the overhead light. The diary lay open on the table between us, its cracked leather cover stark against the polished wood, and Luna's fingers hovered above the pages like she wasn't sure she wanted to touch them.

I sat back in my chair, clutching the necklace beneath my shirt like it might leap away if I let it go. Jayce leaned forward, his elbows resting on the table, his usual smirk replaced with a rare look of genuine curiosity.

"Carrow," Luna murmured, her voice barely above a whisper as her eyes darted across the lines of faded, jagged handwriting. "It's here."

"What does it say?" I asked, leaning closer despite the sick feeling churning in my stomach. My voice cracked slightly, but I didn't care. The name had been ringing in my ears since Ramsey said it, and now... now it was staring back at me from the brittle pages of this forgotten diary.

Luna frowned, her brows knitting together as she read aloud. "'Carrow. A name tied to the binding of the necklace... and to its curse.'" Her voice faltered as she glanced up at me, her green eyes sharp with worry. "It doesn't say much else."

I let out a frustrated sigh, the knot in my chest tightening. "That's it? What kind of curse are we talking about? And why did Ramsey say it like it was something he recognized?"

"Hold on," Luna said, flipping carefully to the next page. Her fingers paused on a line near the bottom, her expression darkening as she scanned the text. "There's more. But... it's not good."

Jayce leaned closer, his tone low. "Define 'not good.'"

Luna inhaled sharply and began reading again, her voice slower this time, heavy with the weight of what she was uncovering. "'The necklace is bound by ritual. To break the binding, a sacrifice must be made. If the ritual remains incomplete—if the binding is fractured but not finished—the one sacrificed will be cursed.'"

My throat tightened. "Cursed how?"

Luna's gaze flicked up to meet mine, hesitant but unwavering. "'Cursed with immortality. Deprived of sleep, cursed to roam the earth, plagued by nightmares that twist and hunt endlessly. The cursed will be unable to eat, unable to find rest, driven to suffering until they return to the necklace and the holder to complete the ritual. An eternity of torment.'"

The words hung in the air like poison, suffocating the small space around us. My grip on the necklace tightened, my heart pounding so loudly I was sure they could hear it. The idea of being bound to this... *thing* forever, of being dragged through nightmares and endless suffering—it made my skin crawl.

"So let me get this straight," Jayce said, breaking the silence. His voice was calm, but his hands were balled into fists on the table. "If someone tries to break the curse without finishing the ritual, they get... what? Eternal misery?"

"That's exactly what it says," Luna replied, her tone grim. She closed the diary, her hand lingering on its cover. "And it sounds like the necklace isn't just any artifact—it's the center of it all. Whoever holds it controls the ritual. Controls... everything."

I stared at the table, my thoughts spinning in every direction. Ramsey's distant gaze flashed in my mind, the way he'd whispered the name like it meant something to him, like he was warning me—or remembering something he couldn't forget. "What if Ramsey knows about the curse?" I said quietly, my voice trembling. "What if he knows exactly what this necklace is—and what it can do?"

Jayce shook his head, leaning back in his chair. "If he does, then he's got some explaining to do. Because this?" He pointed to the diary. "This is way more than we signed up for."

Luna folded her arms, her expression hardening. "We can't ignore this. If the diary's right, then this necklace is dangerous. Whatever Ramsey knows, we need to find out. And we need to figure out why this—" She motioned to the pendant hidden beneath my shirt. "—is connected to you."

The necklace pulsed faintly against my skin, its rhythm steady and deliberate, like it was listening. My chest tightened, fear and determination warring within me. I didn't want this. I didn't ask for any of it. But now, it felt like there was no escaping it.

"Let's find out the truth," I said, my voice shaking but resolute. "Before this gets worse."

Immortality. Endless suffering. Bound to the necklace and its holder.

The words circled in my mind like a storm, each one leaving a deeper cut than the last. An eternity of torment, a punishment that no one deserved, no matter what they'd done.

I flipped through the pages of the folklore book in front of me, the dry paper brushing against my fingertips as if it could somehow ground me. It didn't. The thought of being bound to the necklace—to *someone*—forever sent a sharp chill up my spine.

Then it hit me.

My hands trembled, a cold sweat breaking across my skin. The book slipped from my grasp, crashing onto the table with a hollow thud that seemed to echo through the quiet library. My breath caught in my throat as my heart kicked into overdrive, pounding so loud it drowned out everything else.

"Iris?" Jayce's voice cut through the haze, his chair screeching against the floor as he hurried toward me. "Are you okay?"

Luna was there, too, reaching across the table to clasp my hand in hers. "Iris, hon, please say something. What happened?" Her voice was soft, almost pleading, her eyes scanning my face for any sign of what was going on.

But I couldn't say anything—not yet. All I could see was *him*.

Felix. His guarded demeanor, the way his words were always so carefully chosen, and the fact that he was constantly holding something back. The way he'd look at me sometimes— like he was trying to say something without actually saying it. The way I'd never seen him eat a single thing. And that moment at the diner, when he'd called me "human," and I'd brushed it off, distracted by that stupid flare of jealousy for a guy I barely even knew.

All of it clicked. The forest. The nightmares. The pull of the necklace.

Felix wasn't human.

My vision blurred as I stared at the book on the table, my friends' voices fading into the background. My body felt weightless, like I wasn't even sitting there anymore, but drifting through the pieces of the puzzle I'd been too blind to see.

"I need a minute," I murmured, my voice barely audible. My chair scraped back as I stood, their worried faces blurring as I turned and walked away without another word.

The corridors of the library stretched on endlessly, their dim lighting and towering shelves swallowing me whole. My feet carried me aimlessly through the maze of books, my mind racing with thoughts I couldn't hold onto. This couldn't be real. It had to be another nightmare—a vivid, gut-wrenching nightmare that I'd wake up from any second now.

But it wasn't.

This was real, and that made it worse. My fingers grazed the necklace through my shirt, the metal warm, almost pulsing with an energy I didn't understand. The truth was unbearable, clawing at my chest like it wanted to break free. Felix wasn't who I thought he was—wasn't what he seemed.

I needed to see him.

The thought struck like lightning, sharp and unrelenting. I had to go to the mansion. Tonight. I had to find him, had to make him tell me the truth, no matter what it took.

A sharp pain shot through my chest, pulling me out of my spiraling thoughts. My breath hitched, the necklace burning against my skin like it was made of molten fire. The pulse grew louder, faster, an unbearable rhythm pounding through my body as I clutched the pendant, doubling over.

"Ah!" I gasped, my knees buckling as I collapsed to the floor. My vision blurred with tears as I fought to draw air into my lungs, every breath a struggle.

We told you to stay away. Both of you.

The voices were louder than ever, hissing through my mind like venom.

Now enjoy the consequences.

And then they were gone.

The necklace's pulsing stopped abruptly, the heat dissipating as quickly as it had come. I crumpled to the floor, shaking as silent sobs wracked my body. Tears streaked my cheeks, pooling on the dusty floorboards as the weight of the voices' words sank in.

The consequences.

Were they coming for me? For Luna and Jayce? They hadn't done anything but try to help me, and now they were tangled in this mess—my mess. My chest ached with guilt and fear, the emotions spiraling out of control. I wasn't strong enough for this. I didn't even know what "this" was anymore.

The soft sound of footsteps approached, and then I felt familiar arms wrap around me. Luna knelt beside me, her embrace firm but gentle as she stroked my hair, murmuring softly.

"Shh, it's okay, hon," she whispered, her voice thick with emotion. Tears glistened on her cheeks as she pressed her hand against my back, her touch soothing. "We're here. You're not alone."

"I-I just… it's too much," I choked out between sobs. My voice broke, my breath hitching as I struggled to form the words. "I c-can't… I'm not strong enough for this."

"Yes, you are."

Jayce's voice joined hers as he crouched down, wrapping both arms around the two of us. His warmth, his steady presence, was like a lifeline, tethering me to something solid. "You don't have to do this alone, Iris. We're in this together—you know that. We've told you before. You're not alone, and you never will be."

Their words wrapped around me like a shield, their unwavering support a flicker of light in the overwhelming darkness. But the fear didn't disappear—it lingered, settling deep in my chest like an uninvited guest.

The consequences were coming.

And I didn't know if I'd survive them.

We returned to our usual table, the dim light casting heavy shadows across the rows of shelves. The library felt off—like the air had grown thicker, heavier somehow. It could have just been my paranoia talking, but it felt less like a sanctuary and more like something watching us, waiting for us to leave.

Luna let out a sigh as she shut her laptop, the click of the hinge breaking the silence. "I think that's enough for today," she said, her gaze landing on me and lingering longer than I liked.

She tucked the laptop into her bag with deliberate movements, her exhaustion showing in every gesture.

Jayce stood nearby, balancing a stack of books in one hand as he ran his other hand through his hair. His carefree demeanor seemed to have taken a backseat for the day. "I think we all need some rest," he said, his voice softer than usual. His eyes held the same weariness Luna's did—like the weight of what we'd uncovered had finally caught up to him.

"You're right," I said automatically, my words rushed and distant. "The library's closing anyway." But truthfully, I didn't care about rest. It was the last thing on my mind. All I wanted was to leave—and run straight to Felix. Whatever answers he had, I was going to demand them. I couldn't wait any longer.

"We'll all take a break from researching for the rest of the week," Luna added, her tone firm as her eyes flicked from Jayce to me. "We need it. *You* need it."

Her insistence grated against my nerves, though I knew she was just worried. I let out a heavy sigh, my fingers gripping the edge of the table. "Sounds good," I mumbled, trying to sound convincing, even as my thoughts raced ahead of me. My gaze drifted to the diary still lying on the table, its worn leather cover cracked and faded under the light. *I can't leave it here.*

"Is it okay if I take it with me?" I asked, my voice steady but insistent. My hand reached out to brush against the cool, rough texture of the book, the connection immediate and grounding.

Jayce frowned, his protectiveness shining through as he set the stack of books down. "Are you sure?" he asked, his concern evident in the tilt of his head. "You should take a break—you don't have to carry this with you."

I shook my head firmly, my grip on the diary tightening. "It's okay. Honestly, I just... I want to read more on my own. I promise I'll rest—I just need to figure this out." My voice softened, my fingertips tracing the edges of the cover like it might whisper its secrets to me if I held it close enough.

Luna hesitated, her gaze flicking between the diary and me. Her lips pressed together, her worry etched into her face. "If you're okay with it," she said finally, her tone reluctant. "Just don't overdo it, okay?"

"I won't," I promised, though I wasn't sure I meant it. I tucked the diary into my bag with deliberate care, the weight of it settling against my side like an anchor.

The three of us packed up in silence, the library's gloom pressing around us as we headed for the exit. My mind was already miles away, fixated on the mansion. Felix was waiting, whether he knew it or not, and tonight, I wasn't leaving without answers.

The library door creaked shut behind us, the final echo swallowed by the relentless patter of rain on the pavement. Night had descended fully, blanketing the streets in shadows broken only by the occasional flicker of a streetlight. The rain came down in heavy sheets, cold and unyielding, soaking through my jacket in seconds as I stepped onto the sidewalk. The chill bit at my skin, but it barely registered. My thoughts were too loud— too chaotic—to notice.

Jayce huddled closer under his umbrella, nudging Luna as they exchanged quiet words about catching a ride home. Their voices faded into the background as I stared into the distance, my fingers brushing against the edge of the diary in my bag. The weight of it felt heavier now, like it had absorbed the secrets it carried and was daring me to open it again.

"Iris, are you sure you're okay?" Jayce's voice broke through my haze. I turned to find him watching me closely, his brow furrowed in concern. Luna stood next to him, her expression mirroring his.

"I'm fine," I lied, forcing a half-hearted smile. The truth was far from fine—I didn't even know where to start unpacking everything in my head. But I couldn't let them see that, not now. Not when I was about to step into something even bigger.

"We'll text you when we get home," Luna said, her voice softer now. "Please don't stay up all night. You need rest, too."

"I will," I replied automatically, though we both knew it was a promise I wouldn't keep. The rain soaked through my hair, plastering it to my forehead as I adjusted my bag and nodded toward them. "Get home safe."

Jayce's concerned gaze lingered for a moment before he nodded and turned away, leading Luna toward the parked car waiting at the curb. Their silhouettes disappeared into the night, leaving me alone in the rain-soaked darkness.

The rain hadn't let up since we left the library, a steady downpour soaking through my clothes and turning the streets into gleaming rivers beneath the streetlights. The path to the mansion seemed longer than I expected, stretching endlessly as the cold seeped into my skin. I pulled my jacket tighter around me, my boots splashing through puddles as I approached the towering gates.

The gate swung open easily, and I made my way up the gravel path. The mansion was massive, its darkened windows and intricate stonework looming above me like something out of a forgotten dream. The glow from the porch light was faint but enough to guide my steps, and I paused at the front door, hesitating for just a moment before knocking.

The sound echoed faintly, and the door opened almost immediately. Felix stood there, leaning casually against the frame, his ever-present smirk tugging at the corners of his lips. His expression was light, playful, but as his eyes landed on me, they shifted—softening as a hint of concern flickered in their depths.

"Well, well," he said, his voice carrying that familiar edge of amusement. "Didn't think you'd actually show. Though... you look like you took a swim on the way here."

"I walked," I replied, trying to sound composed despite the chill running through me. My hair was plastered to my face, droplets rolling off the ends and onto the floor. The soaked fabric of my jacket clung to my arms uncomfortably, but I didn't move to adjust it. I was too busy watching the way Felix's smirk faltered for half a second, his gaze lingering on the wet strands of my hair and the rain-soaked jacket.

Without a word, he stepped back, holding the door open wider. "Come in before you freeze to death," he said, his tone dropping slightly, the playful edge muted.

I stepped inside, the warmth of the mansion's interior immediately wrapping around me. The space was elegant and grand, with high ceilings and polished floors, but it didn't feel intimidating. Instead, there was something oddly welcoming about it, like it was meant to be lived in despite its size.

Felix closed the door behind me, his gaze flicking over me again, though he didn't say anything about the rain this time. He gestured toward the hallway. "You want a towel or something, or are you planning to drip all over the place?"

I rolled my eyes but felt a faint smile tug at my lips involuntarily. "I'm fine."

"Sure you are," he muttered, but he didn't press the issue. His footsteps were light as he walked ahead, leading me deeper into the mansion.

As Felix led the way through the hall, I found myself holding my breath without realizing it. The mansion was quieter than I'd expected—eerily so—with only the soft echoes of our footsteps breaking the silence. The air carried a faint chill, a contrast to the warmth I felt earlier when I'd first stepped inside. It wasn't cold, exactly, but it felt heavier here, as though the walls themselves were keeping secrets they didn't want to share.

The living room was breathtaking in a way that made me pause just past the threshold. It wasn't just the scale of it—the vaulted ceilings that seemed to stretch endlessly upward, or the walls lined with intricate wood paneling that looked centuries old. It was the details, the things that seemed too deliberate to be accidental.

A grand fireplace took up nearly an entire wall, its mantle carved with ornate designs that seemed to shift as the flickering flames danced. Above it hung a massive, oil-painted portrait of a man in regal attire—stern, solemn, and unfamiliar. A set of leather armchairs and a matching sofa, dark and weathered, were arranged around the fireplace, their placement meticulous and uninviting, like they were meant to be admired but never touched.

On the far side of the room, the walls were lined with towering bookshelves crammed with volumes that ranged from pristine to crumbling. The spines were all mismatched, some titles embossed in gold while others were faded beyond recognition, giving the impression that the collection had been assembled over lifetimes rather than years. A small ladder leaned against one shelf, its polished wood gleaming faintly in the firelight.

The ceiling was adorned with a crystal chandelier that looked like it belonged in a museum. Its prisms scattered fragments of light across the room, catching on the polished floor and the edges of the furniture. The chandelier's glow mixed with the firelight, creating shadows that seemed to breathe along the walls.

Felix gestured toward the sofa, his usual smirk firmly in place, though I could see a flicker of something else in his eyes—concern, maybe? "Make yourself comfortable," he said lightly, though his tone lacked the teasing edge I'd grown used to. "You look like you've been through it."

I didn't answer immediately, too absorbed in the overwhelming sense of the room itself. It felt like it was watching me—or maybe I was imagining it, letting the weight of everything that had happened earlier cloud my thoughts. I sat down tentatively, the leather cold against my skin as I adjusted the strap of my bag and tried to avoid looking directly at Felix.

"You sure this isn't overkill?" I asked finally, my voice quiet but steady, nodding toward the massive chandelier and the portrait above the fireplace.

Felix chuckled, dropping into the armchair opposite me and stretching out as though he owned the world. "It's a bit much, isn't it? Not exactly my choice of décor, but you get used to it." His eyes flicked to the fire, and for a brief moment, his smirk faltered.

The room was imposing, suffocating in its grandeur, but there was something about it—something beneath the surface—that felt more alive than it should. The flicker of the flames, the faint hum of the chandelier, the way the shadows seemed to move just beyond the edge of sight—it felt deliberate. Intentional. Like the room was warning me not to linger too long.

CHAPTER XI

Three Hundred Years

While I was sitting on the couch, I kept looking at the room around me. Felix's voice brought me back from my thoughts.

"I'll be right back," he said, his eyes never leaving me. He stood from the chair and disappeared into one of the mansion's halls. I stood, taking the jacket off me, and walked slowly to the fireplace, letting the heat warm up my body. I closed my eyes, letting the familiar feeling of warmth get to my bones, letting my body relax to the sound of the rain outside. I started reciting in my mind what I would tell him until the faint sounds of steps coming my way snapped me back.

Felix stood there, a few inches from me, his arm stretched out to me with a towel and in his other hand a cup of hot tea. His eyes averted mine for an instant. "Here," he said. I took a step forward, trying to find his eyes. He confused me with his change in demeanor. He could be so cold and guarded, but also, he had this soft side to him that I still couldn't quite decipher. I couldn't deny how drawn I am to him, either by the necklace – or something else– and I couldn't turn back from him.

I grabbed the towel from him and wrapped it around my neck, then I took the tea, grazing my fingertips slightly against his skin. I felt like electricity shocked through me with the small touch. It was very different from the first time we touched; this was in the real world, real touch. I kept thinking about how soft his hands were and how warm and comforting they felt. I could tell he felt it too by the look in his eyes, slightly widened, and how fast he removed his hand, like something had shocked him.

With hesitation, he dragged himself to the armchair and took a seat. He cleared his throat. "I didn't think you'd actually come," he admitted, his voice quieter now, almost hesitant.

I did the same as I sat down on the couch across from him. "You invited me here," I said nonchalantly. The small quiver in my voice betrayed any bit of confidence I was trying to show.

My nervousness was enough to make him smirk once again. I ignored it and took a sip of my tea. It was a delicious ginger tea, and its distinctive warm, spicy, and slightly sweet taste made me feel better.

"You're quiet," he said, his voice light and teasing, though there was an edge to it. He leaned forward slightly, resting his elbows on his knees as his light eyes settled on me. "Is this the part where you start interrogating me?"

I swallowed hard, gripping the mug tightly. My mind was racing, but I couldn't shake the feeling that he was trying to distract me—trying to keep me from noticing the way his fingers tapped restlessly against the edge of the chair.

"Not exactly," I replied, my voice steadier than I expected. "But I do want answers, Felix. Real answers. No riddles, no cryptic one-liners. Just the truth."

His smirk stretched wider, but it didn't light up his eyes. If anything, it only made them darker, more guarded. "I figured you didn't come all the way here just to swap research notes," he murmured, his voice low enough that it barely broke through the crackle of the fire.

Then came the laugh—not one of those playful, mischievous ones I'd grown used to, but something empty, sharp-edged. It lingered in the air, humorless and hollow. "You make it sound so simple," he continued, leaning back as though he had all the time in the world, his arms resting lazily over the sides of the chair. His gaze flickered back to the fire. "But truth, Iris... It's never black and white. Most of the time, it's just... gray."

There was something in his tone—something quiet but unshakable, like he'd been sitting with this truth for far longer than he cared to admit. It was that realization, more than his words, that sent a shiver down my spine.

I gathered the courage to break the silence, my voice cutting through the air like a knife. "Felix, how old are you?" I asked, the words laced with the anticipation that had been building inside me since I walked into the mansion.

He looked up sharply, caught off guard by the sudden question. For a moment, his brows furrowed, confusion flashing across his face before his expression softened into something more familiar. The playful smile tugged at the corner of his lips—the one he always wore when he wanted to deflect. "Twenty-five," he replied simply, his tone casual, almost amused.

But I wasn't about to let him sidestep the truth. "For how long?" I pressed, my gaze unwavering, locking onto his.

The smile vanished in an instant. His jaw tightened, the amusement draining from his face as though I'd struck a nerve he didn't know he had. His eyes darted away from mine, avoiding my stare completely, and the silence that followed was deafening.

I leaned forward, my voice firm, though my heart felt like it was pounding out of my chest. "How long have you been twenty-five?"

The question lingered, heavy in the air between us, demanding an answer he wasn't ready to give. But I wasn't backing down—not this time. I needed the truth, no matter how uncomfortable it was.

"So, you know," he whispered, barely audible.

The fire in the living room cracked softly as if trying to fill the void. Shadows flickered along the walls, shifting as the flames danced, their glow casting the room in shades of gold and charcoal. The weight of the silence pressed down on me, more suffocating than the rain outside. Even the air felt thicker here, heavy with unspoken words.

Felix stood and walked near the grand fireplace, his figure illuminated by the warm light. His back was turned to me, his posture tense in a way I hadn't seen before. Normally, he carried himself with ease—like the world was something he owned. But tonight, his shoulders seemed to sag, his head bowed slightly, as though he was holding something too heavy to share.

"Felix," I said, my voice breaking through the quiet. The sound seemed to echo, bouncing off the high ceilings. "What aren't you telling me?"

He didn't respond right away. His hand rested on the mantel, his fingers curling slightly against the carved wood as he stared into the fire. When he finally exhaled, the sound was sharp, almost brittle, like it carried the weight of an entire history.

"This wasn't supposed to happen to me," he said finally, his voice low and bitter. The flames caught his profile as he turned, revealing a look I hadn't seen before—haunted, broken in ways I couldn't even begin to understand. His usual smirk was gone, replaced by a shadow of vulnerability that made my chest tighten.

He let out a humorless laugh, the kind that twisted in the air and left a bitter taste behind. "I didn't choose this. Just like you didn't."

The words hung between us, heavy and undeniable. His eyes lingered on mine, dark and unreadable, and yet there was something raw in his expression that made me take a step closer. Felix, the man who always seemed unshakable, now stood before me like someone stripped of everything but pain. And I couldn't look away.

He lingered by the fireplace for what felt like an eternity, his gaze fixed on the dancing flames as though they held the answers he was struggling to give. His hand tightened slightly on the mantel, his knuckles whitening under the pressure, before he finally let out a slow, uneven breath.

"It's time I tell you a story," he said softly, his voice dipping lower as though the weight of the words was too heavy to bear. His eyes flickered with something unspoken—something raw and fragile—that settled over his face the moment the sentence left his lips. The sadness there was unmistakable, as if the act of saying it out loud had reopened an old wound he'd long since tried to forget.

I leaned forward just slightly, my posture rigid but my eyes locked onto Felix. My gaze flicked over the subtle shifts in his expression—the sadness lingering in his eyes, the tension in his jaw—as he seemed to wrestle with the words before speaking them.

I couldn't take my eyes off him. The Felix I knew—the one who always seemed so in control, so untouchable—was nowhere to be found. Instead, he looked... human. Vulnerable, even. It was like I was seeing a different version of him for the first time, one he didn't let slip often, if ever.

My chest tightened as the silence dragged on, thick and suffocating, but I stayed quiet, waiting. The room felt heavier somehow, like even the mansion itself had paused to listen. My thoughts raced, trying to guess what he was about to say, but no amount of guessing could prepare me for what was coming. And I knew that, deep down. So I let the silence linger. I let him take his time.

Because when Felix finally spoke, I wanted to be ready. I needed to be ready.

"As you may have noticed," he added, trying to inject humor, "I'm from England." The joke was weak, falling flat as the sadness in his tone swallowed the light of the moment. He let out a slow, uneven sigh, his shoulders drooping like the weight of his memories was pressing down on him. "And to answer your earlier question... I've been twenty-five for roughly three hundred years. Give or take. I stopped counting about thirty years ago."

His eyes flicked toward me, locking onto mine with a penetrating intensity, like he was searching for something—permission to continue, maybe, or just reassurance that I was ready to hear what he had to say. The firelight danced across his angular features, casting shifting shadows that made him look both younger and impossibly old. I nodded silently, the lump in my throat making words impossible. My encouragement was quiet but certain.

Felix's gaze drifted back to the fire, its golden light reflecting in his eyes as though he could burn the memories away simply by staring into the flames. "I grew up in an orphanage," he began, his voice quieter now, tinged with a raw vulnerability that made the air in the room feel heavier. "There were hundreds of us—kids who'd lost their parents under strange circumstances. My dad died when I was little, and my mum... she couldn't take care of me anymore. She gave me to the church—or at least that's what I was told."

He paused, his fingers curling slightly against the edge of the mantel. The flickering flames bathed his expression in warmth, but they couldn't soften the lines of pain etched into his face. "When I was twelve, I was adopted by a wealthy German family—one of the richest in England at the time. They already had two sons: Henry, the eldest, and Axel, who was my age. My... father, Conrad Lehman, was a powerful man. Ruthless. No one dared to cross him." There was the faintest tremor in his voice as he said the name Conrad, and his jaw tightened as though the mere mention of it left a bad taste in his mouth.

"At first, for the most part, though, I was happy," Felix continued, his voice softening as a ghost of a smile tugged at his lips. "I loved my brothers. We'd spend hours playing in the backyard, getting into trouble, and driving Henry mad with our antics. Axel and I were inseparable—partners in crime. It was fun," he added, the smile flickering brighter for just a second before fading into a shadow. "Conrad was strict, yes, but I had everything I'd ever wanted. A family. His wife, Anneliese, treated me like her own son. She was the kindest woman I'd ever known. For the first time, I felt... at peace. I had a home. A family to call my own."

Felix shifted then, moving toward the window as though the memories were pulling him closer to the storm outside. The rain was still pouring, streaking the glass with silver lines that reflected faint flashes of lightning. He stood there for a moment, his silhouette outlined by the dim light, before turning back to me. His dark hair caught the glow, slick and neat despite the tension that weighed on him.

"When I turned twenty-four, my family suddenly moved to the U.S.—to Rockport. This," he said, motioning to the room around us, "was our home. At first, it was difficult. I couldn't adjust, no matter how hard I tried. The city felt strange, unfamiliar. Every night, my father would host gatherings in this room. Men I didn't recognize would arrive, drink, and talk in hushed tones that I wasn't allowed to overhear. I didn't think much of it then. I thought it was just business."

His voice grew quieter as he ran a hand through his hair, his gaze dropping to the floor. "A few weeks after we arrived, I was introduced to the Hart family—the people my father had been meeting with. Specifically, to their youngest daughter, Eleanor." The way he said her name made something twist painfully in my chest. His lips curved into a faint smile that was almost wistful. "She was... breathtaking. The most beautiful girl I'd ever seen. Kind, funny, with a smile that could light up the darkest room. Whenever I was with her, I couldn't stop smiling. She had this way of making everything... brighter."

A strange unease settled in the pit of my stomach as he spoke about her, and I couldn't shake the thought. Did he still love her? Did he still miss her?

"I was happy," he said, but his voice cracked, betraying the truth underneath. "But I was naïve. I was young and in love, and I didn't see what was coming." He sighed deeply, his shoulders rising and falling in one slow, measured motion. "A year later, we were set to be married. I was... excited. I thought we'd have forever."

The storm outside seemed to grow louder, the rain pounding against the windows as Felix's tone grew heavier. "But everything went wrong. On the day of the wedding, she stood there in her gown, wearing this ruby necklace I'd never seen before. It was stunning, but... something felt strange. She wasn't smiling. Her eyes looked... terrified. When the priest asked if she would take me as her husband, she turned to me, and all she said was one word: 'Run.'"

Felix's voice trembled as he spoke, his hands balling into fists at his sides. "She grabbed my hand, and we ran. I didn't know what was happening, but I followed her. I trusted her." He paused, his breathing uneven. "But we didn't get far. Our fathers caught up to us. Her father grabbed her by the hair and yanked her to the ground. She screamed, begged me to keep running, but I couldn't leave her. I tried to reach for her, but Henry—my brother—held me back. He wouldn't even look at me.

"Then... I watched her die." His voice broke completely, the words barely audible. "Her father... slit her throat. One clean motion. She fell to the ground, lifeless, and I... I couldn't do anything. I screamed her name, over and over, but she was gone."

Felix turned to me then, his eyes filled with a pain that felt endless. "Henry looked at me and said, 'I'm sorry, brother.' And then... he stabbed me. Right in the chest."

The rain outside seemed to echo the grief in his voice as he looked away, his jaw tightening once again. "The last thing I saw was Conrad, staring at me as my life drained away. When I woke up, I was alone. Covered in blood. And Eleanor..." His voice faltered, tears glistening in his eyes. "She was still there. Still lifeless. But the necklace... it was gone."

He paused, his breathing uneven as he tried to steady himself. "I came back here—to the mansion. Barely alive. I hid behind a pillar, overhearing their conversation. They said the ritual had failed. They said I wasn't supposed to be sacrificed... because I wasn't his blood."

His voice dropped to a whisper. "I wasn't adopted out of kindness. I was adopted to die. Nothing more."

Felix fell silent, his breath shallow as a single tear rolled down his cheek. My heart felt like it was breaking into pieces as I stared at him—at this version of him I had never seen. He was no longer the confident, untouchable man I thought I knew. He was someone broken. Someone grieving. Someone who had carried centuries of pain and still managed to stand.

"When I said I didn't choose this," he said, his voice low and rough, "I meant it. None of this was supposed to be my life. I had plans once—dreams, goals... normal things. Things people take for granted." He shook his head slightly, a bitter smile tugging at the corner of his lips. "But that all ended the moment that happened to me. And there was no escaping it, no undoing it."

I stayed silent, frozen in place as his words settled in the air between us. Felix didn't look at me, didn't seem to need to, as he continued.

"It's like the world keeps spinning, but you're stuck," he said, his fingers tapping rhythmically against the mantel like the movement grounded him. "You watch everyone else move forward, change, grow, but you're left behind. It's endless. And then there are the nightmares—they're not just dreams.

They're... different. They're vivid, consuming. And the hunger—it's not the kind you can satisfy. It's constant, gnawing, unrelenting."

I wanted to say something, to ask the questions swirling in my mind, but I couldn't bring myself to interrupt him. There was something about the way he spoke, raw and unguarded, that felt fragile—like any interruption might shatter it completely.

He turned slowly, his gaze finally meeting mine. The firelight danced across his face, highlighting the sharp angles of his cheekbones and the hollow look in his eyes. "Do you know what it's like to be stuck? To feel like time has passed you by? You don't belong anywhere anymore—not to this world, not to anyone. That's what it is, Iris. That's the truth."

His voice cracked slightly, and the vulnerability in it made my throat tighten. Felix—the man who always seemed so sure of himself, so untouchable—looked lost.

"This wasn't supposed to happen to me," he said again, softer now. His gaze dropped to the floor, his expression darkening further. "And it wasn't supposed to happen to you. But now it's here, and you can't ignore it. Not anymore."

The weight of his words pressed against my chest, and I realized with startling clarity that Felix wasn't just warning me. He wasn't just giving me answers. He was preparing me for what was coming. But the look in his eyes told me it wasn't something I wanted to face.

The room felt as though it had frozen in time—only the faint sound of the rain outside breaking the suffocating silence that followed Felix's story. His words echoed in my mind, each detail carving itself deeper into my thoughts, leaving me shaken.

But something stood out, something I hadn't fully registered at first.

The Hart family.

I couldn't breathe, my chest tightening as the realization hit me like a wave. The Hart family wasn't just a name. It was *my* family. My grandparents, my father, the ones who shaped the legacy of everything I knew. How could I not have seen it before? Every puzzle piece I'd tried so desperately to fit together suddenly snapped into place, and the picture it formed made my stomach twist violently.

Felix turned to face me, his light eyes steady, as though he was anticipating the moment I would connect the dots. He wasn't surprised by the realization—it was clear he already knew. He'd known from the beginning.

"I take it you've finally figured it out," he said, his voice quiet but carrying a weight that made me flinch. The corner of his mouth twitched as though he was trying to form a smile, but it didn't come. "Your family, Iris. They're Harts. The same ones. And Eleanor... she was your ancestor."

My breath caught, the tightness in my chest growing unbearable. "Why didn't you tell me?" I asked, my voice shaky as the words came tumbling out.

Felix turned back toward the window, watching the rain streak across the glass. "Would it have changed anything?" he said simply, his tone calm but not unkind. "Knowing sooner wouldn't have undone any of it. And I wasn't sure if... you were ready to hear it."

I felt my knees weaken, and I sat down heavily on the sofa, my head spinning. The necklace. The diary. The ritual. It was all tangled together, connected through threads I hadn't even begun to unravel. And now, this—this impossible connection to Felix, to Eleanor, to everything that had happened centuries ago.

"I don't even know what to say," I admitted, my voice barely above a whisper.

He turned back toward me, his expression softening slightly. "There's nothing you *can* say," he replied, his voice quieter now. "This isn't your fault, Iris. You weren't alive then. You had no control over what they did."

I shook my head, gripping my knees tightly as I tried to steady myself. "But it's my family. It's my name. My legacy. I don't know... I don't know what they did, but—"

"They destroyed everything," Felix interrupted, his voice cutting through my stumbling words like a blade. His tone wasn't angry, but it was raw, full of frustration and pain. "They took Eleanor from me. They took my life. And for what? Power? Control? I don't even know anymore. I stopped trying to make sense of it a long time ago."

My vision blurred as tears welled up in my eyes, and I looked away, unable to meet his gaze. "Felix... I'm sorry."

"For what?" he asked sharply, his voice dipping lower. "You didn't do this, Iris. You weren't even alive."

"But it's my family," I said again, the weight of the words pressing against me. "They... they did this to you. They hurt you. How can I carry that? How can I make it right?"

Felix's expression softened, and for a moment, his vulnerability broke through the pain etched on his face. "It's not yours to fix," he said, his voice quieter now, like he didn't want to scare me away. "But you're tied to it now—whether you want to be or not."

I lifted my head, the tears slipping down my cheeks as I looked at him. He stood there, his posture tense but somehow steady, carrying the weight of centuries like it was a part of him. And even though I knew I couldn't undo his pain, couldn't rewrite his history, one thing became clear.

I wasn't going to let him carry it alone.

I hesitated, the words catching in my throat as my hands fidgeted in my lap. My fingers twisted around each other restlessly, and my eyes darted to the floor, avoiding his gaze. "I-I don't want you to do this alone…" I finally managed, my voice shaky and uncertain.

Felix let out a quiet breath, his gaze softening for a moment. "I didn't think you'd actually come," he said, his voice quieter now, almost tentative. There was something raw about the way he said it, like he hadn't decided whether he was relieved or disappointed. "Not after everything that's happened. I figured you'd keep your distance—and maybe that would've been better."

"Why?" I asked, leaning forward slightly despite the weight in my chest. The warmth of the fire flickered across his profile as I searched his face for answers. "Why would it be better for me to stay away?"

He didn't answer right away. His fingers drummed lightly against the window's mantel, the rhythm oddly steady, like it was the only thing keeping him grounded. Finally, he looked back at me, his eyes shadowed with something I couldn't quite place. "Because this... thing—this connection," he said carefully, his voice low and deliberate, "it's not simple, Iris. It's dangerous. And I don't want you to get caught up in something you can't escape."

His words hung between us, charged with meaning, and my chest tightened as I struggled to hold his gaze. For all the layers of mystery that always seemed to surround Felix, there was no mistaking the sincerity in his tone now. This wasn't just a warning—it was a plea.

I didn't think. I couldn't. My body moved on its own, driven by something I didn't fully understand but couldn't ignore. Felix's words lingered in the air, heavy and raw, wrapping around my thoughts and pulling me toward him. Before I realized what I was doing, I was on my feet, closing the distance between us with a steady but urgent pace.

He didn't turn to look at me—not at first. His focus remained on the rain-streaked window, the faint light of the storm casting sharp angles across his features. His shoulders were tense, his posture rigid, and I could almost feel the weight he carried pressing down on him. The sight of him like this—silent, guarded, yet somehow vulnerable—sent a pang through my chest that I couldn't ignore.

When I reached him, my hands moved instinctively. My arms slid around him, wrapping him tightly, pulling him close in a way that felt unshakably right. My head rested against his chest, and for a moment, I let myself drown in his warmth, in the steady sound of his heartbeat beneath the layers of fabric. The world outside—the storm, the fire, the room—faded into the background. There was only him.

His breath hitched. I felt it in the way his chest rose sharply beneath my cheek, the way his entire body seemed to freeze under my touch. For a moment, he didn't move, and I wondered if I had made a mistake. But I couldn't pull away— not now, not when my feelings had become so tangled with his pain that I could barely tell the two apart.

And then, slowly, he exhaled. The tension in his body melted, his frame softening as though he was finally letting go of something he'd held onto for far too long. His hand hesitated for the briefest moment before resting gently on my shoulder, the touch light but deliberate, like he wasn't sure if he deserved to hold onto me.

"Iris," he whispered, my name slipping from his lips like a quiet confession. There was something different in the way he said it this time—something unguarded, something fragile. It wasn't just a name; it was an anchor, tying us to this moment, to each other.

I closed my eyes, my fingers tightening around the fabric of his shirt as the emotions inside me swirled together—sadness for everything he had endured, anger at the world that had hurt him, and something deeper that I wasn't ready to name but couldn't deny. It was in the way my heart raced whenever he looked at me, in the way his voice lingered in my thoughts long after he was gone. And now, it was in the way I didn't want to let him go, not even for a second.

"You don't have to do this alone," I murmured against his chest, my voice trembling but firm. "I'm here, Felix. I don't care how dangerous it is—I'm not going anywhere."

He didn't answer right away. His hand on my shoulder tightened slightly, and I felt the faintest shift as his head tilted down, his breath warm against the top of my hair. When he finally spoke, his voice was so quiet I almost didn't hear it.

"You shouldn't have to do this, Iris," he said, the bitterness from earlier replaced with something softer, almost mournful. "You shouldn't be here, tied to any of this... tied to me."

"But I am," I said, pulling back just enough to look up at him. His eyes met mine, and for the first time, the walls he always kept so carefully constructed seemed to crack. "And I'm not sorry for it."

He stared at me, his expression unreadable but his eyes searching, as though trying to find something in mine. The storm outside raged on, lightning flashing briefly, illuminating the emotions flickering across his face. Pain. Regret. And something else, something quiet but unmistakable.

"Why?" he asked, his voice barely above a whisper. There was no teasing edge to his question, no sarcasm. Just raw, vulnerable curiosity. "Why would you stay?"

I hesitated, my chest tightening as I tried to find the words. "Because... I can't walk away from this. From you. I can't explain it, but... I feel like I was meant to find you, Felix. Like we're connected somehow, and not just because of the necklace. And I don't want to lose that."

His hand moved then, slowly, hesitantly, until it cupped my cheek. His touch was warm, careful, like he was afraid I might break if he wasn't gentle enough. His eyes softened, and for a moment, the sadness in them ebbed, replaced by something brighter, something that made my heart stutter in my chest.

"You're not what I expected, Iris," he said, his voice quieter now, tinged with something I couldn't quite name. "But maybe, you're exactly what I needed."

I didn't know what to say, so I didn't say anything at all. Instead, I stayed there, my head against his chest, his hand still resting on my cheek, as the storm outside continued to rage and the fire crackled softly behind us. And for the first time in what felt like forever, I didn't feel alone. And maybe, just maybe, neither did he.

CHAPTER XII

Through Fire and Storm

Felix and I stayed up all night, the storm outside becoming nothing more than a distant hum, blending with the occasional crackle of the fire. For once, the necklace resting against my chest didn't dominate my thoughts. We didn't talk about the twisted legacy of our families or the horrors chasing us. We didn't talk about curses or rituals or the inexplicable gravity that had tied us together.

Instead, we talked about ourselves—the parts of us untouched by the chaos. It started small. Felix told me about his favorite books, the ones he'd carried with him through the centuries, their pages worn and edges frayed. I told him about the summer I spent trying—and failing—to learn how to surf, and how I'd fallen in love with the ocean anyway.

We shared little things, fleeting moments of joy and loss that made us feel almost human again. Felix had a dry, understated sense of humor that kept catching me off guard, pulling genuine laughter out of me in a way I hadn't felt in ages. His stories carried a nostalgic warmth, even when they were tinged with sadness. I couldn't stop myself from leaning closer as he spoke, drawn in by the way his words unfolded like threads of an intricate tapestry.

At some point, I started noticing the way his eyes softened when he looked at me—the way his guarded exterior seemed to slip away bit by bit, revealing layers I hadn't seen before. His voice, low and steady, had a way of making the world feel smaller, like everything beyond the walls of this room was just background noise. And the more we talked, the more I couldn't help but feel that strange pull between us deepening.

For hours, it was just the two of us, cocooned in the warmth of the living room, the storm continuing to rage outside. I didn't think about the danger waiting for me, or the nightmares I'd woken up to countless times before. For the first time, the weight of my family's legacy didn't feel so suffocating.

It was just me and Felix.

Two wounded souls, bound by a strange, inexplicable force that neither of us fully understood but couldn't deny. And for once, I didn't feel alone in it.

His voice dipped lower as the fire began to die down, his words slowing, the exhaustion creeping into both of us. But I didn't care—I could've stayed there forever, listening to him, letting his presence ground me.

Destiny was a cruel thing. It had pushed us together in the most chaotic, impossible way. But in that moment, sitting there with Felix, I couldn't bring myself to regret it.

As the fire dimmed further, casting the room in softer shadows, my thoughts began to shift. Felix had fallen silent for a moment, his gaze lingering on the remnants of the storm outside, but I couldn't stop my own mind from wandering. It wasn't about the intimacy we had just shared, the quiet comfort of talking with him. It was something else—something heavier that I'd been holding onto, unsure of whether I should say it aloud.

I thought about my mom.

The memory came rushing back, sharper now that I had the chance to reflect on it, and its weight sat heavy in my chest. Her reaction to the necklace hadn't made sense before—not until now. I had brushed off the fear in her voice, the way her hand trembled as she reached for the pendant only to pull back as if it burned her. But after everything Felix had told me tonight—about Eleanor, about the history we were both tied to—I couldn't ignore it anymore.

I looked over at him, his posture still relaxed, but his gaze sharp as he glanced my way. He wasn't oblivious; he could sense that something was turning inside me, that the silence I had kept so far was about to break.

"There's something I haven't told you," I said softly, my fingers tightening around the strap of my bag.

Felix straightened slightly, his full attention shifting to me. "What is it?" he asked, his voice steady but careful, as though he didn't want to push too hard.

I hesitated, the lump in my throat making it difficult to speak. But the memory of my mom's reaction kept pushing to the forefront, demanding to be acknowledged. "When my mom saw the necklace for the first time... she reacted like she knew. Like she'd seen it before."

Felix's brows furrowed, his blue eyes narrowing slightly as he processed my words. He didn't say anything right away, waiting for me to continue.

"She asked where I got it," I said, my voice trembling slightly as I forced myself to meet his gaze. "Her voice—it wasn't just curiosity. She was scared, Felix. I didn't understand it at the time, but now... now it makes sense. She knows something. She knows more than she's letting on."

Felix exhaled sharply, his fingers tapping rhythmically against the armrest of his chair as he stared at me. "Did she say anything else?" he asked, his voice quiet but intense.

I shook my head, gripping my bag tighter. "Not much. She just told me to be careful. I thought she was being overprotective, you know, the way moms are. But now I think there's more to it. I think she knows about the necklace. Maybe she even knows about Eleanor."

Felix's jaw tightened slightly, his expression darkening as his gaze drifted to the fire. "If she knows, then she's been keeping it from you deliberately," he said, his tone steady but laced with frustration. "And that means she knows how dangerous this all is."

I swallowed hard, the weight of his words settling heavily in my chest. "What should I do?" I asked quietly, the vulnerability in my voice catching me off guard.

Felix looked back at me, his sharp blue eyes searching mine. There was something unspoken in his gaze—a mixture of sympathy and resolve that made my chest tighten. "You have to talk to her," he said, his voice softer now. "You need answers, Iris. And if your mom has them, you need to find out."

I nodded slowly, though the thought of confronting her sent a wave of anxiety coursing through me. The diary sat heavy in my lap, its worn leather cover cool under my fingertips, as if daring me to open it again.

Felix leaned forward slightly, his gaze steady. "You brought the diary, didn't you?"

"Yes," I said, my voice quieter now. "I thought it might help. I thought maybe there's something in here that explains what's going on. Something that ties everything together."

Felix's lips pressed into a thin line, and he nodded. "Then let's start there," he said firmly. "You need all the pieces, Iris. And I'll help you find them."

The diary sat heavily between us on the coffee table, its worn leather cover dimmed by years of wear but still holding an unexplainable weight. Felix sat across from me, his gaze steady but guarded as the storm outside faded into a soft patter. The firelight flickered over the room, and my fingers hesitated over the edges of the book as though it might burn me.

"You ready?" Felix asked quietly, his voice cutting through the stillness like a blade. There was no rush, no impatience—just a calm steadiness that somehow made me feel braver than I was.

I nodded, swallowing the lump in my throat. "Yeah."

Reaching forward, I placed my hand on the diary, its cool leather grounding me as I prepared to open it. Felix leaned forward as well, his hand brushing against mine as he moved to hold the other side. The moment his fingers touched the book, a sudden, sharp pulse radiated through the room.

The necklace around my neck began to glow.

I gasped, my free hand instinctively clutching the pendant as its light intensified, spilling over the room like liquid gold. The warmth was immediate, seeping into my skin and filling my chest with an unfamiliar energy that left me breathless.

Felix's reaction was swift—his head snapped toward the necklace, his eyes narrowing as the glow reflected in them. "Iris," he said sharply, his voice steady but laced with urgency. "What's happening?"

"I—I don't know," I stammered, my voice trembling as the necklace's pulse quickened against my skin. "It's never done this before."

Felix released the diary, and his focus was entirely on me now. His hand hovered near the pendant, hesitant, as though he wasn't sure if touching it would make things worse. "Is it... hurting you?" he asked, his voice softening slightly.

"No," I managed, shaking my head. "It's warm, but it doesn't hurt."

The glow seemed to ebb slightly, dimming enough for me to catch my breath. Felix's hand dropped to his side, but his eyes stayed fixed on the necklace, his expression unreadable.

"I don't think it liked us both touching the diary," he said finally, his tone cautious.

I nodded slowly, the necklace's soft hum still reverberating through me. It felt like it was alive, reacting not just to me but to Felix, too. Whatever this connection was, it clearly wasn't something either of us fully understood.

I let out a shaky breath, my fingers still clutching the pendant as I glanced back at the diary. "Before we keep going, there's something else I need to tell you," I said, my voice quiet but firm.

Felix's eyes flicked to mine, his expression sharp again. "What is it?"

I hesitated, my pulse pounding in my ears. "I found something... in my research," I began, my words halting as I tried to organize my thoughts. "It was this name. Carrow. I wasn't sure what it meant at first, but it kept coming up, connected to rituals and curses. I think it might be tied to the necklace."

The moment I said it, Felix's entire demeanor changed. His body tensed, his jaw tightening as his eyes darkened. He leaned back slightly, his arms crossing over his chest as though trying to shield himself.

"Where did you hear that name?" he asked, his voice low and serious.

My brows furrowed as I tried to recall the exact moment. "It was something I read, but... I've also heard it somewhere else," I said, the pieces slowly clicking into place. "My boss. He saw my necklace one day, and he... he said it. He just looked at me, like he was in some kind of trance, and said, 'Carrow.' It wasn't casual, Felix. It was like he felt something when he saw the pendant."

Felix's gaze sharpened, his tension growing palpable as he processed my words. For a long moment, he didn't say anything, his fingers still resting on the arm of his chair, drumming lightly as though debating how much to reveal.

"Carrow isn't just a name," he said finally, his voice quieter now but carrying a weight that made my chest tighten. "It's... it's a place. A prison, in a sense, but not the kind you're thinking of. It's ancient and hidden, and it doesn't hold people— it holds... something worse."

His words sent a cold shiver down my spine, but I forced myself to stay steady. "What kind of prison?" I asked softly, the unease in my voice impossible to hide.

Felix hesitated again, his jaw tightening as he shifted slightly in his chair. "I'm not sure how much I can tell you," he admitted, his voice low but strained. "But what you need to know is that the necklace—it's the key. Without it, Carrow stays sealed. And with it..." He stopped, his gaze locking onto mine, the tension in his expression almost unbearable. "With it, Carrow opens."

My breath hitched as his words sank in, and I clutched the pendant tighter, as if that could somehow stop it from glowing again. "Felix, if this is the key, then why... why would it be here? Why would it be tied to Eleanor and to me?"

He shook his head slightly, his frustration evident. "That's what we need to figure out," he said firmly. "But, Iris, you need to be careful. Carrow isn't just a place—it's a danger. And if your boss is already reacting to the necklace..." He trailed off, his dark eyes narrowing. "We may not have much time."

The glow of the necklace had dimmed, but its weight against my chest felt heavier somehow, as though it was aware of what we were about to uncover. Felix shifted closer, his sharp features illuminated by the flickering firelight. The tension between us was palpable, but we both knew that there was no turning back now.

With a deep breath, I opened the diary. The spine creaked softly, and the scent of aged paper wafted upward, faint but distinct. My fingers traced the faded handwriting on the first page, the loops and curves of the letters elegant but hurried, as though the writer had been racing against time to commit their thoughts to the page.

The entries were fragmented and disjointed, but as I flipped through the pages, a pattern began to emerge. The handwriting changed over time—different authors, different voices—all connected by the same recurring fear. Mentions of Carrow were scattered throughout, the name underlined or circled in frantic strokes.

"Here," I said, pointing to an entry that caught my eye. Felix leaned in, his dark eyes scanning the words as I read them aloud.

"'The key must never fall into the wrong hands. Carrow is a prison not meant to be opened. The horrors locked within would consume the world.'" My voice wavered as I reached the end of the sentence, my fingers trembling slightly against the paper.

Felix's jaw tightened, his gaze darkening as he absorbed the words. "They knew," he said quietly, his voice laced with frustration. "Whoever wrote this—they knew what Carrow was. They knew the danger."

I nodded, flipping to the next page, where more frantic writing covered the margins. "'The necklace is the lock and the key. It binds to the bloodline, passing from one to the next. Those who wear it are marked.'"

I froze, the weight of the words sinking in as the room seemed to close in around me. "Marked," I whispered, my hand instinctively going to the pendant resting against my skin.

Felix glanced at me, his expression unreadable but tense. "It's not just a key," he said, his voice low. "It's a tether. A connection to Carrow and... to whatever it's holding back."

The fire crackled softly, the only sound in the room as the implications of his words settled over us. My mind raced, trying to piece together the fragments of the diary's warnings with everything Felix had told me.

I turned another page, and my heart skipped a beat as I saw the name scrawled in bold letters: Eleanor Hart. The ink was darker here, the letters etched deeply into the paper as though the writer had been desperate to make the name stand out.

Felix tensed beside me, his breath catching audibly. "Eleanor," he murmured, the name slipping from his lips like a broken prayer.

The entry below her name was brief but chilling. "'The necklace was passed to Eleanor to protect her. To protect us all. But it failed. She is lost, and now the burden falls to her bloodline.'"

I felt a chill run down my spine, and I glanced at Felix, his expression shadowed with pain. "It's me," I said softly, the realization sinking in like a stone. "It's my bloodline."

Felix nodded slowly, his gaze fixed on the diary. "The Harts knew about Carrow, Iris. They knew the risk, the responsibility. And somehow... it's all led to you."

I closed the diary gently, the weight of its contents pressing down on me. The pieces were beginning to come together, but they formed a picture more terrifying than I'd anticipated. The necklace, the prison, the curse—it was all connected, and somehow I was at the center of it.

"Iris," Felix said, his voice pulling me from my thoughts. "If Carrow is stirring, if the necklace is reacting to it, then we don't have much time. We need to figure out why it's happening—and how to stop it."

I nodded, my resolve hardening despite the fear twisting in my gut. "Then we keep going," I said firmly. "We figure this out. Together."

His eyes softened slightly, a flicker of something unspoken passing between us. "Together," he agreed.

The hour was impossibly late, the kind of stillness only found deep into the night, settling over the room. Felix and I had been taking turns reading the diary, combing through its faded pages for anything—*anything*—that might help us untangle the mystery we were caught in. Right now, it was his turn.

His eyes were fixed on the yellowed paper, scanning each line with an intensity that made the world outside the diary seem nonexistent. The firelight painted his features in soft, golden hues, highlighting the sharp angles of his jaw and the way his brows furrowed slightly when he concentrated. I couldn't help but notice the little things—how his fingers turned the pages with a quiet grace, or the way he bit down on his lower lip every so often, completely lost in the words. The light in the room made his eyes seem softer, warmer, like embers glowing faintly in the dark.

I didn't realize I'd been staring until his voice broke the silence.

"You're staring," he said, that familiar smirk tugging at the corner of his lips, though his eyes stayed glued to the diary.

My breath caught, and my eyes widened. Heat rushed to my cheeks, and I quickly turned my gaze away, pretending to find the texture of the sofa remarkably interesting. "I wasn't—" I stammered, cutting myself off because the denial felt ridiculous even to me. "I mean, sorry... I just... spaced out."

The smirk lingered on his lips, but he didn't press the matter, his focus drifting back to the diary as though nothing had happened. But my heart wouldn't stop its awkward, unsteady rhythm, and I fidgeted slightly, trying to shake off the embarrassment.

The room was quieter now, the sound of turning pages and the faint crackle of the fire the only things filling the space. My eyelids were growing heavier with every passing moment, my body succumbing to the weight of exhaustion. I yawned quietly, barely able to stifle it, and shivered as a chill crept over me. My clothes were still damp from the rain earlier, the cold air biting at my skin.

Felix glanced up at me then, his gaze shifting from the diary to where I sat curled on the couch. His smirk softened into something gentler, his lips curving into the faintest smile. "Tired?" he asked, his voice lower now, laced with a quiet concern I hadn't expected.

I rubbed my eyes, letting out another yawn before nodding. "Yeah, a little," I admitted, my voice barely above a whisper. I avoided looking directly at him, not trusting myself not to melt under the weight of his gaze.

He closed the diary gently, setting it aside as he stood. His movements were fluid and effortless, and he crossed the room to where I sat before crouching down so we were eye level. His expression softened further, and for a moment, the distance between us felt impossibly small.

"You should get some rest," he said, his voice quiet but firm. "You've had a long day, and you're no use to either of us if you can't keep your eyes open."

I let out a soft laugh, though it sounded more like a sigh. "I guess you're right," I muttered, my lips curving into a faint smile despite my exhaustion.

Felix stood again, reaching for one of the blankets draped over the back of the couch. He unfolded it with practiced ease before draping it over my shoulders. The fabric was warm and soft, and it chased away the chill that had seeped into my bones.

"Stay here," he said softly, his gaze lingering on mine for just a second longer than it needed to. "I'll keep reading for a while longer. If I find anything... I'll wake you."

I nodded, my heart fluttering unexpectedly at the way he said it. There was no teasing smirk, no clever remark—just quiet sincerity. And as I let my eyes close, the warmth of the blanket and the steady sound of Felix's quiet movements lulling me to sleep, I couldn't help but feel the smallest flicker of safety in the chaos.

It wasn't much. But it was enough.

The fire had burned low, casting the room in a dim, golden glow that softened the sharp edges of everything around us. The storm had quieted to a gentle drizzle, and the rhythmic patter of rain against the window added to the sense of calm that had settled between us. As though time itself had been holding its breath, for the first time I wasn't consumed by fear or the constant hum of unanswered questions. Instead, I let myself focus on Felix—the quiet strength he carried, the weight he so obviously bore, but I never let it consume him.

I wasn't sure when I drifted off, but my eyes had only been closed for a few minutes when I felt a presence near me. Blinking drowsily, I opened my eyes to find Felix crouched beside the couch, his gaze soft as he studied me.

"I thought you were going to let me sleep," I murmured, my voice thick with exhaustion.

He chuckled softly, the sound low and almost musical in the quiet room. "You were shivering," he said simply, motioning toward the blanket he had already tucked around me. "I just wanted to make sure you were warm enough."

I smiled faintly, my cheeks warming at the thoughtfulness behind his words. "Thanks," I said softly, pulling the blanket tighter around me.

Felix didn't move right away. Instead, he stayed crouched beside me, his dark eyes lingering on mine. There was something unspoken in his gaze, something that made my chest tighten and my pulse quicken. I couldn't look away, even though part of me felt like I should. It was too much, too intense. But at the same time, it was... grounding.

"You should try to get some rest," he said eventually, his voice gentle but firm. "You've been through a lot today."

"So have you," I countered, my voice steadier now as I fought back the sleep tugging at my eyelids. "You don't have to keep looking after me, you know. I'm not as fragile as I look."

His lips quirked into a faint smirk, the familiar expression returning like a balm to the tension in the air. "I never said you were fragile," he replied smoothly. "But that doesn't mean you don't need someone watching your back every now and then."

I rolled my eyes, a soft laugh escaping my lips. "Is that your way of saying you've got my back?"

He tilted his head slightly, considering my words. "I think it goes both ways, doesn't it?" he said, his tone lighter now, though there was still a hint of something deeper beneath the surface. "I've got yours, and you've got mine. Whether we like it or not."

That took me by surprise. I hadn't expected him to say it so plainly, and I found myself smiling despite the exhaustion settling over me. "Yeah," I agreed softly. "I guess it does."

Felix stood then, his movements fluid and effortless as he made his way back to the chair he had been occupying earlier. He picked up the diary again, flipping back to the page he'd been reading before. But this time, as he leaned over the book, his gaze flicked toward me every so often, as if making sure I was still there—still okay.

I curled deeper into the blanket, watching him as he worked. The firelight cast shadows across his face, highlighting the sharp lines of his jaw and the intensity in his eyes as they moved across the page. Despite everything—the danger, the uncertainty, the weight of what lay ahead—I felt a strange sense of peace.

The fire had dwindled to faint embers, casting the room in muted shades of gold and copper. The storm outside was little more than a whisper now, its gentle rhythm blending into the quiet of the night. Felix sat in his chair, the diary open in his hands, his focus unwavering as he skimmed through its pages.

I watched him quietly, tucked under the blanket he'd given me, my body curled into the corner of the sofa. Something about the way he sat—the effortless way he carried himself— made it impossible not to notice him. The faint glow of the fire softened the sharpness of his features, and the crease in his brow as he concentrated hinted at something deeper, something private.

For a moment, I let myself wonder about him—not just about the pain he carried or the centuries of history behind his calm demeanor. I wondered about Felix, the man who had managed to slip past my defenses without me realizing it. There was a quiet strength to him, a sense of control that felt unshakable. And yet, there were cracks—moments where the weight of everything he had endured shone through. Those cracks made him feel real in a way that took my breath away.

I didn't realize I was staring until he spoke, his voice smooth and laced with faint amusement. "You're staring again," he said, his lips curving into a familiar smirk without lifting his gaze from the diary.

Heat rushed to my cheeks, and I hurried to look away, my fingers tightening around the edge of the blanket. "Sorry," I muttered, my voice barely audible.

His smirk deepened slightly, though he still didn't look up. "You really don't have to apologize, Iris," he said casually, the faintest edge of teasing in his tone. "It's not like I mind."

I rolled my eyes, though the blush in my cheeks remained stubbornly present. "Do you ever stop?" I asked, trying to sound exasperated but failing miserably.

Finally, Felix looked up from the diary, his eyes meeting mine with an intensity that made my breath hitch. The smirk softened into something more genuine, and he leaned back slightly, the book still balanced in his hands.

"Not when you make it so easy," he said, his tone playful but not unkind.

I scoffed quietly, shaking my head as a faint smile tugged at the corners of my lips. Despite my best efforts, I couldn't stay annoyed at him—not when he looked at me like that.

The silence stretched between us again, comfortable and warm, and I let myself relax against the cushions of the sofa. My exhaustion was still present, tugging at the edges of my mind, but I couldn't bring myself to close my eyes. Not yet.

Felix's gaze lingered on me for a moment longer before returning to the diary, his expression shifting back to one of focus. I watched him quietly, taking in the subtle details—the way his fingers moved over the pages, the way his lashes cast faint shadows against his cheeks.

It was strange, this quiet intimacy between us. Strange, but... comforting. Felix and I were two people caught in something far bigger than ourselves, bound by a history we didn't ask for. And yet, here we were—just two people trying to make sense of it together.

"Iris," Felix said suddenly, breaking the silence. His voice was softer now, thoughtful.

"Yeah?" I asked, tilting my head slightly to look at him.

He hesitated for a moment, his gaze flicking back to me. "I don't say this often, but... I'm glad you're here. I don't think I'd be doing this if it weren't for you."

The words broke through my defenses , and my chest tightened as a strange warmth spread through me. There was no teasing smirk this time, no clever remark—just sincerity.

"I'm glad I'm here too," I said quietly, my voice steady but soft.

And in that moment, surrounded by the glow of the fire and the remnants of the storm, I realized something. Felix wasn't just a part of this mystery I was trying to solve. He wasn't just someone tied to my family's legacy or the horrors of Carrow.

Felix was becoming *something more.*

And as I watched him, I couldn't shake the feeling that destiny—or whatever force had brought us together—had chosen us for a reason.

Two wounded souls. Two keys to a puzzle we hadn't yet solved. And whatever comes next, we were facing it together.

CHAPTER XIII

Resonance

The morning light filtered softly through the pale curtains, casting warm streaks across my face and coaxing my eyes open. At first, I squinted against the brightness, reluctant to leave the cocoon of half-sleep. But as the world sharpened into focus, I shifted onto my back, stretching lazily, my arms reaching high above my head. The slight stiffness in my body reminded me of the long, exhausting day before—one that had left my thoughts spinning long after I had closed my eyes.

It wasn't until I lowered my arms that I realized something was different. My gaze darted around the room, and a jolt of unfamiliarity tightened in my chest. I wasn't home. The room surrounding me was pristine—*too* pristine. The king-sized bed beneath me felt far larger than any bed I'd ever slept in, its surface covered by a thick, luxurious comforter that practically swallowed me whole. The fabric was smooth and warm, a soft contrast to the cool air brushing against my skin.

I sat up, startled, my fingers curling reflexively into the comforter's folds as I scanned the space with wide eyes. The walls were painted a calming shade of cream, their surfaces free of clutter or imperfections. A pair of nightstands flanked the bed, each perfectly symmetrical with polished wood surfaces and neatly arranged objects—a clock on one side, a lamp on the other. The lamp's soft golden glow added a touch of warmth to the clean, organized space.

The floor beneath the bed was made of polished dark wood, gleaming faintly in the morning light. A large woven rug stretched across the space, its muted tones grounding the room with a sense of understated elegance. Everything here—the crisp lines, the perfectly positioned curtains, the matching set of drawers against the opposite wall—was immaculate, almost unnervingly so. It felt like a place untouched by chaos, a sanctuary meticulously maintained.

I inhaled deeply, trying to steady my racing thoughts as my gaze landed on a single chair positioned near the window. Its placement was deliberate, facing the curtains where sunlight streamed in. A small stack of books rested on its seat, their spines perfectly aligned. Felix had an eye for order that bordered on perfection.

And yet, something about the room didn't feel cold or sterile. The warmth in its design, the subtle softness in the details, hinted at care. It wasn't just tidy—it was *intentional*.

I rubbed my hands over my face, trying to shake off the lingering haze of sleep. How had I gotten here? My thoughts were muddled, bits and pieces of the night before surfacing in fragments. The rain, the storm, Felix... Felix.

The tension in my chest eased slightly at the memory of him, and I exhaled shakily. He must've brought me here—this place, this room. I glanced at the nightstand closest to me, my gaze landing on the diary resting atop its polished surface. Its worn leather cover stood out sharply against the neatness of the room, a reminder of everything we had uncovered, everything still waiting for us to face.

Pulling the comforter tighter around me, I swung my legs over the edge of the bed. The chill of the polished floor against my bare feet sent a shiver up my spine, but I barely noticed it. My mind was too busy racing, trying to piece together the pieces Felix hadn't yet shared with me.

I stepped out of the bedroom, the blanket still draped over my shoulders like a shield from the lingering chill. The faint sound of distant birds outside hinted at how early it was, but my thoughts were too scattered to pay attention to the time. I needed to find Felix.

The hallway beyond the bedroom was just as neat and orderly as the room itself—walls painted the same soothing shade of cream, lined with framed sketches and muted landscapes. A tall vase sat on a side table near the door, its arrangement of dried flowers untouched and perfectly symmetrical. Every detail seemed deliberate, but none of it felt lived in. It was as if the house was frozen in time, waiting for something to stir it awake.

I glanced down the corridor, the faint hum of quiet settling over me. Where was Felix? The diary, the necklace, and Carrow—they all felt like they were pressing against my chest, heavy and suffocating.

The stairs were just ahead, their smooth, dark wood matching the flooring upstairs. I took them carefully, my hands brushing against the railing as I made my way down. The lower level opened into a wide foyer, its space just as pristine as everything else. The light streaming through the tall windows bathed the room in a golden glow, but it felt oddly distant, like it couldn't quite reach the warmth of the house itself.

My gaze landed on the living room, where the remnants of the fire from the night before still lingered in the hearth, faint and flickering. Felix wasn't there.

"Felix?" I called softly, my voice barely rising above the quiet.

There was no answer.

Instead, I followed the faint sound that carried through the house—a melody, soft and mournful, drifting upward like a whisper.

My breath caught as I recognized the music for what it was, a piano. The notes were deliberate, aching, each one lingering in the air before giving way to the next. It was as though the instrument itself was speaking, telling a story too heavy for words.

The melody grew clearer with each step, and the tension in my chest grew tighter, sharper. It was beautiful—a haunting kind of beautiful that resonated somewhere deep within me, pulling at emotions I hadn't realized were there.

I stepped further into the house, glancing toward the study tucked behind the living room. The heavy doors were slightly ajar, and I hesitated for a moment before pushing them open. The room smelled faintly of aged wood and leather, the space lit by morning light filtering through the curtains. Shelves lined the walls, packed with books whose spines ranged from worn to pristine, their titles barely discernible in the dim light.

And there he was.

Felix was seated at the piano, his hands gliding over the keys with a grace that made my breath hitch. His posture was steady but relaxed, his shoulders slightly slumped as though he were letting himself sink into the music. The sunlight streaming through the window illuminated him, catching the edges of his dark hair and the faint shadows along his sharp jawline.

I froze in the doorway, the melody washing over me like a wave. It wasn't the image of Felix that rooted me to the spot—it was the way he played. The way his fingers moved, deliberate but unguarded, each note carrying an ache that seemed to spill from somewhere deep within him. He wasn't just playing the piano. He was pouring himself into it, letting the music say what he wouldn't.

The final note lingered in the air, a faint hum that left the room suspended in its wake. Felix didn't look up right away, his hands resting lightly on the keys as though reluctant to pull away. But then he glanced over his shoulder, catching sight of me standing awkwardly near the door.

"How long have you been standing there?" he asked, his voice low but tinged with faint amusement.

"Not long," I admitted, stepping into the room cautiously. My pulse quickened under his gaze, but I pushed through the nerves. "I didn't know you played."

Felix shrugged, turning back to the piano as he pressed a single key lightly. The sound echoed faintly before fading. "It's something I've kept with me over the years," he said. "Something that helps... when there's too much in my head."

I moved closer, my gaze drifting over the piano's smooth black surface, the way it gleamed in the sunlight. "It's beautiful," I said softly, my voice barely above a whisper.

Felix glanced at me again, his lips curving into the faintest smile. "You think so?"

I nodded, my chest tightening slightly as I searched for the right words. "It's... haunting," I said finally. "The way you play—it's like you're telling a story."

Felix's smile faded slightly, replaced by something quieter, something deeper. "Maybe I am," he said simply.

The silence between us stretched, and I hesitated, unsure of whether to press him further. But the way he sat there, his shoulders heavy, his expression shadowed, made me step closer.

"You don't have to keep everything inside, Felix," I said gently.

He exhaled softly, his fingers tracing the edge of the keys without pressing them. "I've spent centuries keeping everything inside," he said quietly, his voice tinged with something raw. "It's... safer that way."

"For you or for everyone else?" I challenged, my tone firm but not unkind.

Felix looked at me, his dark eyes meeting mine with an intensity that made my breath hitch. "Both," he admitted.

"Well, you don't have to anymore," I countered, my voice firmer now. "I'm here, Felix. And whatever this is— whatever Carrow is—we're going to face it together."

He turned toward me fully then, his blue eyes locking onto mine. There was something in his gaze that made my pulse quicken. He didn't speak right away, but the silence between us felt charged, electric.

"I'm not sure you understand what you're signing up for," he said finally, his voice low but steady. "This isn't just some mystery to solve, Iris. It's dangerous. And if you get caught up in it..."

"I'm already caught up in it," I said firmly, stepping closer. "I can't walk away from this, even if I wanted to. So stop trying to protect me, Felix. Stop shutting me out."

"You really don't make things easy, do you?" he said, a faint smile tugging at the corner of his lips.

"I never claimed to," I replied, my own lips curving into a small smile.

Felix shook his head, his smirk softening into something more genuine. "You're stubborn," he said quietly, his tone lighter now.

"And you're impossible," I shot back, my smile growing.

"So..." I began, my voice tentative as I tried to fill the quiet space between us. "I didn't expect your room to be so nice."

I was sitting beside him on the piano bench, the smooth surface of the keys cool under my fingertips as I traced them idly. The melody he had been playing moments earlier still lingered faintly in the air, though the silence was settling in now, wrapping around us like a blanket.

Felix scoffed, the sound light but teasing. "I never said that was my room," he said, his tone laced with playful mischief.

He turned slightly toward me, his dark eyes catching the light from the window, and I realized just how close we were—

our bodies barely inches apart. My throat tightened, and I gulped, suddenly aware of how stupid my comment had been.

"Oh," I stammered, shifting uncomfortably on the stool. "I'm sorry... I didn't mean to assume."

I started to move, ready to stand and put some distance between us, but before I could even get halfway up, I felt his hand wrap around my arm—a firm but gentle grip that stopped me in my tracks.

"Don't be so touchy," Felix chuckled, his laugh low and soft, like a faint melody itself. "I was just messing with you."

His smile didn't falter, the teasing edge lingering in his expression as he released my arm. I could feel the blush creeping up my cheeks, the warmth spreading as my embarrassment grew. I couldn't bring myself to look directly at him, too flustered by the proximity and his casual ease.

"Shut up," I muttered, barely managing to meet his gaze before I swung my hand out and lightly punched his arm.

He laughed harder at that, his amusement breaking through the tension in the room like sunlight through clouds. It was infectious, and despite my embarrassment, I found myself laughing with him, the sound blending into the quiet melody still echoing faintly from the piano.

Felix leaned back slightly, his smirk still firmly in place as he watched me try to recover from my embarrassment. His fingers lightly brushed over the piano keys, playing a few soft notes that filled the room like a teasing echo of his laughter.

"For the record," he said casually, tilting his head slightly, "it *is* my room."

I froze mid-laugh, my eyes snapping to his. "Wait, what?" I blurted. "You just said it wasn't!"

"I said I never *claimed* it was," he corrected smoothly, his smirk growing even more infuriatingly smug. "I never said it wasn't, either."

I stared at him, my mouth hanging open for a moment before I groaned, dragging my hands down my face. "You're impossible," I muttered, shaking my head as I tried to bite back a smile.

"Impossible?" Felix repeated, his tone dripping with mock offense. "I think you mean charmingly unpredictable."

"Annoyingly unpredictable," I shot back, crossing my arms.

He laughed at that, a warm, low sound that sent a strange flutter through my chest. "You're fun to mess with, you know that?" he said, turning back toward the piano and playing a lighthearted melody that matched his teasing mood.

"Well, I'm glad you're enjoying yourself," I said, rolling my eyes. "Meanwhile, I'm over here trying to figure out how I keep walking into these traps."

Felix glanced at me out of the corner of his eye, his smirk softening slightly. "Maybe you just like the company," he said, his tone quieter now, though the teasing edge was still there.

My cheeks warmed at his words, and I quickly looked away, focusing on the piano keys as though they held the secrets of the universe. Before I could come up with a witty response—or any response, for that matter—my phone buzzed on the table nearby, breaking the moment.

Grateful for the distraction, I reached over and grabbed it, unlocking the screen to check the notification. My heart sank as I saw the time. "Oh no," I muttered, my stomach flipping.

"What?" Felix asked, his fingers pausing on the keys.

"I'm late for work," I said, groaning as I slumped back against the piano bench. "I was supposed to be there half an hour ago. Mr. Ramsey is going to kill me."

Felix raised an eyebrow, leaning back slightly as he rested his hands on his thighs. "Who's Mr. Ramsey?"

"My boss," I explained, running a hand through my hair. "He's not exactly the forgiving type, especially when it comes to being late. I don't even have a good excuse!"

Felix tilted his head, studying me for a moment before a faint smile tugged at his lips. "Iris," he said, his tone calm and deliberate, "do you really think work is more important than figuring out what's happening with the necklace and Carrow?"

I hesitated, my fingers tightening around my phone. "I mean, I can't just not show up. I have responsibilities—"

"Responsibilities like answering phones and dealing with whatever mundane tasks Mr. Ramsey throws at you?" Felix interrupted, his smirk returning. "I hate to break it to you, but I think stopping an ancient curse takes precedence over cleaning coffee mugs."

I frowned, my mind torn between the guilt of skipping work and the undeniable weight of everything Felix and I were trying to uncover. "It's not that simple," I said, though even I wasn't entirely convinced by my own words.

Felix sighed, leaning closer until our faces were only inches apart. "Iris," he said softly, his keen gaze locking onto mine, "we both know this is bigger than a nine-to-five job. You can take one day. Just one. And if it makes you feel better, call him. Tell him you're sick. But you need to stay here. We have more important things to do."

I stared at him, my chest tightening as his words sank in. He was right, of course—how could I justify prioritizing work over everything we'd uncovered? Over everything that was still waiting for us to figure out?

With a heavy sigh, I nodded, pulling up Mr. Ramsey's number on my phone. "You owe me for this," I muttered, glancing at Felix as I hit the call button.

"I'll consider it," he said with a small laugh, leaning back against the piano as I held the phone to my ear.

The line rang twice before Mr. Ramsey picked up, his voice sharp as always. "Iris, you're late," he barked without so much as a greeting.

"I know, I know," I said quickly, my voice dropping into my best 'sickly' tone. "I'm really sorry, Mr. Ramsey, but I'm not feeling well. I think I might have caught something—I didn't want to come in and risk getting anyone else sick."

There was a pause on the other end, and I held my breath, bracing myself for the inevitable lecture. Instead, Mr. Ramsey sighed heavily. "Fine," he said gruffly. "But you'd better be back tomorrow, Iris. We're short-staffed as it is."

"Of course," I said, relief flooding through me. "Thank you, Mr. Ramsey. I really appreciate it."

He muttered something unintelligible before hanging up, and I set my phone down with a sigh of relief.

"Well?" Felix asked, his smirk widening.

"He bought it," I said, giving him a pointed look. "But you're still not off the hook for making me skip."

Felix chuckled, his hands brushing lightly over the piano keys as he met my gaze. "Trust me," he said, his voice steady but warm, "you're right where you need to be."

And for the first time all morning, I believed him.

After a long, quiet moment, Felix rose to his feet, the faint sound of the piano keys brushing against the silence as his movements broke the stillness in the room. He looked at me, his dark eyes steady and unreadable, and extended his hand.

"I guess it's time to get back to work," he said, his voice calm but weighted with purpose.

I hesitated briefly, my gaze flicking to his hand and then back to his face. There was something in the way he stood there—an unspoken resolve, a quiet confidence that made my chest tighten. I reached out, slipping my fingers into his, the warmth of his touch grounding me as I nodded.

"Yeah," I said softly, the word carrying more conviction than I realized.

Felix's grip tightened slightly, not too much, but enough to steady me as I stood. For a brief moment, the room felt suspended, the weight of everything still lingering but somehow less suffocating. I didn't know exactly what lay ahead, but with him beside me, it felt just a little more manageable.

And as I followed him forward, our hands brushing as he let go, I felt the stirrings of something stronger than fear—hope.

CHAPTER XIV

Inheritance of Pain

Felix's room was just as pristine as the rest of the house—minimalistic yet inviting, with dark wood accents and soft, earthy tones. The sunlight streamed through the partially drawn curtains, highlighting the neatness of everything. A polished desk sat against one wall, its surface free of clutter except for a single notebook and a fountain pen. A stack of books was lined up perfectly on a nearby shelf, their spines worn but carefully arranged. It was almost hard to believe this space belonged to someone who seemed to carry centuries of chaos and pain with him.

I sat cross-legged on the edge of his neatly made bed, the diary resting in my lap. Felix was perched in the chair by the desk, one leg propped up on the other as he flipped through another book he'd retrieved from the shelves. His expression was focused, his cobalt stare scanning each page with a quiet intensity.

"So," I began, breaking the silence, "where do we start? The diary's a mess of fragmented entries, and I don't even know if what's in there is enough to piece anything together."

Felix glanced up, the faintest hint of a smirk tugging at his lips. "We start by not overthinking," he said, his tone calm but edged with amusement. "The pieces are there—we just have to find the connections."

I huffed softly, opening the diary and skimming its pages for what felt like the hundredth time. "Easy for you to say," I muttered. "You're probably used to this kind of thing."

"Used to ancient curses and unraveling centuries-old mysteries?" Felix teased, raising an eyebrow. "Hardly."

I shot him a look, unable to keep the small smile from creeping onto my face. "You know what I mean."

Before he could respond, my phone buzzed on the bed beside me, the vibration making me jump slightly. I frowned, setting the diary aside as I reached for it. The screen lit up with Luna's name, and my heart sank.

Felix noticed my change in demeanor immediately, his expression shifting into something more serious. "Who is it?" he asked.

"Luna," I said, swiping to answer.

I pressed the phone to my ear, already bracing myself. Luna didn't usually call unless it was something important. "Hey, Luna," I said quickly. "What's up?"

"*What's up?*" Luna repeated, her voice laced with concern. "Iris, are you okay? I went to the café this morning, and Tessa said you called in sick. You never call in sick."

I winced, glancing at Felix, who was now watching me with a faintly curious expression. "Yeah, I'm fine," I said, trying to sound convincing. "I just... wasn't feeling great, so I thought it'd be better to stay home."

Luna didn't buy it. "Are you sure? You sounded fine yesterday when we talked. Did something happen after you left?"

I hesitated, my fingers tightening slightly around the phone. Luna's concern was genuine, and it was making me feel guilty for keeping her in the dark. But there was no way I could explain everything over the phone—especially not with Felix sitting a few feet away, his presence a constant reminder of the enormity of what I was dealing with.

"Luna, I need to talk to you and Jayce," I said finally, my voice lowering as though someone else might overhear. "It's... important. Can you meet me tonight?"

"Tonight?" Luna repeated, sounding both confused and wary. "I mean, sure, but what's going on? Where do you want to meet?"

My eyes flicked to Felix, who tilted his head slightly as though he could sense the direction this was going. "There's a place," I said carefully, glancing around the room. "It's... hard to explain over the phone, but it's not far. Can you and Jayce come there? I'll send you the address."

Luna was quiet for a moment, and I could practically hear her mind racing on the other end of the line. "You're being really cryptic," she said finally. "But yeah, okay. I'll talk to Jayce and let him know. Are you sure you're okay, though?"

"I'm fine," I said, though the words felt heavy in my mouth. "I promise, I'll explain everything tonight."

"Okay," Luna said reluctantly. "Just... don't do anything stupid, okay? And call me if you need anything."

"I will," I assured her before hanging up.

When I set the phone down, Felix raised an eyebrow, his curiosity evident. "Friends of yours?" he asked casually, though there was an edge to his tone that I couldn't quite place.

"Yeah," I said, running a hand through my hair. "Luna and Jayce. They're the only people I trust enough to tell about this."

Felix leaned back slightly in his chair, his expression thoughtful. "And you're bringing them *here*?"

I nodded, meeting his gaze. "They need to know. If I'm going to figure this out—if we're going to figure this out—I can't keep them in the dark. They might be able to help."

Felix didn't respond right away, his jaw tightening slightly as he considered my words. Finally, he nodded, though his reluctance was clear. "Alright," he said, his tone neutral. "But if they're coming here, they need to be prepared. This isn't just some old mansion, Iris. There are things about this place that..." He trailed off, his gaze dropping to the floor.

"I'll explain as much as I can before they get here," I said softly. "But they need to see it for themselves. They need to understand what we're dealing with."

Felix looked at me for a long moment before sighing, the tension in his posture easing slightly. "You're stubborn, you know that?" he said, a faint smirk tugging at his lips.

I smiled, the weight on my chest lifting just slightly. "You're just figuring that out now?"

The afternoon sunlight streamed through the curtains, casting soft patterns across the pristine surfaces of Felix's room. The air felt still, carrying the kind of quiet weight that seemed to belong to the space. Felix was seated by his desk, his eyes locked onto the diary as though he could will it to reveal answers.

The tension in his posture hadn't eased for hours. His shoulders were tight, his fingers drumming absently against the edge of the desk, and I could tell that whatever he had uncovered on those pages wasn't sitting well with him. Sunlight grazed his features, highlighting the faint lines of concentration etched across his face. The orderly neatness of the room only made the unease in the air feel sharper, like a storm brewing beneath a calm surface.

I sat cross-legged on the bed, the soft comforter bunched around me as I watched him. My own thoughts felt tangled, a mess of curiosity and dread. The diary held so many fragmented truths, so many pieces of a puzzle we were struggling to assemble. But whatever Felix had found, it was weighing on him. And if it was weighing on Felix, I knew it had to be bad.

"I think we should take a break," I said softly, breaking the silence.

Felix didn't look up, his fingers tapping lightly against the cover of the diary. "We don't have time for a break," he replied, his tone clipped.

"You haven't said a word since you read that last entry," I pointed out, leaning forward slightly. "Felix, what did it say?"

His jaw tightened, and I could see the muscle there twitch as he debated whether or not to answer me. For a moment, it seemed like he was going to brush me off, but then he sighed, his shoulders sagging slightly as the fight left him.

"It mentioned your family," he admitted, his voice low. "The Harts. They weren't just involved in the creation of the necklace—they were the ones who turned it into what it is now. They're the reason it's tied to Carrow."

I felt a chill creep down my spine, but I pushed through the unease. "What do you mean? What did they do?"

Felix finally met my gaze, his eyes clouded with anger, sadness, maybe even regret. "They weren't just trying to protect Eleanor," he said quietly. "They were trying to use her. The necklace wasn't just a safeguard—it was a tool. A way to control what's inside Carrow. And when she refused to follow their plans..." He trailed off, his jaw tightening again.

"What?" I pressed, my voice barely above a whisper.

"They sacrificed her," he said, the words sharp and bitter. "Your family—her own father—sacrificed her to the curse to ensure the necklace stayed bound to their bloodline."

The room felt colder suddenly, the weight of his words pressing down on me. "I didn't know," I said softly, the lump in my throat making it hard to speak. "Felix, I swear, I didn't know."

"I know," he said quickly, his voice softening. But the tension in his posture didn't ease, and I could see the lingering resentment in his expression. "It's not you, Iris. It's them. Your family—your ancestors—they did this. And I can't... I can't just let that go."

His words stung, even though I knew they weren't meant to hurt me. "I'm not them," I said, my voice trembling slightly.

"I know that," he said, his tone sharper now as though he was trying to convince himself as much as me. "But it doesn't make it any easier. Every time I look at you, I see her. I see Eleanor, and I see what they did to her. And then I remember that you're tied to all of this, just like she was. And I—" He stopped, his voice catching.

"You what?" I asked, leaning forward despite the tension between us.

Felix's gaze dropped to the floor, his shoulders slumping. "I don't want you to end up like her," he said finally, his voice barely audible. "I don't want to lose you, too."

His admission hit me like a punch to the gut, and for a moment, I didn't know what to say. Felix had always been guarded, keeping me at arm's length even as we worked together to unravel the mystery of the necklace and Carrow. But this— this was different. This was him letting me in, even if just a little, and it felt like a crack in the armor he had built around himself.

"You don't have to lose me," I said softly, my voice steady despite the emotions swirling inside me. "Felix, I'm not going anywhere. I'm in this with you, whether you like it or not."

He looked up at me then, his eyes searching mine for something—reassurance, maybe, or a reason to believe me. "You say that now," he said quietly. "But you don't know what you're up against."

"Then tell me," I challenged, sitting up straighter. "Stop shutting me out, Felix. If you don't trust me, if you don't let me help you, how are we supposed to do this together?"

He let out a frustrated sigh, running a hand through his dark hair as he leaned back in his chair. "It's not about trust," he said, his voice tight. "It's about protecting you. If you knew the things I've seen—you'd understand why I'm trying to keep you at a distance."

I shook my head, my resolve hardening. "I don't need your protection, Felix," I said firmly. "I need you to let me in. I need you to stop carrying this on your own. Because whether you like it or not, I'm already a part of this. I have been since the day I had put this necklace on."

The air in the room felt heavier, charged with something I couldn't quite name. Felix had been quiet for what felt like an eternity, his gaze flickering between the diary and the floor, his thoughts clearly elsewhere. And then, without warning, he moved.

He closed the space between us in a single, deliberate step, his presence suddenly overwhelming. My breath caught as he stood right in front of me, his face mere inches from mine. His blue eyes locked onto mine, piercing through every wall I'd ever built, and I felt like he could see everything—every thought, every fear, every feeling I was trying so desperately to keep hidden.

His gaze dropped, traveling from my eyes to my lips, lingering there for a moment that felt an eternity had passed. My heart was pounding so loudly I was sure he could hear it, each beat echoing in my ears as the tension between us grew unbearable.

Felix's hand moved slowly, his fingers brushing against mine before trailing up my arm. The touch was light, almost hesitant, but it sent a shiver through me that I couldn't suppress.

His body shifted closer, the warmth of him wrapping around me like a cocoon, and I felt my cheeks flush, the heat spreading as my pulse raced faster with every second that passed.

I was lost in his eyes—those impossibly blue eyes that seemed to hold the weight of centuries and yet still managed to look at me like I was the only thing that mattered. His hand reached my face, his fingers brushing against my cheek before cupping it gently. The warmth of his touch was grounding, but it only made the storm inside me swirl faster.

We stood there in silence, the rhythm of our heartbeats filling the room, louder than any words could have been. I couldn't look away, couldn't move, couldn't breathe. Something inside me was shifting, bubbling to the surface with an intensity that left me dizzy.

I lifted my hand, placing it over his, the warmth wrapped around me with unexpected ease. I let my eyes drift shut for a breath of a moment, letting it sink in, letting myself dissolve into the quiet gravity of his touch. My fingers curled slightly, holding him there as I stared at him, taking in every detail—the sharp lines of his jaw, the faint crease in his brow, the way his lips parted slightly as he exhaled. He was beautiful, in a way that felt almost unreal. And he made me feel something I never thought I would—something I wasn't sure I was ready for.

Felix bit his bottom lip, his gaze roaming over my face as though he was memorizing every inch of it. His eyes were a storm of emotions—desire, maybe even lust, but also fear and hesitation. Concern flickered there, too, like he was fighting against something he couldn't control.

His brow furrowed, and he let out a quiet sigh, his hand starting to drop as he turned away. The sudden loss of his touch sent a pang through my chest, and before I could think, I reached out, grabbing his wrist and stopping him in his tracks.

But I couldn't let him go.

"Don't," I whispered, my voice trembling but firm.

Felix froze, his gaze snapping back to mine. For a moment, neither of us moved, the tension between us crackling like electricity. And then, slowly, he turned back toward me, his free hand lifting to brush a strand of hair away from my face.

"Iris," he murmured, my name slipping from his lips like a confession.

I didn't respond—not with words, anyway. Instead, I leaned in, closing the final gap between us. My lips brushed against his, tentative at first, but the moment they met, the world seemed to tilt on its axis.

Felix's hand slid back to my cheek, his fingers curling slightly as he deepened the kiss. His other hand moved to my waist, pulling me closer until there was no space left between us. The warmth of him, the way he held me, the way his lips moved against mine—it was overwhelming, intoxicating, and I couldn't get enough.

Every emotion I'd been trying to suppress came rushing to the surface, crashing over me like a wave. The fear, the uncertainty, the undeniable pull I felt toward him—it all melted away, replaced by something raw and unfiltered.

His kiss was soft but insistent, a perfect balance of tenderness and urgency that left me breathless. My hands found their way to his chest, my fingers curling into the fabric of his shirt as I tried to steady myself. But there was no steadying myself—not when every part of me felt like it was on fire, like I was unraveling and coming alive all at once.

Felix's lips parted slightly, and I felt the faintest brush of his breath against mine, sending a shiver down my spine. His hand at my waist tightened, grounding me even as the rest of the world seemed to fade away.

When we finally pulled apart, our foreheads rested against each other, our breaths mingling in the quiet of the room. Felix's eyes searched mine, his expression conflicted but unguarded.

"This changes everything," he said softly, his voice barely above a whisper.

"I know," I replied, my own voice trembling.

And as we stood there, the weight of what had just happened settling over us, I realized that nothing would ever be the same.

For a moment, the room felt suspended, like the air itself was holding its breath. Felix's forehead rested against mine, our breaths still mingling in the quiet that followed the kiss. My heart pounded against my chest, each beat reverberating through me as though trying to fill the silence. I couldn't think, couldn't move—everything inside me was tangled in the overwhelming rush of what had just happened.

Felix pulled back just slightly, enough to put space between us but not enough to break the spell entirely. His hand lingered on my cheek, his thumb brushing gently against my skin, as though he was afraid to let go. His eyes searched mine, a storm of emotions flickering in their depths—confusion, yearning, fear. It was like he was trying to make sense of what we'd just done, the way we'd crossed a line we could never uncross.

"I shouldn't have..." Felix began, his voice low and unsteady. He shook his head slightly, his brow furrowing as though he was trying to pull himself back together. "I shouldn't have done that."

The words stung more than I expected them to, like a cold wind cutting through the warmth still lingering from his touch. "Why?" I asked softly, my voice trembling despite my best efforts to keep it steady. "Felix, why would you say that?"

He closed his eyes briefly, exhaling a shaky breath before meeting my gaze again. "Because it's dangerous," he said, his tone filled with quiet frustration. "This—us—whatever this is... it can't happen, Iris. You don't understand how much is at stake."

The vulnerability in his voice made my chest ache, but his words only fueled the confusion swirling inside me. "You don't get to decide that for me," I said firmly, my hand still wrapped around his wrist. "You keep telling me how dangerous everything is, how much you're trying to protect me—but you never let me choose. You never let me decide for myself."

Felix's jaw tightened, his expression conflicted. "You don't know what you're asking for," he said quietly, his gaze dropping to the space between us. "I've lived with this—this curse—for centuries. It doesn't leave room for anything else. It can't."

I shook my head, refusing to let him retreat into himself again. "That's not your choice to make, Felix," I said, my voice soft but unwavering. "If I'm already in this—if I'm already tied to the necklace, to Carrow, to *you*—then you don't get to push me away every time you get scared."

His eyes snapped back to mine at that, a flicker of something raw and unguarded flashing across his face. "I'm not scared," he said, though the words sounded hollow even to him.

"Yes, you are," I said, the heat of my emotions breaking through. "You're scared of letting yourself care, of letting yourself feel something because you think it'll make everything worse. But it won't, Felix. It won't."

He let out a quiet, humorless laugh, his hand finally dropping from my face as he turned away. The loss of his touch was immediate, a sharp contrast to the warmth that had just been there. "You don't get it," he said, his voice low and strained. "It's not about me. It's about you. If anything happens to you because of this... because of me... I couldn't—" He stopped himself, his voice breaking slightly, and I realized just how deeply this fear of his ran.

I reached out again, my hand finding his arm. "Felix, look at me," I said gently.

He hesitated, his muscles tensing under my touch, but after a moment, he turned back toward me. His eyes were guarded now, the vulnerability slipping behind the walls he so carefully maintained. But he was still there, still listening.

"I'm not going anywhere," I said, my voice quiet but firm. "I don't care how dangerous it is or how much you think I need protecting. I'm here, Felix. And I'm not giving up on this— on you."

His gaze searched mine, and for a moment, I thought he might argue, might tell me again that I didn't understand. But instead, he let out a quiet sigh, his shoulders relaxing slightly as the tension began to ease from his posture.

"You're stubborn," he said softly, a faint smirk tugging at the corner of his lips despite everything.

"You say that a lot," I replied, my own lips curving into a small, tentative smile.

The quiet between us shifted then, the weight of the moment settling into something steadier, more grounded. There were still so many questions, so many things left unsaid. But for now, in the quiet warmth of the room, it felt like enough.

The quiet in the room lingered, wrapping around us like a fragile thread that neither of us dared to break. Felix's faint smirk had faded, replaced by a thoughtful look that softened the sharp edges of his usual guarded expression. I could see the weight still pressing on him—the uncertainty, the conflict—but for the first time, it felt like he was letting me shoulder even the smallest part of it.

"You know," I said, leaning back slightly but keeping my gaze locked on his, "for someone who claims they're good at keeping people out, you're not doing a great job right now."

Felix raised an eyebrow, the faintest flicker of amusement breaking through his otherwise serious demeanor. "And yet, somehow, you keep finding ways to get in," he replied, his tone teasing but laced with something warmer, something deeper.

I smiled faintly, crossing my arms as I sat on the edge of his bed. "Maybe you're letting me," I said softly.

His gaze faltered for a moment, as though my words had struck a chord he wasn't ready to acknowledge. He looked away, his jaw tightening briefly before he let out a quiet sigh. "Maybe I am," he admitted, his voice barely above a whisper.

That caught me off guard, and for a moment, I didn't know what to say. Felix wasn't the type to admit things easily, especially when it came to emotions. But here he was, letting me into the parts of him he usually kept hidden, and it felt like standing on the edge of something vast and terrifying.

"You don't have to keep doing this alone," I said gently, my voice steady but soft. "I know you think you have to—because of the curse, because of Carrow, because of everything—but you don't. Felix, you don't have to keep shutting me out. I'll keep reminding you until you accept it"

Felix's shoulders tensed slightly, his eyes darkening as he turned back to me. "It's not that simple," he said, his voice tinged with frustration. "I've lived with this for so long, Iris. It's... it's part of me. I don't even know how to let someone in anymore."

"You're doing it right now," I said, leaning forward slightly. "And it doesn't have to be perfect or easy or anything like that. It just has to be real. That's enough."

Felix's gaze softened, his guarded walls slipping just a little more. "You make it sound so easy," he said quietly, his lips curving into a faint smile that didn't quite reach his eyes.

"It's not," I admitted. "But it's worth it."

The silence stretched again, comfortable but charged, and I could feel the shift between us—something deeper, more vulnerable taking root. Felix let out another quiet sigh, his fingers brushing absently against the fabric of his shirt as though he was trying to ground himself.

"Why do you keep doing this?" he asked finally, his voice tinged with quiet curiosity. "Why do you keep pushing, even when I tell you it's dangerous?"

"Because I care," I said simply, the words spilling out before I could stop them. "And because I see you, Felix. Not just the curse, not just the centuries of pain or the walls you've built—I see *you*. And I think you deserve to let someone in."

Felix stared at me, his expression unguarded now, his blue eyes searching mine as though he was looking for something he couldn't quite put into words. And for a moment, I thought he might say something—might let himself admit something he hadn't before.

But instead, he reached out, his fingers brushing lightly against my hand before curling around it. His touch was warm, steady, grounding, and it sent a shiver through me that I couldn't suppress. He didn't speak, but he didn't have to—his actions said enough.

And as the light streamed through the room, illuminating the space between us, I realized something. Felix wasn't just letting me in. He was choosing to stay, even if it scared him.

We decided to put the research on pause until tonight, when Luna and Jayce arrived. Well, more like *I* decided. Felix had been reluctant, his jaw tightening the way it always did when he disagreed but didn't want to argue. He'd eventually given me that tiny nod of begrudging acceptance, though I could tell he wasn't thrilled about it.

I couldn't blame him. When Luna and Jayce showed up tonight, they'd have so many questions—especially when they saw Felix. These were questions I wasn't fully ready to answer. But I knew I had to. If I wanted them to be a part of this, to help me unravel the truth about Carrow, I needed to stop hiding behind half-truths and just be honest. I had to tell them about Felix, about the diary, and, most terrifying of all, about what we'd found out about my family.

Still, for the first time in weeks, I realized I was feeling... good. Better than I'd felt in a while, actually. Maybe it was because of Felix—or maybe it was the fact that, for once, I hadn't woken up from a nightmare. Being here, in this strange, impossibly clean house with him, seemed to keep them at bay. It was always that way when I was with Felix—either no nightmares at all, or the recurring dream of the forest. The one where I met him over and over, like some secret thread connecting us across a distance I didn't fully understand.

Whatever the reason, it was a relief not to wake up drenched in sweat, haunted by shadows of things I couldn't quite remember. For now, I was content to let that part of my life sit in the background.

A loud rumble broke through the calm, startling me out of my thoughts. I froze, heat creeping into my cheeks as I realized it was my stomach. Great. So much for looking composed and thoughtful.

Felix, of course, didn't miss a thing. Sitting in the armchair near the window, flipping absentmindedly through a book, he glanced up with the faintest curve of a smirk tugging at his lips. "Hungry?" he asked, his voice calm but laced with just enough amusement to make me want to disappear.

"I'm fine," I said quickly, crossing my arms as though that might silence my stomach.

Felix raised an eyebrow, setting the book down on the small table beside him. "That didn't sound 'fine,'" he teased, leaning back in his chair with that infuriatingly casual confidence of his. "When's the last time you ate something?"

"I don't know, like... last night," I mumbled, avoiding his gaze.

Felix let out a soft sigh, standing gracefully and heading toward the door. "Come on," he said, motioning for me to follow.

"Where are we going?" I asked, even though my feet were already moving, apparently deciding to obey him without consulting my brain.

"To get you some food," he said simply, glancing over his shoulder. "Unless you'd prefer to starve while pretending you're fine?"

I rolled my eyes but couldn't stop the small smile tugging at the corners of my lips. "You're impossible, you know that?"

"So I've been told," he replied, his smirk widening as he led the way down the hall.

The kitchen, like everything else in the house, was immaculately clean. Not a speck of dust, not a single thing out of place. It made me hesitate in the doorway, half-afraid I'd ruin the perfection just by breathing too loudly.

Felix, on the other hand, seemed completely at ease as he opened the fridge and began pulling out ingredients. "What do you feel like eating?" he asked over his shoulder, his tone casual.

I shrugged, leaning against the counter. "Surprise me."

His lips twitched, like he found that answer amusing, but he didn't comment. Instead, he started pulling together a simple but surprisingly enticing meal. Watching him work was... unexpected. There was a quiet precision to the way he moved, like he'd done this a thousand times before and could do it with his eyes closed.

"You know," I said, crossing my arms as I watched him, "I didn't take you for the cooking type."

Felix glanced at me, his expression unreadable. "I've had a lot of time to pick up some skills," he said vaguely, his focus returning to the task at hand.

I didn't push him for more, but I couldn't help the curiosity bubbling up inside me. There was so much about him I didn't know—so much he kept just out of reach. But right now, as the scent of food began to fill the air and his movements softened the edges of his usual guarded demeanor, I found myself wanting to know.

And maybe, tonight, I'd finally get some answers—not just for me, but for Luna and Jayce, too.

Felix glanced at the stove, his movements careful as he adjusted the heat on the pan and stirred the contents. The kitchen smelled amazing already, but it was clear he was taking his time. It wasn't surprising; Felix didn't strike me as the type to rush things—not in the kitchen, not with anything.

"This is going to take a little while," he said casually, glancing over his shoulder at me. His voice was calm, steady, like he'd already decided this conversation was going somewhere. "If you want, you can use the bathroom in my room to shower. It's all yours."

I blinked, caught off guard by the suggestion. "Your bathroom?" I asked, leaning against the counter with an eyebrow raised.

Felix smirked faintly, turning back to his work on the stove. "Yes, my bathroom. I promise it's clean," he said, the teasing note in his voice impossible to miss.

"Wow, generous offer," I shot back, crossing my arms as I eyed him.

"You're welcome," he replied smoothly, flipping something in the pan with a practiced ease that made me wonder how he was this effortlessly skilled at so many random things.

"And what am I supposed to wear after?" I asked, narrowing my eyes at him as a smile tugged at my lips.

Felix didn't miss a beat. "You can grab something from my closet," he said simply, setting the spatula down and turning slightly to face me. "There are clean clothes in there—you can pick whatever you want."

I stared at him for a moment, unsure if he was serious. The idea of rooting around in Felix's closet felt weird, but there wasn't any judgment in his tone, and there was no teasing smirk waiting for me to react. He was being oddly matter-of-fact about it, which somehow made it stranger.

"Are you sure?" I asked cautiously, crossing my arms tighter as I leaned against the counter.

Felix let out a soft sigh, raising an eyebrow as he looked at me. "Iris, it's not a trap. Just go shower," he said, his voice light but edged with the faintest hint of impatience. "You'll feel better after. Besides,"—he motioned toward the stove with a smirk—"if you're planning to sit here and stare at me until the food's done, it's going to be a long wait."

I rolled my eyes, though I couldn't stop the small laugh that slipped out. "Fine," I said, pushing off the counter and heading for the door. "But if you poison me with whatever you're cooking, I'll know it was deliberate."

Felix chuckled, turning back to his work. "You'll survive," he said easily, his voice carrying a warmth that followed me out of the kitchen.

As I stepped into Felix's room, the same neatness I'd noticed earlier washed over me again. The bathroom was just off to the side, its door slightly ajar to reveal the pristine space beyond—a large glass shower, polished tile floors, and faint traces of what smelled like cedar and mint lingering in the air.

I grabbed a towel from the neatly stacked shelf and stepped inside, the warmth of the steam beginning to relax the tension I hadn't even realized I was carrying. As the water cascaded over me, I let myself pause for just a moment, letting the events of the last twenty-four hours sink in. Felix, the diary, the truth about my family, tonight with Luna and Jayce—it was all tangled in my mind, weaving together into something impossibly big.

But for now, in the quiet solitude of the shower, I let it all fade.

When I stepped out and wrapped myself in the towel, I wandered over to Felix's closet with a hesitant glance at the neatly organized shelves. His clothes were hung perfectly, his shirts arranged by color and style—because of course, they were—and I couldn't help but wonder what I was even looking for.

Eventually, I settled on a plain black shirt and soft sweatpants that felt surprisingly comfortable. Slipping into them, I glanced at myself in the mirror, the faint blush still lingering in my cheeks. Felix's scent clung faintly to the fabric—clean, subtle, like cedar and something darker, something warmer—and it sent an unexpected flutter through my chest.

Pushing the thought aside, I gathered my damp hair into a loose braid and headed back toward the kitchen, the faint sound of sizzling filling the air as I approached. Felix glanced up as I entered, his smirk returning at the sight of me.

"Feeling better?" he asked casually, setting a plate down on the counter as he motioned for me to sit.

"A little," I admitted, sliding onto the stool and eyeing the food. It looked—and smelled—amazing, which was infuriating because I'd really wanted an excuse to call him out for something.

"Good," Felix said, his smirk widening as he handed me a fork. "Now eat. You're unbearable when you're hungry."

I glared at him, though I couldn't help the smile that tugged at my lips. "You're lucky this smells good," I muttered, digging in.

CHAPTER XV

Truth and Nightmares

The moment I tasted the first bite, I was done for. Felix had made some sort of grilled chicken, paired with perfectly seasoned roasted vegetables, and a side of fluffy rice that melted in my mouth. The flavors were bold but balanced, the kind of dish that made you want to close your eyes and savor every bite. I wasn't sure if he'd grown up with a chef in the house or if centuries of practice had given him an edge, but whatever it was, Felix could cook. And it wasn't fair.

"This is amazing," I said, staring at him in disbelief as I took another bite. "Seriously, how are you this good at everything? Do you moonlight as a five-star chef when you're not unraveling ancient curses?"

Felix smirked from where he sat across the table, his posture relaxed but somehow still carrying that air of effortless composure. "I aim to impress," he said smoothly, though there was a hint of amusement in his tone.

"Well, mission accomplished," I muttered, focusing on my plate again. I wasn't usually the type to gush over food, but this deserved it. "If I didn't know better, I'd say you're trying to distract me from all the chaos we're dealing with."

Felix leaned back slightly, folding his arms across his chest as he watched me. "Is it working?"

"Absolutely," I admitted without hesitation, cutting into another piece of chicken. "Unfortunately for you, I can multitask. Food doesn't stop me from asking questions."

"Somehow, I knew that was coming," Felix replied, his smirk widening just enough to be infuriating.

I set down my fork, my gaze steady as I leaned forward slightly. "Don't you feel uncomfortable?" I asked softly.

Felix's brow furrowed, the smirk slipping away as he tilted his head. "With what?"

"With all of this," I said, motioning vaguely toward the room and the house beyond. "Not just the food—but living here. Being in this house, where everything happened."

He didn't answer right away, his jaw tightening as he stared down at the table. His expression shifted, the faint tension in his shoulders growing more pronounced, and I knew I'd hit on something heavy.

"It's not easy," Felix said finally, his voice quieter now. "There's no shortage of memories here. Some of them are harder to face than others."

His gaze drifted to the window, his blue eyes shadowed by something I couldn't quite place. "But it's familiar," he continued. "And familiarity... it's a strange kind of comfort, even when it's tied to pain."

I studied him for a moment, the weight in his words settling over me. Felix wasn't the type to talk about himself—not really. But the way he said it, the way his voice faltered just slightly, told me there was so much more beneath the surface.

"And the food?" I asked gently, pushing a little further. "Doesn't it bother you that you can't—" I hesitated, suddenly feeling like I was treading on thin ice. "That you can't eat?"

Felix's lips pressed into a thin line, and for a moment, I thought he might brush the question off entirely. But instead, he let out a soft sigh, his gaze dropping to the table. "It doesn't bother me as much as you might think," he said quietly. "Not anymore, at least. I can still cook. I can still smell it. That's enough."

"But it's not the same," I said softly, my chest tightening as I watched him. "Doesn't it feel... lonely?"

Felix's eyes flicked back to mine, and for a moment, I thought he might snap at me. But instead, his gaze softened, the tension in his posture easing just slightly. "Loneliness comes with the territory," he said, his voice steady but tinged with a quiet sadness. "It's been this way for a long time. You learn to adapt."

The words felt heavier than they should have, and I fought the urge to reach across the table, to tell him he didn't have to deal with it alone anymore. But I knew better than to push him further—at least for now.

I cleared my throat, shifting gears as I took another bite of the food. "What about your family?" I asked cautiously. "Do you know what happened to them after... after everything?"

Felix stiffened slightly, the tension returning to his shoulders as he leaned back in his chair. "No," he said simply, his voice edged with something sharper now. "I didn't stay long enough to find out."

"You never tried to—" I started, but Felix cut me off with a shake of his head.

"I couldn't," he said firmly, his gaze darkening. "It wasn't just about the curse—it was about the choices they made. The things they were willing to sacrifice. I couldn't be a part of that anymore."

I swallowed hard, the weight of his words settling over me. Felix's family wasn't just tied to Carrow—they'd been part of its creation, part of the horrors sealed within. And the more I learned, the clearer it became that he wasn't just haunted by the curse—he was haunted by them.

"I'm sorry," I said quietly, my voice barely above a whisper.

Felix's lips twitched into the faintest hint of a smile—small, fleeting, but real. "You don't need to be," he said, his tone softening. "None of this is your fault."

And as we sat there, the remains of lunch between us, I realized just how much Felix carried—and just how far he was willing to go to keep me from carrying any of it myself.

The food had been nothing short of amazing, but it left me feeling strangely heavy—not just in my body, but in my mind too. I sat back in my chair, letting out a satisfied sigh as I rubbed my hands over my face. The weight of the morning, the tension of the past few days, and the sheer emotional rollercoaster of being here with Felix were finally catching up to me.

Felix leaned against the counter, watching me with that unreadable expression of his. "You look exhausted," he said, the faintest hint of teasing in his tone.

"I'm fine," I said automatically, though even I didn't believe it.

He raised an eyebrow, setting his plate in the sink with deliberate precision. "You've been running on fumes since you got here, Iris. You can barely keep your eyes open."

I opened my mouth to argue, but a yawn slipped out instead, completely betraying me. Felix's smirk deepened, and I glared at him halfheartedly. "Alright, fine," I muttered, standing up. "Maybe I'll just rest for a little bit. But only until Luna and Jayce get here."

"Good idea," Felix said, nodding toward the hallway. "The bed in my room is more comfortable than the couch, if you're not opposed."

I hesitated for a moment, but the thought of curling up in that ridiculously neat, comfortable room was too tempting to resist. "You're not just trying to get me out of your way, are you?" I asked, narrowing my eyes.

Felix chuckled softly, shaking his head. "I think we both know I'd win that argument, but no. I'm not."

I rolled my eyes, the corners of my lips tugging into a small smile despite my exhaustion. "Fine. Wake me up if anything happens, okay?"

He nodded, his smirk softening into something closer to a smile. "I will."

The dream started the way it always did—with the forest. The trees loomed high above me, their branches tangled in a dense, shadowed canopy that seemed to press down on everything below. The air was damp, carrying the faint scent of moss and earth, and the faint crunch of leaves beneath my feet was the only sound.

But this time, something felt different. The forest wasn't just quiet—it was *still*, unnaturally so. There was no wind, no rustling of leaves, no distant chirp of birds. It was as though the entire world was holding its breath.

And then, I saw her.

A figure stood at the edge of the clearing, illuminated by a soft, otherworldly glow that made her seem as though she'd stepped out of a dream. Her dark hair cascaded over her shoulders in loose waves, glinting faintly in the strange light. Her skin was smooth and pale, almost luminous, and her sharp, high cheekbones gave her an ethereal beauty that felt both striking and haunting. But it was her eyes that caught me—piercing and impossibly bright, like they held the weight of the world and a thousand secrets.

She was beautiful in a way that didn't feel real, like something out of a story I couldn't fully remember. But there was something else too, something in the way she stood there—still and yet commanding, fragile and yet unyielding—that sent a shiver through me.

"Iris," she said, her voice carrying across the stillness like a whisper and a warning all at once.

I took a hesitant step toward her, my heart pounding in my chest. "Who are you?" I asked, my voice shaky.

She didn't answer right away, her gaze flicking over me as though searching for something. Finally, she spoke again, her tone urgent and deliberate. "Eleanor Hart."

The name hit me like a wave, crashing over me and leaving me breathless. "Eleanor?" I echoed, my voice barely audible. "You're... Eleanor?"

Eleanor Hart. My ancestor, the woman that was sacrificed by her own family and Felix's first love.

She nodded, taking a step closer. The faint glow surrounding her flickered slightly, like a candle caught in an unexpected draft. "You're in danger," she said, her voice trembling.

My stomach dropped, the weight of her words sinking in immediately. "Danger from what?" I asked, stepping closer. "What's happening?"

Eleanor's expression darkened, her brows furrowing as she glanced over her shoulder, as though checking for something—or someone. When she looked back at me, her voice was softer, almost desperate. "It's stirring, Iris. Whatever's been sealed away… it's waking up."

Her words sent a shiver down my spine, the hairs on the back of my neck standing on end. "Carrow," I murmured, my voice barely audible.

Eleanor nodded again, her piercing gaze locking onto mine. "You don't understand," she said, her voice trembling. "It's not just the curse. It's not just the necklace. It's *everything*. They'll come for you, Iris. You need to be ready."

"Who?" I asked, my voice rising with panic. "Who's coming for me?"

Before she could answer, the glow around her faltered completely, and a shadow swept across the clearing, swallowing the light. Eleanor's eyes widened, her face twisting with fear. "Wake up," she said sharply, her voice cutting through the darkness. "Iris, *wake up!*"

I shot up in bed, my chest heaving as I gasped for breath. The room was quiet, the faint afternoon light streaming through the curtains. My heart pounded in my ears, the remnants of the dream still clinging to me like cobwebs.

Eleanor's warning echoed in my mind, her voice urgent and unshakable: *You need to be ready.*

It wasn't just the dream—it was the voice, the warning, the way Eleanor's name had echoed in my mind as though it had been carved there. My hands trembled as I pushed the hair out of my face, my skin damp and clammy. I couldn't shake the image of her—glowing, otherworldly, and yet so unmistakably human. And the fear in her voice…

I didn't hear the door open, but I felt Felix's presence before I saw him. He appeared in the doorway, his silhouette sharp against the soft glow of the hall light. His brow was furrowed, his gaze steady as he took in the state I was in.

"You're awake," he said softly, his voice steady but edged with concern. "Are you alright?"

I shook my head, trying to speak but finding that my words refused to cooperate. Instead, I let out a shaky breath, clutching the edge of the blanket as though it might anchor me. "I... I had a dream," I said finally, my voice barely above a whisper. "It felt... different."

Felix stepped further into the room, his movements careful, deliberate. He didn't press me for more, didn't try to fill the silence with empty words. He simply waited, his presence grounding me in a way I hadn't expected.

"She was there," I continued, my gaze dropping to the blanket as I struggled to make sense of the swirling thoughts in my head. "She told me her name—Eleanor Hart. She warned me about something... something waking up. She said I'm in danger."

Felix stiffened slightly, his jaw tightening as he processed my words. I could see the flicker of something in his eyes— recognition, maybe, or unease—but he didn't let it show. Instead, he nodded faintly, his gaze softening as it settled on me.

"Iris," he said gently, his voice steady and calm. "It was just a dream."

"No," I said quickly, shaking my head. "It wasn't. It was more than that. It felt... real. Like she was really there, trying to talk to me, trying to warn me."

Felix didn't argue, but the tension in his shoulders was impossible to ignore. "Dreams can feel real," he said cautiously. "Especially here, with everything that's been happening."

"But what if it wasn't just a dream?" I asked, my voice trembling. "What if she was trying to help me? What if—" I stopped myself, my chest tightening as the fear began to creep back in.

Felix moved closer, his steps silent on the polished floor, and sat on the edge of the bed beside me. He didn't speak right away, but his presence was steady, unshakable. The warmth of him so close to me made the fear less suffocating, though it didn't vanish entirely.

I looked up at him, my eyes pleading even as my voice faltered. "Can you stay here?" I asked softly. "Just... for a little while. I don't want to go back to sleep alone."

Felix hesitated, his gaze flicking over me as though he was weighing the request carefully. For a moment, I thought he might refuse, might remind me of the boundaries he'd so carefully maintained since we met. But then, slowly, he nodded.

"Alright," he said, his voice softer now. "I'll stay."

Relief flooded through me, but it didn't erase the lingering fear. Felix moved to sit more comfortably, his back resting against the headboard as I lay back down. I pulled the blanket up to my chin, my body curling slightly toward him as the exhaustion began to pull at me again.

"You don't have to worry," Felix said quietly, his voice low and steady. "I'm here."

Something about his words—simple but sincere—made the tension in my chest ease just a little. As my eyelids grew heavy again, I let myself focus on his presence, on the quiet sound of his breathing and the steady rhythm of his heartbeat.

When I opened my eyes, the first thing I noticed was warmth—steady, soothing warmth that radiated from beneath me and wrapped around me like an embrace I didn't knoe I needed. The faint scent of cedar and something darker, something inherently *Felix*, filled my senses, grounding me before I was even fully awake. It took me a moment to realize why everything felt so... different. And then it hit me.

I wasn't lying on the bed anymore. Instead, my head was resting on Felix's chest, his arms loosely cradling me as though it were the most natural thing in the world. His hand moved in slow, rhythmic circles against my back, the motion gentle yet deliberate, as if he was trying to keep me calm even in sleep. My entire body froze, my breath catching in my throat as the weight of the moment sank in.

I tilted my head up, and my gaze collided with his. Felix was already looking down at me, his piercing blue eyes softened by something I couldn't quite place. His expression wasn't guarded like it so often was—it was... open, quietly thoughtful, and just a little conflicted. But his hand didn't stop moving; his touch was steady and reassuring, like he was anchoring me to the present.

"You fell asleep," he said softly, his voice barely above a whisper. "You were restless for a while. I thought this might help."

My cheeks burned with the realization of just how close we were, how I had practically curled into him like a cat seeking comfort. "I—uh—" My voice caught, and I looked away quickly, unable to handle the intensity of his gaze. "I didn't mean to... I mean, you didn't have to—"

"It's fine," Felix interrupted, his tone calm, patient. "You needed it."

The sincerity in his voice made my chest tighten, and despite my flustered state, I couldn't ignore the way his presence made me feel—safe, steady, like I wasn't carrying all of this alone anymore. My heart was racing for an entirely different reason now, and I hated how much I liked it.

"I didn't think you could be this... warm," I admitted softly, my voice trembling as I forced myself to look back at him. "You're always so distant, so guarded. But this... this feels... nice."

The faintest flicker of surprise passed over his face—or uncertainty—but he didn't pull away. If anything, his touch softened, his hand brushing against my back with a tenderness that made my pulse quicken.

"I don't do this often," Felix said after a moment, his voice quieter now, like he was revealing a truth he hadn't meant to share. "Letting people in. It's... complicated."

"I know," I said quickly, my words rushing out before I could stop them. "I know it's complicated, and I know this probably isn't easy for you. But I... I like it. Being with you like this. It makes me feel like I'm not completely losing my mind."

Felix's lips twitched into a faint smile—not his usual smug, teasing smirk, but something softer, something almost vulnerable. "You're not losing your mind," he said gently, his hand stilling for a moment before resuming its slow circles.

"You're just... human. And being human means needing someone else sometimes. Even if it's me."

I laughed softly, the sound barely more than a breath as I let my head rest against him again. "Even if it's you," I murmured, closing my eyes. "Especially if it's you."

Felix's hand moved, his fingers brushing against my hair as his other hand steadied me lightly against his chest. I felt the shift between us—the quiet pull of something unspoken growing stronger, settling into the charged space between our breaths. When I tilted my head to look up at him again, the intensity in his gaze stopped my heart.

Felix's thumb brushed against my cheek, his movements slow and deliberate, as though giving me a chance to pull away. But I didn't. My breathing hitched as he leaned closer, his gaze flicking from my eyes to my lips and back again, the hesitation breaking just enough to close the distance.

My eyes fluttered shut, the anticipation tightening in my chest as his lips hovered so close to mine, the faint brush of his breath sending shivers down my spine. And then—

The phone buzzed, loud and sharp, cutting through the fragile moment like a blade. I jerked back, my pulse still racing, as Felix exhaled slowly, his hand falling to the side. His jaw tightened, and I saw the faint flicker of frustration in his eyes before his guarded expression slipped back into place.

My cheeks burned as I reached for the phone, avoiding Felix's gaze entirely. Luna's name flashed across the screen, and a mix of relief and regret flooded through me as I pressed the answer button.

"Luna," I said quickly, my voice unsteady and far too loud.

"Hey," her voice came through the line, bright and familiar but tinged with curiosity. "Jayce and I are on our way. We should be there in about twenty minutes. You ready?"

I glanced at Felix, whose expression was unreadable now, his blue eyes shadowed by something I couldn't name. "Yeah," I said hurriedly, my voice firmer than I felt. "I'm ready."

"Good," Luna said, a smile in her voice. "Because we have so many questions, Iris. You'd better be ready to start explaining."

I forced a laugh, though my chest felt tight as I ended the call and set the phone down. The fragile intimacy that had filled the room moments before was shattered, replaced by the looming weight of everything I still had to face. But even as I straightened the blanket and tried to collect myself, I couldn't forget the way Felix had looked at me, the way his touch had lingered just a little too long.

"Twenty minutes," I said softly, my voice quieter now as I looked at him. "You ready for this?"

Felix's lips curved into a faint smirk, though the tension in his posture hadn't fully eased. "I'm always ready," he said simply.

But even as he spoke, I couldn't shake the feeling that this—letting my friends meet Felix, and everything it would bring—was just the beginning.

I paced back and forth in the living room, the plush rug muffling the sound of my footsteps as my thoughts spiraled into chaos. How was I supposed to explain everything to Luna and Jayce—everything that had happened yesterday? Well, *not everything*, I thought, cheeks flushing at the memory of the kiss and the almost-kiss with Felix. That little detail was staying locked away in the furthest corner of my mind, thank you very much.

Felix, as usual, looked completely unbothered. He was lounging in the armchair like he owned the place—which, to be fair, he kind of did—his head propped up on one fist while his other hand rested casually on the armrest. One leg was crossed over the other, and his sharp blue eyes followed my every movement, an amused smirk tugging at the corner of his lips.

"Iris," he drawled, finally breaking the tense silence, "if you keep this up, you're going to wear a hole in my floor."

I glared at him, throwing my hands up in frustration. "I'm sorry, okay? I'm just nervous! I don't know how to tell them all of this." My voice rose slightly, a mix of anxiety and exasperation as I resumed pacing.

Felix let out a long, dramatic sigh, his smirk softening as he clasped his hands on his knees and stood up. He moved with that same maddening grace he always did, crossing the room in a few quick strides before stepping directly into my path. His hands settled on my shoulders, stopping me in my tracks.

"Iris," he said firmly, his deep voice cutting through my racing thoughts. He leaned down slightly, meeting my gaze with an intensity that made my breath hitch. His hands rubbed soothing circles against my arms, and the faintest hint of a smile curved his lips. "You know I'm not particularly fond of this idea of yours, but..." He paused, his face inching just a little closer, the warmth of his presence wrapping around me like a shield. "If they're your friends, they'll understand. So don't stress, alright?"

Before I could respond, he leaned in and pressed a soft, fleeting kiss to my forehead. My cheeks flared instantly, the sensation both calming and electrifying all at once. Felix didn't seem fazed—of course, he didn't—but I barely had time to process the moment before a sharp knock echoed through the house.

I jolted back as the sound broke through the tension, and Felix reluctantly let go of my arms, rolling his eyes as if the interruption had personally offended him. I shot him a look, silently asking *what was that*, but he just shrugged, his expression unreadable.

"Don't look at me like that," he said, a hint of amusement in his voice. "You heard the door."

I shook my head, motioning for him to answer it. He sighed—because apparently everything was a chore for him— and started toward the door, his steps slow and deliberate. I followed a few paces behind, my heart still racing for reasons I didn't want to examine too closely.

The door swung open to reveal Luna, standing there with her hands on her hips and an exasperated expression that immediately made my stomach twist. "Iris," she started, her voice sharp with impatience, "you better tell me—" Her words cut off abruptly as Jayce, standing behind her, nudged her arm and tilted his head toward Felix.

Luna's eyes widened as she finally registered the tall, dark-haired figure leaning casually against the doorframe. Felix's smirk was already firmly in place, but there was something sharper about it now, his piercing gaze flickering with recognition as he sized them up.

"Well, hello there," he said smoothly, his voice like velvet as his eyes swept from Luna to Jayce. "You must be Iris's friends."

Luna blinked, clearly caught off guard, while Jayce's brow furrowed slightly as he stepped closer. Felix's smirk deepened, turning darker, and his eyes lingered just a beat too long as he gestured for them to come inside. "Come on in."

I hovered a few feet back, feeling my pulse spike as Felix stepped aside to let them enter. As Luna and Jayce moved past him, Felix shifted, his arm snaking around my waist in one swift, fluid motion. My head snapped toward him, my eyes wide with disbelief as I realized what he'd just done.

I wasn't the only one who noticed. Luna stopped dead in her tracks, her mouth falling open as her gaze darted from Felix's arm around me to my face. Jayce's expression mirrored hers—equal parts shock and confusion—and for a moment, the three of us just stood there, frozen in mutual disbelief.

"Um... guys, this is Felix," I said, my voice higher than usual as I attempted to regain some semblance of control. As soon as the words left my mouth, Felix's grip on my waist tightened ever so slightly, his smirk never wavering.

"Pleasure to meet you," Felix said, his voice calm but carrying an undercurrent of something almost predatory. It wasn't threatening, exactly, but there was a caution in his tone that sent shivers down my spine. "I've heard so much about you."

Luna's eyes narrowed, suspicion flickering across her face as she crossed her arms. "I'll bet you have," she muttered, her tone sharp as a knife.

Jayce, ever the diplomat, stepped forward with a strained but polite smile. "Nice to meet you," he said, though his gaze lingered on Felix's arm around me before flicking back to my face. "So... you've been keeping busy, huh, Iris?"

I laughed nervously, stepping out of Felix's grip and putting a bit of space between us. "Yeah, uh... there's a lot to explain," I said quickly, avoiding their gazes as I motioned toward the living room. "Why don't we sit down?"

Luna raised an eyebrow but followed my lead, her sharp eyes never leaving Felix as she walked past him. Jayce hesitated for half a second before following her, leaving me alone with Felix for just a moment.

"That went well," Felix said quietly, his smirk turning playful as he leaned down slightly, his voice low enough that only I could hear. "Your friends are charming."

I shot him a glare, my cheeks still burning. "Behave," I hissed, turning on my heel to follow Luna and Jayce into the living room.

We all settled into the living room, though the tension in the air was enough to make the space feel suffocating. Jayce and Luna perched on the couch, Jayce's arm casually slung over her shoulders while Luna sat stiffly, her arms crossed and her gaze locked on Felix. Her glare was sharp enough to cut steel—her hostility palpable—and it made my stomach twist.

Felix and I sat in separate armchairs facing them, an intentional choice that somehow still didn't make things feel less awkward. Felix, ever the picture of calm, leaned back slightly in his seat, but I could see the faint glimmer of amusement in his eyes as he clocked Luna's icy demeanor.

"If you wanted us to meet at the mansion," Luna said, her tone sharp and cutting, "you shouldn't have been so cryptic about it." Her eyes stayed glued to Felix the entire time, her gaze brimming with distrust.

I swallowed hard, my nerves bubbling to the surface. Luna was rarely this hostile—especially with strangers. Felix hadn't done anything to warrant this reaction from her, but the way she looked at him... it felt off.

Jayce let out a nervous laugh, shooting me an apologetic glance before turning to Luna. "Babe, don't be like that," he said, nudging her closer to him. "We were both worried about her, but she's fine. More than fine," he added, his lips twitching into a teasing grin as he glanced at me. "By the way—nice clothes." He raised his eyebrows suggestively, clearly enjoying his own joke.

I shot him a death glare, silently warning him to stop before he dug himself into an even deeper hole. Felix, unsurprisingly, let out a low chuckle at my reaction, his smirk widening just enough to be exasperating.

Luna, however, stayed quiet, her sharp gaze never leaving Felix. The silence stretched uncomfortably, and I realized I needed to break it before things got worse.

"I'm sorry I didn't call you guys sooner," I said, my voice softer now, guilt creeping into my tone. I'd been so caught up with Felix—and everything else—that I hadn't thought about how worried they must have been. "But I can explain everything."

Jayce and Luna both turned to me, their expressions expectant but wary. I took a deep breath, trying to steady the racing of my heart as I gathered my thoughts.

"Last night, after I left the library... things got a little hectic," I began, my voice trembling slightly. "There's something I haven't told you guys. But I need you to have an open mind."

Jayce nodded encouragingly, his usual easygoing demeanor softening into something gentler. Luna tilted her head slightly, the suspicion in her eyes giving way to intrigue—but it was clear she was still on edge.

"You know about the nightmares, the voices, and the necklace," I continued, hesitating for just a moment before pushing forward. "But I haven't told you about the... other dreams."

Luna's brow furrowed, concern flashing across her features for the first time since she'd arrived. Both of them knew how bad the nightmares were, how much they had taken a toll on me—and the mention of more dreams clearly set off alarm bells for them.

"They started a few weeks ago," I said, my voice trembling slightly. "Sometimes they'd come before a nightmare, sometimes they'd replace them altogether. In these dreams, I'm always in a forest. And there's always someone with me."

My gaze flicked to Felix instinctively, drawn to him unwillingly. His expression was calm, his features carefully neutral—but I could sense the faint tension beneath the surface. Concern, maybe. Or something darker.

"That's how I met Felix," I finished softly, my voice trailing off.

Jayce's jaw dropped, his mouth hanging open as he stared at me like I'd just grown an extra head. "Wait—what?" he asked, his voice rising slightly. "So you met... in a dream?" He motioned between Felix and me, disbelief written all over his face. "And now you're here. And the man of your dreams happens to be the new guy at the creepy mansion?" He turned to Felix, adding quickly, "No offense."

Felix's jaw tightened subtly, though his expression remained outwardly unbothered. "None taken," he said evenly, his voice flat but deep. He glanced at me, his piercing gaze questioning, as if asking *Seriously?*

I shot him an apologetic smile, silently pleading for him to let it slide.

"You could say that," I said, addressing Jayce's question. "But it's not that simple—"

Before I could finish, Luna—who had been silent up until now—finally spoke, her voice colder than the winter wind. "So you're the immortal," she said, her eyes narrowing as they bore into Felix. "The one cursed by the ruby."

Felix stiffened instantly, the tension in his posture rising like a tidal wave. I could feel the shift in the room, the sharp edge of suspicion cutting through his calm demeanor as he leaned back slightly in his chair. His smirk—the one that had been lingering all morning—slipped away, replaced by a darker, more defensive expression.

"I am," he said smoothly, though there was an undercurrent of caution in his voice. His piercing gaze locked onto Luna, sharper than I'd ever seen it. "But how would you know that?" His tone darkened, his focus unrelenting as he leaned forward. "Is there something you'd like to share, *love*?"

Luna fidgeted, her confidence faltering as she glanced between me and Jayce, clearly caught off guard. "I—I just put two and two together," she said quickly, her voice wavering slightly. Her eyes found mine, pleading for understanding. "We read it yesterday in the diary, remember, Iris?"

I blinked, her words settling in as I tried to make sense of the whirlwind of tension surrounding us. But the way Felix looked at her, the guarded suspicion in his gaze—her hostile behavior. It was overwhelming.

Felix's gaze stayed locked on Luna, his sharp blue eyes unwavering as he leaned forward slightly, the tension in the room thick enough to choke on. The faint smirk tugging at his lips earlier had faded completely, replaced by an expression that was far darker, far more calculating. Even seated, he managed to radiate an air of quiet authority—dangerous and unrelenting.

Luna didn't shrink under his scrutiny, but I could see her confidence beginning to waver. She fidgeted slightly, her fingers tapping a nervous rhythm against her arm as she glanced at Jayce, then back at me. "I told you," she said quickly, her voice trembling just enough to make Felix's brow arch. "I just put two and two together. It wasn't... it wasn't that hard."

Felix leaned back into his chair, crossing his arms as he regarded her with a mixture of suspicion and curiosity. "Hmm," he murmured, the sound low and smooth, carrying just enough weight to make Luna squirm. "And what else did you put together, love?" His words dripped with something that wasn't quite malice, but it wasn't kind either.

"Felix," I said softly, my voice barely audible over the tension. "Don't."

He didn't look at me, but the slightest twitch of his jaw told me he'd heard. The faint edge in his expression softened—just slightly—but the intensity in his gaze didn't falter.

Jayce, sensing the precariousness of the situation, let out a small, strained laugh. "Alright, everyone, let's take a breather," he said, gesturing vaguely between Felix and Luna. "No need for the standoff. We're all on the same team, right?"

Felix's lips twitched into a small, humorless smile as he glanced at Jayce. "That remains to be seen."

Jayce blinked, clearly unprepared for Felix's cutting response, but before he could say anything more, I stepped in, my heart pounding as I tried to ease the tension. "Stop, both of you," I said firmly, my gaze flicking between Felix and Luna. "This isn't helping. We don't have time for... whatever this is." I gestured between them, frustration bubbling in my chest. "We need to focus."

Felix exhaled through his nose, the sound heavy but controlled, as he leaned back in his chair. Luna stayed tense, her gaze darting to me briefly before settling back on Felix, but the sharpness in her features dulled slightly. It wasn't much, but it was enough.

"Fine," Felix said finally, his voice low and steady. "But don't think I didn't notice your slip."

"Slip?" Luna repeated, her eyes narrowing defensively.

Felix's smirk returned, colder now, as he tilted his head. "The ruby."

I stiffened, my stomach dropping as Luna froze, her face turning pale for a brief moment before she swallowed hard and tried to recover. "It was in the diary," she said quickly, her words coming out in a rush. "We read that part yesterday, with Iris."

"We did," I said slowly, though Luna's reaction left me uneasy. There was something she wasn't saying—something she was trying to bury under the pretense of nonchalance. Felix knew it too, and the way he looked at her, like he was picking her apart piece by piece, made my skin crawl.

But whatever Luna was hiding, it wasn't something we could unpack right now—not when we had bigger issues to deal with.

"Enough," I said firmly, forcing my voice to sound steadier than I felt. "We don't have time for this. We need answers, and the only place we're going to get them is the diary—or the mansion itself."

Jayce nodded quickly, his expression relieved to have a plan to latch onto. "Right, research. That's what we're here for." He glanced between me and Felix, his gaze lingering on the tension that still hung in the air. "Let's figure out what's going on before we lose track of the point."

Felix stood, his movements smooth and deliberate, as he glanced at me with a look that was just shy of approval. "I'll fetch the diary," he said simply, his voice calm but carrying the faintest edge of authority.

Luna let out a quiet huff, clearly still irritated, but she didn't argue as Felix strode out of the room. Jayce shifted beside her, leaning in slightly as he murmured something I couldn't catch. Luna rolled her eyes but softened just enough to make me think she might settle down—at least for now.

I sank back into my chair, the weight of everything pressing down on me as I rubbed my hands over my face. Felix wasn't wrong to question Luna, but the way he did it—so sharp, so merciless—made it clear just how deeply the suspicions ran on both sides. And Luna's reaction... whatever that was about, I'd have to deal with it sooner or later.

For now, though, the focus had to be on the diary—and what secrets it held about Carrow, Felix, and the curse.

CHAPTER XVI

The Curse Binds Us

Felix returned to the living room, the diary tucked under his arm as he stepped inside with his usual air of quiet authority. His expression was calm, almost unreadable, but there was a subtle tension in the way his shoulders were set—the kind of tension that made me wonder just how much he'd pieced together from Luna's earlier reaction.

He handed the diary to me without a word, his piercing gaze briefly flicking to Jayce and Luna before settling back on me. I took it carefully, my fingers brushing against the worn leather cover as a wave of uncertainty washed over me. This was it—the moment I had to tell them everything. And I wasn't entirely sure how to start.

I glanced at Jayce and Luna, both of them watching me intently. Jayce had leaned forward slightly, his arms resting on his knees, while Luna sat stiffly, her posture tense as she crossed her arms. Felix, meanwhile, moved to his chair and sank into it, his focus shifting entirely to me as if silently urging me to speak.

"Okay," I said finally, my voice trembling slightly as I flipped the diary open. "There's... a lot we need to talk about."

Jayce raised an eyebrow, his expression expectant but still tinged with uncertainty. Luna's gaze flicked to Felix, then back to me, the suspicion in her eyes softened just enough to make me think she might listen.

I exhaled slowly, grounding myself as I began to explain. "Felix and I found something in the diary last night. Something about my family—and about the necklace."

Jayce straightened slightly, his brows furrowing in confusion. "Your family?" he repeated, his tone cautious. "What does your family have to do with the necklace?"

"It's tied to them," I said, my voice steadier now as I flipped to one of the marked pages. "It's tied to the Hart family—and to the curse."

Luna's expression shifted, intrigue flickering across her face as she uncrossed her arms. Jayce leaned back slightly, his lips pressing into a thin line as he processed my words.

"My ancestors were involved in the creation of the curse," I continued, my stomach twisting as the truth finally settled on my shoulders. "They were connected to Carrow—to everything that's sealed away. They... they weren't just victims of the curse. They were part of it."

Jayce blinked, his mouth falling open slightly in shock. "Wait, what?" he asked, his voice rising. "Are you saying your family was responsible for the curse?"

"Not exactly," I said quickly, shaking my head. "But they were part of what created it. The necklace—it was designed to tie the curse to their bloodline, to keep Carrow sealed. And that connection... it's passed down through generations. That's why it's tied to me."

Luna let out a sharp breath, her posture tensing again as she turned her attention fully to Felix. "And him?" she asked, her tone cold. "Where does he fit into all of this?"

Felix's jaw tightened, his expression darkening slightly, but he didn't respond. Instead, he glanced at me, silently asking me to handle this part.

I hesitated, glancing down at the diary before looking back at Luna and Jayce. "Felix is tied to the curse, too," I said softly, my voice heavy. "He's been cursed for centuries—trapped by the same magic that created the necklace. And because the necklace is tied to my family, it's tied to him too."

Jayce let out a low whistle, his expression a mixture of awe and disbelief. "So... you're connected. Through the curse."

"Yes," Felix said finally, his voice deep and steady. He leaned forward slightly, his sharp gaze locking onto Jayce and Luna. "The curse binds us. It's why Iris is here now—and why we're both tied to Carrow."

Luna stared at him, her lips pressing into a thin line as she considered his words. She looked like she wanted to say something—like she wanted to challenge him—but instead, she turned her attention back to me. "And the diary?" she asked, her voice softer now but still cautious. "What else does it say?"

I glanced at Felix, his expression unreadable, before flipping to another marked page. "It's fragmented," I said, running my fingers over the faded text. "But it mentions the curse and the necklace—how it was created, how it ties to the Harts. And it talks about Eleanor. She was part of it too."

I carefully avoided mentioning one glaring detail—the tangled history between Felix's family and mine. The fact that our families were connected in ways that made this entire situation feel even more impossible. I didn't tell them about how Felix had almost married Eleanor before it all went horribly wrong. I left out how they were both betrayed and slaughtered by the same family that cursed us, chaining our lives to this shadowed legacy.

That wasn't my story to share—not entirely. If Felix wanted to bring it up, to lay out the full weight of what had happened, that was his choice to make. And judging by the tension simmering beneath his calm facade, I wasn't about to push him to do it now.

Luna frowned, intrigue flickering across her face as she tilted her head slightly. "Eleanor?"

"Eleanor Hart," Felix said, his voice calm but carrying the faintest edge. "She was involved in the events that led to the curse—and she's tied to the necklace."

Jayce shifted, his brows furrowing as he glanced between me and Felix. "And what does this have to do with the mansion?"

Felix exhaled slowly, his piercing gaze steady. "Everything. The mansion is part of Carrow's history—it's where the curse began. If we want answers, we'll find them here."

Luna let out another sharp breath, her eyes narrowing slightly. "And you trust him to help you figure this out?" she asked, her gaze flicking to me.

"Yes," I said firmly, meeting her gaze head-on. "I do."

She didn't respond, but the faint softening in her expression told me she wasn't entirely opposed to the idea—at least for now.

Jayce nodded, his lips curving into a small, strained smile. "Alright. Let's figure this out. The sooner, the better."

Felix leaned back slightly, his smirk returning as he glanced at me. "Looks like we're all in agreement."

But even as the group settled into the plan, I couldn't shake the feeling that the secrets tied to Carrow—and to us—ran far deeper than any of us could imagine.

We all eventually agreed to get to work, the tension in the room settling into a fragile truce. Luna and Jayce moved to the table in the living room, her laptop open and glowing faintly as she typed furiously, pulling up whatever she could about the Hart family and the mansion. Jayce leaned over her shoulder, offering input here and there, though his focus drifted between Luna and the room at large, like he was keeping a wary eye on things.

Felix and I, meanwhile, took the couch. I had the diary open in my lap, its worn pages faintly scented with old paper and ink. Felix sat beside me, his shoulder brushing mine as he leaned over to scan the text. He was quiet, his expression calm and composed, but I could feel the intensity radiating off him—the weight of his focus as he traced the fragmented words alongside me.

As the minutes passed, my mind began to drift. The words in the diary blurred slightly, replaced by flashes of memory. I couldn't stop thinking about those dreams—about the forest, the way Felix always seemed to find me there, no matter how lost I felt. It had always been so vivid, so real, and now, with him sitting beside me, the line between dreams and reality felt thinner than ever.

I turned to him, curiosity bubbling to the surface. "Felix," I said softly, my voice breaking the silence between us.

He glanced at me, his blue eyes sharp but patient. "Yes?"

I hesitated for a moment, unsure how to phrase the question swirling in my mind. "If you don't sleep," I began, my voice cautious, "how could we meet in the dreams? How is that even possible?"

Felix's expression shifted, his calm facade cracking just slightly as something flickered in his gaze—surprise, maybe, or something deeper. He leaned back slightly, his arms resting casually on the back of the couch as he regarded me thoughtfully.

"The dreams," he said slowly, his voice low and measured, "aren't exactly dreams. At least, not for me."

I frowned, my curiosity deepening. "What do you mean?"

He exhaled quietly, his gaze drifting to the diary for a moment before returning to me. "The connection between us— the curse—it bridges the gap between waking and... whatever state I exist in." He paused, his expression softening slightly. "When you dream, you open a door. And I... I step through."

I stared at him, the weight of his words settling over me like a heavy blanket. "So, you were never really dreaming?" I asked, my voice barely above a whisper.

"No," he admitted, his tone soft but firm. "But it felt real enough, didn't it?"

I nodded slowly, the pieces falling into place in my mind. The forest, the way he always seemed to know exactly what I was thinking, what I needed—it all made sense now, in a way that only added to the strange, impossible connection between us.

Before I could say anything more, I caught a movement out of the corner of my eye. I turned, my gaze landing on Luna, who was staring at Felix with an intensity that bordered on hostile. Her jaw was tight, her fingers curled into her palm as she sat stiffly beside Jayce, who seemed oblivious to her growing tension.

I exhaled quietly, glancing at Felix, who had clearly noticed but chose not to react. "I'll be right back," I said softly, standing up and giving him a small smile that I hoped was reassuring.

Felix nodded, his expression calm but knowing, and I made my way to Luna. "Hey," I said, my voice low enough that Jayce wouldn't hear. "Can I talk to you for a minute? In the kitchen?"

Luna's eyes darted to mine, a flicker of surprise crossing her face before she nodded reluctantly. She stood, following me into the kitchen, where the tension felt less suffocating but no less present.

"What's going on with you?" I asked once we were alone, my voice firm but gentle. "What's your problem with him?"

Luna crossed her arms, her posture defensive as she leaned against the counter. "I don't know," she admitted, her voice quieter than I expected. "There's just... something about him. I can't put my finger on it, but I don't think I can trust him."

I frowned, her words sending a pang of frustration through me. "Luna, he's been nothing but helpful," I said, my tone softening as I tried to make her understand. "He's helped me figure so much out already—about the necklace, the curse, everything. And he's connected to all of this the same way I am. If I trust him, you can too."

Luna hesitated, her gaze dropping to the floor as she shifted uncomfortably. "I'm just worried about you," she said finally, her voice quieter now. "This is all... a lot. And he's a part of it—this chaos you're caught up in."

"I know," I said gently, stepping closer and placing a hand on her arm. "But he's part of it for me, too. I'm not saying it's easy, but I trust him, Luna. And I need you to trust me."

Luna looked at me, her eyes searching mine for a long moment before she exhaled, the tension in her posture easing. "I'm sorry," she said softly, her tone filled with sincerity. "I didn't mean to make things harder for you. I just... I'll trust you. And your judgment."

"Thank you," I said, relief washing over me as I pulled her into a hug. She stiffened slightly at first but relaxed quickly, her arms wrapping around me in return.

"We'll figure this out," she said quietly, her voice steadier now. "Together."

"Together," I echoed, a small smile tugging at my lips.

As we pulled apart and made our way back to the living room, I couldn't help but feel a flicker of hope. Despite the tension, the doubts, and the impossible weight of everything we were facing, we were still standing. Still fighting. And for now, that was exactly what I needed.

The room was quiet except for the faint sound of Luna's typing, the occasional rustle of paper as Felix flipped through the diary, and Jayce muttering under his breath as he scanned a webpage. We had settled into the rhythm of researching, everyone focused on finding something—anything—that could bring us closer to answers.

"Wait," Jayce said suddenly, his voice cutting through the silence. He leaned closer to Luna's laptop, squinting at the screen as his fingers traced something on the page. "I think I found something."

Luna tilted her head, her curiosity showing, as she shifted the laptop slightly so she could read over his shoulder. "What is it?" she asked, her tone sharp but intrigued.

Jayce rubbed his chin thoughtfully, his brow furrowing. "It's... some kind of reference. It doesn't mention Carrow by name, but it sounds similar. It talks about a prison—a place meant to hold beings so powerful they could destroy the world if they got out. It says there's a key, something meant to keep the prison sealed."

Felix and I both glanced up, the diary momentarily forgotten as we shifted our attention to Jayce. "A key," I repeated, my voice steady but cautious. "What does it say about the key?"

Jayce exhaled, his frustration evident as his fingers tapped against the table. "Not much. It says if the key is used incorrectly, the prison... I don't know. It doesn't completely open, but it doesn't stay sealed either. It ends up in some kind of limbo—not closed, not open."

Felix's jaw tightened, his expression darkening slightly as he processed the information. "Limbo," he murmured, his voice low. "That would make it far worse. The beings inside wouldn't be fully contained, but they wouldn't be entirely free either. It would destabilize everything."

Luna nodded, her gaze flicking between Jayce and Felix as she leaned back in her chair. "So basically, it would make things even more dangerous," she said bluntly. "Great. Just what we need."

I frowned, the weight of their words pressing down on me. "The necklace," I said softly, my voice carrying just enough conviction to draw their attention. "We know it's the key. But we don't know how it works—or what could happen if we use it wrong."

Luna sighed, her frustration bubbling to the surface. "We need more information," she said, shaking her head. "Half-truths and fragmented explanations aren't going to cut it. If this key really is tied to Carrow, we need to know exactly how it works."

"Agreed," Felix said, his tone calm but edged with determination. "But we're not going to find it online. If this prison is tied to Carrow and the curse, the answers will be in the diary—or the mansion."

I nodded, flipping back to the diary in my lap. Felix leaned closer, his gaze sharpening as we scanned the pages together, both of us searching for anything that could explain the connection—the key, the curse, or something deeper.

And then, I saw it.

"Felix," I said quietly, my voice trembling as my finger traced the edge of a passage hidden between faded lines of text. "Look at this."

He leaned in, his sharp blue eyes narrowing as he read the delicate handwriting alongside me. It was written in the same script as before—Eleanor's script—but the words were faint, almost like they had been deliberately obscured. "Breaking the curse," he murmured, his voice barely above a whisper.

Luna and Jayce turned to us, their expressions shifting as curiosity replaced the tension lingering in the room. "What does it say?" Luna asked, her voice softer now, less guarded.

"It's incomplete," Felix said, his tone heavy with frustration. "But it mentions breaking the curse. Eleanor wrote it—she must have been trying to figure it out before she..." He stopped, his jaw tightening as his gaze darkened.

I frowned, my fingers brushing against the text as I searched for more clarity. "Do you think she knew how?" I asked softly, glancing at Felix.

Felix's gaze froze, and his hand hovered over the page for a moment before tracing the date scrawled at the bottom of the entry. "September 14th, 1693," he said quietly, his voice heavy with something unspoken. "The day of the wedding, and my birthday."

I blinked, confusion flashing across my face as I tried to piece together his words. "The wedding?" I repeated, my voice hesitant.

Felix nodded, his expression tightening as he leaned back slightly, his gaze dropping to the diary. "It's the day Eleanor and I died."

The weight of his admission settled over the room like a storm cloud, thick and suffocating. Luna and Jayce exchanged a glance, their expressions softening but confusion arising in their faces. They didn't know about the wedding, but that didn't stop Jayce from giving some reassurance. "She must have been trying to stop it," Jayce said gently, his voice steadier now. "To stop the curse before... before everything happened."

Felix nodded faintly, his gaze dropping to the diary as he exhaled slowly. "She was close," he said quietly, his voice steady but tinged with quiet sorrow. "But not close enough."

I placed a hand on his arm, the tension in my chest tightening as I met his gaze. "We'll figure it out," I said softly, my voice filled with determination.

Felix's lips twitched into the faintest hint of a smile—small and fleeting.

As we settled back into our research, the weight of Eleanor's unfinished work hung over us like a shadow. The answers were close, but the question remained—were we ready for what came next?

Luna leaned back in her chair, letting out a sigh as she ran a hand through her hair. "Well," she said finally, her voice softer but still edged with determination. "If Eleanor started this, then maybe we can finish it. But we're going to need more than what's here."

"The mansion holds its own secrets," Felix said, his smirk returning just enough to give the moment some levity. "If there's anything left behind—anything Eleanor missed—we'll find it."

"And if we don't?" Luna asked, her voice tight with the faintest trace of doubt.

Felix's gaze flicked to her, his smirk fading into something sharper. "We will," he said simply. "Why do you think I moved back?"

The room felt heavy, the air thick with the weight of unspoken questions and the tension of everything we'd uncovered. The four of us exchanged a look, each of us carrying the burden of realization in our own way. Whatever waited for us in the mansion, whatever truths and dangers it held, we knew one thing for certain:

We weren't done yet.

CHAPTER XVII

Crust and Conundrums

As the night dragged on, hunger finally caught up to us. Our brains were tired from hours of scanning through endless pages and screens, and the tempting idea of ordering pizza floated into the conversation. Felix, of course, was less than thrilled.

"Really?" he said, his tone dripping with exasperation. "You could have at least let me cook something."

"Come on, man," Jayce replied, brushing him off with a wave of his hand as he scrolled through his phone. "You're not the only one with taste buds, and we're starving."

Luna chimed in, barely looking up from her laptop. "It's pizza, not poison. We'll survive." Her casual dismissal only deepened Felix's scowl, and his annoyance was so palpable I thought he might start pacing.

I couldn't help but notice the quiet laugh that bubbled up at his reaction, the way his jaw tightened and his shoulders squared like he was about to wage war against a cardboard box. It was... oddly endearing. Felix rarely let his irritation show, but when he did, it was almost adorable.

The pizza arrived in less than twenty minutes, and we all gathered in the dimly lit living room, the warmth of the boxes cutting through the eerie chill of the mansion. Jayce and Luna grabbed slices with a kind of desperation that came from pure exhaustion, while I savored mine slowly, deliberately. Felix, predictably, abstained, his sharp blue eyes flicking between us like he was silently judging every bite.

Jayce, chewing through his second slice, tilted his head toward Felix. "So, what's the deal?" he asked, his tone casual but curious. "Why don't you eat? Is it the curse?"

Felix's lips twitched into a faint smirk, though there was no humor in it. His gaze shifted to Jayce, steady and unyielding. "Yes," he said simply, his voice deep and calm. "Anything I try to eat turns to ash the moment it touches my mouth."

Jayce froze, his slice hovering halfway to his mouth as he processed Felix's words. "Ash?" he echoed, his brow furrowing. "That's... unsettling."

Felix shrugged, leaning back in his chair. "It is what it is," he said smoothly, though the faint tension in his jaw told me the subject wasn't as simple for him as he let on.

"Guess you won't be joining us for pizza then," Jayce muttered awkwardly, setting his slice back down and shooting me a quick glance as if to gauge my reaction.

I bit back another laugh, shaking my head slightly. "No, he won't," I said, offering Felix a small smile despite the heaviness of the topic. "But it hasn't stopped him from glaring at us like we're committing a crime."

Felix let out a low chuckle, his smirk softening just enough to lighten the mood. "Pizza isn't a crime," he said, his voice carrying just a hint of amusement. "But you lot have questionable priorities."

The fatigue hit us hard as we ate, visible in the slump of our shoulders and the slower rhythm of our conversations. The research had reached a dead end for now, the clues fragmented and elusive. It was clear we weren't going to uncover anything else tonight, and calling it a day was our only option.

"I think we'd better get going," Jayce said, tossing the crust of his last slice into the box. He glanced at Luna, who was nearly asleep where she sat, her head resting against her hand.

"That sounds like heaven," Luna muttered, her voice heavy with exhaustion. She stood slowly and made her way to me, pulling me into an unexpectedly tight hug. Her arms wrapped around me like she was reluctant to let go, and for a moment, I just stood there, soaking in the quiet comfort of her presence.

She squeezed me tightly before pulling back, her gaze steady and serious. "Call me," she said firmly, her eyes holding mine as though she wanted me to promise. Then she turned to address the group, her voice softening slightly. "We'll regroup soon."

Jayce was next, his usual energy dulled by the weight of the day, but he still managed a grin as he came over to give me a side hug. He glanced between Felix and me, his smile turning mischievous, and I could practically see the teasing comment forming in his mind.

I rolled my eyes, giving him a light shove toward the door. "Stop with the looks. Just go."

Jayce laughed, sending me a playful wink before grabbing his coat. "Alright, alright. See you soon, Iris."

Luna offered a small wave as they stepped into the doorway, their figures silhouetted against the night outside. The mansion seemed quieter after they left, the absence of their voices making the space feel even larger, even emptier.

I stood there for a moment, watching their silhouettes disappear down the driveway before closing the heavy door behind them. The quiet settled over me like a weight, and as I turned back to Felix, who remained seated on the couch, I realized just how much tonight had taken out of all of us—except him.

I threw myself onto the couch, letting out a heavy sigh as my head leaned back, resting against the plush cushions. Exhaustion tugged at my every muscle, the weight of the day settling into my chest. Felix stood a few feet away, his hands buried in the pockets of his dark slacks. He was watching me, as usual, his sharp blue eyes steady and unreadable.

"I thought they'd never leave," he said, his tone casual, almost detached, but there was a faint edge of amusement beneath it. I tilted my head up to look at him, catching the signature smirk already tugging at the corners of his mouth.

I rolled my eyes, resisting the urge to throw one of the decorative pillows at him. "You'd like them if you gave them a chance," I said, though I couldn't keep the exasperation out of my voice. Felix could be impossible sometimes—charming, infuriating, and impossibly closed-off all at once.

He crossed the room with fluid, effortless grace, settling onto the opposite end of the couch. His posture was relaxed, one arm resting casually on the back of the seat as he faced me. "I don't think Luna likes me very much," he said, his smirk softening but not disappearing entirely.

I shifted, pulling my legs up to sit cross-legged as I faced him. "I don't know why she acted like that," I admitted, tilting my head slightly. "She's normally so sweet." Confusion crept into my voice, the memory of Luna's sharp demeanor replaying in my mind.

Felix's gaze flicked toward the fireplace, the flames casting flickering shadows across his face. "I think she's hiding something," he said, his tone calm but edged with quiet suspicion. "But she's not ready to share it."

There was something in his eyes—an intensity that told me his thoughts ran deeper than he was letting on. But whatever he suspected, he wasn't ready to lay it all out yet, and I wasn't about to push him.

My thoughts drifted back to the day's discoveries, the weight of everything we'd uncovered settling over me like a storm cloud. The diary, the necklace, the secrets tied to my family—it was all too much. And then there was my mom, her strange reaction to the necklace looming in the back of my mind like an unanswered question.

"I should talk to my mom," I murmured, the words escaping before I could stop them. Felix turned his head sharply, his brows furrowing as he studied me.

"What are you thinking?" he asked, his tone calm but curious, like he was trying to unravel my thoughts piece by piece.

I pushed myself up from the couch, shaking my head as I tried to collect myself. "I think I should get going," I said, brushing my hands against my jeans as I started toward the door.

I barely made it two steps before I felt the firm grip of Felix's hand on my arm. His touch stopped me in my tracks, and I turned to face him, my heart racing as his piercing gaze locked onto mine. The feeling in his eyes was indescribable—soft, almost sad, but layered with something deeper that made my stomach flip and heat rise to my cheeks.

"Leaving so soon?" he asked, his voice low and playful, but his smirk didn't reach his eyes. His hands slid to my waist, pulling me closer until our bodies were only inches apart.

"As much as I'd like to stay," I said, my voice wavering slightly as his presence overwhelmed me, "I believe I'd be taking advantage of your hospitality." A small smile tugged at my lips as I rested my hands on his chest, my fingers brushing against the fabric of his shirt. My eyes traced the lines of his face, the features I'd become far too attached to—the sharpness of his jaw, the way his lips curled ever so slightly, the impossible depth in his eyes.

Felix's gaze traveled over my face, his hesitation visible in the way his lips pressed together, the way his fingers flexed lightly against my waist. He bit his bottom lip, just barely, as if fighting the words sitting on the edge of his tongue. His eyes flicked between mine, taking in every detail as though committing them to memory.

I broke the tension, forcing a laugh to escape my lips. "Besides, I can't escape my job forever," I said, my tone lighter. "And I need to go to my apartment for fresh clothes."

Felix's hands loosened reluctantly, sliding away from my waist as he took a small step back. I hated how empty the space between us felt, how cold the air seemed without him close to me.

"I could go with you," he said suddenly, his voice steady but serious.

"To my job?" I let out a laugh, shaking my head. "Well, it's not like you've never been."

"To talk to your mom," he clarified, his tone serious now, his expression searching for any reaction from me.

I froze, his words striking me with the force of a tidal wave. My thoughts raced, panic fluttering in my chest as I tried to imagine how I could ever explain Felix to her—who he was, why he was here with me, why our lives were tangled in ways I couldn't untangle.

"Felix," I started, but the words stuck in my throat, uncertainty gnawing at the edges of my resolve. How could I possibly make sense of this? How could I explain the inexplicable?

I froze, my body rooted to the spot as Felix's words hung between us. His eyes, a tumult of unspoken emotions, searched mine. I could feel the vulnerability radiating from him, a quiet plea painted in the soft sadness behind his cool facade. My heart pounded as I struggled for words.

For a long, suspended moment, neither of us spoke. The only sound was the slow, steady beat of my heart echoing the uncertainty in my mind. Finally, I whispered, "Felix, what do you mean? How do you expect me to explain... you—us—to my mom?"

He shifted slightly, his hands still in his pockets, and took a step closer until we stood nearly side by side. "I'm not saying you have to justify my presence," he said, his voice low and earnest, "but if there's any part of this life you want to continue embracing—the secrets, the curses, the chaos—I want to help you carry it, even if that means being with you when you talk to your mom."

I looked down, my thoughts a tangle of fear and longing. What would it mean for her to see him there with me? The idea sent my stomach into knots. And yet, there was something undeniably magnetic about him—an unspoken promise that he understood the darkness as well as the light in my life.

"I'm terrified," I confessed, my voice barely a whisper. "I don't know how I'll ever explain who you are, why you're here. How can I tell her that you're not just a part of some curse, but—"

"Please, Iris," Felix interrupted gently, stepping even closer so that our shoulders brushed. "I know the truth is messy. My past intertwines with yours in ways that defy explanation. But I'm here because I care. And I want to be there for you—even in the worst moments."

His words, heavy with sincerity, made my heart ache. I searched his eyes, finding there a well of regret, a longing for redemption, and something tender that made me want to lean in. Yet the practical part of my mind insisted this conversation was far too complicated to resolve here and now.

I exhaled shakily, "Felix, I—I need to do this on my own. I'm scared of dragging you into something that might shatter everything. My mother... she won't understand."

He tilted his head, his gaze softening. "Understanding isn't something you can force, Iris. But I believe in being honest about who we are. I won't stand in the way if you need space, but I also won't let you face the storm alone." His voice, though quiet, carried an assurance that sent warmth spiraling through me.

I hesitated, torn between the pull of his presence and the responsibilities I feared. The silence stretched as I cradled the tumultuous hope and fear in my chest. "I want to believe that," I murmured, "but it scares me how complicated everything is."

Felix reached out, gently lifting my chin so that our eyes met. "Sometimes the most complicated truths are the ones that matter most. I'm not asking you to explain me to your mom right now, but just... consider that I'm here, not to complicate your world, but to help you understand it." His touch was soft, his gaze pleading for trust without demanding it.

I felt a shiver run through me—a mix of trepidation and something resembling comfort. For a long moment, I simply looked at him, letting the truth in his eyes and the quiet intensity of his voice unravel the knots of uncertainty within me.

Finally, I whispered, "Maybe you're right. I can't keep running from this... from us." My voice, though small, was laced with a promise, fragile and tentative.

Felix's lips curved into the faintest of smiles—a smile that carried both hope and sorrow. "I'll be here, whenever you're ready," he said, his tone soft but unyielding.

In that quiet space between fear and trust, our shared vulnerability lingered, binding us closer in the unspoken understanding that we were both adrift in a world full of secrets. And even though the path ahead was shrouded in uncertainty, for now, we clung to each other, silently promising that we wouldn't let the darkness swallow us whole.

My mind was a jumble of secrets and uncertainties, and I knew I needed to clear my head. "I'll be heading home now," I said softly, my voice wavering with the weight of it all.

Felix's eyes, still filled with that unspoken tenderness, flickered with concern as he stepped forward. "Let me drive you," he offered, his tone warm yet insistent.

I shook my head, a slight smile tugging at my lips despite the storm inside me. "I'd rather walk tonight," I replied. "I need the time to think, to process everything."

He paused for a moment, studying my face as if trying to decide whether to press further or respect my space. Finally, his expression softened further. "If you need anything—anything at all—call me," he said quietly.

I hesitated, glancing at him with a mix of amusement and exasperation. "I don't even have your number," I teased, though beneath the banter lay real uncertainty.

Felix chuckled softly and fished my phone from my pocket. With a playful glint in his eyes, he tapped out a few quick numbers before handing the device to me. "There. Now you have my number," he said, his voice light but with a gentle seriousness beneath it. Then, leaning in as if sharing a secret, he added with a teasing smile, "And if anything happens, we can always meet in your dreams."

His remark, as enigmatic as ever, sent a flutter through me—a reminder that no matter how tangled our lives became, there was always this strange, undeniable connection that defied logic. I took his number, the closeness of the moment lingering like a promise, even as I stepped back into the solitude of the night.

The walk home was quiet, the kind of quiet that made every footstep feel louder than it should. The cold night air scraped against my skin, sharp and biting, but I barely noticed. My head was spinning—thoughts crashing into each other, looping back to every moment, every clue. I was scared. Scared of what would happen when the truth finally came out and refused to be ignored.

But fear wasn't going to stop me. Not now. Whatever came next, I was ready to face it. I had to. And if there was one thing I knew for sure, it was this: Felix was right. He was with me. And somehow, that made everything feel just a little less impossible.

When I finally stepped into my apartment, the clock had already ticked past midnight. Exhaustion clung to me like a second skin, weighing down every step as I closed the door behind me and leaned against it for a moment. The quiet of the space felt almost deafening after the intensity of the mansion, but it was a relief, nonetheless.

I shuffled toward my bedroom, my feet dragging slightly against the floor. The bathroom light flickered on with a soft hum, and I caught my reflection in the mirror. I looked like a complete mess—my hair disheveled, dark circles under my eyes, and a faint smudge of dirt on my cheek that I hadn't even noticed until now. But what stood out the most was the oversized shirt and sweatpants I was still wearing—Felix's clothes.

They hung loosely on me, the fabric soft and worn in a way that felt oddly comforting. His scent lingered faintly on them, a mix of cedar and something darker, something uniquely him. It wrapped around me like a ghost of his presence, and for a moment, I just stood there, staring at myself in the mirror, unsure of how to feel.

With a sigh, I peeled off the borrowed clothes and folded them neatly, placing them on the edge of my bed. "I'll wash them tomorrow," I murmured to myself, though the thought of returning them stirred something bittersweet in my chest. Shaking off the feeling, I slipped into my pajamas and crawled into bed, the weight of the day pulling me under almost immediately.

The dream came quickly, pulling me into its grasp before I even realized I'd fallen asleep. My grandmother's house loomed before me, shrouded in a thick, suffocating fog that seemed heavier than ever. The air was cold, biting against my skin, and a shiver ran down my spine as I took a hesitant step forward.

"Not again," I whispered, my voice barely audible over the oppressive silence. Fear coiled in my chest, tightening with every step I took toward the front porch. The door was wide open this time, its dark interior beckoning me like a predator luring its prey. They were waiting—I could feel it—and yet, I couldn't stop myself from walking straight into their trap.

As I crossed the threshold, the air shifted, growing heavier and colder with each passing second. The door slammed shut behind me with a deafening bang, and I jolted, my heart leaping into my throat. My breath came in shallow gasps as the darkness pressed in around me, suffocating and unrelenting.

And then, I felt it.

A presence so dark, so malevolent, that the hairs on the back of my neck stood on end. My palms grew slick with sweat as the oppressive energy closed in, and my knees buckled beneath me, sending me crashing to the ground. A shadowy figure emerged from the darkness, its form shifting and writhing like smoke given life. It loomed over me, its sheer force pushing me back as I scrambled to put distance between us.

"This is your last warning", it hissed, its voice ancient and otherworldly, echoing through the empty space like a thousand whispers layered on top of one another. The figure circled me, its movements slow and deliberate, as though savoring my fear. *"Leave it alone. Stop probing."*

My chest tightened, fear clawing at my throat, but something inside me refused to back down. "Then just leave me alone!" I shouted, my voice trembling but laced with defiance. The words echoed in the silence, a fragile challenge against the overwhelming darkness.

The creature laughed, a sound so twisted and diabolical that it sent a chill racing down my spine. *"Feeling brave, aren't you?"* it sneered, its form shifting closer, its shadowy tendrils reaching out toward me. *"I need you, and you will comply. Both of you will."*

Its laughter grew louder, more menacing, as it closed the distance between us. My body froze, paralyzed by the sheer weight of its presence, and I could feel the darkness pressing against my skin, suffocating and inescapable.

I shot up in bed, my chest heaving as I gasped for air. Sweat clung to my skin, my hair damp and sticking to my forehead. My hands trembled as I clutched the blanket, my heart pounding so hard it felt like it might burst from my chest. The room was dark and quiet, but the echoes of the creature's laughter still rang in my ears, its words etched into my mind like a brand.

I braced myself, my breaths coming in shallow bursts as I tried to shake off the lingering terror. I'd never been so scared—not like this. Whatever that thing was, it wasn't just a figment of my imagination. It was real, and it was coming for me.

And for Felix.

The alarm buzzed, sharp and sudden, snapping me put of the spiral in my head, dragging me back to the world outside my thoughts, its insistent beeping slicing through the dim haze of a restless night. With bleary eyes, I reached over to silence it, the cool glow of the clock reminding me it was already past dawn. Every muscle in my body felt weighed down, as if I'd been carrying the burdens of the night with me into the new day.

Dragging myself out of bed, I shuffled through the motions of my morning routine, my movements mechanical, detached. I pulled my hair into a quick ponytail, grabbed a clean pair of slightly ripped jeans paired with a simple black top and a plaid shirt to finish my look. I put on my combat boots and headed straight to the café, trying to shake off the unease that clung to me. The walk there was quiet, the streets still waking up, though I couldn't help but feel that familiar sense of eyes watching me. Paranoia—or something more? I didn't want to dwell on it.

When I arrived, the café was unusually calm, the hum of the espresso machine and the occasional clink of cups filling the space. Customers trickled in slowly, and for the first time in days, the slower pace felt like a blessing. I took orders, brewed coffee, and cleaned tables, all while keeping my mind busy with thoughts of what I needed to do next.

Still, I couldn't ignore Mr. Ramsey. He lingered behind the counter, his posture stiff, his dark eyes darting to me every now and then. It wasn't the usual glance a boss might give to ensure everything was running smoothly—it was heavier. I tried to shrug it off at first, but every time I caught his gaze, I could feel its weight.

Finally, I couldn't take it anymore. I walked to the counter during a lull, the usual courage bubbling up after days of being submerged in mysteries I was desperate to untangle. "Mr. Ramsey," I said, my voice steady but cautious, "You've been watching me all morning. Is there something you want to say?"

He straightened, his brows furrowing as he considered my words. For a moment, he said nothing, his lips pressed into a thin line. Then, with a faint sigh, he leaned closer, his voice low and deliberate. "Be careful, Iris. Carrow is stirring."

The words sent a shiver down my spine. My heart skipped a beat as I tried to parse their meaning. I hadn't mentioned Carrow to him, and yet here he was, as if he knew every dark corner of the curse I was slowly piecing together.

"How—" I started, my voice trembling.

Mr. Ramsey cut me off with a sharp look. "It doesn't matter," he said, his tone firm but not unkind. "Just be careful. Keep your head down, and don't let yourself get tangled in what doesn't concern you."

I stared at him, the words swirling in my head like a storm, begging for clarity he clearly wasn't willing to give. "That's not an answer," I said, frustration creeping into my voice. "If you know something, you need to tell me—"

Before I could press him further, he dismissed me with a curt nod. "Back to work," he said, returning to his papers as quickly as he'd shifted his attention.

Still shaken, I stepped outside during my break, the crisp air doing little to calm my racing thoughts. I pulled out my phone, my fingers trembling slightly as I dialed my mom's number. The line rang twice before she picked up, her voice warm but a little distracted. "Iris?"

"Mom," I said, my voice quieter than I meant it to be. "I need to talk to you. Are you free? It's important."

There was a pause, and I could almost hear her concern through the phone. "Is everything alright?" she asked, her tone tinged with worry.

"It's... complicated," I admitted. "But I really need to talk to you."

"Alright," she said softly. "Come by Saturday morning. I'll be here."

As I hung up, the weight of the conversation settled over me like a heavy blanket. Between the ominous warnings from my dream and Mr. Ramsey's cryptic comments, I could feel the threads of the mystery tightening around me. And as much as I wanted answers, I couldn't shake the feeling that they would only lead me deeper into the darkness.

As I lowered the phone from my ear, my mom's agreement still hanging in the air, I hesitated on the café's small stoop. The conversation felt inevitable, unavoidable, but the idea of facing it alone made my stomach twist into knots. My thoughts drifted, unbidden, back to Felix. His words from last night echoed in my mind: *"To talk to your mom."*

I pulled my phone from my pocket, my fingers trembling as I unlocked it. Felix had given me his number in that moment—playful as always, but beneath the teasing, there had been a sincerity, a quiet offer of support that I hadn't fully appreciated until now. My heart beat faster as I opened my contacts, scrolling down to the new addition I'd added just before leaving the mansion.

His name stared back at me, stark and unassuming against the screen: *Felix.*

I stared at it for what felt like forever, my thumb hovering over the call button. The memory of his hands on my waist, the way his eyes softened when he looked at me, flashed through my mind. His presence was steady, grounding, even when everything else felt like it was slipping out of my control. And more than anything, I realized, I needed that steadiness right now.

Taking a deep breath, I tapped the call icon and pressed the phone to my ear. It rang once—twice—before his familiar, smooth voice came through the line. "Iris," he said, his tone laced with a mix of curiosity and amusement. "Couldn't stay away?"

I rolled my eyes, though a small smile tugged at my lips despite the tension coiled in my chest. "Felix," I said, trying to keep my voice steady. "I— I thought about what you said. About going with me to talk to my mom."

There was a pause, just long enough for me to wonder if he was going to tease me, but his voice was calm and serious when he replied. "And?"

"I think I want you to come with me," I said, the words tumbling out in a rush. "I don't know if I can do this on my own. And honestly, I don't want to."

The line went quiet for a moment, and I could almost picture him, leaning against some shadowy corner of the mansion, his sharp blue eyes narrowing thoughtfully. When he finally spoke, his voice was softer than I expected. "Alright," he said simply. "When do we leave?"

"Saturday morning," I replied, a mix of relief and nervous energy flooding through me. "I don't work Saturdays, so it's the perfect opportunity."

"Good," Felix said, his tone shifting into something lighter, almost playful. "I'll be ready. And Iris?"

"Yeah?"

"I'm glad you called," he said, the sincerity in his voice sending a shiver down my spine.

I smiled, the unease in my chest loosened, replaced by a quiet sense of reassurance. Whatever happened next, I wouldn't face it alone. For better or worse, Felix would be by my side—and for now, that was enough.

CHAPTER XVII

Killer Saturday

Saturday morning arrived with the weight of an entire week pressing down on me. The moment my eyes fluttered open, the anxiety I had worked so hard to suppress came rushing back, wrapping itself tightly around my chest like an unwelcome reminder. I lay in bed for a moment, staring at the ceiling as the light from the window spilled across the room. The promise I made to myself echoed in my mind—I would face this, no matter how much it scared me. But knowing that didn't make the task ahead any less daunting.

Dragging myself out of bed, I moved through my morning routine slowly, my hands trembling slightly as I reached for the coffee pot and my phone. The air in my apartment felt heavier than usual, as though the walls themselves could sense the unease within me. By the time I slipped on my jacket, the knot in my stomach had only tightened, twisting painfully as I glanced at the clock. It was time.

A low hum greeted me as I stepped outside—Felix's car idling at the curb like a shadow waiting for me. He was there, leaning casually against the driver's side door, his hands tucked into the pockets of his jacket. The sight of him brought a strange mix of emotions—relief, comfort, and the tiniest spark of something lighter that I didn't dare name.

He straightened when he saw me, his sharp blue eyes narrowing slightly as he studied my face. "Ready?" he asked, his voice low, steady, and carrying just the faintest hint of concern.

I forced a smile, though it didn't quite reach my eyes. "As ready as I'll ever be," I said, trying to sound more confident than I felt.

Felix didn't press me, didn't fill the moment with empty reassurances or idle chatter. He simply nodded, his gaze lingering on me for a moment longer before he climbed back into the driver's seat. I slipped into the passenger side, feeling the cool leather beneath me as he started the engine. His quiet presence was grounding in a way I hadn't realized I needed.

The drive was a strange blend of too short and too long, every moment thick with unspoken words and the tension building in my chest. The trees blurred by the windows, their bare branches swaying in the gentle breeze as we made our way through the familiar streets. Felix didn't say much, but every now and then, I caught him glancing at me—his gaze soft and steady, as if silently reminding me that he was here, that I wasn't alone.

I couldn't bring myself to say anything, afraid my voice might betray the whirlwind of emotions swirling inside me. Instead, I stared out the window, my fingers twisting in my lap as the distance to my mom's house grew shorter and shorter.

Finally, Felix broke the silence. "You don't have to face her alone," he said, his voice calm but laced with quiet intensity. "Whatever happens, I'll be there."

I turned to him, my throat tightening as I met his gaze. There was a sincerity in his eyes, a quiet promise that felt unshakable. And for the first time in days, I believed him.

As we pulled up to the familiar house, its white shutters and brick walls standing unchanged, the knot in my stomach twisted even tighter. Felix slowed the car to a stop, his hands resting lightly on the steering wheel as he looked over at me. He didn't say anything, but the look in his eyes was enough—a silent reassurance that no matter what came next, I wouldn't face it alone.

I took a deep breath, gripping the door handle as I prepared to step into the unknown. The weight of the moment pressed down on me, but Felix's presence beside me was a steady force, keeping me grounded. And as I opened the door and stepped out onto the driveway, I knew that whatever lay ahead, I would face it—with him by my side.

The walk up to the front door felt like an eternity. The crunch of gravel beneath our shoes was loud in the silence, and every step seemed heavier than the last. My mom's house, with its neat white shutters and weathered brick exterior, looked almost exactly as I remembered—but there was something different today. Something heavier, more ominous, hanging in the air. Or maybe that was just me.

Felix walked beside me, his presence steady but quiet. He didn't say a word, but I could feel the weight of his gaze on me every now and then, like he was silently measuring my resolve. I wrapped my arms tightly around myself, the chill in the air biting through my jacket and into my skin, though I wasn't sure if it was the weather or my nerves.

When we reached the porch, I paused, my eyes landing on the faded doormat with the words "Welcome Home" barely visible anymore. I swallowed hard, the knot in my stomach twisting tighter as I raised my hand to knock. Felix stood beside me, his hands tucked into his pockets, his posture relaxed—but there was a faint tension in his shoulders, an alertness that told me he was anything but calm.

The sound of my knuckles against the door felt thunderous in the quiet, and I resisted the urge to step back. My breath hitched as I heard footsteps from within, slow and deliberate. The familiar creak of the hinges sent a shiver down my spine, and then the door opened, revealing my mom standing there.

She looked... tired. Her usually bright eyes were dulled, her smile strained as it tugged at the corners of her lips. Her hair was pulled back in a loose bun, and she wore a cardigan that seemed to swallow her slight frame. There was something in her face—something heavy and sad—that made my chest tighten with guilt.

"Iris," she said softly, her smile faltering for a moment as she studied me. "You look exhausted." Her voice was gentle, but I could hear the concern hidden beneath the words.

I tried to smile, though I knew it probably looked more like a grimace. "Hi, Mom," I said, my voice quieter than I intended. "Thanks for letting me come by."

Her eyes softened, and for a moment, it felt like the tension in the air had lifted—but only for a moment. Her gaze shifted, landing on Felix, who stood just behind me, his expression composed but guarded. Her brow furrowed, confusion flickering across her face as she looked from me to him and back again. The guardedness in her stance was unmistakable, her posture stiffening as she took him in.

"And... who is this?" she asked, her tone cautious, almost wary.

I hesitated, my chest tightening as I glanced at Felix, whose eyes met mine with a calm steadiness that felt oddly reassuring. "This is Felix," I said, forcing the words out before I could second-guess them. "He's... a friend. He's been helping me with—well, with everything."

My mom's gaze didn't leave Felix, her lips pressing into a thin line as she studied him. There was something in her eyes, something I couldn't quite place—a flicker of recognition, maybe, or suspicion. "Helping you," she repeated, her tone neutral but carrying an edge I couldn't ignore.

Felix, to his credit, didn't flinch under her scrutiny. He nodded slightly, his expression polite but distant. "It's nice to meet you, Mrs. Hart," he said, his voice smooth and even.

Her eyes narrowed just barely, a subtle tightening of her jaw that might have gone unnoticed by anyone else—but I saw it. I saw the hesitation, the guardedness that was suddenly so prominent in her demeanor. "Nice to meet you, Felix," she said, though her tone carried none of the warmth it usually did when meeting someone new.

The silence that followed was suffocating, stretching out into an unbearable moment that left me feeling trapped between them. I cleared my throat, forcing myself to step forward. "Mom, can we talk? There's... a lot I need to tell you."

She blinked, her gaze shifting back to me, and the faint sadness in her eyes returned. "Of course," she said softly, stepping aside to let us in. "Come in."

As Felix and I stepped over the threshold, the weight of the house settled over me like a blanket, its familiar walls and furniture suddenly feeling foreign. My mom's guarded expression lingered in the back of my mind, a quiet reminder that this conversation wasn't going to be easy.

We followed her into the cozy kitchen, its familiar warmth a stark contrast to the chill of the front porch. The worn wooden table was laid out with mismatched mugs and a small vase of faded wildflowers, and as we all sat down, my mom busied herself with the kettle. The soft hum of the appliance mixed with the quiet clinking of cutlery as she poured tea into each cup. The aroma of herbal tea filled the room—lavender and chamomile, soothing yet laced with an unspoken melancholy.

"Sit down," she said softly, gesturing toward the wooden chairs by the table. Felix and I settled into our seats, his posture calm and composed, while I fidgeted, unable to keep still. "I'll get us something warm," she said gently, offering a smile that didn't quite reach her tired eyes.

Felix took the mug in his hands, the warmth of the tea curling into the air between us. He lifted it to his lips and took a slow sip, his expression thoughtful but unreadable. The simple motion grounded me somehow, a reminder of how effortlessly he seemed to fit into the strangest of situations. I stared down at my own mug, the swirling steam making my already scattered thoughts blur even further.

My mom settled into her seat across from us, her hands wrapped around her cup as she looked at me with tired, searching eyes. She seemed to be bracing herself, though for what, I wasn't entirely sure yet.

I stared into my cup, the swirling steam blurring the edges of the room for a moment. The silence offered no answers, so I cleared my throat. "Mom," I began tentatively, "I need to ask you something... about the necklace." My voice trembled slightly, the words feeling too heavy to say aloud, yet necessary.

Her expression shifted instantly, her hands tightening around the mug as her gaze dropped to the table. I saw the tension in her shoulders, the way her lips pressed into a thin line. "The necklace," she echoed softly, her voice tinged with something I couldn't quite name—pain, maybe, or regret.

I nodded, leaning forward slightly. "When I had it on recently... I saw your reaction. You looked so upset, almost like you knew something I didn't. Why did you react like that?"

Her brow furrowed, and she hesitated, her eyes darting to Felix for the briefest of moments before returning to me. "Iris, I didn't mean to upset you," she said softly, her voice carrying a mix of guilt and uncertainty. "It's just... that necklace, it reminded me of things I'd rather forget. It's always been in the family and passed down for generations, but no one ever really spoke about why. I guess I've always felt uneasy about it."

Her words struck me in a way I hadn't expected. "Uneasy?" I repeated, my voice trembling slightly. "Do you think it's dangerous?"

She shook her head, her hands gripping the mug more tightly. "I don't know. I just know that it carries weight—history. There's something about it that feels... heavy. When I saw it on you, all those old feelings came rushing back. I reacted without thinking."

Felix's gaze lingered on her, his expression calm but alert. He didn't say anything, allowing the moment to belong to us, but his presence was a quiet reassurance I hadn't realized I needed.

I reached out, resting my hand over hers on the table. "Mom, I don't think it's just history," I said softly, my voice steady despite the emotions bubbling up inside me. "I think it's connected to something bigger—something about our family."

"Iris," my mom said suddenly, breaking the silence. "Have you ever wondered about your dad's side of the family?"

The question threw me off. "Not really," I said slowly. "Why?"

She set her mug down, her gaze flicking briefly to the necklace. "They had... traditions," she said carefully, her tone measured. "Things I never really understood. Your dad didn't talk about them much, but I always thought there was more to it. More than I knew."

My chest tightened as her words sank in. The necklace now felt heavier, the weight of its history pressing harder against me.

"What kind of traditions?" I asked, my voice barely a whisper.

My mom shook her head, her expression thoughtful but distant. "I don't know," she admitted. "But I always got the feeling it was important—to them, anyway. Maybe more than it should have been."

She squeezed my hand gently, her tired eyes searching mine. "Iris, I wish I could give you the answers you're looking for," she said, her voice heavy with regret. "But I don't know. All I know is that the necklace has always been part of us, but why or how... I just don't know."

The honesty in her voice was both frustrating and heartbreaking. I glanced at Felix, who remained quiet, his sharp eyes flicking between us like he was piecing together a puzzle.

"It's just... that necklace, it carries memories I don't talk about often. It reminds me of your father—and your grandmother."

I sat up straighter, the mention of my grandmother pulling at something deep inside me. "Grandma?" I asked, confusion flickering across my face. "What do you mean?"

She sighed, her shoulders sagging as if the weight of those memories had suddenly become unbearable. "She gave me that necklace as a wedding gift," she said, her voice trembling slightly.

"She said it had always been passed down through the family. I thought it was just an heirloom—something special because it had been hers."

She paused, staring into her tea like it might offer her strength. "But your father... when he saw me with it, he told me to get rid of it. He said we should sell it, that it wasn't something I should keep."

Felix tilted his head slightly, his sharp gaze honing in on her words. He took another sip of his tea, his silence somehow urging her to continue.

I frowned, my heart racing. "Why would he say that?" I asked, my voice trembling. "Was he worried about something?"

Her lips pressed together tightly, and I could see the conflict in her eyes—the hesitation, the fear. "He never explained," she admitted quietly. "He just said the necklace was... wrong. I didn't understand at the time, but he looked so worried, so shaken, that I couldn't ignore it. I kept it hidden after that, locked away in a drawer. Until I decided to sell it a few weeks before your dad died"

She shook her head, her gaze lifting to meet mine. "I wish I could help you, Iris," she said softly. "I only know that your father never wanted it near us, and I respected that. But when I saw you wearing it... it felt like all those old fears came rushing back."

I glanced at Felix, who had remained silent through it all, his sharp eyes flicking between my mom and me like he was piecing together a puzzle. His presence grounded me, a quiet reassurance amid the storm of emotions threatening to pull me under.

The silence in the kitchen was interrupted by a knock at the door, sharp and unexpected. All three of us turned our heads toward the sound, my mom's expression shifting to one of confusion as she stood up from her chair.

Felix finally spoke for the first time since we'd sat down, his voice calm but laced with suspicion. "Were you expecting someone, ma'am?" he asked, his tone polite but guarded.

My mom shook her head, her brows furrowing slightly. "No," she said, her voice tinged with uncertainty. "Saturdays are for me and Iris. I never invite anybody over."

She started walking toward the door, her steps slow and deliberate, disappearing from view as she rounded the corner. I glanced at Felix, whose sharp blue eyes remained locked on the spot where my mom had vanished. His posture had shifted slightly, his shoulders tense, as though he were bracing for something.

A moment later, my mom's voice called out, shaky and strained. "Iris! Come here!"

The urgency in her tone sent a chill down my spine, and I shot up from my chair, Felix following close behind. We hurried toward the source of her voice, my heart pounding as we entered the living room.

There, standing in the middle of the room, was Mandy— my mom's neighbor and longtime friend. But something was wrong. Her posture was rigid, her movements unnatural, and her eyes... her eyes were dark, almost black, as though the light had been drained from them. In her hand, she held a knife, the blade glinting ominously in the dim light.

"Mandy?" I said, my voice trembling as I took a cautious step forward. "What are you doing?"

She didn't respond. Instead, she turned her head slowly, her gaze locking onto me with an intensity that made my blood run cold. When she spoke, her voice wasn't her own—it was deeper, distorted, and filled with malice. "You should have stayed away," she hissed, her words cutting through the air like a blade. "You're meddling in things you don't understand."

Felix stepped in front of me, his presence steady and protective. "Let her go," he said firmly, his voice calm but carrying an edge of warning. "Whatever you're doing, it stops now."

Mandy—or whatever was controlling her—laughed, the sound twisted and unnatural. "*You think you can stop me?*" she sneered, her grip tightening on the knife. "*You have no idea what you're dealing with.*"

My mom stood frozen, her face pale as she stared at Mandy, her hands trembling at her sides. "Mandy, please," she whispered, her voice barely audible. "This isn't you."

Mandy's dark gaze flicked to my mom, and for a moment, her expression softened, as though the real Mandy was fighting to break through. But it was fleeting, and the darkness returned, consuming her once more. "*You've been warned,*" she said, her voice low and menacing while holding the knife against my mom's neck. "*Stay away from the necklace. Stay away from Carrow.*"

With one swift motion, the knife moved like a whisper across her skin. Time seemed to stop when her eyes widened as they found mine, full of everything she couldn't say. The sound of my mom's body hitting the floor echoed in my ears, louder than anything I'd ever heard. It was like the world had stopped spinning, the air sucked out of the room. My heart plummeted, a hollow ache spreading through my chest as the realization of what had just happened crashed over me. My knees buckled, and I crumpled to the ground, my hands trembling as they reached out toward her lifeless form.

A single line drawn in red – that's how she ended my mom's story.

Tears blurred my vision, hot and relentless as they streamed down my face. They fell freely, soaking into the fabric of my jeans as I sobbed, my cries raw and broken. "Mom!" I screamed, my voice cracking under the weight of my grief. "Mom, no!"

Felix stood frozen, his face pale and his eyes wide with shock. He looked like he'd been turned to stone, his body rigid and unmoving as he stared at the scene before us. But when my sobs grew louder, more desperate, something in him seemed to snap. He moved quickly, crossing the room in a few long strides before dropping to his knees beside me.

"Iris," he said, his voice low and urgent as he wrapped his arms around me. His grip was firm but gentle, his hands steady as he pulled me close, shielding me from the sight of my mom's still body. "Don't look," he murmured, his voice breaking slightly. "Don't look."

I buried my face in his chest, my tears soaking into his shirt as I clung to him. My whole body shook with the force of my sobs, my mind unable to process the horror of what had just happened. Felix held me tightly, his presence grounding me even as the world around us seemed to crumble. I was too late – too late to save her – and now she was gone.

Behind him, Mandy's body convulsed violently, her limbs jerking as though she were a puppet on tangled strings. The knife slipped from her grasp, clattering to the floor with a metallic thud. Her movements grew more erratic, her head snapping back as a guttural sound escaped her lips. And then, just as suddenly as it had started, it stopped. Her body went limp, collapsing to the floor in a heap.

The room fell into an eerie silence, the tension so thick it was suffocating. Felix's arms tightened around me, his breathing shallow as he turned his head to glance at Mandy's motionless form. "She's out cold," he said quietly, his voice strained. "Whatever was controlling her... it's gone."

I pulled back slightly, my hands clutching at his shirt as I looked up at him, my vision still blurred with tears. "What just happened?" I whispered, my voice trembling. "Why did this happen?"

Felix's jaw tightened, his eyes darkening as he looked back at Mandy. "I don't know," he admitted, his voice low and grim. "But this wasn't her. Something else was controlling her."

I shivered, the weight of his words settling over me like a heavy blanket. My gaze flicked to my mom, and a fresh wave of grief threatened to pull me under. "She's gone," I choked out, my voice barely audible. "She's really gone."

Felix's expression softened, and he reached up to brush a strand of hair from my face. "I'm so sorry, Iris," he said, his voice filled with quiet sorrow. "I'm so, so sorry."

The room felt impossibly still, the only sound the faint hum of the refrigerator in the corner. Mandy lay motionless on the floor, her chest rising and falling in shallow breaths.

Whatever had taken control of her was gone, but the damage it had done was irreversible.

As I sat there, cradled in Felix's arms, the weight of everything that had happened pressed down on me, threatening to crush me. But somewhere, deep in the back of my mind, a spark of determination flickered. This wasn't over. Whatever had done this—whatever had taken my mom from me—it wasn't going to get away with it.

I wiped at my tears, my hands trembling as I pulled away from Felix. "We need to figure out what's going on," I said, my voice shaky but resolute. "We need to stop this."

Felix nodded, his expression hardening as he stood and offered me his hand. "We will," he said firmly. "I promise you, Iris. We'll stop this."

I took his hand, letting him pull me to my feet. My legs felt weak, my body heavy with grief, but I forced myself to stand. There was no time to fall apart—not now. Not when there were still so many unanswered questions.

The drive was steeped in silence, broken only by the hum of the car's engine and the rhythmic sound of the tires gliding over the asphalt. I stared blankly out the window, my face pressed against the cool glass as tears slipped down my cheeks, one after another, threatening to never stop. The world outside blurred—a haze of muted colors and indistinct shapes that mirrored the chaos swirling in my chest. My hands rested limply in my lap, trembling slightly, still too numb to process what had happened.

Felix sat beside me, his grip firm on the steering wheel, his jaw clenched as he focused on the road. He hadn't spoken since we'd left my mom's house, but I could feel the weight of his gaze flicking toward me every so often. It wasn't intrusive—it was steady, grounding, as though he was silently reminding me that I wasn't alone, even if the emptiness inside me said otherwise.

The sleek interior of his car—a black Audi A8—wrapped us in quiet luxury, its leather seats and polished surfaces offering a stark contrast to the turmoil inside me. The gentle hum of the engine was soothing, yet even that couldn't erase the heaviness pressing down on my chest. Felix's car fit him perfectly: sharp, commanding, and understated in a way that spoke volumes.

"We can't just leave her" I said, wipping some runaway tears of my face. "She doesn't deserve that."

Felix turned to look at me "I'll take care of it" he said, reaching for my hand. I didn't say a word—just gave a slow, deliberate nod, the kind that carried more weight than any sentence I could've strung together. My throat was tight, my chest heavier than I wanted to admit, but I trusted him. I trusted that he'd take care of her. That trust gave me permission to step back, just for a moment, and let myself feel everything. The ache. The fear. The love. I needed that final goodbye—not rushed, not interrupted—just one last chance to hold her in my heart before everything changed forever.

The trees thickened as we neared the mansion, their shadows stretching long and ominous in the fading light of the late afternoon. I shivered despite the warmth of the car, my body tense as the memories played on a loop in my mind—my mom's voice, her face, Mandy's twisted expression as she spoke in that inhuman tone. I squeezed my eyes shut, willing the images to fade, but they clung to me like a second skin.

"Iris," Felix said finally, his voice soft but edged with resolve. It was the first word he'd spoken since we got into the car, and its sound broke through the fog in my mind. "You shouldn't go back to work. Not for a few days, at least."

I turned my head slightly, my bloodshot eyes meeting his for a fleeting moment before I looked away again. "Felix," I started, my voice hoarse and unsteady from crying, "I can't just stop working. I need something—anything—to keep me grounded."

He exhaled sharply, gripping the wheel a little tighter. "I understand," he said, though there was a tension in his voice that told me he didn't agree. "But it's not safe for you to be out there right now. What happened today—what we saw—it wasn't random. Someone or something wanted to hurt you. Staying at the mansion for a few days is the safest option."

His words hung heavy in the air, and I bit my lip, trying to suppress the wave of guilt and fear rising in my chest. "I don't want to hide," I said quietly, my voice barely audible over the hum of the car. "I can't just sit around and do nothing while everything falls apart."

Felix glanced at me again, his expression softening. "I'm not asking you to do nothing," he said gently. "I'm asking you to let me help you. To give yourself the space to grieve and to figure out what we're dealing with. The answers won't come from drowning yourself in work."

His voice cracked slightly on the last word, and I could see the weight he was carrying too—the guilt, the frustration, the helplessness. It mirrored my own in ways I didn't want to admit. I took a shaky breath, my fingers gripping the edge of my seat as I struggled to find the words.

"It's just... hard," I admitted, my voice trembling. "Hard to feel like there's nothing left to hold onto."

Felix's hands tightened on the wheel, his jaw clenching briefly before he spoke again. "Then let me be something to hold onto," he said, his voice barely above a whisper. "Stay at the mansion for a few days. It's not forever—it's just until we figure out our next move."

I looked over at him, the raw emotion in his voice catching me off guard. Felix rarely let his walls down, and hearing that vulnerability made something shift inside me. I nodded slowly, my throat too tight to form words, and his expression softened, the faintest hint of relief flickering across his face.

The mansion loomed in the distance, its silhouette dark and foreboding against the twilight sky. As Felix pulled into the long, winding driveway, I felt a shiver run through me, though I wasn't sure if it was from the chill in the air or the knowledge that this place, with all its shadows and secrets, was now my refuge.

He parked the car neatly in front of the mansion's sprawling entrance, the black Audi A8 gleaming faintly under the golden light spilling through the towering windows. Felix turned to me, his sharp blue eyes locking onto mine with quiet determination. "I'll do everything I can to keep you safe," he said, his voice steady. "But I need you to trust me."

I nodded again, my hands trembling as I reached for the door handle. The mansion seemed to watch us as we approached, its windows glinting faintly in the dim light. Felix opened the door for me, his presence a steadying force as I stepped inside.

The weight of the day hadn't lifted—it still pressed heavily on my chest, threatening to crush me—but for the first time since it happened, I felt the smallest glimmer of hope. Felix was right. I couldn't face this alone.

And as the door closed behind us, sealing us inside the dim, echoing halls of the mansion, I realized I didn't have to.

The mansion's dimly lit foyer stretched out before us like a shadowed maze, its grandiose walls etched with intricate carvings that seemed to whisper their own secrets. The air was cooler here, the faint scent of aged wood and stone lingering beneath the chill. My footsteps echoed faintly as Felix led me through the space, his broad frame steady and unyielding as he moved forward. I clung to his presence like a lifeline, each step pulling me deeper into the heart of this strange refuge.

We paused in the living room, where the fireplace crackled softly, casting flickering orange light against the velvet curtains and heavy furniture. The room seemed impossibly vast, yet suffocatingly intimate all at once, the kind of space that could swallow you whole if you weren't careful. Felix turned to me, his sharp blue eyes cutting through the gloom as he gestured for me to sit.

"Make yourself comfortable," he said quietly, his voice steady but carrying a hint of hesitation. "I'll grab something warm to drink."

I nodded, my throat too tight for words, and sank into the armchair closest to the fire. It was plush and worn, the upholstery faded in places where time had left its mark. My trembling hands rested on the armrests, the flickering light dancing across my fingers like restless shadows.

Felix disappeared into the kitchen, the faint clinking of mugs and utensils filling the silence for a brief moment. The mansion felt alive somehow, its walls pulsing with an energy that was equal parts ominous and protective. I wrapped my arms around myself, pulling my knees up to my chest as the weight of the day pressed harder against me.

When Felix returned, he carried two steaming mugs of tea, the aroma of chamomile and honey curling through the air. He set one on the table in front of me, then sank into the chair opposite to mine, his posture relaxed but his expression guarded. He studied me for a long moment, his gaze unwavering as if he were trying to gauge the depth of my pain.

"You're safe here," he said softly, his voice barely above a whisper. "Nothing will touch you while you're under this roof."

I nodded again, but the knot in my chest didn't loosen. The idea of safety felt foreign now, like something distant and unreachable. My hands shook slightly as I reached for the mug, the warmth seeping into my palms as I tried to steady my breathing.

"I still can't believe it," I murmured, my voice trembling as I stared into the tea. "She's gone. My mom's gone."

Felix leaned forward, his elbows resting on his knees as he clasped his hands together. His face was etched with sorrow, though it wasn't the kind of grief you wear for yourself—it was for me. "Iris," he began, his voice steady but filled with a quiet intensity, "I know nothing I say can take away your pain. But you're not alone in this. We'll figure out what's happening together."

I met his gaze, my tear-streaked face illuminated by the firelight. There was a conviction in his eyes that made something inside me flicker—hope, maybe, or at least the promise of it. "It's too much," I admitted, my voice breaking. "I don't even know where to start."

Felix's lips pressed into a thin line as he leaned back, his fingers tapping lightly against the armrest. "Start by staying here for a few days," he said firmly. "You need time to process everything. To grieve. The answers will come, but only if you're in the right place to face them."

His words settled over me like a blanket, heavy and comforting all at once. The flickering firelight cast long shadows across his face, highlighting the sharp angles of his jaw and the subtle furrow in his brow. He looked so sure, so steady, and I couldn't help but feel drawn to that strength, even as my own felt like it was slipping away.

I took another sip of tea, the warmth soothing my throat, but doing little to calm the storm inside me. "It feels like the world's falling apart," I said quietly, my voice barely above a whisper.

Felix tilted his head slightly, his sharp gaze softening. "It may feel that way now," he said gently, "but you're stronger than you think. You've already come this far, and you're still standing."

I wanted to argue, to tell him I wasn't strong, that I felt like I was crumbling with every passing second. But the sincerity in his voice stopped me, the quiet reassurance sinking into the cracks of my broken resolve.

As the fire crackled and the tea grew colder, the mansion seemed to wrap around us, its shadows offering a strange kind of comfort. And though the weight of the day still pressed heavily on my chest, Felix's presence anchored me, his steady voice pulling me back from the edge.

CHAPTER XVIII

Surprise

The days blurred together after that terrible morning, each one suffocating in its quiet weight. The reality of my mother's absence settled over me like an immovable fog, pressing down on every breath, every thought, every corner of Felix's room where I had hidden myself away.

Felix kept his promise. Somehow, he pulled together a quiet funeral—just the two of us, no crowd, no noise. It was raining that day, the kind of steady, relentless rain that felt personal. Like the sky understood what I was feeling and decided to cry with me. The drops slid down my cheeks, mixing with tears I didn't bother to hide. It was simple, raw, and exactly what she deserved. And in that moment, standing beside Felix, I knew I wasn't alone in my grief.The comforters became my cocoon, shielding me from the world outside—a world I wasn't ready to face. Food had lost its appeal, even water felt like an unnecessary effort.

Felix was patient and more understanding than I deserved, as he gave me space to grieve in my own twisted way. He had spent hours trying to be unobtrusive, filling the air with his steady presence but never pressing me to do more than I could handle. He called Mr. Ramsey to explain my situation— a call I couldn't bring myself to make—and my boss, with more kindness than I expected, cleared me from work for the time being. "Take the time to grieve," Mr. Ramsey had said.

Grieve. The word felt bitter and sour in my mouth. It was a word I thought I had defeated years ago when my father passed. But now it clawed its way back into my life, mocking me with its permanence. It was funny in a tragic sort of way, how grief always felt like an enemy you'd outrun, only to find it waiting around the corner, relentless and cruel.

The knock on the door startled me, cutting through the thick haze of my thoughts. It was soft, tentative—Felix's knock. "Come in," I said, my voice weak and barely audible.

The door creaked open, revealing Felix on the other side. He stepped into the room with the careful grace he always carried, his expression shadowed but flickering with a quiet determination. I knew he had spent the last few nights immersed in his own research, diving deeper into the chaos that had entangled our lives. He hadn't wanted to burden me with the details, insisting that I needed to rest, but now there was something different in his eyes. Something hopeful.

He crossed the room and sat on the edge of the bed, his shoulders relaxed but his posture alert. "I need you to come downstairs in fifteen minutes," he said, his voice steady but threaded with quiet encouragement. His eyes held mine, radiating an unspoken plea.

"Do I have to?" I murmured, the exhaustion in my voice evident.

Felix sighed, his lips pressing into a faint line before softening into the smallest smile. "I would love for you to," he said, his hand finding mine, his touch warm and grounding. "I know how you feel, but this—this isn't healthy. You can't keep shutting the world out like this."

His gaze softened further, so full of tenderness it nearly broke something inside me. "Besides," he added, his voice lighter, "I have a surprise for you."

"Felix," I replied, dragging his name out with the weight of my weariness, "you know I don't like surprises."

He smirked, the hint of a tease flashing in his eyes. "Just trust me," he said firmly, his tone leaving no room for argument. "Now, go shower and put on the clothes I left for you. They're in the closet." He stood, straightened his jacket, and walked to the door without hesitation, leaving me to my silence.

I wanted to argue, to pull the comforter tighter around me and hide away like I had been, but something about the look in his eyes lingered. It tugged at me, pushed against the heavy fog that had swallowed me whole. With a reluctant sigh, I rose from the bed, dragging myself toward the bathroom like someone half-dreaming.

The shower was hot and steaming, the water wrapping around me like an embrace. I closed my eyes, letting the heat melt the tension in my muscles, hoping it would somehow wash away the sadness clinging to my skin. For a few fleeting minutes, the steam and silence were a refuge, a fragile reprieve from the weight of the past few days.

When I finally stepped out, my skin flushed from the heat, I padded to the closet as Felix had instructed. I hesitated for a moment, staring at the door as though opening it might reveal more than I was ready to see. Then, with trembling fingers, I slid it open.

Inside of it was a dress, it was carefully hung, its light blue fabric catching the soft glow of the moonlight spilling through the mansion's tall windows. The floral patterns immediately stood out, delicate yet vibrant—a harmony of yellows, pinks, and whites woven across the soft material, each bloom almost seeming alive in the silvery light.

The bodice was fitted, with wide shoulder straps and a sweetheart neckline that gave it an air of timeless elegance. As my fingers traced the seams, I admired the craftsmanship, the way the dress hugged the top and then cascaded into a full skirt. It wasn't just any skirt—it flowed all the way down to the ankles, the fabric gathered into a ruffled hem that seemed to shimmer faintly, moving with a whisper at the slightest touch.

It was undeniably beautiful, almost too beautiful for someone like me to wear, especially tonight. But as I stood there holding it, I couldn't help but wonder why Felix had picked this specific dress. It felt intentional, as though every detail had been chosen with care. There was something almost comforting in that thought, like a piece of normalcy amidst the chaos. Yet, there was also something about the dress—its elegance, its fragility—that made me feel exposed, as though wearing it would tell the world more about me than I was ready to share.

I was lost for words. How had Felix known? How had he chosen something so perfect, so alive, when I felt anything but?

I traced my fingers lightly over the fabric of the dress, its softness contrasting sharply with the weight pressing down on me. Felix's choice felt deliberate—so deliberate that it made my chest tighten with an unfamiliar emotion. He'd left this for me, left it knowing what I needed before I could even admit it myself. It wasn't just a dress; it was an invitation, a quiet plea to step out of the cocoon I'd wrapped myself in and try, even if only for a moment, to breathe again.

I clutched the dress to my chest, the floral patterns brushing against my skin, and swallowed the lump rising in my throat. Was it possible to feel both overwhelmed and comforted all at once? The quiet elegance of the garment made me feel seen, like Felix had chosen it because he understood what I might need at that moment. And yet, the idea of putting it on felt daunting, like a step I wasn't sure I was ready to take.

After a moment of standing frozen in the closet's glow, I turned away and began to dress. The light blue fabric slid over me like a second skin, enveloping me in its delicate embrace. The floral designs came alive against the curve of my body, a vivid contrast to the quiet grief I carried inside. When I turned toward the mirror, my breath caught. It wasn't that the dress transformed me—it wasn't magic—but it felt like it held a piece of something I'd lost, something I didn't even know I needed to find.

I ran my hands down the ruffled hem of the skirt, smoothing it out as though trying to calm my nerves. Felix's voice echoed in my mind: *Just trust me.* The memory brought a faint smile to my lips—something I hadn't felt in days. Maybe he was right. Maybe trust was all I needed tonight.

I stood in front of the mirror, the dress draped gracefully over me, its light blue fabric flowing like water around my frame. It was breathtaking, almost too perfect, and the thought of pairing it with the mess my hair had become over the past few days made me cringe. Felix had taken the time to pick this out for me—he'd thought about it, cared enough to make sure I had something beautiful. The least I could do was try to look like I deserved it.

Sighing softly, I grabbed the brush from the vanity and began to work through the tangles, each stroke feeling like a small step toward reclaiming something I'd lost. I twisted and pinned sections here and there, letting the soft waves frame my face in a way that felt effortless, yet intentional. It wasn't perfect, but it was enough—enough to feel like I wasn't hiding anymore. Enough to face whatever Felix had planned with a flicker of confidence.

The dress moved with me as I walked through the mansion, the fabric brushing softly against my legs like a whisper of reassurance. The air in the house felt different tonight—

warmer, quieter, as though the shadows themselves were holding their breath. My fingers trailed along the smooth wooden railing of the staircase as I descended, the faint echo of my footsteps filling the vast, empty halls.

I wasn't entirely sure where I was supposed to go, but I followed the soft glow of light spilling from the corridor ahead. The flicker of candles drew me like a moth, each step closer pulling me out of the haze I'd been stuck in for days. By the time I reached the kitchen, I froze, my breath catching at the sight before me.

The table had been transformed into something out of a dream. A crisp white tablecloth draped over the surface, its pristine folds catching the warm light of the candles set in ornate holders. In the center was a small bouquet of red roses, their petals vivid against the dim surroundings. The fragrance of the flowers mingled with the subtle aroma of the food waiting on delicate china plates. A glass of wine, its deep crimson hues glinting in the candlelight, sat invitingly on one side of the table.

But Felix wasn't there.

Instead, a single note sat propped up against one of the glasses, the elegant handwriting instantly recognizable as his. My heartbeat quickened as I stepped closer, my heels clicking softly on the polished floor. I picked up the note, the faint scent of parchment brushing against me as I read the words scrawled in deliberate, precise strokes:

"Take your time. Eat. When you're ready, come to the living room. There's more waiting for you."

A small smile tugged at my lips, the first in what felt like an eternity. Felix's thoughtfulness was... overwhelming in a way I wasn't entirely sure how to process. He hadn't said anything grand or dramatic—just left me with food, wine, and the promise of something more. But it was enough.

I sat down slowly, the chair creaking softly beneath me as I adjusted the folds of the dress. The soft clink of the silverware and the gentle rustle of the roses in their vase filled the silence. The food was simple but elegant, the flavors warming me in a way I hadn't realized I needed. Each bite was a reminder that I was still here, still breathing, still capable of feeling something other than grief.

The wine left a comforting warmth in its wake, its rich taste lingering on my tongue as I gazed at the roses. They were beautiful, vibrant, and alive—everything I hadn't felt in days. But here, in the soft glow of candlelight, surrounded by the quiet care Felix had so deliberately crafted, I felt a flicker of something different. Not joy, not yet, but... peace. A fragile, fleeting peace.

When I'd finished the meal, I wiped my hands on the napkin, my gaze drifting back to the note. *Come to the living room.* The words lingered in my mind, their simplicity a quiet promise that something else awaited me. I stood, the chair scraping lightly against the floor, and smoothed the dress over my hips. The roses' scent followed me as I turned toward the corridor, the faint buzz of anticipation threading through my chest.

The soft hum of the mansion's energy seemed to guide me as I walked, each step echoing in the stillness. The living room's heavy wooden doors were slightly ajar, a faint golden glow spilling through the crack. I pushed the door open gently, my breath catching as I stepped inside.

And there he was. Felix stood near the fireplace, his tall frame cast in golden light, the flicker of flames dancing in his sharp blue eyes. The faintest smile touched his lips as his gaze met mine, and for a moment, the rest of the world fell away.

He was dressed in a crisp white shirt with subtle blue stripes running neatly through the fabric. The sleeves were rolled up to his elbows, revealing the lines of his forearms in an almost effortless display of casual elegance. His navy blue trousers fit him perfectly, tailored in a way that spoke of both refinement and ease. A brown leather belt and matching polished leather shoes tied the look together, understated but undeniably sophisticated. He looked composed, impeccable, and yet somehow relaxed, like he'd just stepped out of another time—one where grace and composure were effortless requirements.

For a moment, I just stood there, taking him in. Felix always carried himself with a quiet authority, but tonight, there was something different. He exuded a kind of warmth, a subtle energy that seemed woven into every detail of his appearance.

His eyes met mine, those striking blues softening when they landed on my face. A small smile tugged at the corner of his lips as he stepped toward me, closing the space between us. "You look stunning, Iris," he said, his voice low and steady. The sincerity in his words hit me like a gust of wind, leaving me slightly off-balance.

I felt my cheeks flush, my hands unconsciously smoothing the soft folds of my dress. "Thank you," I murmured, my voice a bit quieter than I meant it to be. "You don't look too bad yourself."

That earned me the faintest smirk, one that flickered briefly across his face before he extended his hand. "There's more to the evening. Come."

He led me toward the small table by the fireplace, its surface adorned with simple yet elegant touches. A bouquet of roses rested in the center, their rich red petals unfurling delicately in the flickering glow of the fire. Two wine glasses sat ready beside a deep bottle of crimson wine, the light catching the glass and casting faint streaks of color onto the white tablecloth. It was breathtakingly beautiful—thoughtful in a way that made my chest tighten.

I turned to Felix, my voice catching slightly as I spoke. "You planned all this?"

"Of course," he said simply, pulling out a chair for me. "I wanted tonight to be special. For you."

I sat down, the warmth of the fire wrapping around me like an embrace. Felix poured the wine with quiet precision, sliding a glass toward me before taking his own seat across the table. The candlelight illuminated his features, and for a moment, I forgot the chaos that had been pressing down on us. All I could see was the soft flicker of light in his eyes, the faint curve of his lips as he watched me.

The night was perfect. Every dish, every detail, seemed designed to draw me back to the present, away from the heavy weight of grief. Felix didn't talk much—he didn't need to. His quiet presence was enough, grounding and steadying me in a way I hadn't realized I needed.

When we finished, I sat back in my chair, the warmth of the wine spreading through my chest. Felix stood slowly, his movements deliberate, and extended his hand toward me again. "Dance with me," he said softly, the request so simple, yet carrying a weight that made my breath hitch.

The melody shifted then, and the unmistakable tune of *The Way You Look Tonight* filled the air. It's timeless elegance wrapped around us like the faint glow of the fire, stirring something deep and unfamiliar in my chest. I hesitated, looking up at him with wide eyes. "Felix, I—"

"You don't have to be perfect," he interrupted gently, the faintest smile tugging at his lips. "Just trust me."

I took his hand, letting him pull me to my feet. His other hand rested lightly on my waist, his movements slow and deliberate as he guided me into the rhythm of the song. The music wrapped around us, the soft, crooning melody weaving through the room as Felix led me through the steps.

At first, I stumbled, my feet awkward and unsure against the polished floor. But Felix was patient, his grip steady, his voice low and soothing. "You're doing fine," he murmured, his blue eyes locked onto mine. "Just let go."

And I did. Slowly, I felt myself relax into him, my movements becoming fluid as I let him guide me. The skirt of my dress swirled with each turn, catching the light like rippling water. The warmth of the fire, the faint scent of roses, the quiet intensity in Felix's gaze—it all melted together, creating a moment that felt impossibly surreal.

As the song reached its crescendo, Felix spun me gently, his hand firm and sure as he pulled me back into his arms. I laughed softly, the sound unfamiliar but welcome, and when the music faded into silence, we didn't move. His hand lingered on my waist, mine still entwined with his. For a moment, the rest of the world ceased to exist.

"You didn't tell me you could dance," I said finally, my voice soft and teasing.

Felix's lips curved into a faint smirk. "There's a lot I haven't told you," He replied, his voice quiet but warm.

And as the fire crackled softly in the background, I realized I didn't mind waiting to discover the rest of his secrets. Not tonight. Not with him.

The fire crackled softly in the background, its warm glow casting flickering shadows across the room. Felix's hand lingered on my waist, his touch steady and grounding, while his other hand still held mine, our fingers loosely intertwined. The air between us felt charged, heavy with something unspoken, something that had been building quietly for days, maybe even weeks.

His blue eyes searched mine, their intensity making it impossible to look away. There was a softness there, a vulnerability that he rarely let slip through the cracks of his carefully composed exterior. And then, just for a moment, his gaze flicked downward—to my lips—and I saw it. That subtle, almost imperceptible movement as he bit his bottom lip, his teeth catching it briefly before releasing it. It was a habit of his, one I'd noticed before, but tonight it felt different. Tonight, it felt like a question.

My breath hitched, my heart pounding so loudly I was sure he could hear it. The space between us seemed to shrink, the world narrowing until it was just him and me, the firelight wrapping around us like a cocoon. His hand on my waist tightened slightly, pulling me just a fraction closer, and I felt his warmth, the steady rise and fall of his chest as he exhaled.

"Iris," he murmured, my name barely more than a whisper on his lips. There was something in the way he said it, something that made my knees feel weak and my pulse race. He didn't move right away, though. He just stood there, his gaze locked on mine, as if waiting for permission, for some sign that I wanted this as much as he did.

And I did. God, I did.

I tilted my head slightly, my fingers tightening around his as I leaned in, closing the last sliver of space between us. That was all it took. Felix's lips met mine, soft and warm and impossibly gentle at first, as though he were afraid I might break. But then the kiss deepened, his hand sliding from my waist to the small of my back, pulling me flush against him.

The world tilted, the firelight spinning in my peripheral vision as I lost myself in him. His other hand released mine, his fingers threading through my hair with a tenderness that made my chest ache. There was nothing rushed about the way he kissed me—every movement was deliberate, like he was savoring the moment, like he wanted to memorize the way we fit together.

I felt his lips part slightly, the faintest brush of his teeth against my bottom lip, and a shiver ran down my spine. It wasn't just a kiss—it was a conversation, a promise, a thousand unspoken words exchanged in the space of a heartbeat. My hands found their way to his chest, the fabric of his shirt soft beneath my fingers as I clung to him, afraid that if I let go, the moment might shatter.

When we finally broke apart, it wasn't because we wanted to—it was because we had to. My forehead rested against his, our breaths mingling in the small space between us as we tried to steady ourselves. Felix's eyes fluttered open, and the way he looked at me—like I was the only thing in the world that mattered—made my heart ache in the best possible way.

"You're incredible," he said softly, his voice rough around the edges, like he was struggling to find the right words. His thumb brushed against my cheek, his touch featherlight. "I don't think you even realize it."

I didn't know what to say, so I didn't say anything. Instead, I leaned into him, letting the warmth of his embrace and the steady beat of his heart against mine speak for me. The fire crackled again, the sound grounding us as the rest of the world slowly came back into focus.

But even as the moment passed, I knew something had shifted between us. This wasn't just a kiss—it was the beginning of something bigger, something neither of us could ignore.

The fire crackled softly in the background, its warm glow casting flickering shadows across the room. Felix's hand lingered on my waist, his touch steady and grounding, anchoring me to the moment. I could feel the steady rise and fall of his chest against mine, could hear the faint sound of his breathing as it began to even out. But his eyes—they stayed on mine, unwavering and impossibly blue, studying me like I was the only thing in the room worth noticing.

Time seemed to stretch, the rest of the mansion fading into the quiet hum of the fire. I didn't dare move, afraid that breaking the silence would somehow shatter whatever fragile connection had formed between us. But Felix, as always, carried a sense of certainty that I couldn't help but be drawn to.

"I didn't plan on that happening," he said softly, his voice steady but tinged with a quiet vulnerability that caught me off guard. He hesitated for a fraction of a second, his gaze flickering to my lips again before returning to my eyes. "But I'm not sorry it did."

His words made my chest tighten, the raw honesty of them sinking in deeper than I expected. I swallowed, my hands still resting lightly against his chest, the fabric of his shirt warm beneath my fingertips. "Neither am I," I admitted, my voice barely above a whisper.

Felix's lips curved into a faint smile, his fingers brushing against the small of my back. "Good," he murmured, his thumb grazing a slow, deliberate circle against the fabric of my dress. "Because if I'm being honest, I've been thinking about doing that again since the last time."

I felt my cheeks flush, heat spreading across my skin as I tried to process his words. "You have?" I asked, the disbelief clear in my voice.

His smirk deepened, the familiar glint of amusement flashing in his eyes. "Iris," he said, tilting his head slightly, "how could I not? Look at you."

I laughed softly, the sound almost foreign after everything that had happened in the past few days. "You're impossible, you know that?" I teased, though my voice betrayed the fluttering feeling in my chest.

"Maybe," he replied, his tone light but edged with sincerity. "But if being impossible gets me moments like this, I think I can live with it."

I wanted to say something, to find the words that would match the quiet intensity of the moment, but nothing felt right. Instead, I leaned into him, resting my forehead against his as I closed my eyes. The warmth of his skin, the quiet strength in his hold—it was enough. For now, it was enough.

We stayed like that for a while, the fire crackling softly in the background as the room seemed to exhale around us. It was a fragile peace, but it was real, and I found myself clinging to it, letting it fill the spaces that grief and chaos had carved out of me.

Eventually, Felix shifted, his hand trailing lightly down my arm before he took a step back. The absence of his touch left a faint ache, but his gaze held the same steady warmth as before. "There's something else I want to show you," he said, his voice breaking the quiet without shattering it.

"What is it?" I asked, curious.

His lips twitched into another faint smirk, and he extended his hand toward me. "Trust me."

The words were simple, but they carried a weight that made my heart skip. Without hesitation, I placed my hand in his, his fingers curling around mine as he led me toward the hallway. The faint hum of the fire faded behind us, replaced by the quiet echoes of our footsteps against the polished floor.

I didn't know what Felix had planned, but for the first time in days, I didn't feel the weight of needing to know. With him by my side, the answers could wait.

Felix led me down the mansion's dimly lit hallway, his hand warm and steady in mine. The soft hum of our footsteps against the polished floor was the only sound as the faint glow of candlelight spilled from the space ahead. My heart fluttered with quiet anticipation, the lingering warmth of his earlier words and the memory of our kiss wrapping around me like a protective layer. Whatever he had planned, I already knew it was going to be something that would leave me breathless.

When we reached the doorway, he paused, turning to me with a faint smirk tugging at the corner of his lips. "Ready?" he asked, his voice low and even, but carrying an undeniable spark of excitement.

I nodded, my grip tightening on his hand. "Ready," I said, though my voice barely carried above a whisper.

Felix pushed the door open with deliberate ease, and the sight before me took my breath away. The room was bathed in soft, golden light from the dozens of candles lining every surface, their flickering flames casting delicate shadows that danced across the walls. A small table stood in the center of the room, draped in an ivory cloth and adorned with roses—deep red, vibrant yellow, and soft pink—all arranged in elegant perfection. The subtle aroma of the flowers mixed with the warm scent of vanilla from the candles created a space that felt impossibly intimate and serene.

But my gaze froze on what sat atop the table. A small cake, white and pristine, with delicate frosting roses blooming along its edges. The words "Happy Birthday, Iris" were scrawled in elegant script across the top, the light catching the faint shimmer of the icing.

My mouth fell open, a soft gasp escaping before I could stop it. "Felix," I began, my voice unsteady, "how did you—how did you know?"

He smiled, stepping closer as he let my hand fall gently from his grasp. "You have friends who care about you," he said casually, like it was the most obvious thing in the world. "Luna and Jayce texted you this morning while you were asleep. I happened to check your phone when they kept popping up."

I blinked, stunned not only by the revelation but by how casually he said it, as if remembering my birthday was the easiest thing he'd ever done. "You—you saw their messages?" I stammered, still processing everything.

Felix nodded, his smile deepening. "They didn't say much, just a simple 'Happy Birthday' and how much they wished they could see you. I figured it was something worth celebrating." He gestured to the room, his blue eyes softening as they lingered on me. "Even if you weren't planning to."

The knot in my chest loosened just slightly, replaced by an ache that felt almost like gratitude. Felix hadn't just remembered—he'd gone out of his way to make this a moment I would never forget, despite everything else we'd been through. And somehow, he'd done it in the quiet, thoughtful way that was so undeniably him.

I turned back to the table, my fingers brushing lightly against the edge of the cloth. "Felix, I don't know what to say," I murmured, my voice catching on the lump rising in my throat.

"You don't have to say anything," he replied, stepping beside me. His hand found the small of my back again, steady and grounding. "Just let me make tonight about you."

I glanced up at him, the sincerity in his gaze sending a fresh wave of warmth through me. For the first time in days, I felt something lighter, something like hope. And as the firelight danced across his face, I knew that whatever chaos awaited us beyond these walls, tonight, at least, I wasn't worried.

I turned back to Felix, the weight of the evening pressing softly against my chest—a mix of gratitude, warmth, and something else I wasn't entirely ready to name. The flickering candlelight danced across his face, and he looked at me with an expression I couldn't quite decipher, somewhere between steady calm and quiet intensity.

"Thank you," I said finally, my voice barely above a whisper. The words felt small compared to everything he'd done tonight, but they carried every ounce of sincerity I had.

Felix's lips curved into a faint smile, his eyes softening as he stepped closer, his presence steady and grounding. "You don't have to thank me, Iris," he murmured, his voice as warm and quiet as the firelight surrounding us. "You deserve this."

The air between us felt heavier again, charged with an unspoken energy that made my breath catch. He reached up slowly, his hand brushing against my cheek, his thumb grazing my skin in a touch so light it sent shivers down my spine. The way he looked at me in that moment, like I was something precious, made my heart ache in the best possible way.

I didn't realize I was leaning into him until his face was just inches from mine. His gaze flicked down to my lips, lingering for the briefest of moments, before his eyes met mine again, silently asking permission. And just like before, I gave it without a word.

His lips brushed against mine softly, a fleeting kiss that was as much a question as it was a promise. It wasn't hurried or desperate—it was gentle, careful, like he wanted to savor every second of it. My hands found their way to his chest, the fabric of his shirt warm beneath my fingers, and I felt his breath hitch slightly, just enough to make my pulse race.

When he pulled back, his forehead rested lightly against mine, his eyes still closed as if he wasn't ready to let the moment end. Neither was I.

"Happy birthday, Iris," he whispered, the words so quiet they were almost swallowed by the space between us. But they hung there, heavy and sincere, wrapping around me like the faint glow of the candles.

For the first time in what felt like forever, I allowed myself to smile—soft, small, but real. "Thank you," I said again, this time with more certainty.

And as the fire crackled softly and the roses filled the air with their delicate scent, I knew this night would stay with me, etched into my memory like a moment I could return to whenever the darkness felt too heavy to bear.

Everything seemed to fall into place, even with the ever-present darkness that haunted us, lingering in the edges of every moment. For the first time in what felt like months, I smiled—a real, unforced smile that reached somewhere deep inside me. It was a warmth I hadn't thought I would feel again. And it was all because of him.

I thought about the evening, about how much care Felix had poured into every detail, how he had done everything in his quiet, deliberate way to make me feel better. It wasn't just the effort; it was the way he truly saw me, the way he made the weight of everything seem just a little lighter.

Something felt different now. Something had shifted, settled into a place I hadn't expected, but I knew with quiet certainty.

I loved Felix.

CHAPTER XIX

The Weight of Letting Go

The morning light filtered softly through the heavy curtains in Felix's room, casting muted shadows across the polished wooden floors and the intricate patterns of the rug beneath my feet. I sat by the window, curled up in the armchair, the fabric of the light blue dress Felix had given me still swayed gently in the breeze drifting through the cracked window. It fluttered gently, like it hadn't quite let go of the night before. My fingers traced absent circles along the hem, my thoughts drifting as the memories of Felix's warmth and his quiet sincerity stayed with me.

It was the first morning that didn't feel suffocating since everything had happened. The weight in my chest hadn't disappeared—it was still there, an ache that I wasn't sure would ever fully leave—but it felt lighter now, less like a burden and more like something I could carry, even if only for a little while. Felix had done that for me. His presence, his care, his relentless thoughtfulness—it had all worked to pull me out of the darkness I'd been drowning in.

The quiet sound of footsteps approached from the hallway, steady and deliberate, and moments later, there was a soft knock at the door. It opened before I could respond, Felix stepping inside with his usual calm demeanor. Today, he wore a different outfit—another crisp white shirt paired with dark gray slacks, his sleeves rolled neatly to his elbows as always. He had a way of making simplicity look like elegance, as though he didn't even have to try.

"Good morning," he said, his voice low and smooth as he crossed the room toward me. There was a faint trace of a smile on his lips, warm but restrained, like he was testing the waters.

"Morning," I replied softly, setting aside the dress's hem as I shifted in the chair to face him. "Did you sleep?"

He paused for half a moment, his gaze catching mine, before the faintest smirk curved his lips. "You know I don't sleep," he said, his tone light but carrying a deeper undercurrent.

I blinked, realizing my question had been more out of habit than intention. "Right," I murmured, a bit flustered. "Still, you seem… rested."

Felix stepped closer, leaning against the back of the chair opposite mine, his sharp blue gaze steady as it studied me. "It's a skill," he said casually, though the way his eyes softened hinted at something more. "What about you?"

I hesitated, trying to decide how honest to be. "Better than I expected," I admitted finally, my voice quieter now. "It wasn't perfect, but... last night helped."

Felix's lips twitched slightly, his faint smile deepening. "Good," he said. "That's what I was hoping for."

There was a pause between us, the kind of silence that felt like it was holding something unspoken. Felix tilted his head slightly, his eyes narrowing just a fraction, as though he was debating whether or not to say what was on his mind. When he finally spoke, his voice was careful but firm.

"Iris," he began, "there's something else you should know."

I straightened in my seat, my pulse quickening. "What is it?" I asked, the words slipping out before I could stop them.

He hesitated again, and then, with his typical calm resolve, he stepped forward, resting his hand lightly on the edge of the table near me. "It's not just about what happened the other day," he said. "There's something bigger—something we need to understand before we can move forward."

His words sent a shiver down my spine, the faint undercurrent of urgency in his voice making my chest tighten. "You've found something," I said, my mind already racing.

Felix nodded, his gaze unwavering. "I've been digging into it all—Mandy, the necklace, your grandmother's connection. There are pieces of a puzzle here, and I think it's time we start putting them together."

I swallowed hard, my hands clenching slightly against the armrest. The weight that had eased the night before came rushing back, heavier and more chaotic than ever. "What are you saying?" I asked, my voice trembling.

Felix's expression softened, and he reached out, resting his hand lightly on my arm. His touch was steady, grounding, as his blue eyes searched mine. "I'm saying that whatever happened to Mandy, whatever your father feared about that necklace—it's still in play. And it's time we figure out why."

The resolve in his voice made something stir inside me— fear, yes, but also determination. Felix had been my anchor through the chaos, and if he believed we could find answers, then maybe, just maybe, I could believe it too.

The late morning sun filtered through the tall windows of the mansion, casting streaks of light onto the grand hallway. I sat at the edge of the plush armchair in the sitting room, my hands folded tightly in my lap as I waited for Felix to return. My thoughts felt heavy, swirling with a mix of gratitude and resolve, and I wasn't sure how to put them into words.

Felix stepped into the room, his footsteps as quiet and purposeful as always. He paused when he saw me sitting there, his sharp blue eyes softening slightly as they met mine. He must've noticed the weight behind my expression because he didn't say anything right away. Instead, he crossed the room and took a seat in the chair opposite me, resting his elbows on his knees as he leaned forward slightly.

"Iris," he said finally, his voice calm but threaded with something deeper, something concerned. "What's on your mind?"

I took a deep breath, my fingers fidgeting with the fabric of my dress, before I forced myself to meet his gaze. "I think it's time I go home," I said softly, the words catching in my throat. "I've been here long enough, and I need to figure out how to move forward. On my own."

Felix's expression didn't change immediately. He was quiet, his gaze steady as he let my words sink in. But I could see the tension in his jaw, the way his hands clasped together just a bit tighter. "You don't have to rush this," he said carefully. "You've been through a lot, Iris. Staying here isn't a sign of weakness."

"I know that," I said quickly, my voice gentler now. "But I need this. You've done so much for me, Felix. More than I could ever thank you for. You've been… everything I needed when I didn't even know what that was. But I can't stay here forever. I need to find a way to face what's waiting for me outside."

His jaw tightened briefly before he exhaled, leaning back slightly in his chair. "And you're sure you're ready for that?" he asked, his eyes searching mine for any hint of doubt. "Being alone right now… It's not exactly safe."

"I know," I admitted, my hands tightening in my lap. "And I'm not saying it's going to be easy. But I can't hide here forever. If I don't do this now, I might never feel ready."

Felix ran a hand through his hair, his usual calm demeanor cracking just slightly as he studied me. "Iris, I don't like the idea of you being on your own right now," he said, his voice quieter but no less firm. "Not after everything that's happened. You're still in the middle of this, whether you want to be or not."

I leaned forward, reaching out to place my hand over his. His skin was warm, his fingers still beneath mine as I looked at him. "I won't be completely alone," I said gently. "Luna and Jayce are just a text away. And if anything happens, I know I can count on you."

His lips pressed into a thin line, the reluctance in his eyes clear, but he didn't argue. Instead, he turned his hand over, letting his fingers curl around mine. "If that's what you need," he said after a long pause, "then I won't stop you. But promise me something."

"Anything," I said, my voice steady.

"Promise me you'll call if anything feels off," he said firmly, his grip on my hand tightening just slightly. "No matter how small it seems. I'll come. No questions asked."

"I promise," I said, my voice soft but resolute. "Thank you, Felix. For everything."

He nodded, his gaze lingering on mine for a moment longer before he stood, his hand still holding mine as he guided me toward the entrance of the mansion. The air felt different as we walked, heavier somehow, the weight of the decision settling in with each step.

When we reached the grand double doors, Felix paused, turning to face me. His expression was unreadable, his sharp features softened just enough to let that flicker of concern show through. "Are you sure about this?" he asked one last time, his voice low but steady.

I nodded, a faint smile tugging at my lips as I squeezed his hand. "I need this," I said simply.

Felix's lips twitched into the faintest of smiles, though it didn't quite reach his eyes. "Then take care of yourself," he said quietly. "And don't forget your promise."

"I won't," I assured him.

He released my hand reluctantly, and I turned toward the path that led down from the mansion, the quiet hum of the world outside waiting just beyond the iron gates. As I stepped forward, I couldn't help but glance back, my heart tugging at the sight of Felix standing there, framed by the grandeur of the mansion's entrance. He didn't move, his sharp blue eyes fixed on me as though committing this moment to memory.

And then I turned back to the path, the soft crunch of gravel underfoot as I walked, my thoughts swirling with a mix of uncertainty and resolve. The weight of what lay ahead was heavy, but I knew I wasn't truly alone. Not with Felix just a call away.

The walk home started out uneventful, the streets of the city alive with their usual hum of noise and motion. Cars sped past, their headlights streaking across the pavement as the sky dipped into shades of deepening gray. I pulled my jacket tighter around me, the weight of my conversation with Felix still heavy in my chest. I'd promised him I would be okay, that I could handle being on my own again—but as I neared my apartment, a flicker of unease began to creep up my spine.

It started small, just a tingling sensation at the back of my neck. I glanced over my shoulder, half expecting to see someone trailing behind me, but the sidewalk was empty. Still, the feeling didn't fade. My pulse quickened, the sound of my boots hitting the concrete echoing louder in my ears as I picked up my pace. The shadows seemed to stretch unnaturally, darkened corners of alleyways yawning wide as though waiting to swallow me whole.

I told myself it was nothing, just my imagination running wild after everything I'd been through. But the weight of someone—or something—watching me lingered, settling into my chest like a stone. My apartment building came into view, its familiar outline doing little to ease the tension coiling in my stomach. I practically ran the last block, fumbling with my keys as I reached the door.

The lock clicked, and I shoved the door open, stepping inside and slamming it shut behind me. My chest heaved as I leaned back against the door, my heart racing in my ears. The unease didn't go away, though. It clung to me, a heavy shroud that refused to lift even as I turned on the lights and scanned the room. Everything seemed normal—quiet, untouched—but the feeling wouldn't leave.

Then came the knock. A loud, sudden bang against the door sent a jolt of terror through me.

I froze, my hand gripping the edge of the counter for support as my breath caught in my throat. It was too loud, too forceful—nothing like the polite knock of a neighbor or delivery person. Slowly, I turned toward the door, my legs shaking beneath me as I took a hesitant step forward. "Hello?" I called out, my voice trembling.

The knock came again, harder this time, followed by a low, guttural sound that made the hair on the back of my neck stand on end. Before I could react, the door splintered inward, the wood cracking like brittle ice as it flew off its hinges. I flew backwards, my back hitting the floor with a hard thump. A scream lodged in my throat as a dark figure emerged through the broken frame.

It wasn't human—not entirely. Its body was twisted, shadow-like tendrils writhing around its form as though it were barely contained. Its eyes glowed with an unnatural light, pale and menacing as they fixed on me. The air in the room seemed to grow colder, the shadows deepening around us as it stepped forward.

"You cannot stop it," the creature growled, hovering over me, its voice a chilling echo that reverberated through the room. "The darkness is coming. Carrow stirs, and soon, all will fall."

I backed away, my heart hammering so loudly I could barely hear its words. My apartment was a whirlwind of chaos—furniture overturned, glass shattering as the creature moved closer, its tendrils lashing out and tearing through the room like knives. My mind screamed at me to run, but my feet felt rooted to the spot, fear holding me captive.

The creature lunged, and instinct took over. I turned and bolted toward the door, stumbling over the debris as I scrambled outside. My breath came in ragged gasps, my vision blurred as I sprinted down the hall, the sound of the creature's pursuit close behind. Its guttural growls echoed off the walls, a sinister reminder that it wasn't far.

"Leave me alone!" I shouted, my voice cracking with desperation as I stumbled down the stairs, my only thought to escape. "Go away!" The piercing pain growing with every step.

The necklace around my neck began to glow faintly, its warmth pressing against my skin. I clutched it instinctively, the familiar sensation grounding me as I stumbled out onto the street. The creature followed, its shadowy form stretching unnaturally beneath the glow of the streetlights. It hissed, the sound like nails on a chalkboard, and I turned to face it, my chest heaving.

"Disappear!" I yelled, my voice shaking but loud enough to echo through the empty street.

The necklace flared to life, its glow intensifying until it bathed the entire street in brilliant light. The creature screamed, a sound of pure rage and agony, as the light enveloped it. Its shadowy form began to dissolve, the tendrils disintegrating into specks of ash that scattered in the wind. The glow grew brighter still, forcing me to shield my eyes until, finally, the street fell silent.

When I opened my eyes, the creature was gone. The necklace hung heavily around my neck, its light fading back to a faint shimmer. My knees buckled, and I sank to the pavement, trembling and gasping for air. The street was quiet again, eerily so, and the weight of what had just happened pressed down on me.

I didn't know what the necklace had done or why it had reacted the way it did, but one thing was clear: the darkness wasn't just coming—it was already here.

I sat there on the cold pavement, clutching the necklace tightly in my trembling hands as the world spun around me. My breaths came in ragged gasps, each one struggling to fill my lungs. The streetlights above cast pools of golden light across the deserted road, but they felt distant, too far away to offer any comfort. My heart pounded in my chest, the fading glow of the necklace still imprinted in my mind.

The silence was suddenly broken by a voice calling out my name. "Iris!"

It was sharp, urgent, and familiar. I turned my head sluggishly, my thoughts scattered like shards of glass. Luna. She was running toward me, her long hair whipping behind her as she sprinted down the street. Her voice carried a mixture of relief and panic, and I tried to focus, to pull myself back to reality.

When she reached me, Luna dropped to her knees, her hands immediately reaching out to steady me. "Oh my god, Iris," she breathed, her voice trembling as she scanned me from head to toe. "What happened? Are you hurt?"

I opened my mouth, but the words wouldn't come. My throat felt tight, my mind still reeling from what had just happened. My fingers clutched the necklace even tighter, as if letting go would invite the shadows back.

"Iris, talk to me," Luna said, her voice softer now but no less insistent. "I've been worried sick. You haven't answered your phone, and I didn't know if you were okay."

I forced myself to meet her eyes, the concern in them cutting through the fog in my mind. "I was… I was attacked," I managed to whisper, my voice shaking so badly that the words barely came out.

Luna's face paled, her hands gripping my arms firmly as though trying to anchor me. "Attacked? By who? What happened?"

I shook my head, unable to find the words to explain. How could I tell her about the creature, about the way it spoke of darkness and destruction, about the way it dissolved into ash under the glow of the necklace? It sounded impossible, even to me.

"Luna," I whispered, my voice breaking. "It—it destroyed everything."

Her eyes widened, a flicker of fear crossing her face before she masked it with determination. "You're coming with me," she said firmly, her tone leaving no room for argument. "We're not staying out here. We need to talk—somewhere safe."

I tried to protest, but the words caught in my throat, replaced by a fresh wave of terror as the memory of the shadows clawed at the edges of my mind. Luna didn't wait for me to respond. She helped me to my feet, her movements careful and steady, and wrapped her arm around my shoulders, holding me close.

"You're going to be okay," she murmured, her voice resolute even as her own fear crept in. "I promise. But we need to figure out what's going on—together."

As she guided me away from the wreckage of my apartment, the necklace pressed heavily against my chest, its faint warmth a reminder of the impossible light that had saved me.

The woods were eerily quiet as we approached the cabin, the towering trees casting long shadows across the forest floor. The cabin itself was small and unassuming, its wooden frame weathered with age but sturdy against the encroaching darkness. Luna walked ahead, her steps purposeful but not rushed, her gaze flicking back to me every so often to make sure I was still following.

"This place belonged to my family," Luna said as we reached the front steps. Her voice was steady, but I could hear the faint edge of tension beneath it. "It's safe here. No one knows about it."

I nodded, clutching the necklace around my neck tightly as my eyes darted around the clearing. Safe was what I needed, but something at the back of my mind was unsettled. The cabin felt welcoming enough, but the air seemed heavier here, charged with something I couldn't quite put into words. I pushed the thought aside. Luna had always looked out for me, and now, when I needed her most, she was here. I couldn't let paranoia cloud that.

Inside the cabin, the warmth of the space wrapped around me like a blanket. The small hearth burned softly, the scent of wood smoke filling the air. Luna moved toward the small kitchenette, her movements hurried but practiced as she pulled out mugs and filled them with something steaming.

"Here," she said, handing me a mug as she sat down across from me. "Drink this. It'll help."

The warmth of the mug seeped into my fingers, grounding me as I curled up on the worn couch. Luna sat opposite, her expression guarded, as though she were debating something. She looked nervous, her hands gripping the edge of the chair tightly enough that her knuckles turned white.

"Iris," she began, her voice softer now, tentative. "I need to tell you something."

I frowned, sitting up slightly as I studied her face. "What is it?" I asked, my voice quieter than I'd intended.

Luna opened her mouth to respond, but the faint sound of something outside interrupted her. A rustling, low and deliberate, like someone—or something—moving through the underbrush. I stiffened, the mug shaking slightly in my grip as adrenaline surged through my veins.

"What was that?" I whispered, my heart pounding.

Luna was on her feet in an instant, her hand outstretched toward me. "Iris, don't—"

But I was already moving. I set the mug down shakily and bolted for the door, my mind racing as I yanked it open and stepped into the cool night air. The forest stretched out before me, dark and endless, the shadows pooling at the edges of the trees. Luna followed close behind, her footsteps quick as she tried to catch up to me.

"Iris, wait!" she called, her voice sharp with worry.

I stopped abruptly, my breath catching as my gaze landed on a figure standing just beyond the clearing. It was Felix. His tall frame was silhouetted against the faint moonlight, his familiar presence cutting through the tension in my chest. He looked… shocked, his blue eyes wide as they darted between me and Luna.

"What are you doing here?" I asked, my voice breaking under the weight of both fear and relief.

Felix turned toward us slowly, his expression confused. "I could ask you the same," he replied, his voice steady but tinged with something uncertain. "I didn't expect to see you here."

Luna's hand found my arm, her grip firm as she stepped forward, her own expression clouded with a mix of worry and something unreadable. "Felix," she said carefully, her voice level but carrying an edge, "why are you out here?"

He hesitated, his gaze flicking between us as he studied the tension on our faces. "I was… looking for Iris," he admitted after a moment. "You weren't answering your phone, and I—" He paused, his jaw tightening briefly before he continued, "I didn't want to leave you alone, and I started walking until I got here…"

Something about his words—his presence, the concern etched into every inch of him—made my chest tighten. Luna's grip on my arm softened slightly, but she didn't let go, her attention fixed on Felix as though she were waiting for an explanation.

The three of us stood there in the clearing, the weight of the unspoken settling heavily around us. The shadows stretched, the faint rustling of leaves the only sound as the tension between us grew. I glanced at Felix, his blue eyes searching mine, and the unsettled feeling from earlier returned, stronger than ever.

Felix paced relentlessly across the clearing, his steps sharp and measured, his figure cutting through the stillness of the night like a restless shadow. His hand tangled repeatedly in his hair, the movement reflecting the storm raging in his mind. His face was alive with emotion—a volatile mix of shock, confusion, and something deeper, closer to fear. Every glance he threw at Luna and me was quick, almost desperate, as though he was trying to make sense of the impossible reality unfolding in front of him.

I stood rooted to the spot just outside the cabin, my arms folded tightly against myself, as if trying to guard against the piercing cold of the woods. My heart thundered in my chest, the disbelief flooding every corner of my being. Felix was here— standing just outside Luna's family cabin—and I couldn't begin to comprehend how or why.

"Felix," I finally managed, forcing the words through the knot in my throat. "How did you get here? This is Luna's family cabin."

He turned to face me, the desperation flashing in his sharp blue eyes striking me like a physical blow. His voice wavered as he answered, cracking under the weight of uncertainty. "Iris, love, I have no idea," he admitted, his gaze locking onto mine as though it was the only steady thing around him. "I was just thinking about finding you. That's all. And then—somehow—I ended up here."

Before I could even attempt to process his words, Luna scoffed audibly beside me, her stance shifting to one of skepticism as her arms crossed tightly over her chest. Her eyebrows arched high, her tone cutting as she echoed Felix. "Love?" she repeated incredulously, as though the term itself offended her.

I shot Luna a warning glare, desperate to hold her off from escalating things any further. My patience was already thin, but Luna had always been the type to push boundaries. "Luna, stop," I said firmly, my voice steady despite the chaos spiraling around us. "We've talked about this. You know I trust him."

Felix's pacing halted, and with a purposeful stride, he closed the space between us. His movements were swift and resolute, his presence intense as he addressed Luna directly. "She can trust me," he said, his voice unwavering and sharp. "But can she trust you? Have you told her who you really are?"

Luna's posture faltered. The confidence she had moments ago slipped away like water through her fingers. She stiffened under Felix's gaze, her brows furrowing deeply as unease clouded her features. Her lips pressed together in a thin line, her eyes darting between Felix and the ground, as though she were searching for some kind of escape.

"I should've known," Felix muttered under his breath, his sharp gaze narrowing as it fixed firmly on Luna. His voice dropped to a low, biting whisper, the accusation cutting through the tense silence like a blade. "You look just like her."

A sickening wave of confusion and dread crashed over me, rooting me to the spot. "Like who?" I asked, the trembling in my voice betraying my attempt to stay composed. "Felix, what are you talking about?"

Felix didn't answer immediately. Instead, he turned to me, his movements slow and deliberate, as though he was bracing himself for the impact of his next words. He rested a steady hand on my arm, the warmth of his touch grounding me in the moment. "Iris," he said softly, his tone coaxing but urgent. "Look around you. Doesn't this place feel familiar?"

I shifted my gaze to the towering trees that surrounded us, their shadows stretching long and dark against the faint moonlight. The clearing was bathed in muted silvers and grays, the forest carrying an almost haunting stillness. The soft, rhythmic sound of the river nearby reached my ears, a distant melody that stirred something deep in my chest. My heart seized as realization struck—the place was familiar, more familiar than I could rationally explain. I had been here before. I had seen it in my dreams, the dreams where Felix first appeared to me.

I turned to Luna slowly, my stomach twisting as disbelief etched itself into every fiber of my being. "You knew," I whispered, my voice barely audible against the weight of the revelation. "You knew all of this—the cabin, the forest, Felix—you knew it all along, didn't you?"

Luna flinched, her defenses crumbling further as her gaze dropped to the ground. "Iris, listen to me," she said cautiously, raising her hands as if to pacify me. "Remember I told you there was something I needed to tell you? It's all connected—to this place, to the curse, to you."

"She's a witch," Felix interrupted, his voice sharp and resolute. The word cut through Luna's attempt at explanation, slamming into me with all the weight of a truth too big to ignore.

I froze, the breath leaving my lungs as the revelation settled heavily in my mind. A witch. Luna was a witch. My grip on reality felt dangerously thin, as anger and betrayal swelled uncontrollably in my chest. "Luna," I said slowly, my voice shaking despite my attempt at control, "is it true? Are you... a witch?"

Luna's shoulders dropped, defeat flickering across her expression as she nodded hesitantly. "Yes," she said quietly, her words heavy with regret. "I'm a descendant of the witch who worked with the Hart family—the one tied to the curse. My family has carried this legacy for generations. I'm trying to end it, to break the curse once and for all."

The anger bubbling inside me exploded into words I couldn't hold back. "And you didn't think to tell me?" I snapped, stepping back as betrayal hardened my voice. "You've been hiding this from me? Helping me while keeping the truth hidden? Does Jayce even know?"

"No," Luna said quickly, shaking her head. "Jayce doesn't know either. I've kept it hidden from everyone because I didn't want people to see me differently. But everything I've done has been for you—to protect you, to help you end this."

My chest tightened further, the bitterness in my throat making it impossible to hold back. "And Felix?" I said sharply, motioning toward him. "You thought he was the enemy, didn't you? You thought he'd try to stop you?"

Luna hesitated, her gaze darting briefly to Felix before she sighed. "I didn't know his intentions," she admitted. "I thought he might try to interfere, but…"

"But I want the curse broken too," Felix said, his voice steady as he interrupted her. His sharp gaze fixed firmly on Luna, the weight of his conviction clear in every word. "I want this to end—for Iris, for myself. You think this hasn't been a prison for me, Luna? I've been tied to this for longer than you can imagine. If you're trying to end it, then I'm with you."

The tension in the clearing was suffocating, every unspoken word pressing down on us like an invisible force. Luna's defensiveness melted further, her posture softening as she studied Felix with reluctant understanding. The fear in her expression shifted, replaced by quiet resolution.

"Iris," Luna said finally, her voice softer as she turned to me. "I'm sorry. For not telling you sooner. For keeping this from you."

I swallowed hard, my emotions swirling too fast to grasp. But the sincerity in her voice pierced through the anger, forcing me to consider what lay beneath her words. "No more secrets," I said firmly, glancing between both of them. "If we're going to do this, we need to do it together. All of us. That means no more lies."

Felix nodded, the steadiness in his gaze making something in me shift. Luna followed, her relief evident as she reached tentatively toward me. The three of us stood there, the impossible weight of the curse pressing down heavily on our shoulders. But for the first time, hope stirred beneath it—a fragile, fleeting hope that maybe, just maybe, we could end this. Together.

"We need to talk to Jayce," I said, my voice steady despite the uncertainty swirling in my chest.

"Agreed," Luna replied quickly, her tone resolute as she reached for my hand. Her grip was warm and reassuring, grounding me in a way I hadn't realized I needed. I glanced at her, grateful for the silent strength she always seemed to carry, even when everything felt like it was falling apart.

The park stretched out in quiet serenity, its paths winding through patches of grass bathed in the golden light of late afternoon. The fountain gurgled softly behind us, the sound blending with the faint rustle of leaves swaying in the breeze. Though the world around us felt calm, the tension within our small group was impossible to ignore. We were gathered near the edge of the fountain, the urgency of why we were here hanging heavily between us.

Jayce leaned casually against the fountain's rim, his arms crossed as he glanced between us, the sharp frown on his face betraying his confusion. "What's going on?" he asked, his voice edged with impatience. "You said this was urgent, but I don't even know what this is about."

Luna exchanged a quick look with me and Felix, her hesitance clear as she fiddled with the edge of her sleeve. Her determination to see this through was stronger than the nerves she felt; I could see it in the way she straightened her shoulders. She took a deep breath before finally turning to Jayce. "I need to tell you something," she said quietly.

Jayce raised an eyebrow, his gaze sharpening. "What is it?"

Luna paused for a moment, her knuckles white as she gripped her sleeve. "I'm… a witch," she said, her voice soft but resolute. "I'm a descendant of the witch who worked with the Hart family—the one tied to the curse. It's my family's legacy, and I've been trying to break it."

Jayce stared at her, stunned into silence. His arms fell to his sides as he tried to process her words, disbelief etched into every line of his face. "You're what?" he asked finally, his voice rising with incredulity. "You're saying you're a witch? How— how is that even possible?"

Luna didn't flinch at his tone. She simply nodded, her determination unwavering despite his reaction. "It's true. My family has carried this legacy for generations, and I've kept it hidden—for obvious reasons. But this curse… it needs to end. That's why I've been helping Iris."

Jayce glanced at me, his eyes searching for some sort of explanation, confirmation that what she was saying wasn't as impossible as it sounded. "Iris?" he asked, his voice softer now. "Did you know about this?"

I nodded reluctantly, my fingers brushing against the necklace at my throat as I tried to ground myself. "Yes, I knew," I admitted, my voice steady but heavy. "She told me last night."

"And you didn't think to tell me?" Jayce asked, his frustration laced with disbelief.

"I didn't think it mattered at the time," I replied, my voice growing firmer. "But it's not just that. There's something else I need to tell you. Something happened to me last night."

Felix, who had been standing quietly beside me, instantly stiffened. His sharp blue eyes darted toward me, his brows pulling together in alarm. "What do you mean 'something happened'?" he demanded, his voice low but tense.

I exhaled, glancing between them. "I was attacked," I said quietly, the words heavy as they left my mouth.

Jayce's eyes widened in disbelief. Felix, on the other hand, took a step closer, his posture rigid with barely contained anger. "Attacked?" he echoed sharply. "By whom? And you didn't think to tell me?"

"It wasn't a person," I said quickly, shaking my head. "It was—it was something else. Something shadow-like. It destroyed my apartment, Felix. I barely made it out alive."

Felix's jaw clenched, his fingers curling into fists as he paced a few steps away, then back again. "Iris," he said, his voice rising slightly, "why didn't you tell me sooner? You should've called me immediately!"

Luna placed a calming hand on my arm, her touch light but grounding. "Felix, let her finish," she said, her tone steady but edged with a hint of authority. "This is bigger than any of us thought. It's why we went to the cabin."

I glanced at her, thankful for the reprieve, then continued. "The necklace… it did something. When I told the creature to leave, it started glowing—brighter than it's ever been. The light—it completely disintegrated the shadow. That's why I went to Luna's family cabin. I needed somewhere safe."

Jayce stepped forward, his expression stunned as he tried to process my words. "The necklace," he murmured, his eyes flicking toward the faintly shimmering pendant at my throat. "It reacted?"

"Yes," I said, nodding. "It saved me."

Felix, however, wasn't as calm. His pacing grew more frantic, his hands running through his hair as frustration simmered beneath his sharp gaze. "This is exactly why you shouldn't be alone," he said, his voice cracking under the weight of his emotions. "I told you, Iris. You're not safe out there."

"Felix—" I started, but he cut me off.

"You shouldn't have gone home," he continued, his tone harsher now. "You should've stayed at the mansion. With me. This wouldn't have happened if you'd listened!"

I felt my own frustration flare, the heat of his words stoking the embers of my own anger. "Felix, stop," I said firmly, stepping toward him. "I need you to step away for a moment. We need to talk."

Felix hesitated, his chest rising and falling heavily as he met my gaze. His jaw tightened, but after a tense moment, he nodded and followed me a few paces away, leaving Jayce and Luna by the fountain. The air between us crackled with unspoken tension, his restless energy palpable as he turned to me.

"Iris," he started, his voice calmer but still laced with urgency. "You should've told me. You shouldn't have tried to handle this on your own."

He took a deep breath, his voice quieter now but still filled with urgency. "I'm just trying to keep you safe."

"I know that," I replied, my voice shaking. "But you can't keep treating me like I'm fragile. I can't hide forever, Felix. I need to figure this out, and I need you to trust me."

Felix's hands dropped to his sides, his shoulders slumping slightly as he stared at me. "I'm not trying to treat you like you're fragile," he said softly, his voice breaking. "I'm trying to protect you because I can't lose you. I can't, Iris."

The vulnerability in his voice hit me like a tidal wave, washing away my frustration and replacing it with something deeper. I took a step closer, my breath catching as his blue eyes met mine.

"I love you," Felix said suddenly, the words raw and unfiltered. "I've loved you since the moment I met you. And that's why I'm terrified. Because you mean everything to me."

The weight of his confession struck me with all the force of a tidal wave, leaving me momentarily breathless. My heart fluttered wildly, a sudden rush of warmth spreading through my chest as his words sank in. *I love you.* The three simple words echoed in my mind, filling the spaces between my doubts and fears. It was like everything had shifted in that instant, the air charged with something fragile yet profound. Butterflies stirred in my stomach, their fluttering chaos unsettling but strangely exhilarating. I had imagined this moment—wondered, hoped— but hearing it from him? It left me speechless.

Felix's sharp blue eyes stayed locked on mine, unguarded and filled with an earnest vulnerability that made my pulse race. I felt myself struggle to form words, my cheeks warming as the weight of his gaze held me captive. "Felix," I began, my voice barely above a whisper, "I…"

He stepped closer, his hand reaching for mine. The warmth of his fingers sent shivers through me as they curled gently around mine, grounding me in the moment. His touch was steady, reassuring, but the depth in his expression left me feeling small and shy. I swallowed hard, my lips trembling as the truth I'd been holding in finally tumbled out. "I… I love you too," I confessed, my voice so quiet I wasn't sure he'd even heard me.

For a heartbeat, Felix didn't move, his sharp gaze locked on mine as though time itself had paused. Then, his lips curved into a genuine smile, the kind that softened the edges of his usually intense features and made him look impossibly kind. Relief flooded his expression, mixed with something deeper—a quiet joy that made the butterflies in my stomach flutter even harder. His hand tightened slightly around mine, grounding me further as his smile lingered, warm and unwavering.

"We'll do this together," Felix said softly, his voice steady but carrying an undeniable tenderness now. The simple word felt like a promise, unshakable and full of meaning.

When we returned to the group, the air between us had shifted subtly, the unspoken connection lingering like a thread tying us together. The weight of the alliance settled heavily on our shoulders as Luna and Jayce waited for us by the fountain. It wasn't going to be easy—none of it would be—but as we stood there, united, I felt a quiet certainty begin to bloom. Together, we had a chance to face the darkness. Together, we could fight it.

CHAPTER XX

Blood for Balance

The mansion felt colder than ever, despite the warmth that radiated from the crackling fireplace in the sitting room. The shadows that danced along the ornate wallpaper seemed heavier, darker, as though they were lingering too long in the corners of the room. Felix stood near the far window, his back rigid, his blue eyes trained on the fading light beyond the glass. Luna had positioned herself at the center table, pouring over her journal with meticulous care, the yellowed pages spread across the surface like maps to a destination none of us wanted to reach. Jayce leaned against the wall, his arms crossed tightly, his face etched with a tension that bordered on anger. I sat closest to the fireplace, my fingers curled loosely around the necklace at my throat, its warmth pulsing faintly against my skin.

It had been hours since we arrived at the mansion. Hours of deciphering records, combing through pages that were barely legible, chasing threads that seemed to lead to nowhere. But now, as Luna lifted her gaze from the journal to meet mine, I knew the search had taken a dark turn.

"There's a cost," Luna said quietly, her voice steady despite the tremor in her hands. She didn't look at Jayce, as though she knew his expression would only add weight to the confession. "To break the curse."

The air in the room seemed to grow heavier, pressing against my chest as her words settled over us. My pulse quickened, the faint warmth of the necklace doing little to calm the unease that had begun to spread. "What kind of cost?" I asked, my voice barely above a whisper.

Luna hesitated, her fingers brushing against the edges of the journal as she glanced at Felix, then Jayce, before finally returning her focus to me. "A life," she said simply. "The curse was sealed with a life, and it can only be undone with one."

For a moment, the room fell into silence, the crackle of the fire the only sound as the weight of her revelation pressed down on us. Felix turned abruptly, his blue eyes blazing as he took a step forward. "No," he said sharply, his voice cutting through the quiet. "There has to be another way."

"There isn't," Luna replied, her tone firm but edged with regret. "I've searched every record in my family's archives. The only way to break the curse is to offer a life in exchange."

Jayce uncrossed his arms, stepping away from the wall with frustration written across every line of his face. "And you're just telling us this now?" he demanded, his voice rising. "After everything, after you've been keeping secrets about being a witch, now you tell us the only solution is sacrifice? What else aren't you telling us, Luna?"

Luna flinched, her expression tightening as she turned to face him. "I told you everything I know," she said defensively, her voice trembling. "I didn't want to believe it either, Jayce. But the records are clear. This curse—it wasn't just a spell. It was bound with blood, and it can only be undone the same way."

Jayce scoffed, shaking his head as he ran a hand through his hair. "Convenient," he muttered bitterly. "And who exactly is supposed to pay this price? Have you decided that already too?"

Luna's gaze dropped to the journal, her silence louder than any answer she could have given. Felix stiffened beside me, his jaw tightening as he took another step forward. "The Hart descendant," he said darkly, his tone low and filled with unspoken fury. "Is that what you're saying?"

Luna met his gaze reluctantly, her voice barely audible as she replied, "Yes."

All eyes turned to me, the weight of their stares suffocating. My chest tightened, my fingers trembling slightly as I clutched the necklace closer. The air felt impossibly thick, every breath a struggle as the enormity of her words settled over me. "You mean me," I said finally, my voice hollow.

Felix crossed the space between us in an instant, his hands gripping my arms as he knelt in front of me. "You're not doing this," he said firmly, his blue eyes locked on mine. "I won't let you, Iris."

Jayce slammed his hand against the edge of the table, the sound echoing through the room. "How are we supposed to make this kind of choice?" he demanded, his voice shaking with frustration. "We're talking about sacrificing someone. This isn't something we can just decide!"

"There is no choice," Felix snapped, his voice rising as he turned to glare at Jayce. "Iris isn't doing this. End of story."

"That's not your call to make," Jayce shot back, his tone sharp. "You're not the one tied to this curse."

"You think this curse hasn't affected me?" Felix spat, his voice cracking. "You think I don't know what it means to suffer because of it?"

Before I could interrupt, Luna's voice cut through the tension. "Enough!" she snapped, slamming her hands down on the journal. "None of this is Felix's fault—or Iris's! We're here because of Carrow, because of the curse. This isn't about blame, Jayce."

Jayce's glare shifted toward her, his frustration spilling out unchecked. "And you? You've known about all of this—been keeping secrets—and now you want to act like you're the authority on what we should do? How am I supposed to trust anything you say?"

Luna straightened, her expression hardening. "I didn't tell you because I didn't want you dragged into this. Do you think I wanted you to have to make choices like this? If you knew, you would've been in danger—"

"I'm in danger now!" Jayce shot back. "Because of everything you hid. And don't pretend you were doing this for me. This has always been about your family and fixing what they broke."

The tension between them crackled, thick and unbearable, as Luna stepped forward, her voice quieter but no less intense. "You're angry, and I understand that," she said. "But I didn't do this to hurt you. I did this to protect you."

"Well, it didn't work, did it?" Jayce muttered, turning away as he ran a hand through his hair again.

Before Luna could respond, Felix's voice broke through, softer but firm. "Iris," he said, turning his attention back to me. His blue eyes searched mine, his tone trembling slightly. "Please—"

"I don't know what to do," I interrupted, my words breaking under the weight of my emotions. "I don't know how to make this choice. But if breaking the curse is the only way to stop Carrow..."

"No," Felix said quickly, his voice hardening again. "We'll find another way. I won't let you sacrifice yourself."

Luna stepped forward cautiously, her expression heavy with regret. "There isn't another way," she said softly. "I wish there were, but the curse—it demands balance. It was made with blood, and it can only be undone the same way."

Felix clenched his fists, his frustration evident in every line of his posture. "Then I'll do it," he said suddenly, his voice steady but filled with determination. "If a life is required, take mine."

I froze, my heart lurching as his words hung in the air. "Felix, no," I whispered, my voice breaking. "You can't—"

"I can," he replied, his blue eyes softening as he turned to me. "I would do anything to protect you, Iris. Anything."

Tears pricked at the corners of my eyes, the ache in my chest unbearable as I stared at him. The weight of his offer settled heavily over me, compounding the impossible choice that had already threatened to break me. Luna and Jayce stood in tense silence, their expressions torn between disbelief and grief.

The fire crackled softly in the hearth, its warmth a distant comfort as the reality of the curse pressed down on us. A life. A sacrifice. And as I looked at Felix, his resolve clear, the necklace pulsing faintly against my skin, I knew there was no escaping this decision. It would demand more from us than we were ready to give.

The room felt impossibly heavy, the crackle of the fire doing little to ease the suffocating tension that filled the air. Felix stood in front of me, his sharp blue eyes unwavering, his jaw set with fierce determination. His words echoed in my head, impossibly bold, impossibly selfless: *If a life is required, take mine.*

It was as though the world had stopped for a moment, every sound drowned out by the thundering of my heartbeat. My fingers trembled around the necklace at my throat, the warmth of it pulsing faintly as if trying to anchor me. Luna froze where she stood, her hand resting on the open journal, her expression torn between shock and frustration. Jayce let out a sharp exhale, his disbelief radiating through the room as he stared at Felix.

"You can't do this," I said finally, my voice breaking under the weight of my emotions. "Felix, it doesn't work like that."

Felix's gaze softened as it landed on me, but his resolve didn't waver. "It has to," he said firmly, his voice steady. "I'm not letting you sacrifice yourself, Iris. If there's even a chance—"

"There's not," Luna interrupted, her tone cutting but not unkind. She stepped forward, gripping the edge of the journal as her eyes narrowed at Felix. "The curse makes you immortal. Don't you get it? Even if you wanted to, you couldn't sacrifice yourself. The curse won't allow it."

Felix stiffened, his lips pressing into a thin line as his jaw tightened. For the first time, his confidence seemed to falter, a flicker of doubt crossing his expression. "That can't be true," he said, his voice quieter but still insistent. "There has to be a way for me to—"

"There isn't," Luna said, her voice rising with frustration. "The curse keeps you bound. It won't let you die. That's part of the reason you've suffered for so long."

Jayce let out a humorless laugh from where he stood. "Immortal," he muttered, shaking his head. "Great. So not only do you want to throw yourself on the sword, but it wouldn't even do anything? That's just perfect."

Felix shot him a glare, his frustration sparking like a live wire. "Do you think I want this?" he snapped, his voice sharp. "You think I enjoy being tied to this curse, knowing what it's done—to me, to her, to everyone?"

"Then stop pretending you're the hero who can fix it all," Jayce retorted, his tone bitter. "Because clearly, you can't."

"That's enough!" Luna interjected, her voice commanding as she stepped between them. "This isn't about you two fighting over who gets to play the martyr. This is about the curse—and Iris."

At her words, Felix's anger seemed to shift, his focus returning to me. His expression softened, but the desperation in his eyes hadn't faded. "Iris," he said quietly, "we can find another way. There has to be something we're missing."

I shook my head, my chest tightening as I looked at him. "Felix, you heard Luna," I said softly. "Even if you could, it wouldn't work. The curse doesn't work that way."

"But there has to be another way," he insisted, his voice breaking slightly. "I can't lose you, Iris. I can't."

The raw vulnerability in his voice cut through me, making my breath hitch. I reached out, my hand brushing against his arm, grounding him just enough to still his restless energy. "I'm not going anywhere," I said firmly, my voice trembling but resolute. "Not yet. We'll figure this out."

Felix stared at me for a long moment, his blue eyes searching mine as though trying to find reassurance in the chaos. Slowly, he nodded, though the tension in his shoulders didn't fully ease.

Jayce let out another exhale, leaning heavily against the wall as he raked a hand through his hair. "This whole thing is insane," he muttered. "Sacrifices, immortality, curses. How do we even fight something like this?"

"We don't have all the answers yet," Luna said, her tone softer now as she looked between him and me. "But we need to keep looking. There has to be a way to break this without losing anyone."

"And if there isn't?" Jayce asked, his voice quieter now, almost resigned.

Luna's gaze flickered to me, then Felix, her expression unreadable. "Then we'll cross that bridge when we get there," she said finally. "But for now, we plan. We don't give up."

The fire crackled faintly in the hearth, the only sound in the room as her words settled over us. The weight of the curse, of the impossible choice we might have to make, pressed down on all of us like a storm waiting to break. And as I looked at Felix, his resolve was unwavering despite everything, and I felt the ache in my chest deepen.

We were running out of time, and the cost of breaking the curse was greater than any of us was ready to face.

The mansion had grown quiet, the tension that had consumed us earlier lingering like an unseen shadow. The fire in the hearth had burned low, its embers casting faint orange glows across the sitting room. Felix had retreated to the farthest corner, his back turned as he stared out the window, lost in thought. Jayce had taken refuge in the armchair closest to the door, his frustration evident in the way he leaned forward, elbows on his knees, his hands clasped tightly as though holding back the storm inside him.

I stood near the fireplace, staring into the smoldering embers, my mind swirling with the impossible choice that loomed ahead. Luna's voice broke through the silence, hesitant yet steady.

"Iris," she said softly, her voice just loud enough to pull me from my thoughts. "Can we talk?"

I turned toward her, surprised by the vulnerability in her tone. She stood near the doorway, her hands clasped in front of her, her gaze flickering between me and the floor as though she was afraid to meet my eyes.

"Of course," I replied, though the unease in my chest grew. I followed her as she led me down the hallway, the ornate patterns on the walls blurring together as my thoughts remained focused on Luna's unusual behavior. She stopped at a small alcove near the grand staircase, where the light from the chandelier overhead illuminated the space in a soft, golden glow.

Luna hesitated, her back turned to me as she stared at the intricate carvings on the banister. When she finally turned to face me, her expression was heavy with something I couldn't quite place—regret, sadness, perhaps both.

"Iris," she began, her voice trembling slightly, "I need to tell you something. Something I've been carrying for a long time."

I frowned, the unease twisting tighter in my chest as I nodded for her to continue. "What is it?"

She took a deep breath, her gaze flickering to the floor as though the words were too heavy to speak while looking at me. "When I first met you," she said quietly, "I didn't become your friend because I wanted to. I… I did it because you're a Hart."

Her confession hit me like a physical blow, my breath catching as her words sank in. "What?" I asked, my voice barely audible.

Luna's shoulders sank, her hands trembling slightly as she clasped them tighter. "My family has carried the pain of the curse for generations," she explained, her voice breaking. "And I blamed the Harts for all of it. I thought… I thought if I could get close to you, I could find a way to take revenge. To make your family pay for everything mine has endured."

The ache in my chest deepened, a sharp mix of anger and betrayal surging through me. "Luna," I said, forcing the words out despite the lump rising in my throat, "you used me?"

She flinched, tears pooling in her eyes as she shook her head. "That's how it started," she admitted, her voice cracking. "But it didn't take long for me to see who you really are. You're not like the rest of the Harts, Iris. You're kind, genuine, brave… Everything I didn't expect. And I realized I didn't want revenge anymore. I wanted to help you."

Her words hung in the air, and for a moment, I didn't know how to respond. The betrayal stung, but there was something raw and honest about her confession that tugged at my heart. I could see the pain in her eyes, the guilt she carried, the way she struggled to meet my gaze.

"I'm so sorry," Luna whispered, tears spilling down her cheeks as she buried her face in her hands. "I never wanted to hurt you. I never wanted you to feel like you were being used. But I understand if you hate me now. If you don't want to trust me anymore."

I stood frozen, my heart aching at the sight of her falling apart in front of me. She had carried this secret for so long, hiding it even as we grew closer, even as she stood by my side. Slowly, I reached out, my hand brushing against her shoulder, grounding her just enough for her to lift her tear-streaked face toward me.

"I don't hate you, Luna," I said softly, my voice trembling. "You hurt me, yes, but I can see how much you regret it. And I believe you—about wanting to help. You've been there for me in ways no one else has. That means something."

Luna blinked, her tears continuing to fall as she stared at me in disbelief. "You forgive me?" she asked, her voice barely above a whisper.

I nodded, the knot in my chest loosening slightly as I offered her the faintest of smiles. "I forgive you," I said. "But no more secrets, okay? If we're going to get through this, we have to trust each other completely."

Her expression crumbled into something resembling relief, and she nodded furiously, her trembling hands wiping at her cheeks. "Okay," she said, her voice breaking. "No more secrets. I promise."

We stood there in the alcove, the golden light wrapping around us as Luna's tears slowly dried, and the tension between us began to ease. I felt the bond of our friendship strengthen in that moment, forged in truth and vulnerability. Whatever lay ahead—whatever the curse demanded—I knew Luna and I would face it together.

The fire in the sitting room burned low, its soft light flickering across the shadowed walls of the mansion as the atmosphere shifted once more. The tension had eased slightly after Luna's heartfelt confession, but the looming weight of the curse and the unanswered questions kept us on edge. Felix leaned against the farthest corner of the room, his sharp gaze fixed on the window, while Jayce paced, his frustration simmering beneath the surface. Luna sat at the table, her hands resting lightly on the journal, her eyes occasionally flicking toward me. I stood near the hearth, the warmth of the necklace grounding me as I tried to gather my thoughts.

"We need a plan," Luna said suddenly, her voice steady despite the tremor of exhaustion in her tone. She straightened in her chair, pulling the journal closer as her gaze shifted between all of us. "We're running out of time, and Carrow's influence is growing. If we don't act soon, the curse will consume everything."

Jayce stopped pacing, turning toward her with a sharp expression. "Act how?" he asked, his voice clipped. "The only 'plan' we've heard so far involves sacrificing someone, and I don't think any of us are ready to make that kind of decision."

Luna sighed, her shoulders sinking slightly as she met his gaze. "I know," she said softly. "But we can't afford to waste time arguing. We need to figure out what the curse is doing—how Carrow is connected—and if there's any way to weaken him before we make the ultimate decision."

Felix turned from the window, his blue eyes narrowing as he stepped closer. "You said the curse reacts to balance," he said, his tone thoughtful but tense. "If that's true, then Carrow's power must have a source. Something that anchors it."

Luna nodded, her attention shifting back to the journal. "That's what I've been trying to figure out," she admitted. "The records mention Carrow's connection to the witch who created the curse. Her lifeblood was used to bind him, but there are hints of something else—something deeper. If we can find that, maybe we can break the curse without a sacrifice."

Jayce crossed his arms, his frustration giving way to curiosity as he leaned closer. "And where exactly do we start looking for this 'deeper connection'?" he asked. "The witch is long gone, and Carrow isn't exactly handing out clues."

"There's a place," Luna said after a moment, her voice quieter now. She hesitated, her gaze flickering to Felix before landing on me. "It's tied to the curse—the site where the binding took place. It's dangerous, but if we go there, we might find answers."

Felix's jaw tightened, his posture straightening as he stared at her. "You think going to the source of the curse is a good idea?" he asked, his tone sharp. "Carrow's power will be strongest there. If we're wrong about this…"

"I know it's a risk," Luna replied firmly, her tone unwavering. "But it's the only lead we have."

Jayce exhaled sharply, running a hand through his hair as he paced again. "Of course it is," he muttered under his breath. "It's always the dangerous places with you, Luna."

Luna shot him a pointed look, her frustration resurfacing. "You can sit here and sulk, or you can help us figure this out," she said, her voice tense but steady. "Your choice."

Jayce stopped pacing, his glare softening slightly as he turned toward her. "I'm here," he said after a moment, his voice quieter now. "Don't act like I'm not."

The tension between them crackled, but Luna's gaze softened just enough for her attention to shift back to the journal. "If we're going to do this, we need to prepare," she said finally. "The binding site is deep in the forest, near the old river. Carrow's influence will be strongest there, so we'll need the necklace to counteract it. And Jayce..." Her gaze flickered toward him. "We'll need your protection."

Jayce nodded, though his expression remained guarded. "Fine," he said. "But if this goes sideways..."

"We'll handle it," Felix interrupted, his voice steady but laced with tension. He turned to me, his blue eyes softening slightly as they met mine. "Iris, are you sure about this?"

I took a deep breath, the necklace warming against my skin as I nodded. "If it gets us answers," I said softly, "it's worth the risk."

The fire crackled faintly, the shadows flickering as the weight of the decision settled over us. Together, we would face the curse's source, confront Carrow's influence, and uncover the truth behind the binding. The path ahead was treacherous, but with Luna's knowledge, Felix's resolve, Jayce's strength, and the necklace's power, I knew we had a chance—a slim, fleeting chance to end this nightmare once and for all.

The hours that followed were a blur of preparation. The mansion echoed with the sound of quiet footsteps and hushed voices as we gathered supplies and pieced together everything we knew. Luna focused intently on her journal, flipping through the pages with a precision that hinted at her determination. Jayce disappeared briefly before returning with a sturdy flashlight and a small bag that clanked faintly, likely holding supplies to defend us in case of trouble. Felix stayed near me, his protective energy unwavering as he watched my movements with an intensity that left my heart aching.

"We'll leave at dawn," Luna said as she leaned against the table, her finger tracing the map sketched across one of the journal's pages. "The binding site is deep in the forest, near the old river. The path isn't easy—it's overgrown, and the closer we get to the site, the more likely Carrow's influence will try to stop us."

Jayce scoffed softly, his arms crossed as he leaned against the wall. "Great. So we're walking straight into a cursed heartland with no clue what we're going to find."

"Not no clue," Luna replied sharply, her gaze snapping to him. "We know Carrow's power will be strongest there. We know the necklace reacts to him. And we know it's the only place that might give us answers."

Jayce's lips twitched into something close to a smirk, but the frustration in his voice was clear. "Sounds like a solid plan."

Luna clenched her jaw, her knuckles white where they gripped the journal. "If you're so ready to give up, then don't come," she said, her tone low but biting. "But if you want to do something useful, stop acting like everything is doomed before we even try."

Jayce's expression darkened, his frustration spilling out unchecked. "Oh, I'm here, Luna," he said bitterly. "I just don't like walking blindly into a trap."

Luna stepped closer, her voice dropping as she stared him down. "Then maybe you should've asked about the curse earlier instead of assuming you didn't need to know."

Jayce opened his mouth to respond, but Felix's voice cut through their argument like a blade. "Enough," he said sharply, his tone commanding. His blue eyes flicked briefly to Luna and Jayce, their tension thick and crackling, before turning toward me. "We don't have time for this."

Luna exhaled, her shoulders sagging slightly as she stepped back. Jayce huffed softly but didn't say anything further, his glare fixed on the floor as he turned away. The room fell into silence again, the weight of their argument lingering like an unseen force.

I glanced toward Luna, her expression tight as she refocused on the journal. "Are you sure about this?" I asked softly, breaking the quiet.

She looked up, her gaze meeting mine for a moment before nodding. "It's the only lead we have," she said, her voice steady despite the exhaustion etched across her features. "If we don't act now, the curse will keep getting stronger, and Carrow will become unstoppable."

Felix stepped closer to me, placing my hand in his. His sharp gaze softening slightly as he studied my face. "You don't have to do this," he said quietly, his voice low enough that only I could hear. "We can find another way."

I shook my head, my fingers brushing against the necklace at my throat as its warmth pulsed faintly against my skin. "If we don't try," I said softly, "we'll lose what little chance we have."

Felix's jaw tightened, but he didn't argue. He stepped back, his presence steady and grounding as we turned our attention back to the journal and the map Luna had drawn.

The hours passed, and dawn arrived too quickly. The faint light of morning crept through the mansion's windows, casting long shadows across the grand halls. We gathered in the entryway, our supplies packed, and our purpose as strong as it could be despite the uncertainty ahead.

Luna adjusted the strap of her bag, her movements precise as she glanced at each of us. "Are we all ready?" she asked, her voice steady but edged with tension.

Jayce nodded, though his expression remained guarded. Felix's blue eyes lingered on me, his protective energy unwavering as he placed a reassuring hand on my shoulder. "We'll be right here," he said softly.

I nodded, my fingers tightening around the necklace as its warmth steadied me. The weight of the journey ahead pressed heavily on my chest, but I knew we couldn't afford to hesitate. Together, we stepped out into the cool morning air, the forest stretching before us like a labyrinth of shadows.

The path to the binding site would test every bond, every ounce of strength we had left. But as we walked forward, the faint pulse of the necklace against my skin reminded me of one thing: we still had hope.

The forest enveloped us as we pressed forward, the overgrown path winding deeper into its twisted depths. The towering trees above blocked out nearly all light, their interwoven branches clawing at the crimson sky that loomed ominously overhead. Shadows grew thicker with every step, stretching unnaturally across the ground as though trying to pull us back. The air itself felt alive, charged with an energy that buzzed faintly against my skin. The pulse of the necklace grew stronger with each passing moment, syncing to the thundering rhythm of my heart.

Felix walked ahead of me, his sharp gaze scanning every corner, every flicker of movement in the underbrush. I could see the tension in his shoulders, the protective stance he'd adopted since we began this journey. Luna moved with purpose just behind me, clutching her journal tightly, her focus unwavering despite the unease etched across her face. Jayce trailed behind, his flashlight slicing through the oppressive darkness, his jaw clenched as his frustration battled his determination.

The path grew treacherous the closer we came to the binding site. The gnarled roots twisted and rose from the ground like skeletal fingers, while the brambles snagged at our clothes with every step. The sound of the river—which had been soft and melodic in the distance—now roared like a beast, the water churning and surging as though consumed by the same wrath that painted the sky above. I forced myself to keep moving, even as the coldness seeped into my bones and the faint warmth of the necklace wavered.

As the clearing came into view, the air shifted sharply, growing heavier and colder than ever. The towering trees around us seemed to lean inward, their warped and claw-like branches forming an almost impenetrable barrier. At the center of the clearing stood the altar—a massive stone relic worn with age, its surface cracked and etched with ancient symbols that shimmered faintly in the blood-red light.

Felix stopped abruptly, his arm outstretched to block my path. "We're here," he said, his voice low but sharp with tension. He turned toward the clearing, his sharp blue eyes narrowing as he scanned the space ahead. "And something's waiting for us."

I followed his gaze, and my breath caught in my throat. The sky above the clearing was alive with shadowy forms, twisting and writhing like smoke caught in a storm. The red light pulsated ominously, casting long, shifting shadows across the warped trees that encircled the space. The river gleamed black as pitch, its surface unnaturally still, as if bracing for something to rise from its depths.

"This is it," Luna said, stepping beside me. Her voice trembled slightly, but her determination didn't waver. "This is where the curse began."

Jayce pushed past us, his flashlight cutting across the altar as his gaze darted around the clearing. "So, what now?" he asked, his tone biting. "We just stand here and hope for a miracle?"

A low, guttural sound rumbled through the clearing, cutting through the eerie silence. The ground trembled beneath us, cracks splintering out from the edges of the altar. The shadows above twisted violently, coiling together before plunging into the earth. The river rippled suddenly, sending waves lapping against the shore, though no wind disturbed the surface.

And then, it emerged—a figure shrouded in darkness that writhed and shifted like living smoke. Its towering form was skeletal and grotesque, its limbs impossibly long, its molten gold eyes piercing through the gloom. Every step it took split the earth beneath it, the ground itself seeming to reject its presence.

Carrow's manifestation.

My pulse thundered as I stumbled back, the heat of the necklace against my skin rising sharply, almost unbearably. Felix moved in front of me without hesitation, his body taut, his stance defensive. "Stay behind me," he ordered, his voice low but steady.

The creature's voice was an echoing chorus, layered and distorted, sending chills down my spine. "You should not have come here," it said, its golden eyes narrowing. "The curse cannot be broken. It is eternal."

"We didn't come here to leave," Luna shot back, stepping forward as she clutched the journal tightly. Her voice was steady, though the fear in her eyes betrayed her. "We came to end this. To stop you."

The creature snarled, the sound reverberating through the clearing like the growl of a monstrous beast. Shadows spilled from its form, stretching across the clearing and clawing toward us. The air grew colder still, and the red sky above darkened further, streaks of black spilling across its surface like a plague.

Jayce moved quickly, pulling salt from his bag and scattering it in a sharp line across the ground. "Keep it back," he said sharply, his voice commanding as he darted around the edges of the clearing. "Don't let it get past us."

But the shadows lunged, splitting and twisting as they surged forward, bypassing the salt and spilling toward the forest's edge. My heart leapt as I realized what lay beyond. "The town is nearby," I said, my voice trembling as the memory surfaced. "If those shadows reach it—"

"They won't," Felix said firmly, his tone hard with resolve. "We stop it here."

The creature's golden eyes turned toward me, narrowing as it raised one long, clawed hand. The shadows swirled and stretched farther, their sinister tendrils reaching in the direction of the town.

"You cannot stop the inevitable," the creature said, its voice colder now, more menacing. "The darkness will consume all."

"No!" I shouted, clutching the necklace tightly as its heat intensified, spreading through my chest. The pulse grew stronger, the glow building from deep within the pendant. The shadows recoiled slightly, flickering against the growing light.

Chaos erupted in the clearing as the shadows lunged once more, splitting into frenzied movements that threatened to overwhelm us. Felix moved with sharp precision, staying close to me as he pushed back against the onslaught. Jayce fought fiercely near the clearing's edge, wielding a crude iron blade and scattering salt in wide arcs to slow the advance. Luna stood at the center of the chaos, her voice rising as she shouted ancient words from the journal, the power of the incantations causing the shadows to writhe and recoil.

The manifestation stepped closer, its form flickering and warping as the light from the necklace grew brighter. The golden eyes never left me, its focus locked as though drawn to the energy emanating from the pendant.

"Iris!" Luna shouted, her voice breaking through the chaos. "The necklace—use it!"

I didn't know how, but as the light within the necklace grew brighter, hotter, I felt a wave of clarity wash over me. The shadows recoiled from the glow, and the creature snarled, its form flickering as though struggling to maintain its presence.

This was our chance—to stop it here, to protect the town, and to stand our ground against Carrow's power.

And then, as Luna flipped a page and gasped audibly, her voice broke through the cacophony: "Wait!" she shouted, her tone frantic. "It's not just Carrow—it's the curse itself!"

"What are you talking about?" Felix shouted back, his gaze darting to her even as he drove back a tendril of shadow.

"It's tied to something deeper," Luna replied, her voice trembling. "There's another binding—another layer. If we don't stop it, the curse won't just consume the Harts. It will consume everything."

Her words hit like a thunderclap, and the weight of her revelation sank into the chaos like a stone. The binding wasn't just a prison for Carrow—it was spreading. The curse, unchecked, could destroy not only us but the entire town and beyond.

"This is bigger than us," I whispered, the heat of the necklace reaching a searing intensity. The glow spilled across the clearing, pushing back the shadows and illuminating the creature's grotesque form. Its golden eyes narrowed, flickering as though destabilized by the light.

We weren't just fighting Carrow. We were fighting the very fabric of the curse itself.

CHAPTER XXI

The Cracked Mirror

The forest had erupted into chaos, and the town wasn't spared. Shadows spilled from the binding site, stretching far beyond the clearing, twisting through the trees and into the streets. They moved with unnatural speed, their tendrils lashing out and splintering buildings, shattering streetlamps, and disrupting the stillness that had once defined the town's quiet charm. Screams pierced the air as people fled, desperate to escape the creeping darkness.

We sprinted through the streets, our breaths ragged, our bodies aching from the confrontation in the clearing. Felix led the way, his pace relentless, his sharp gaze fixed ahead as he scanned for any sign of safety. Luna clutched her journal tightly to her chest, her movements quick and purposeful despite the panic that flickered in her eyes. Jayce stayed close, his flashlight cutting through the gloom as he threw frantic glances over his shoulder. And I… I followed the rhythmic pulse of the necklace, its warmth growing stronger, hotter, as the chaos surged around us.

The shadows clawed at the edges of the town, twisting and writhing like living things. The red sky above cast an eerie glow over the streets, its unnatural light making the darkness all the more sinister. The air was thick, heavy with Carrow's influence, and every step felt like walking through a storm.

The first tendril of shadow lashed out, shattering the window of a boutique just ahead of us. Felix grabbed my arm, pulling me back just as shards of glass rained down onto the pavement. "Keep moving!" he shouted, his voice cutting through the panic.

Another tendril shot toward us from the alleyway, twisting and whipping violently. I raised the necklace instinctively, the heat of it searing against my skin as its light flared. The shadow recoiled, writhing as though in pain, and Luna let out a sharp breath.

"You're pushing it back!" she exclaimed, her voice trembling with urgency. "Iris, you can stop it!"

I clutched the necklace tighter, the heat almost unbearable now as its glow spread farther, brighter. The shadows recoiled again, but their movements grew faster, more frenzied, as though resisting the light. Felix grabbed my shoulder, his voice low and urgent. "We can't stay here," he said. "The necklace is working, but there are too many of them."

Jayce darted ahead, shouting over his shoulder as he motioned for us to follow. "The café!" he yelled. "Go—now!"

We followed with the shadows lunging toward us with every step, their twisted forms growing darker, denser, as we neared the center of town. The streets were in disarray, the once-familiar storefronts now scarred by the chaos. My chest burned as I raised the necklace again, its light flaring once more as I pushed back another tendril that whipped toward Felix.

"We're almost there!" Luna shouted, her voice breaking as we turned the corner. The café's warm lights glowed faintly ahead, flickering as though struggling to withstand the darkness.

And then, we heard it—an unmistakable voice cutting through the chaos with unexpected clarity. "Get inside! Hurry!"

Mr. Ramsey stood at the café's entrance, his usually stern expression twisted with urgency. He waved frantically for us to enter, his voice rising above the roar of the shadows. "Come on—move!"

Felix reached the door first, shoving it open as he motioned for the rest of us to follow. Luna darted inside, clutching her journal tightly, while Jayce paused just long enough to ensure no tendrils were chasing us directly before stepping inside himself. I hesitated for a brief moment, turning back to raise the necklace once more, its searing light forcing the shadows away from the café's entrance.

"Don't be a hero, Iris!" Jayce shouted from inside. "Move!"

I stumbled forward, the heat of the necklace fading slightly as the café's door slammed shut behind us. The warm, familiar smell of coffee and pastries filled the air, a stark contrast to the chaos outside. The small space felt like a sanctuary, its light comforting despite the shouts and screams echoing faintly from the streets beyond.

Mr. Ramsey locked the door, his hands trembling slightly as he turned to face us. "What have you gotten yourselves into?" he demanded, his voice sharp but filled with concern.

Felix glanced at me, his blue eyes softening just enough to offer reassurance. "It's a long story," he said quietly. "But for now, we need to keep the shadows out."

Jayce peered through the window, his jaw tight as he watched the shadows writhe outside. "They're not stopping," he muttered, his frustration evident.

Luna stepped forward, her voice steady despite the fear in her eyes. "They're drawn to the curse," she said, holding up her journal. "And to Carrow's power. But the necklace—it's keeping them back. As long as we have it, we might be able to push them away from the town completely."

The room fell into tense silence, the hum of the refrigerator behind the counter mingling with the distant sound of glass shattering outside. The shadows continued to writhe beyond the windows, their movements chaotic, desperate, as though searching for a way in.

Felix stepped closer, his voice low but steady as he addressed all of us. "We need a plan," he said. "We can't stay here forever. If the necklace can push them back, we need to figure out how to end this—permanently."

The café's interior was dimly lit, its warm ambiance now overshadowed by the chaos roaring through the town outside. The faint scent of coffee and pastries lingered in the air, but it offered little comfort as the shadows continued to claw at the windows. Felix stood near the entrance, his sharp gaze fixed on the writhing forms just beyond the glass, his body taut with vigilance. Jayce remained by the counter, his iron blade still gripped tightly in his hand, his jaw clenched as he surveyed the room. Luna was seated at the corner table, her journal opened, the pages smeared slightly from the sweat on her hands. And I…

I sat just behind the counter, the necklace burning against my skin, its pulse syncing with the frantic rhythm of my heart.

Mr. Ramsey stood in the middle of the café, his usually composed demeanor now strained as he paced between the counter and the door. His face was pale, his eyes darting from us to the shadows outside as though he was assessing the situation—or deliberating something.

"You kids don't know what you're dealing with," he said finally, his voice sharp and filled with tension. "Carrow isn't just some curse you can break. It's… it's bigger than that."

Felix turned sharply, his piercing blue eyes narrowing as he faced Mr. Ramsey. "What else do you know about Carrow?" he demanded, his tone low but urgent. "What are you not telling us?"

Ramsey hesitated, his lips pressing into a thin line as his gaze flickered to me, then Luna, then back to Felix. "I've been keeping it locked away," he admitted, his voice quieter now but no less serious. "For years."

The air in the room seemed to shift, the weight of his confession pressing down on all of us. Luna straightened in her chair, her hands gripping the edges of her journal as she stared at him. "You've been keeping it locked away?" she asked, her voice trembling slightly. "What do you mean?"

Mr. Ramsey sighed heavily, his shoulders slumping as though the burden of the truth had finally become too much to carry. "The café," he said, motioning toward the floor beneath us. "It's built on top of the entrance to Carrow—the prison realm. It's the only thing keeping it sealed—the only thing keeping anyone from trying to free what's locked inside."

Jayce let out a sharp exhale, his frustration radiating through the room as he stepped closer. "You're telling me we've been sitting on top of this thing the whole time?" he snapped. "And you didn't think to tell us?"

"I didn't think it mattered," Ramsey shot back, his tone defensive but tinged with guilt. "Telling anyone would've only put them in danger. Carrow feeds on fear, on desperation. The more people know, the stronger it becomes. I kept it quiet to protect everyone."

Felix stepped closer, his hands clenched into fists at his sides. "Well, it's not quiet anymore," he said darkly, his tone hard. "The shadows are everywhere. The chaos is spreading. How are we supposed to stop it?"

Ramsey hesitated again, his gaze dropping to the floor as though he couldn't bear to meet Felix's sharp stare. "There's only one way," he said finally. "But it's not easy—and it's not safe."

Luna stood, her expression a mix of determination and urgency. "What do you mean?" she asked quickly. "What's the way?"

Ramsey glanced at her and then at me, his lips tightening. "You have to confront it," he said quietly. "You have to go to the entrance."

Jayce scoffed, shaking his head as he paced across the room. "Oh, of course," he muttered bitterly. "Because walking right into the heart of chaos sounds like a great idea."

"It's the only way to weaken it," Ramsey replied sharply, his voice rising slightly. "You don't have to seal it completely—not yet—but you can stop the spread, give yourselves time to find the rest of the answers."

Felix turned back to me, his blue eyes softening slightly as he searched my face. "Iris," he said quietly, "are you sure about this?"

The necklace burned hotter now, its pulse growing stronger, brighter, as though it could sense the decision looming ahead. I swallowed hard, the ache in my chest deepening as I nodded. "If it's the only way," I said softly, "we don't have a choice."

The room was filled with the muted sounds of preparation—bags being packed, supplies gathered, footsteps echoing faintly against the walls of the café. Felix moved with quiet determination near the door, his sharp gaze fixed on the shadows clawing at the windows. Luna flipped hurriedly through her journal, her focus unwavering despite the tension that filled the air. Jayce rummaged through his bag, his movements stiff, his frustration simmering just below the surface. I adjusted the necklace at my throat, its heat pulsing steadily against my skin, a constant reminder of the burden we carried.

Just as we were about to head toward the hidden entrance, Mr. Ramsey stepped forward, his voice cutting through the noise with calm authority. "Stop," he said firmly, raising a hand to halt us. The room fell silent instantly, and we all turned toward him. His expression was grave, his gaze heavy as it swept across the group.

"Only the ones involved in the curse," he continued, his voice low but unwavering. "The ones tied to Carrow—the prison—can go."

His words settled over us like a thundercloud, oppressive and undeniable. Felix stiffened beside me, his posture straightening as Mr. Ramsey's eyes landed on him. And then, his gaze shifted to me, lingering for a moment as the weight of his statement hit me like a physical force.

Felix's blue eyes darted toward mine, and though he said nothing, his presence felt steady, grounding. My breath hitched as the pulse of the necklace grew stronger, hotter, as though it, too, recognized the truth of Ramsey's words. We were the ones bound to the curse. We were the ones who had to face what lay within Carrow's depths. There was no escaping it now.

Ramsey stepped forward, his gaze steady as he met mine. "I'll show you the way," he said, his voice quieter now but filled with resolve. "But you have to be careful. Once you're down there, there's no turning back."

The café fell into tense silence, the hum of the refrigerator behind the counter mingling with the distant sound of glass shattering outside. The shadows clawed at the windows, their movements growing faster, more frenzied, as though they could sense what we were about to do.

Together, we prepared for the next step—a descent into Carrow's entrance, a confrontation with the curse's source. The air felt heavier, the shadows darker, as the reality of what lay ahead settled over us.

And as Mr. Ramsey led us toward the hidden entrance beneath the café, the necklace pulsed hotter, brighter, filling me with a fragile hope that maybe, just maybe, we still had a chance.

The entrance to Carrow lay hidden behind an old, unassuming door tucked away in the back of the storage room, almost forgotten in the chaos of the café's main floor. The door groaned softly as Mr. Ramsey opened it, revealing a narrow stairwell spiraling downward into darkness. The air beyond the doorway was heavy, damp, and cold—a chill that seeped into my bones and sent shivers up my spine. The faint beam of Ramsey's flashlight pierced the gloom, illuminating the ancient, uneven stone steps that stretched into the depths below.

Felix stepped forward without hesitation, his posture tense, his sharp blue eyes scanning the shadows as though daring them to move. I followed him, clutching the necklace at my throat, its warmth grounding me against the cold that wrapped itself around us like a living thing. Ramsey motioned for me to stay close, his expression tight as he adjusted the flashlight's beam and began the descent.

The stairwell twisted and narrowed as we moved deeper, the walls pressing closer together until it felt as though they were breathing. Every step echoed faintly in the enclosed space, a sound that seemed to stretch unnaturally far. The pulse of the necklace grew stronger, syncing to the rhythm of my heartbeat, and its glow illuminated the jagged stone walls, their surface marked with faint, weathered carvings that were impossible to decipher.

"This is it," Ramsey said quietly, his voice low and steady as he led the way. "The entrance to Carrow—the prison realm— is just ahead. Be prepared. The air down there is heavier, and it won't let you forget what you're walking into."

Felix glanced toward me briefly, his jaw tightening as he nodded. "We're ready," he said, though the tension in his voice was unmistakable.

The staircase ended abruptly, opening into a narrow tunnel carved deep into the stone. The air was thicker here, suffused with an oppressive chill that made every breath feel labored. The faint sound of whispers crept through the tunnel, their source impossible to pinpoint. They were soft at first, indistinct murmurs that tugged at the edges of my mind, but as we moved forward, they grew louder, more insistent, though the words remained elusive.

Ramsey didn't falter. His flashlight swept across the floor, revealing more of the worn carvings etched into the stone walls. "Stay close," he instructed, his voice sharp but calm. "The shadows don't sleep down here. If you lose focus, they'll try to separate you."

I tightened my grip on the necklace, its light pushing back the encroaching darkness as the whispers seemed to press closer. Felix stayed close by my side, his movements deliberate, his hand brushing against my arm briefly as though grounding me. The tunnel twisted again, narrowing even further, the walls slick with moisture that glimmered faintly in the glow of the flashlight.

The tunnel opened suddenly, revealing a vast chamber that stretched beyond the reach of Ramsey's flashlight. The air shifted sharply, pressing against my chest with a weight that was almost tangible. The walls were jagged black stone, their surface rippling like liquid in the flickering light. At the center of the chamber stood a massive iron door, its surface etched with ancient symbols that shimmered faintly, their glow reflected in the necklace's light.

"This is the entrance," Ramsey said, his voice quieter now, almost reverent. "Carrow lies beyond that door. Whatever was locked inside remains sealed, but the binding spell is weakening. The shadows are just the beginning."

I stepped forward cautiously, the heat of the necklace flaring as I approached the door. The symbols carved into its surface seemed to pulse faintly, in rhythm with the hum emanating from the pendant. The whispers grew louder, their tone shifting to something darker, more insistent, though their source remained elusive.

Felix moved to stand beside me, his sharp gaze fixed on the door, his jaw tight. "And what happens if the door opens?" he asked, his voice steady but laced with tension.

Ramsey hesitated, his flashlight beam lingering on the glowing symbols. "The prison breaks. Whatever's locked inside will be unleashed," he replied finally, his tone grave. "And once it escapes… there's no going back."

I felt the weight of his words settle heavily in the chamber, the oppressive air pressing harder against my chest.

The pulse of the necklace quickened, its light growing brighter as though in defiance of the darkness surrounding us. Felix's hand brushed against my shoulder briefly, a silent gesture of reassurance that steadied me just enough to breathe.

Ramsey turned to us, his expression hard but resolute. "This isn't a fight," he said. "You're here to understand the truth. To see what's at stake. But you need to move carefully. The shadows won't let you go easily."

The iron door trembled faintly, the symbols glowing brighter as the whispers swelled into a chaotic roar. I clutched the necklace tightly, its heat spreading through my chest, filling me with a fragile sense of purpose.

The descent into Carrow wasn't just a journey into darkness—it was a confrontation with everything the curse had buried, a step closer to the truth that had haunted us all. And as Ramsey led the way into the depths, I knew we were walking toward something far bigger than we could comprehend.

As we stood in the cold, suffocating stillness of the chamber, Mr. Ramsey turned to face us. The faint beam of his flashlight trembled slightly as his fingers tightened around it. His expression was grim, the hesitation clear in the tight set of his jaw.

"I'll keep them at bay," he said, his voice low but steady. There was a weight behind his words, the reluctance etched into every syllable. His gaze flicked between Felix and me, lingering just long enough to betray his unease. "When we go in, you'll find another chamber. That's where it is—the Cracked Mirror."

"The Cracked Mirror?" Felix asked with uncertainty.

Mr. Ramsey nodded, "It will help you find the truth— answers" he hesitated, his lips pressing into a thin line before he added, almost reluctantly, "Just… be prepared. It won't be what you expect."

With a deliberate motion, Mr. Ramsey stepped forward and unfastened the heavy lock on the door. As it creaked open, his hand went to the amulet hanging around his neck—a small, weathered relic that seemed to pulse faintly in the dim light. He had explained earlier that the amulet kept the shadows at bay, forcing them to stay at a distance. They wouldn't attack us, he'd said, but their presence would remain, unsettling and inescapable.

The air shifted as the door swung open, colder and heavier than before, carrying with it a chorus of whispers that echoed softly around us. The sound wasn't loud, but it was insistent—a constant reminder that the shadows were watching, waiting. Felix stepped inside first, his stance tense but resolute. I followed closely, my fingers tightening around the pendant at my throat as its heat flared faintly in response to the new environment.

Behind us, Ramsey pushed the door shut, the sound reverberating through the chamber like a final toll. It sealed tightly, enclosing us in the suffocating stillness of the space beyond. The whispers remained, weaving through the echoes of our footsteps as we moved forward. The shadows wouldn't strike—but they wanted us to know they were there. Always.

The chamber holding The Cracked Mirror was unlike anything I'd ever seen. The air felt colder, sharper somehow, and it clung to me with a weight that made it hard to breathe. The black stone walls shimmered faintly in the dim light of Mr. Ramsey's flickering flashlight. My pulse quickened as I stepped into the space, the warmth of the necklace flaring sharply, almost as if it knew what was here. Felix walked beside me, his shoulders tense, his sharp blue eyes locked on the jagged glass that towered in the center of the room. Ramsey hung back, hovering just near the entrance, his flashlight steady but his posture strained. He didn't want to be here—I could tell.

The artifact at the center of the room drew my attention immediately. It was tall and jagged, its cracked surface pulsing faintly in rhythm with the necklace at my throat. Its edges gleamed in the dim light, sharp and uneven, while the cracks that marred its surface seemed alive. They rippled and shifted as though something inside the mirror was watching us, waiting. Its reflections weren't normal. Instead of showing the three of us, the mirror held distorted shapes—shadows of things that shouldn't be there, twisting in ways my mind couldn't fully understand.

"That thing's dangerous," Ramsey said suddenly, breaking the silence. His voice was low, almost hushed, and filled with a gravity that made the hair on the back of my neck stand up. "It doesn't just show the truth—it shows everything about the truth. All at once. You don't walk away the same."

I tightened my grip on the necklace, fingers curled so tight my knuckles turned bone-white. The heat of it thrumming through me like a second heartbeat. My eyes flicked to Felix, who was standing a step ahead of me. He was staring at the mirror with a hard, calculating expression, his jaw tight. I didn't know what he was thinking, but the way his fists clenched told me he wasn't about to back down.

"We're here for answers," Felix said firmly. His voice was calm and steady, but there was an edge to it that told me he wasn't going to let Ramsey's warning stop him. "If this thing has them, we're not walking away."

Ramsey shook his head slowly, his face etched with something like fear. "You don't know what you're asking for," he said, his flashlight beam faltering as he glanced toward the mirror. "It doesn't give you what you want—it forces you to see what it wants. The truth doesn't care if you're ready for it."

His words sent a shiver down my spine, but I couldn't stop the pull I felt toward the mirror. The whispers that had been distant and faint ever since we entered Carrow's depths had grown louder, clearer now, as if they were coming from the artifact itself. Each crack seemed to hum faintly, their vibrations tugging at the edges of my mind. The necklace flared hotter against my skin, and I knew—whatever this mirror held, it was tied to the curse. It was tied to me.

"Iris," Felix said quietly, his voice a calm thread of caution. But the pull was too strong. Desperation clawed at my chest, the need for answers overwhelming the fear building in the pit of my stomach.

"I have to," I said, my voice trembling as I took a hesitant step forward. Ramsey's protests faded into the background, my focus narrowing to the jagged glass in front of me. My breath caught as I raised a hand, my fingers trembling as they brushed the cracked surface.

The moment I touched it, the air in the room shifted violently. The mirror shimmered under my hand, its surface rippling like water. The cracks pulsed with an intense light, spreading outward like veins, and the world around me twisted sharply. The whispers surged into a deafening roar, and I was pulled into the mirror's grip.

The visions hit me like a thunderclap, searing and overwhelming. I gasped as the first image overtook me—a woman standing at the altar that had created Carrow. Her face was fierce, her eyes blazing with both rage and desperation. Blood dripped from her hands, pooling around her feet as she carved intricate symbols into the stone. Her voice shook as she chanted, her words trembling with anguish. She wasn't just casting a spell—she was sealing a betrayal, pouring her fury into the creation of a curse that would preserve her bloodline no matter the cost.

The scene shattered, replaced by another just as vivid. I saw Carrow itself—a prison, swirling with dark tendrils that lashed violently against its confines. The void twisted and churned, alive with a force so vast and chaotic that it felt like the very air around me might collapse under its weight. The cracks in the prison weren't just fractures—they were inevitabilities. Carrow was never meant to hold forever.

"Iris!" Felix's voice cut through the chaos, distant and faint. But the visions kept coming.

I saw the town—our quiet little town—engulfed in shadows. The curse spread like wildfire, twisting through the streets, swallowing buildings and people alike. It didn't stop there. The shadows rippled outward, consuming everything in their path, leaving nothing behind but darkness and void.

Then I saw myself. I was standing at the same altar, the necklace blazing with an unbearable light. I was chanting, my voice breaking as the words left me. The heat of the necklace seared into my skin, and my knees buckled under the weight of the light pouring from it. I collapsed, my vision fading as the curse claimed me—the final sacrifice.

"No!" Felix's voice was louder now, sharper, pulling me back from the depths of the visions.

The mirror shimmered violently, and I caught glimpses of him—his immortality laid bare. Felix stood at the edge of Carrow's prison, his body tense, his face twisted in pain. He wasn't just fighting the curse—he was part of it, bound to its creation through his bloodline. I saw the weight of that knowledge crush him, though he didn't falter.

The necklace flared brighter, and the mirror's surface fractured further, the visions splintering into chaos. Felix's hands gripped my arms tightly, yanking me back from the jagged edges of the artifact. My chest heaved as I stumbled into him, the weight of the visions crashing down on me like waves.

Ramsey moved quickly, slamming the mirror shut with a resounding thud. Its surface darkened instantly, the cracks fading into stillness as the roar of the whispers ceased. The room fell into an eerie, suffocating silence.

Felix's hands steadied me, his voice soft but urgent. "Iris, are you okay?" he asked, his sharp eyes searching mine. "Say something."

I nodded faintly, though the images still burned in my mind, etched into me as if they were scars. "I saw it," I whispered, my voice barely audible. "I saw everything."

Ramsey's face was grim as he turned toward us, his flashlight beam catching the still surface of the mirror. "Now you understand," he said, his voice trembling slightly. "Carrow isn't just a prison. It's a doorway. And the thing behind it… it doesn't just want to escape. It wants to destroy the balance. To consume everything."

The truth hung heavily in the room, pressing down on me like a weight I couldn't carry. The warmth of the necklace flickered faintly against my skin, its once steady pulse now weak and uneven.

For the first time, I understood the stakes. The town—the curse—was only a fraction of what we were facing. Our choices wouldn't just ripple through our lives. They would decide everything.

CHAPTER XXI

Carrow's Ultimatum

The steps creaked softly beneath us as we ascended back into the café, the air heavier than it had been before we descended into Carrow's depths. The warmth of the room, the faint hum of the lights, and even the familiar smell of coffee did little to ease the cold weight pressing against my chest. Felix walked just ahead of me, his shoulders stiff and his jaw set, the tension in his body unrelenting. Ramsey followed quietly, his flashlight hanging limply at his side, his eyes dark with the burden of truths he had finally allowed us to uncover.

When we stepped onto the main floor, Luna and Jayce were already there, their faces pinched with concern. Luna shot to her feet the moment she saw us, her journal clutched tightly against her chest. Jayce leaned heavily against the counter, his arms crossed, his gaze sharp and searching as it flicked between me and Felix. I felt their unspoken questions pressing against me like a tide I couldn't hold back.

"What happened down there?" Luna asked, her voice edged with worry. Her wide eyes darted to Felix, then to Ramsey, and finally rested on me. "What did you find?"

For a moment, I couldn't speak. The images from the mirror still haunted me, burned into the back of my mind. The witch's blood pooling around her feet, Carrow's tendrils lashing violently against its prison, the shadows consuming the town and everything beyond it—and my own collapse at the altar, the necklace blazing as it claimed the final sacrifice. My breath hitched, the weight of it threatening to crush me all over again.

Felix stepped in, his voice calm but flat, almost unnervingly controlled. "We found what we were looking for," he said, though his tone betrayed how much it cost him to say it. "We got answers. Just… not the ones we wanted."

The tension in the room pressed down on me like a physical weight as the words sat unspoken between us, heavy and undeniable. Felix avoided my gaze, his sharp blue eyes locked on the floor, his jaw clenching so tightly I thought it might crack. Ramsey lingered near the edge of the group, his expression grim as he fidgeted with the amulet around his neck. Only Luna and Jayce watched me directly, their stares heavy with unspoken questions. I could feel their concern—feel the moment cracking under the strain of what I hadn't said yet.

"There's no other way," I finally forced out, my voice trembling as I broke the silence. I hated how small I sounded, how the truth clawed its way from my chest like glass shards. My hands tightened around the pendant at my throat, its warmth burning against my palms as though it, too, understood the weight of the words. "To break the curse, to stop the shadows, to keep Carrow sealed forever… I have to die."

Luna inhaled sharply, her hand flying to her mouth as she stumbled back a step. The journal she'd been clutching fell to the table with a dull thud, forgotten as she stared at me with wide, disbelieving eyes. "What are you talking about?" she whispered, her voice trembling. "Iris, that—no, there has to be another way."

"There isn't," I said, shaking my head. The images from the mirror burned behind my eyes, vivid and relentless. The altar, the light of the necklace, the final sacrifice—it had shown me everything. Every possible path, every consequence, every ending. There was no other way forward. "The mirror... it showed me everything. The curse needs a sacrifice to seal it for good. If it doesn't get one, the cracks in Carrow will keep spreading. The shadows will scatter. They'll take everything."

Jayce let out a bitter laugh, though there was no humor in the sound. "That's it?" he snapped, his frustration boiling over as he threw his hands in the air. "That's the grand solution? Sacrifice yourself and hope it works?"

"It's not a solution. It's the only way," I said firmly, though my voice cracked at the edges. "It's not about what I want. It's about what has to be done."

"No," Felix said suddenly, his voice sharp as a knife. His posture shifted, his jaw tightening as he finally met my gaze with an intensity that made my chest tighten. "That's not happening."

"Felix—" I started, but he cut me off, his voice rising just enough to make me pause.

"No," he repeated, his tone hard, unyielding. "I don't care what the mirror showed you. I don't care what it said. We're not losing you. We'll find another way."

"There is no other way," I said, my frustration and despair bleeding into my words. "Felix, I saw it—everything. The curse won't stop. It'll destroy the town. It'll destroy everything. If I don't—"

"Then we'll stop it some other way," Felix said, his voice cutting through mine with a fierce determination. His blue eyes burned as they locked onto mine, daring me to argue. "I'll figure it out. We'll figure it out. But you're not doing this, Iris."

"You can't just ignore what the mirror showed her!" Jayce snapped, his frustration spilling over as he turned on Felix. "You think you can fight fate? Do you even hear yourself?"

"I don't care what fate says," Felix bit back, his tone icy and unforgiving. "Fate doesn't get to decide this. We do."

"Felix—" I started again, but the words caught in my throat as the weight of his determination hit me like a tidal wave. I could feel my resolve faltering, the cracks in my composure growing deeper under his unrelenting gaze.

"We're not giving up on you," he said, his voice softer now, though the fire in his eyes didn't waver. "You've carried this curse long enough. Let me carry it for a while."

Luna stepped forward hesitantly, her face pale and her voice trembling as she spoke. "Iris... is it really the only way?" she asked softly, her tone pleading.

I didn't answer her right away. I couldn't. The truth of it felt too big, too raw to say again. My hands shook as I gripped the pendant tighter, its pulse a steady reminder of everything the mirror had shown me. Finally, I nodded, tears pricking at the edges of my eyes. "It is," I whispered. "It's the only way to stop it."

Luna's breath hitched, and Jayce cursed softly under his breath, raking a hand through his hair as he turned away. Ramsey, who had been silent the entire time, finally stepped forward, his voice low and measured. "You're right," he said, his tone filled with resignation. "The mirror doesn't lie. But it doesn't give you the whole picture either. There are always pieces it leaves out."

Felix latched onto Ramsey's words instantly. "Then we'll find those pieces," he said, his voice filled with a renewed determination. "We're not done yet."

I wanted to believe him. I wanted to believe there was something we hadn't seen, some way out of the nightmare that didn't end with me at the altar, the light of the necklace blazing as it consumed me. But the weight of the mirror's vision clung to me, unshakable and suffocating.

I stayed silent as Felix's words hung in the air, the tension between us like a fragile thread threatening to snap. Deep down, I knew he wasn't ready to accept it—not yet. And maybe, just maybe, I wasn't either.

The silence pressed down on us, thick and suffocating, until Felix let out a sharp breath. He dragged a hand through his hair, his frustration evident in the restless motion. "Excuse me," he muttered, his voice low, strained. Without another word, he turned away, his footsteps heavy as he headed into the adjoining room. The faint creak of the floorboards followed his departure, and the tension he left behind settled in his absence, as tangible as the air we were struggling to breathe.

The murmur of voices from the other room faded as I stepped away quietly, careful not to draw attention to myself. Ramsey's voice was steady, trying to reason with Jayce and Luna, but their arguments churned on, a back-and-forth of frustration and desperation. I couldn't listen to it anymore—not the conflicts over inevitability or their futile attempts to invent another way. The truth hung heavy in my mind, its weight settling like a fog over my thoughts, leaving my expression blank. I tried to pretend I was fine, but the terror creeping through me was impossible to ignore.

I eased the door open, my movements deliberate, quiet, as I entered the adjacent room. Felix was there, sitting on the floor with his back pressed against the wall. His knees were drawn up, his hands clasped loosely over them. The light spilling through the tall glass windows painted him in shades of deep red, the glow reflecting the chaos unfurling outside. His gaze was fixed on the scene, unblinking, his face unreadable.

I moved toward him slowly, lowering myself to the floor beside him. Drawing my knees to my chest, I wrapped my arms around them and leaned my head against his shoulder. His warmth grounded me, easing the ache in my chest just slightly. The silence between us stretched, fragile but comforting in its stillness.

"I know what you're thinking," I said softly, my voice barely audible. I avoided his gaze, keeping my eyes fixed on the floor or nowhere at all. I was scared that if I looked at him, I might cry.

He didn't turn to look at me, his head leaning back against the wall as though the weight of his thoughts was too much to carry. "I don't think you do," he murmured, his voice quiet, distant.

We stayed like that for a while, the quiet wrapping around us, broken only by the faint hum of echoes from the room beyond and the muted roar of the chaos outside. My mind wandered, spiraling toward the nightmare awaiting us below. Carrow—or the creatures tied to it—wouldn't stop. They would tear through everything, leaving darkness and destruction in their wake. I wouldn't let that happen. I couldn't.

The thought sparked something in me—a fragile thread of courage. I lifted my head, turning toward Felix as the words poured out of me. "I have to do it, Felix," I said, my voice trembling but resolute.

He finally turned to face me, and the emotion in his eyes shattered me. They glistened, on the verge of tears, raw and defenseless. He shifted, his entire body turning toward me, his hands gripping his knees tightly. "It should be me, Iris," he said, his voice cracking with emotion. "I was supposed to be dead a long time ago. It should be me."

My chest ached as his words sank in, the pain in his voice cutting through me like a knife. "I can't lose you," he continued, his tone trembling. "I've lost too much already—I won't stand to see you die."

The anguish in his voice stirred a deep ache in me. He had suffered so much because of this curse, endured endless pain, loss, and regret. But I had the power to stop it—to end the cycle of suffering once and for all. Slowly, I raised my hand to his cheek, brushing my fingers against his skin. He caught my hand in his and pressed it against his face, his grip firm, desperate. I could see every inch of him fighting against the inevitable.

My gaze dropped to his arms, where his sleeve hung ripped and frayed, exposing fresh cuts and bruises. A dark bruise marred his cheek, its edges stark against his pale skin. Seeing him like this broke something in me; I wanted to heal him, to give him a life free of all of this—even if it meant I wouldn't be in it.

"We don't have another choice," I said, my voice quiet but firm. "You've suffered so much because of my family and their choices. I have the chance to stop it—for you, for me, for everyone suffering right now."

"No," he said, shaking his head sharply. His gaze dropped to the floor as his voice filled with determination. "We'll find another way. One way or another. You won't have to sacrifice yourself."

I hesitated, my heart twisting painfully in my chest. I wanted to believe him, but the truth burned too vividly in my mind. "Then we'll get to that when the time comes," I lied, knowing full well that there was no other choice. But I didn't want him to suffer anymore, not tonight. For now, all I wanted was to hold onto the time we had left. I offered him a small smile, hoping it would ease the sadness in his eyes.

His lips curved into the faintest of smiles, weak but enough to pull me closer. He hugged me tightly, his arms wrapping around me as though he could shield me from the weight pressing down on both of us. I buried my face into the crook of his neck, savoring his warmth, his presence.

We pulled back slowly, our gazes locking as the moment stretched between us, heavy with unspoken words. Felix leaned forward, resting his forehead against mine. His voice came softly, full of raw emotion. "I love you," he said, and the words hit me like a wave.

"I love you too, Felix," I whispered, my voice breaking as tears pricked at the corners of my eyes.

We held each other tightly, and neither of us was willing to let go just yet. Deep down, we both knew this was goodbye, even if Felix wasn't ready to accept it. And in this fragile moment, I couldn't bring myself to say the words aloud.

The room remained still after Felix's quiet confession, his words lingering in the air like threads of something too fragile to grasp. Neither of us moved, our embrace holding the weight of everything that had been left unspoken. But the whispers from outside grew louder, clawing at the edges of my resolve. Time wasn't on our side, and I knew every passing second was one closer to the inevitable.

Reluctantly, I pulled away, his warmth slipping from me as I shifted back. Felix watched me closely, his gaze sharp yet undeniably vulnerable. The red light streaming through the windows painted us both in stark shades—deep shadows that didn't quite hide the pain written across his face. I forced myself to steady my voice, though it trembled with every word. "We should go back," I said softly, motioning toward the door. "They'll need us to plan whatever comes next."

Felix hesitated, his jaw tightening as if to keep himself from saying something he couldn't take back. Finally, he nodded, though his movements were reluctant, almost mechanical. "Yeah," he murmured, his voice barely audible. He rose to his feet first, offering me his hand, the gesture grounding even as the tension lingered between us.

I took it, letting him help me up, and together we made our way back into the other room. The sound of raised voices greeted us immediately—Jayce's sharp frustration clashing with Luna's softer pleading. Ramsey stood between them, his amulet clasped tightly in his hands, his expression grim but resolute. He was attempting, in his own way, to calm them, but it was clear the conflict was wearing on him.

Jayce turned the moment we stepped through the door, his arms crossing as he fixed his sharp gaze on us. "Well?" he said, his tone biting. "Any breakthroughs while you were off having your moment?"

"Jayce," Luna said softly, a note of warning in her voice. She reached for his arm, but he shrugged her off, his frustration burning too brightly to contain.

Felix didn't respond, his own tension simmering just beneath the surface. I stepped forward instead, forcing myself into the space between them. "This isn't helping," I said, my voice steady despite the storm brewing inside me. "We need to focus. The longer we argue, the less time we have to stop Carrow from breaking free."

Jayce scoffed, but Ramsey raised his hand, silencing him with a single motion. "She's right," Ramsey said, his tone calm but firm. "We need a plan. There's no room for hesitation."

The words twisted something inside me. A plan. Every fiber of me screamed that there was only one path forward—that no amount of arguing or desperate searching could change what the mirror had shown me. But still, Felix's determination lingered in my thoughts. I wasn't ready to crush his hope—not yet.

"Whatever plan we make," I said quietly, "it has to stop the shadows from spreading. It has to hold the shadows in Carrow in place. No matter what."

Ramsey nodded slowly, his expression darkening. "I have the means to hold the door," he said, glancing down at the amulet in his hands. "But only for so long. Once the seals weaken further, it will take everything to keep Carrow contained."

Felix stepped forward, his voice cutting through the growing tension. "Then we'll find a way to reinforce the seals," he said, his tone resolute. "There has to be something—another binding spell, another artifact. Something."

Ramsey hesitated, his gaze flicking toward me, then back to Felix. "If there is, it would be down there," he said reluctantly. "Beyond the mirror."

The room grew silent at his words, the weight of them pressing heavily against us. Luna shifted nervously, her hands twisting together as her brows furrowed in worry. "Beyond the mirror," she echoed softly, her voice trembling. "What does that mean?"

"It means Carrow isn't just a prison—it's a labyrinth," Ramsey said grimly. "The mirror is only one piece of it. There are other chambers, other artifacts, other dangers. If you want to reinforce the seals, you'll have to face all of it."

Jayce exhaled sharply, his frustration giving way to something more uncertain. "So, what? We just throw you two into the depths and hope you come out alive? Sounds brilliant."

"It's the only way to find what you need," Ramsey said firmly. "Unless you're prepared to accept the alternative."

His words hung in the air like a storm cloud, dark and oppressive. I could feel Felix's gaze on me, searching for some sign of agreement or resistance. But I stayed quiet, my resolve solidifying as I pieced together the fragments of the future the mirror had shown me.

"If we're going back down," I said finally, "we need to be ready. Whatever's waiting beyond the mirror—it won't let us through easily."

Ramsey nodded, his expression grim. "Then prepare yourselves," he said. "Because once we cross that threshold, there's no turning back."

Luna nodded, her journal pressed tightly to her chest, her expression determined. "Jayce and I will stay here while Mr. Ramsey guides you back down there," she said, glancing between Felix and me. "I'll keep looking for spells in the journal—anything that might help with the chaos. Then, when he returns, he can help me with protection spells, along with Jayce."

Jayce scoffed at her words, his frustration evident in the sharp rise of his shoulders. Still, his gaze softened when he glanced at Luna from the corner of his eye. It was subtle, but I saw it—the same love and worry I had always noticed in him when it came to her. No matter how mad he was, no matter how stubbornly he clung to his hard façade, he cared about her deeply.

"Then it's settled," I said, my voice steady despite the weight pressing against my chest. But as the silence stretched, my thoughts began to spiral. The truth of what lay ahead was suffocating. My palms grew clammy, and a wave of dizziness washed over me as my mind replayed the possibilities of what could happen. I didn't want them to risk their lives for me—not Felix, not Luna, not Jayce. My heart ached at the thought.

"Iris," Luna's voice interrupted my downward spiral, pulling me back to the present. I blinked, turning toward her as she spoke. "I found a communication spell in the journal. It can keep us connected—with each other," she explained, her gaze steady and reassuring.

Her words eased the weight in my chest, if only slightly. At least I wouldn't be alone. Even if something went wrong, I'd be able to reach out to them—at least that much gave me comfort.

Luna quickly turned her focus to the spell, enlisting Mr. Ramsey's help to gather the ingredients. As it turned out, Ramsey had a surprising arsenal of supplies tucked away— ingredients, potions, tools for emergencies like this. He was prepared for everything. I couldn't help but feel a small flicker of gratitude for his readiness, even in such dire circumstances.

Meanwhile, Jayce had retreated to a corner booth. He sat hunched forward, his head resting in his hands, his right leg bouncing restlessly up and down. I hesitated, glancing toward Felix for reassurance. He met my gaze with a small nod, his presence grounding me enough to approach Jayce.

Stopping in front of him, I studied his posture for a moment, then spoke softly, my voice low enough for only him to hear. "Hey… how are you holding up?"

Jayce's head lifted slightly, his expression blank as he looked at me. "What kind of question is that, Iris?" he said, his voice trembling as his gaze flickered downward. He inhaled shakily before meeting my eyes again. "What do you want me to say? Like, 'Hey, I'm fine. I'm so glad the world is being consumed by creepy shadows and that one of my best friends is about to go to her death.' Yeah, right."

His words hit me harder than I'd expected, and my chest ached in response. Jayce was my best friend, and seeing him unravel like this made everything feel even more fragile. Still, I couldn't show how much his pain affected me—I had to be steady for him.

I sat down beside him, resting a hand gently on his back. "Jayce, I know this is hard, but you have to trust that we'll find a way," I said softly, trying to comfort him. My touch seemed to ease some of his tension, though his sadness lingered as he turned to look at me.

"I'm sorry, alright?" Jayce said finally, his voice cracking as tears welled in his eyes. "I just… I just can't bear the thought of losing any of you."

I pulled him into a hug without hesitation, wrapping my arms tightly around him as he let himself break against me. "It's okay," I murmured, my voice steady despite the knot tightening in my chest. We stayed like that for a while, his grip on me unyielding as he let the tears fall.

Eventually, Luna's voice pulled us from the quiet. She stood near the door, her expression soft as she motioned toward us. "We're ready. Come."

I gently eased Jayce back, offering him a small, reassuring smile before standing. Felix and Jayce followed close behind me as we made our way to Mr. Ramsey's office. Inside, the room had been transformed—a white tablecloth stretched across the desk, bowls and candles arranged meticulously atop it. Luna stood waiting, her journal open as she gestured for us to approach.

"Here," she said, motioning toward the table.

I watched as Luna worked quickly and efficiently, mixing the gathered ingredients into a stone bowl. Her voice rose in rhythmic chants, unfamiliar Latin words flowing seamlessly from her lips as she stirred the mixture. The air around us shifted, growing heavier with every passing second, until Luna finally stepped back, the chant coming to an end.

Moving toward us, Luna dipped her finger into the mixture, the cool substance glistening faintly as she drew a rune on each of our foreheads. The moment her finger touched my skin, the rune sent a chill through me, though the sensation was oddly grounding. Luna left her own forehead for last, and as I watched, her rune began to fade, dissolving completely into the air.

"Now we should be able to communicate with each other through our minds," Luna explained, tapping her temple lightly with her index finger. "Just picture the person or people you want to talk to and think of what you want to say."

Her voice filled my head suddenly, breaking through the stillness with startling clarity. "*Like this,*" she said, her tone light with amusement.

I jolted back slightly, startled by the abrupt connection, and Luna chuckled softly in response. "It's simple," she continued. "You'll get used to it."

Her reassurance eased my nerves, and I took a deep breath, centering myself. Whatever lay ahead, at least I wouldn't have to face it alone. Luna's spell would keep us connected, and as I glanced toward my friends, a faint flicker of hope stirred within me.

The air was colder this time, heavier as we descended the narrow stairwell. Mr. Ramsey led the way, his amulet clasped tightly in his hand, its faint glow pushing back against the shadows that lingered at the edges of the staircase. Felix moved just behind him, his flashlight casting jagged shadows along the damp stone walls. I followed closely, clutching the necklace at my throat, its steady warmth grounding me against the oppressive weight of the air that seemed to press closer the deeper we went. The door to the depths of Carrow had closed behind us with a finality that sent a shiver down my spine. There was no retreat now, only forward.

The stairwell spiraled downward endlessly, the steps uneven and slick with moisture. Each footfall sent faint echoes reverberating through the enclosed space, blending with the whispers that lingered just at the edge of perception. They were faint at first, indistinct murmurs, but they grew louder with each step, a chorus of sounds that made the hairs on the back of my neck stand on end.

Felix stopped suddenly, glancing back at me and Ramsey. "You okay?" he asked softly, his voice low to avoid carrying too far. Even in the dim light, I could see the tension in his expression, his jaw set in quiet determination.

Ramsey didn't falter, his amulet glowing brighter as the whispers shifted, but he glanced over his shoulder at me, his gaze steady. "She'll be fine," he said, his voice calm but firm. "The necklace will hold for now. Just don't lose focus."

I nodded, though my chest tightened as the whispers grew sharper. "I'm fine," I murmured, though my grip on the necklace tightened. It pulsed faintly in response, as if to reassure me.

We continued downward, the air growing colder still, the oppressive weight thickening around us like a vice. Ramsey's pace remained steady as he led us deeper, his flashlight sweeping ahead to illuminate the narrow walls of the tunnel. The faint glow of his amulet seemed to keep the shadows at bay, though their presence never fully receded. The air felt heavier here, colder, and the faint hum that had been present since we entered grew louder, vibrating in my chest like a second heartbeat.

The landing came suddenly, the spiral stairs opening into the first narrow tunnel that stretched ahead. The walls were carved from the same black stone as before, their surface etched with faint, weathered markings that seemed to ripple in the dim light.

"This is it," Ramsey said quietly, his voice barely above a whisper. "The first chamber is just ahead—where the entrance is."

I swallowed hard, the memory of the Cracked Mirror flickering briefly in my thoughts before giving way to something deeper. Ramsey's words echoed in my mind: the prison realm was beyond the mirror, through the tall double doors hidden in its shadow. The thought of facing whatever lay inside sent a shiver down my spine.

Felix glanced at me, his sharp blue eyes searching mine. "You don't have to—"

"I do," I interrupted, my voice firmer than I felt. "This is the only way. We both know it."

Ramsey hesitated, his amulet glowing faintly in the dim light. "Stay focused," he said finally. "Whatever happens, don't lose sight of what you need to do."

We stepped forward into the tunnel, the whispers growing louder, their tone shifting, more insistent. They seemed to press against my mind, the words just out of reach, slipping through my grasp every time I thought I understood them. Ramsey kept his pace even, his flashlight and amulet pushing back against the encroaching darkness as the tunnel twisted and narrowed.

The passage opened suddenly, the narrow space giving way to the cavernous chamber where the Cracked Mirror loomed. But this time, my eyes didn't linger on its jagged surface. Beyond the mirror, just behind it, stood a set of tall double doors, the black stone polished and smooth, engraved with intricate patterns that pulsed faintly in the flickering light. The air around them shimmered, a faint aura that seemed to hum in time with the necklace at my throat.

Ramsey's amulet flared briefly, its glow pulsing brighter as he stopped just short of the mirror and the doors. He turned to us, his posture stiff, his expression grim. "This is where I leave you," he said finally, his voice steady but heavy with warning. "The necklace will hold the seal long enough for you to enter— but it won't keep you safe once you're inside. That will be up to you."

Felix nodded once, his grip tightening on the flashlight. He glanced at me, his resolve solid despite the tension in his expression. "We'll manage," he said, though his tone carried a weight that mirrored my own apprehension.

Ramsey turned his attention to me, his gaze sharp. "You'll have to unlock the doors yourself," he said. "If I do it, the seal will break completely, and whatever's inside will escape."

I swallowed hard, nodding despite the fear clawing at the edges of my mind. "How?" I asked, my voice trembling.

Ramsey raised his hand, pointing toward the center of the doors. "The necklace will guide you," he said. "When you're close enough, it will start to glow. Once it does, you need to press your palm against the center—here." His finger hovered over the intricate engraving at the heart of the doors. "It will open for you, but you have to be quick. The longer the seal is interrupted, the more unstable the prison becomes."

Felix stiffened beside me, his grip tightening on my arm. "I'll be right there," he said, his voice steady despite the tension simmering beneath it.

Ramsey stepped back, his amulet pulsing faintly in his hand. "Once the doors open, you're on your own," he said firmly. "Whatever happens inside, don't forget why you're here."

The room grew still as his words hung in the air, the hum from the doors growing louder, deeper, resonating through my chest like a second heartbeat. I moved forward hesitantly, my breath shallow as I approached the doors. The whispers surged, louder and more chaotic, pressing against my mind with an intensity that left me reeling. The necklace flared suddenly, its warmth spreading across my chest in steady waves.

Ramsey's voice was calm but urgent. "Now," he said. "Place your palm against the center while it's glowing."

I raised my hand slowly, my palm trembling as the light of the necklace grew brighter, casting faint patterns across the surface of the doors. The engraving pulsed faintly in response, the hum growing louder as my hand connected. The moment my skin touched the smooth stone, the light surged, and the room seemed to shudder violently. The whispers erupted into a deafening roar, the air thickening as the seal began to break.

Behind me, Felix's presence grounded me, his steady grip on my shoulder a reminder that I wasn't alone. And then, with a final surge of light, the doors began to shift, the engravings rippling as the stone parted, revealing the dark labyrinth beyond.

CHAPTER XXII

Fate Beneath the Fractured Sky

Carrow's labyrinth stretched beneath an ominous and alien sky, its towering, jagged black walls exposed to an expanse of glowing green light that pulsed faintly, casting unnatural hues across the maze. The fractured surface of the labyrinth was slick and broken in places, its twisted paths spiraling chaotically in all directions, as though mocking any attempt I made to find clarity or escape. High above me, a massive orange orb—neither sun nor moon—hovered like an unblinking eye, its intense glow bleeding through the green haze of the sky and saturating the labyrinth with surreal, overlapping tones of orange, red, and emerald.

Despite the openness of the space, the atmosphere was suffocating, the towering walls pressing inward as if they were alive, leaning closer with every step I took. The green light refracted strangely as it struck the crumbling structures, warping their shadows into grotesque, twisting forms that seemed to move of their own accord. I couldn't shake the feeling of being watched. The shadows rippled and shifted like ink spilled across uneven ground. They clung to the cracks and crevices of the maze's floor, surging forward and recoiling as though alive— silent sentinels waiting for me to make a mistake.

The air was thick with the stench of decay, sharp and inescapable, mingling with the metallic tang of something burned and bitter. My stomach twisted as I tried not to breathe too deeply. The ground beneath my feet was cracked and uneven, scattered with debris—broken fragments of stone, splinters of wood, shards of glass—that had crunched faintly with every step. The carried, echoing far too loudly, the sharp clatter swallowed by the vast emptiness around me. A faint hum resonated through the air, deep and unrelenting, vibrating through my chest like an unshakable heartbeat.

Even with the open sky stretching above me, Carrow twisted reality, making the vast expanse feel suffocating. Every corridor felt like a snare, twisting and curling at impossible angles. Some had tightened into suffocating passageways, barely wide enough to pass, while others had opened into gaping voids littered with rubble and shadowy shapes lurking just at the edges of my vision. Far off, broken structures jutted into the sky, jagged and skeletal, their edges glowing faintly with the red and blue bleed of the surreal, shifting sky.

The shadows flickered constantly at the edges of my sight, forming strange, shifting shapes that vanished the moment I turned to face them directly. Whispers slid through the cracks in the stone walls, fragments of voices too distorted to make out but persistent enough to gnaw at my mind. The deeper we ventured, the thicker the shadows had become, darker and more restless. The walls seemed to pulse faintly with light, like shallow breaths, drawing us toward the center where the air had thickened and the green glow of the sky deepened, merging with the orange haze until everything was bathed in a sickly, otherworldly glow.

Carrow wasn't just a maze—it was alive. Every corridor, every wall, every shifting shadow carried the weight of its malice, wrapping itself around me with unrelenting pressure. The light of the necklace cast fractured, wavering patterns across the black stone, grotesque reflections that warped and rippled with every movement I made. The open air above offered no solace, no relief. The labyrinth wrapped itself around my mind and body alike, twisting reality until there was no certainty left but its desire to consume.

The labyrinth twisted and narrowed as we continued deeper, the shadows closing in around us with every turn. Felix stayed close, his arm brushing mine, his flashlight carving jagged streaks of light through the encroaching darkness. The whispers were relentless, sliding through the cracks in the black stone walls, their fragmented words pressing against my thoughts. The air was sharp, heavy with the stench of decay, and every step felt like dragging my feet through thick, suffocating silence.

Felix's sharp gaze darted to every corner, his movements tense and deliberate as he scanned for anything lurking in the maze's shadows. His presence kept me steady, though the oppressive hum of the labyrinth threatened to break through my resolve. The necklace at my throat pulsed softly, its warmth comforting despite the suffocating atmosphere. It was the only thing tethering me to the here and now—the one constant against the disorienting weight of Carrow.

The narrow walls abruptly gave way, spilling us into a vast, open expanse. I stopped in my tracks, the sheer scale of the scene taking the breath from my lungs. The alien sky loomed above us, fractured and glowing with surreal hues of green and orange. The air felt colder here, sharper, pressing down like the weight of a storm. And then, as my gaze swept the desolate landscape, I saw it.

The tower.

It rose from the jagged ground like a monolith, its structure angular and imposing, carved from black stone that glimmered faintly under the unnatural light of the sky. The walls were fractured and uneven, jagged edges slicing through the eerie green and orange glow that spilled across its surface. Sharp leaf-like protrusions crowned its top, each one gleaming with the same alien intensity that made the sky pulse above. The base of the tower was surrounded by jagged rocks and crumbled ruins, their surfaces etched with intricate carvings too faint to make out.

A large circular emblem marked the tower's center, its surface glowing faintly as if alive, pulsing with an otherworldly energy that resonated deep in my chest. The intricate designs carved into the tower seemed to ripple with each step we took, the faint hum in the air growing louder. The shadows around its base twisted and shifted, curling up along its jagged edges like living things.

I froze, rooted in place as the fear hit me in an overwhelming wave. My breath caught, and my legs threatened to give out beneath me. The tower felt wrong—alive in a way I couldn't fully comprehend. Its presence seemed to swallow the air, pressing against my thoughts like the whispers that had followed us through the labyrinth. The necklace flared suddenly, its warmth intensifying as the glow grew brighter, illuminating the path ahead.

Felix turned toward me immediately, his flashlight shifting to the tower as his arm wrapped around my shoulders. "Iris," he said softly, his voice low and steady. The tension in his gaze was unmistakable, but his presence grounded me as I instinctively leaned into him, pressing against his shoulder, seeking comfort.

"I can't—" I started, my voice faltering, the words caught in my throat. My fingers clenched around the glowing necklace, its steady pulse barely keeping the fear at bay. Felix tightened his hold on me, his flashlight steady as it traced the jagged edges of the tower.

"We're okay," he murmured, though his tone carried the weight of uncertainty. He adjusted his stance, positioning himself between me and the shadows creeping around the tower's base. His blue eyes flicked back to mine briefly before returning to scan the open space. He wasn't letting anything past him—not the tower, not the labyrinth, not the fear that threatened to consume me.

The hum in the air grew louder with every step forward, the glowing emblem at the center of the tower pulsing in time with the necklace's light. The closer we moved, the heavier the air became, pressing against my lungs, dragging at my limbs. The tower loomed over us, its jagged edges sharp against the fractured sky, its aura a suffocating weight.

Despite the oppressive fear, Felix's steady presence kept me moving, his quiet determination pulling me forward. The tower, with all its malice and unrelenting pull, promised that Carrow's labyrinth wasn't done with us yet.

The closer we got to the tower, the heavier the air grew, thick and suffocating. Every breath felt like a battle, my lungs straining against the oppressive weight. Felix looked the same way, his face pale with effort, yet his eyes carried a fierce resolve. It was like nothing could stop him from finishing this, from finding a way to see us through. I clung to the flicker of his determination, even though the truth hung between us—a silent, unbearable reality. Only one of us would make it out of here.

When we reached the entrance, the massive double doors swung open without a sound, as though the tower had been expecting us. The motion carried an unsettling sense of invitation, a pull that sent shivers down my spine. Felix stopped abruptly, turning to face me, his hand reaching out to grasp mine. His touch was warm despite the air's bitter chill, grounding me in a way that almost made me forget the fear gnawing at my chest. He gave me a small nod of reassurance, his grip tightening for a brief moment before we stepped through the threshold together.

The interior was exactly what I'd expected—creepy, hollow, and dark. Very dark. The faint glow from the necklace did little to cut through the oppressive blackness that swallowed every corner. The walls seemed to stretch infinitely, their jagged surfaces shimmering faintly under the fractured light spilling in from the entrance. The air here was colder than outside, sharper, as if the tower itself breathed an unnatural chill. Shadows twisted and writhed at the edges of the room, recoiling and shifting in a way that made my stomach turn.

But what I didn't expect was the altar.

It loomed in the center of the room, its surface carved from the same rough black stone as the tower. Intricate runes sprawled across it, glowing faintly with a pale green light that pulsed like a heartbeat. Positioned just behind the altar was the cell—massive, towering, its iron bars gleaming faintly under the unnatural light of the room. At least twenty feet tall, its size dwarfed everything else in the space. Even the altar seemed small in comparison. The faint hum that had followed us through the labyrinth grew louder here, vibrating through the air, rattling through my chest.

Whatever the cell held, it was big—and dangerous.

I froze in place, my knees threatening to give out. The glow of the necklace intensified, casting fractured patterns across the altar and the bars of the cell. I didn't dare take another step. My breath came in shallow gasps, and the world narrowed to the eerie light pulsing from the cell, the shadowed shapes shifting behind its bars.

Felix's hand found mine again, pulling me closer to his side. "I've got you," he said quietly, his voice steady, though the tension in his grip betrayed his own fear. His flashlight beam swept across the room, illuminating the altar and the cell in sharper detail. The bars twisted slightly, warping under the light like something inside was pressing against them, eager to break free.

"We need to move," Felix said, his voice firmer now. "Whatever's in there—it's not going to wait."

I nodded, my throat too tight to respond. The necklace flared again, its warmth clashing with the icy chill of the room. Every instinct screamed at me to turn back, but Felix's grip on my hand, the weight of his resolve, pulled me forward. Step by step, we approached the altar, the hum in the air growing louder, more erratic, vibrating through my chest like a second heartbeat.

Something shifted behind the bars, a low rumble vibrating through the cell. It wasn't just dangerous—it was alive.

The glow of the necklace intensified, casting fractured patterns across the jagged black stone. Felix's grip on my hand tightened, his flashlight steady as it swept across the room, but the light seemed to falter against the oppressive darkness that clung to the edges of the space. The cell loomed behind the altar, its towering iron bars twisting faintly, as though something massive was pressing against them from the other side.

I could feel it before I heard it—a presence, vast and suffocating, pressing against my mind like a storm cloud ready to break. The air grew colder, sharper, and the shadows around the cell began to writhe, curling and twisting like living things. My breath hitched as a low, guttural voice echoed through the chamber, deep and resonant, carrying a weight that made my knees threaten to buckle.

"You dare to come here," the voice rumbled, each word dripping with malice. It wasn't loud, but it filled the space, reverberating through the walls, the floor, my very bones. "Fools. Do you think you can stop what has already begun?"

Felix stepped in front of me instinctively, his body tense, his flashlight fixed on the cell. The shadows within shifted, coiling tighter, and for a moment, I thought I saw something— an outline, massive and grotesque, pressing against the bars. My heart pounded in my chest, the glow of the necklace pulsing in time with its rhythm.

"There's no stopping it," the voice continued, a cruel edge creeping into its tone. "The seal weakens with every passing moment. Soon, I will awaken, and your world will drown in darkness. Millions will fall, their screams— a symphony to my power."

I swallowed hard, my throat dry, but Felix didn't flinch. His voice was steady, sharp. "You're not getting out," he said, his words cutting through the oppressive air. "We won't let you."

A low, rumbling laugh echoed from the cell, the sound twisting and warping as it filled the room. "Won't let me?" the creature mocked, its tone dripping with disdain. "You are nothing but insects, scurrying in the shadow of something far greater than you can comprehend. Your defiance is meaningless."

The shadows pressed harder against the bars, and the faint glow of the carvings on the altar flickered, as though struggling to hold their light. The air grew heavier, colder, and the whispers that had followed us through the labyrinth returned, louder now, their fragmented words clawing at the edges of my mind.

"You feel it, don't you?" the voice hissed, softer now, more insidious. "The fear. The doubt. You know you cannot win. You know one of you will fall. Why fight it? Why not surrender to the inevitable?"

I clenched my fists, the warmth of the necklace grounding me against the creature's words. But the fear was there, gnawing at the edges of my resolve. I could feel its presence pressing against me, vast and unrelenting, its malice seeping into every corner of the room.

Felix's hand found mine again, his grip firm, steady. "Don't listen to it," he said quietly, his voice cutting through the oppressive weight of the creature's presence. "It's trying to scare us. That's all it can do."

The creature laughed again, the sound low and rumbling, like distant thunder. "Scare you?" it said, its tone almost amused. "No, little one. I am simply telling you the truth. There is no stopping my awakening. The seal will break, and when it does, your world will burn."

The glow of the necklace flared suddenly, brighter than before, and the carvings on the altar pulsed in response. The creature recoiled slightly, its shadowed form retreating from the bars for a brief moment. The air shifted, the oppressive weight lifting just enough for me to take a full breath.

Felix's gaze flicked to me, his expression resolute. "We need to figure out what to do," he said, his voice low but urgent. "Whatever's holding it back—it's tied to this altar. We have to act fast."

I nodded, my heart pounding as I stepped closer to the altar, the necklace's glow guiding me forward. The creature's voice rose again, louder this time, its tone laced with fury. "You cannot stop me!" it roared, the shadows surging against the bars. "You will fail, as all who came before you have failed!"

"Felix," I murmured, my voice barely audible as I reluctantly let go of his hand. The warmth of his grip faded, leaving the icy chill of the tower pressing down harder against me. My chest tightened, and the words that followed felt like dragging glass across my throat. "You know what we have to do," I said, the trembling in my voice betraying the strength I was desperately trying to hold onto.

He froze, his eyes widening as the meaning of my words sank in. I watched his jaw clench tightly, his entire body rigid with tension. "No," he said, his voice sharp and resolute. The single word carried an edge that cut through the suffocating hum filling the room. It wasn't a denial—it was an objection, a refusal to let the inevitable take hold.

Tears blurred my vision as the silence stretched between us, heavy and unrelenting. I swallowed hard, forcing the words through the ache in my chest. "It's the only option, Felix," I said, my voice cracking as the first tear slipped down my cheek. "If we break the curse…this place will be sealed. Forever."

He turned toward me slowly, his expression a storm of emotions—anger, fear, anguish. "There has to be another way," he said, his voice trembling despite the strength he tried to convey. "You can't ask me to—"

"I'm not asking," I interrupted, the desperation in my voice forcing the words out before I could stop them. "This is what the mirror showed me. This is what it's always been about. There's no other way."

His hands curled into fists at his sides, his gaze flickering between me and the altar, the glow of the necklace casting fractured light across his face. "I won't let you do this," he said finally, his voice low, almost pleading. "There has to be something we haven't seen. Some piece of this we missed."

"The mirror doesn't lie" I said softly, my tears falling freely now. "It showed me what happens if we don't stop it. If we let the curse go unchecked, if we let Carrow break free…" My voice faltered, the weight of the creature's earlier words pressing down on me. "It will consume everything. Millions will die. We can't let that happen."

Felix shook his head, his movements sharp, filled with denial. "It's not fair," he whispered, his gaze dropping to the necklace glowing against my chest. "It shouldn't be you. It should be me."

I took a hesitant step forward, my hand reaching for his arm. "It's always been me," I said gently, my voice breaking under the strain. "From the moment I found this necklace, from the moment the mirror chose me—it's always been me."

The rumble from the cell behind us grew louder, the creature's mocking laughter echoing through the chamber. "Do you see now?" it hissed, its voice laced with malice. "Even your resolve crumbles before me. You cannot win. You cannot escape. This seal will break, and I will be free."

Felix's gaze snapped to the cell, his jaw tightening once more as he stepped in front of me protectively. "Shut up," he spat, his tone sharp, furious. "You're not getting out of here."

The creature laughed again, louder this time, its shadowed form pressing harder against the bars. "Oh, but I am," it said, its tone cruel, taunting. "The question is, how much will you sacrifice to keep me contained? How much will you lose to seal your fate?"

Felix turned back to me, his resolve flickering like the light from his flashlight. "We'll find another way," he said firmly, his voice steady despite the agony in his eyes. "We have to."

I hesitated, the truth of his words and the weight of the creature's malice tearing at me. The glow of the necklace burned brighter against my chest, pulling me toward the altar. The air around us trembled, the carvings on the stone shifting faintly, as though waiting for the decision to be made.

"Felix…" I started, my voice trembling as my hand fell to the necklace. "It's time."

Felix stared at me, his expression lost, his lips parted as though he wanted to speak but couldn't find the words. Then, without warning, he pulled me into his arms, holding me tightly against him. I melted into the embrace, burying my face in his chest, desperate to memorize every detail—the warmth of his touch, the faint scent of him, the steady rhythm of his heartbeat. It was all I had left, and I clung to it like it might somehow keep me whole.

His hand slid gently through my hair, his fingers brushing against my scalp as his face rested against the top of my head. I felt his breath, warm and steady, as though he was trying to ground himself in the moment just as much as I was. Then, slowly, he pulled back just enough to tilt my face toward his. His eyes searched mine, filled with a storm of emotions—fear, anguish, love—and then he kissed me.

It was sweet but desperate, a kiss that carried everything he couldn't say. His lips trembled against mine, and I felt the weight of his emotions pouring into me. Tears streamed down my face as I kissed him back, trying to savor the moment, trying to hold onto it forever. The world around us faded, the oppressive hum of the tower dimming for just a heartbeat as we clung to each other.

But the moment shattered as the creature's laughter echoed through the chamber, sharp and cruel. We pulled away, our heads turning in unison toward the cell. The shadows within writhed violently, pressing against the bars as the voice rose again, mocking us.

"Oh, young love," it sneered, its tone dripping with disdain. "You humans are pathetic." The laughter grew louder, harsher, filling the room with its malice. "Unfortunately, it is too late."

I barely had time to process the words before the creature roared, a sound so deep and guttural it shook the very walls of the tower. The cell exploded with a deafening force, the iron bars shattering and flying outward like shards of glass. The blast threw us back, the impact slamming me into the altar. Pain shot through my body, sharp and unrelenting, and I screamed as the jagged stone bit into my side.

Felix landed a few feet away, his body crumpling against the ground. He groaned as he sat up, his forehead bleeding, the crimson streak stark against his pale skin. My arm throbbed as I tried to push myself upright, the blood dripping from a deep gash just below my elbow. The room spun around me, the hum now a deafening roar, and I struggled to regain my balance.

The creature stepped forward, its massive form emerging from the shadows of the shattered cell. My heart stopped as I looked up at it, fear gripping me so tightly I couldn't breathe.

When it stepped out of the cell, for a moment, time seemed to stop. My breath caught in my throat as the creature's massive form emerged from the shadows. It was humanoid—barely—but everything about it was grotesquely exaggerated. Its shoulders were impossibly broad, its arms long and muscular, ending in clawed hands that twitched like they were eager to rend and tear. Its entire body seemed to ripple with raw power, every movement fluid and unnaturally precise.

Its skin—or whatever it was made of—looked like cracked, rough stone, ridged and jagged in places, as if its very form had been carved from the darkness itself. The surface glimmered faintly under the fractured green and orange light of the sky outside, the cracks pulsing faintly with some inner, otherworldly glow.

But its face—its face was what froze me to the spot. The features were almost human, but twisted and angular, like someone had taken a human skull and warped it into something monstrous. Its glowing eyes burned with a sickly yellow light, boring into me with an intensity that made my blood run cold. It felt as though it could see right through me, peeling back my layers and exposing every fear, every doubt I had buried inside.

It was towering, grotesque, and so profoundly wrong that just looking at it made my stomach twist. As it stepped closer, its movements were eerily graceful, like a predator circling its prey.

The air grew heavier around it, and the faint glow of its eyes seemed to bleed into the room, casting flickering, warped shadows across the walls.

I couldn't move. I couldn't breathe. My hand instinctively clutched the glowing necklace at my throat, its pulsing light the only thing tethering me to reality. The creature tilted its head slightly, as though studying me, and its lips pulled back into something that might have been a smile—if it wasn't so grotesque, so full of malice.

This thing, this being, was the embodiment of destruction. It wasn't just a creature—it was darkness incarnate, a force of unrelenting power that promised ruin and death to anyone in its path. And now, it was free. My heart raced, fear clawing at my chest as I realized the truth: I wasn't ready to face this. Not yet.

A voice broke through the chaos, sharp and desperate, pulling me out of my trance. "Iris! Felix!" Jayce's voice resonated in my mind, frantic and filled with fear. The connection was sudden, jarring, and I could feel his panic as though it were my own.

"Jayce," I managed, my voice trembling as I tried to focus. "What's going on?"

There was silence for a moment, heavy and suffocating, before Jayce's voice broke through again. "Luna! She's…" His words faltered, desperation choking him. "She's…I don't know what to do. She's not responding! I think she's…"

No. It couldn't be. My chest tightened, my heart pounding as the weight of his words sank in. I couldn't lose anyone else. Not Luna. Not her.

My gaze snapped to Felix, who was already looking at me, his expression mirroring the horror I felt. The creature's laughter rose again, louder, crueler, as it stepped closer, its massive form casting a shadow that swallowed the altar. Anger bubbled up inside me, hot and unrelenting, pushing past the fear that had gripped me moments before.

"What did you do?" I screamed, my voice shaking as the tears spilled freely down my face. "WHAT DID YOU DO TO HER?" My whole body trembled, my fists clenched as the rage consumed me. The creature's glowing eyes fixed on me, its laughter fading into a low, rumbling growl.

The necklace burned against my chest, its light flaring brighter than ever, and I knew this was far from over.

The creature's mocking laughter echoed through the chamber, its glowing eyes fixed on me with a cruel, unrelenting intensity. My hands trembled as I clutched the necklace, its warmth burning against my skin, the light flaring brighter with every passing second. Anger bubbled up inside me, hot and uncontainable, pushing past the fear that had gripped me moments before.

"You won't win!" I screamed, my voice cracking as I stepped forward, the necklace blazing in my hand. The creature tilted its head, its grotesque features twisting into something that might have been amusement. The shadows around it writhed violently, curling and twisting like living things.

I didn't wait for it to respond. I raised the necklace, its light surging as I focused all my rage, all my desperation into it. The warmth spread through my chest, a pulsing energy that felt like it might consume me, but I didn't care. I wanted this thing gone. I wanted it erased from existence.

The creature moved faster than I could react. One of its tendrils shot out, a dark, writhing mass that struck me with the force of a battering ram. Pain exploded through my side as I was thrown backward, the necklace slipping from my grasp as I hit the ground hard. My vision blurred, and for a moment, all I could hear was the pounding of my heartbeat in my ears.

"Iris!" Felix's voice cut through the haze, sharp and panicked. I blinked, trying to focus as I saw him sprinting toward me, his flashlight discarded on the ground. The creature's tendrils lashed out again, but Felix dodged them, his movements quick and desperate as he reached for me.

Before he could get to me, the creature's massive hand shot out, grabbing him by the torso and lifting him off the ground like he weighed nothing. Felix struggled, his fists pounding against the creature's unyielding grip, but it didn't even flinch. Its glowing eyes turned toward him, and a low, rumbling laugh escaped its twisted mouth.

"Such fragile things," it sneered, its voice dripping with malice. "You think you can defy me? You think you can stop what's already begun?"

"Let him go!" I screamed, my voice raw as I pushed myself to my feet, every movement sending waves of pain through my body. Tears blurred my vision as I stumbled forward, my hands outstretched. "Please, let him go!"

The creature ignored me, its grip tightening around Felix as he gasped for air. Then, with a sudden, brutal motion, it hurled him toward the altar. Felix's body hit the jagged stone with a sickening thud, and I cried out as I saw the blood spill from the gash on his forehead, pooling on the altar's surface.

"Felix!" I ran to him, my legs shaking beneath me as I dropped to my knees beside him. He groaned, his hand weakly reaching for the edge of the altar as he tried to push himself upright, but his strength failed him. His blood smeared across the carved symbols, the faint glow of the altar intensifying as the crimson liquid seeped into the grooves.

I reached for him, my hands trembling as I tried to pull him closer. My own blood dripped from the gash on my arm, splattering onto the altar alongside his. The moment my blood touched the stone, the symbols flared to life, their glow blinding as the hum in the air grew deafening.

The creature recoiled slightly, its tendrils twitching as the light from the altar spread outward, illuminating the chamber with an intensity that made the shadows retreat. My breath caught as I looked down at the glowing carvings, the patterns shifting and twisting beneath my hands.

And then it hit me—an understanding so sudden and clear it felt like the air had been knocked from my lungs. The altar wasn't just a seal. It was a key. A key that required a sacrifice to lock the creature away forever.

"Iris…" Felix's voice was weak, barely audible, but it pulled me back to the moment. I turned to him, my heart breaking as I saw the pain etched across his face. He was trying to speak, but the words wouldn't come.

The creature roared, its voice shaking the very walls of the tower as it surged forward, its massive form looming over us. The light from the altar flared again, brighter this time, and I knew we didn't have much time.

It loomed over us, its grotesque form towering in the flickering glow of the altar. Shadows twisted around it, surging and recoiling like living extensions of its malice. Felix groaned beside me, his blood streaked across the altar's surface, his strength faltering as he struggled to sit upright. My chest heaved, and my heart thundered as I stared up at the monster, fear clawing at the edges of my mind.

But then, through the storm of terror, clarity struck me like a lightning bolt. This wasn't just about fear—it had never been about fear. This was about power, about control, about standing firm in the face of darkness and refusing to let it win. The necklace burned against my chest, its warmth spreading outward as though responding to my resolve.

I pressed my hand against Felix's shoulder, urging him to stay down. "Felix," I said softly, my voice steadier than I expected. His bleary eyes met mine, wide with pain and desperation. "I've got this," I whispered, my gaze locking onto his. "Trust me."

"Iris—" he started, his voice weak, but I shook my head, cutting him off.

"You have to trust me," I said, the words firm, though tears burned in my eyes. "This is what I'm meant to do."

Felix's jaw tightened, but he nodded faintly, the trust in his eyes breaking my heart all over again. I turned back to the creature, forcing myself to rise to my feet. My legs trembled beneath me, my body screaming in protest, but I stood tall, clutching the glowing necklace tightly in my hand.

The creature tilted its head, its glowing eyes narrowing as it watched me. "Ah, the little hero," it sneered, its voice reverberating through the chamber. "So brave. So foolish."

I ignored its taunts, every ounce of focus narrowing to the warmth radiating from the necklace and the light spreading through my chest. The altar pulsed beneath me, the glow of its carvings growing brighter, matching the necklace's rhythm. I stepped closer, my hand trembling as I lifted the glowing pendant toward the altar.

"You think that trinket will stop me?" the creature hissed, its voice dripping with disdain. "Do you not see? I am inevitable. My power cannot be undone by your feeble attempts."

But I saw it. I saw the way its tendrils hesitated, how the glow from the altar forced the shadows to recoil. It wasn't invincible—not here, not now.

"I'm not afraid of you," I said, my voice quiet but unwavering. The creature's laugh rumbled like thunder, but I didn't stop. "Not anymore."

The necklace flared brighter, blinding in its intensity, and the carvings on the altar seemed to come alive, the runes shifting and twisting under the light. Heat coursed through me, filling me with a power I didn't fully understand but knew I could control. My fear was still there, lingering in the back of my mind, but it no longer controlled me. I gripped the necklace tighter and slammed my other hand down onto the glowing surface of the altar.

The reaction was immediate. Light surged from the altar in a blinding wave, slamming into the creature and forcing it back with a guttural roar. Its tendrils lashed out, but the light burned them away, leaving trails of smoke and ash in the air. The creature recoiled, its twisted form flickering as though it were struggling to hold itself together.

Felix called out my name, his voice faint but filled with urgency. The creature roared again, its massive frame surging forward against the onslaught of light. My knees buckled, the power of the necklace and the altar almost too much to contain, but I held on, focusing everything I had on the light pouring through me.

"You will not win!" I screamed, my voice cracking but fierce, as I pushed against the darkness with everything I had.

The creature's form wavered, its glowing eyes dimming as the light consumed it. For a moment, it seemed to hesitate, its tendrils retreating, its presence weakening. The warmth of the necklace burned brighter, spreading outward in waves, until the chamber was bathed in radiant light.

And then, with one final roar, the creature dissolved into the shadows, its form breaking apart like smoke in the wind. The oppressive weight in the air lifted, the hum of the altar fading into silence.

I collapsed to my knees, the necklace dimming as exhaustion overtook me. Felix's hand found mine, weak but steady, and I clung to him as relief flooded through me.

"I told you," I whispered, my voice trembling as tears streamed down my face. "We can do this."

Felix squeezed my hand, his expression softening despite the pain etched across his face. "You're incredible," he murmured, his voice barely audible.

The altar glowed faintly beneath us, the runes settling into stillness. The creature was gone—for now—but I knew our fight wasn't over. Still, as I knelt beside Felix, his hand in mine, I felt a spark of hope.

For the first time, I felt like I could win.

The silence that followed was deafening, broken only by the soft hum of the altar as its glowing symbols pulsed faintly. I clung to Felix, my chest rising and falling with shallow breaths as exhaustion threatened to pull me under. My mind raced, replaying the moment the creature dissolved into shadows, its roar still ringing in my ears. The weight of its presence lingered like a shadow over my heart.

Felix stirred beside me, his hand tightening slightly around mine. His forehead was still bleeding, the crimson streak vivid against his pale skin, but his blue eyes locked onto mine with a steadiness that warmed me despite the cold air of the chamber.

"You did it," he whispered, his voice hoarse. "I don't know how, but you did."

"No," I said softly, shaking my head. My gaze fell to the altar, its symbols still glowing faintly beneath our blood. "We did."

Felix gave a weak nod, his head falling back against the jagged edge of the altar as he tried to catch his breath. I leaned against him, my head resting on his shoulder, the warmth of his presence grounding me against the lingering terror that threatened to consume me. But I couldn't rest for long. There was still so much I didn't understand—so much that still needed to be done.

The altar's glow intensified briefly, pulling my attention back to the runes etched into its surface. They pulsed rhythmically, their light spreading outward like ripples in water, illuminating the shattered cell and the jagged walls of the chamber. I stared at the patterns, my mind struggling to piece together the fragments of understanding that had come to me earlier. The altar was a seal—a key—and now it was something more.

Felix must have noticed my expression, because he shifted beside me, wincing as he tried to sit up straighter. "What is it?" he asked, his voice laced with concern. "What do you see?"

I reached out, my fingertips brushing against the glowing symbols. The light flared in response, brighter and warmer, spreading up my arm and settling in my chest. The hum of the altar grew louder, filling my ears, but it wasn't an oppressive sound—it was steady, grounding, almost comforting. The realization hit me like a bolt of lightning.

"The altar…" I started, my voice trailing off as the pieces began to click into place. "It's tied to the creature, to the curse. It's not just a seal—it's connected to everything."

Felix frowned, his eyes narrowing as he followed my gaze. "Connected how?"

I turned to him, the words tumbling out in a rush as the clarity solidified in my mind. "The creature draws its power from the curse—from the darkness spreading through the world. But the altar...it's the opposite. It's like a beacon, a channel for something stronger. Something that can stop it." My fingers tightened around the necklace, its glow brightening as if in agreement. "The light isn't just from the altar. It's from us."

Felix's brow furrowed, his gaze flicking between the altar and the necklace. "You mean...?"

"Our blood," I said, my voice steady despite the tremor running through me. "The curse is tied to our bloodline—my bloodline. That's why the mirror showed me. That's why the necklace chose me. But it's not just about me. It's about all of us, everything we've done to get here. It's why you're still standing, Felix. The altar responds to sacrifice—to hope."

Felix was quiet for a moment, his expression unreadable. Then, slowly, he nodded, his hand brushing against mine. "So what do we do?"

I hesitated, the weight of the realization settling over me. The creature might be gone for now, but the altar's glow wasn't just a victory—it was a warning. The light wouldn't last forever. The fight wasn't over.

"We finish what we started," I said, my voice firm as I pushed myself to my feet, ignoring the pain that lanced through my body. The light of the altar and the necklace burned brighter, illuminating the chamber in warm, golden hues. "We seal this place—for good."

Felix stood beside me, his movements slow but deliberate, his eyes filled with the same resolve I felt burning in my chest. The creature's laughter echoed faintly in my mind, a reminder of what was at stake, but I refused to let it take hold. For the first time, I felt like I had the power to fight back—not just for myself, but for everyone who couldn't.

The altar pulsed beneath us, its light casting long shadows against the jagged walls. And as we stood together, facing the darkness head-on, I knew this was the moment everything had been building toward.

The glow of the altar pulsed faintly, casting fractured light across the jagged walls of the chamber. Felix and I stood side by side, our breaths shallow, our bodies aching from the confrontation. The creature was gone, but the oppressive weight of the room hadn't lifted. The air felt thick, heavy, as though the darkness itself was pressing against us, waiting for its moment to strike.

I ran my fingers over the glowing symbols on the altar, their shifting patterns almost hypnotic. My chest tightened as the truth pressed against the edges of my mind, unrelenting. I knew what had to be done. I knew how the curse could be broken and how to seal Carrow for good. It had been clear to me the moment the light of the necklace and the altar intertwined. The answer wasn't hidden—it was glaring at me, demanding the ultimate price.

"It's me," I said softly, my voice trembling as the realization settled heavily in my chest. "I'm the key. My blood— my life—it's the final piece."

Felix stiffened beside me, his hand gripping the edge of the altar so tightly his knuckles turned white. His jaw clenched, and he turned to face me, his sharp blue eyes blazing with determination. "No," he said firmly, the word sharp and absolute. "That's not happening."

"Felix—" I started, but he cut me off with a sharp shake of his head.

"There's something we're missing," he insisted, his voice steady but laced with desperation. "We always figure it out, Iris. Always. This won't end with you dying. I won't let it."

Tears pricked at my eyes as I watched him, his resolve unshakable even as the weight of the moment pressed down on both of us. I wanted to believe him. I wanted to find another way to keep fighting, but the altar's light told a different story. The carvings beneath my blood and Felix's pulsed with energy, their rhythm steady and unrelenting. They knew what had to be done, even if Felix refused to accept it.

"Felix," I said softly, my voice breaking, "I've seen it. The mirror showed me everything. The only way to stop this, to seal Carrow forever, is—"

"No!" he snapped, his voice louder now, echoing through the chamber. "We're not doing this your way, Iris. Not this time."

The whispers returned then, faint at first, sliding through the cracks in the walls like threads of malice. My breath caught as the sound grew louder, sharper, filling the room with fragmented voices that clawed at the edges of my mind.

Felix's gaze darted to the shadows, his body tensing. "Do you hear that?"

I nodded, my fingers curling around the necklace as the whispers grew chaotic. The light from the altar flickered, dimming slightly as the room grew darker, the shadows pressing closer. The air felt heavier, colder, and my chest tightened as a roar shook the chamber.

"I will kill you first," the voice thundered, filled with rage and malice. The sound reverberated through the walls, and my knees threatened to buckle beneath its weight. The shadows surged forward, twisting violently as something massive and jagged emerged from the depths of the room.

My heart stopped as I saw it—a tendril of shadow, sharp and writhing, hurtling toward me with terrifying speed. I froze, my mind screaming at me to move, but my body refused to obey. The necklace flared brightly, its light casting fractured beams through the darkness, but it wasn't enough to stop the tendril's advance.

"Iris!" Felix's voice cut through the chaos, sharp and desperate. He moved faster than I could react, stepping in front of me just as the tendril struck. The jagged shadow pierced through his stomach, the force of the impact throwing him backward, ripping the necklace from my neck as he fell. His cry of pain echoed through the chamber, and I screamed as I watched him collapse to the ground, blood spilling from the wound.

"Felix!" I dropped to my knees beside him, my hands trembling as I pressed them against his stomach, trying to stem the flow of blood. Tears blurred my vision as his blood seeped through my fingers, pooling on the altar beneath him. His face was pale, his breaths shallow, but his eyes found mine, filled with pain and defiance.

The shadows twisted violently, the roar of the creature filling the room once more. "You cannot stop me," it hissed, its voice dripping with malice. "You will fall!"

Felix groaned, his hand weakly reaching for mine. "Iris…" he whispered, his voice barely audible. "You have to finish this. It requires a sacrifice, use me."

"No," I said, shaking my head as tears spilled down my cheeks. "I can't—I can't do this without you."

"You can," Felix said, his voice trembling as his gaze locked onto mine. His lips curled into a faint, almost fragile smile, the kind that carried more pain than reassurance. "I'm immortal, remember?" His words faltered, his breath hitching as he coughed, the sound raw and strained. Blood stained his lips, but he pushed through, his determination unwavering.

"If I finally die because of the shadows…" He paused, his chest rising and falling unevenly as he struggled to speak. His hand weakly reached for mine, his fingers brushing against my skin. "I'll be happy to die… so you can live."

His words hit me like a blow, sharp and unrelenting, and tears blurred my vision as I stared at him. The faint glow of the altar illuminated his pale face, the blood pooling beneath him stark against the jagged stone. He was trying to be strong, trying to give me the courage I needed, but all I could see was the pain etched into every line of his expression. My heart ached, torn between the desperation to save him and the weight of the choice I knew I had to make.

The light from the altar flared suddenly, brighter than before, and the runes began to shift beneath Felix's blood. The hum in the air grew louder, vibrating through the chamber as the carvings pulsed with energy. My breath caught as I realized what was happening—the altar was responding to the sacrifice, to the blood that had been spilled.

"Iris…" Felix's voice was weak, barely audible, but it pulled me back to the moment. I turned to him, my heart breaking as I saw the pain etched across his face. He was trying to speak, but the words wouldn't come.

The creature roared again, its massive form surging forward against the light of the altar. The hum grew louder, the glow brighter, and I knew we didn't have much time.

The necklace lay discarded on the ground, its faint glow flickering like a dying ember. My hands trembled as I reached for it, the cold metal biting against my skin as I lifted it carefully. Felix's blood still stained the altar, pooling around the glowing runes that pulsed with an intensity that seemed to match the pounding of my heart. I placed the necklace on the altar, its ruby centerpiece catching the light as the humming intensified, vibrating through the air like a second heartbeat. The glow spread outward, brighter and sharper, illuminating the jagged walls of the chamber.

I turned quickly, my legs shaking beneath me as I sprinted toward the backpack we had brought. My fingers fumbled with the zipper, my breath hitching as I pulled out the knife we had packed before coming here. Its blade gleamed under the fractured light of the altar, sharp and unyielding. I ran back to Felix, my chest tightening as I dropped to my knees beside him.

He lay motionless, his eyes closed, his face pale, but his chest still rose and fell in shallow breaths. Relief washed over me, but it was fleeting. The shadows twisted violently at the edges of the room, recoiling and surging as the light from the altar grew brighter. The guttural voice hissed again, cutting through the hum with a venomous edge.

"You wouldn't dare," it sneered, the confidence in its tone sending shivers down my spine. "He will live. If you do it, he dies."

That was the breaking point. I clenched my fists, my jaw tightening as the weight of every loss settled squarely on my shoulders. My dad, my mom—gone. Taken by forces I couldn't control, ripped from my life while I stood helpless. Defenseless.

Not this time.

This time, the story would change. The fury in my chest burned hotter than the fear, igniting something I hadn't felt in a long time: resolve. I wouldn't stand idly by, watching as the people I loved were torn away from me. Not again. If there was even the smallest chance I could fight back, I would take it. Whatever it took, whatever it cost—this time, I'd make sure no one else slipped through my grasp. Not while I still had the strength to act.

I turned to the shadows, my grip tightening around the knife as the room seemed to grow darker despite the altar's light. My heart pounded, the weight of the creature's words pressing against me, but I refused to let it take hold. I clenched my jaw, my voice steady despite the tremor running through me.

"Go to hell," I spat, and with that, I pressed the blade into my abdomen.

Pain erupted from the wound, sharp and all-consuming, stealing the breath from my lungs. My vision blurred as the ruby in the necklace shattered, the shards scattering across the altar like fragments of light. The humming reached a fever pitch, the glow of the altar flaring so brightly it was almost blinding. My knees buckled, and I collapsed to the ground beside Felix, the knife slipping from my grasp.

My hand found his, trembling as I clung to him with the last of my strength. Tears streamed down my face, my breath hitching with every word. "I love you," I whispered, my voice barely audible. "I always will."

A high-pitched screech filled the chamber, piercing and relentless, as the shadows surged violently. The air turned chaotic, a raging wind tearing through the room like a tornado, scattering debris and light in every direction. I covered my ears, the sound unbearable, as an explosion of light erupted from the altar, consuming everything in its path. The brilliance was blinding, and then—silence.

The shadows were gone. The whispers had vanished. The room was still, almost peaceful, as the glow of the altar dimmed to a soft, steady light. My body felt numb, the pain fading into a distant ache as exhaustion pulled at me. My eyelids grew heavy, and I fought to keep them open, but the weight was too much.

Through the haze, I saw a brilliant figure standing before me, its form radiant and ethereal. I blinked, my vision struggling to focus as the figure approached. Slowly, the details came into view, and I recognized her—Eleanor. She crouched beside Felix, her hand brushing gently through his hair. His expression was calm, his eyes closed, his breathing steady. She whispered something to him, her voice soft and soothing, though I couldn't make out the words.

Eleanor turned to me, her movements graceful as she stood and walked toward me. She knelt beside me, her gaze meeting mine, and I could barely make out the faint smile on her face. Her hand touched the wound where the knife had been, and the pain disappeared entirely, replaced by a warmth that spread through my chest.

"You did good, Iris," she said softly, her voice steady and kind.

And just like that, my eyes closed, the world fading into peaceful darkness.

CHAPTER XXIII

Sealed

Light returned to me slowly, hazy and fragmented, as though I were awakening from a deep dream. My body was weightless, no longer tied to the crushing exhaustion or searing pain I had endured. For a moment, I wasn't sure if I was even alive. The world around me was quiet—eerily so—but it carried a sense of calm, like the final breath of a storm that had ravaged everything in its path.

The jagged walls of the chamber had vanished. Instead, a faint golden glow surrounded me, shimmering like the surface of a still pond kissed by sunlight. My feet were on solid ground, yet I felt untethered, floating in a space that felt neither here nor there.

"Where…?" The word caught in my throat, my voice faint, barely audible. I didn't recognize where I was, but at the same time, it felt achingly familiar, as though I had been here before in dreams I could never quite remember upon waking.

Then I saw her again—Eleanor. She stood at the edge of the glowing expanse, her radiant figure illuminated by the same light that surrounded me. Her presence was serene, her expression calm yet filled with a depth of emotion that made my chest ache. As she stepped closer, the golden light seemed to follow her, wrapping around her like a gentle halo.

"You did it, Iris," she said softly, her voice steady and warm. "Carrow has been sealed."

Her words washed over me, sinking into my mind with a weight I wasn't prepared for. Relief surged through me, followed by guilt. "But Felix…" I stammered, my breath hitching as the memory of his injury came rushing back. "He… he was hurt. He—"

Eleanor raised a hand, her gentle touch cutting off my words as she rested her palm lightly against my shoulder. Her gaze held mine, filled with a quiet understanding that steadied my fraying thoughts. "He will live," she said. "The bond you share saved him, just as it saved the world."

I blinked, the meaning of her words settling over me like a heavy blanket. My sacrifice, my blood—it had been meant to seal Carrow and the darkness it contained. And yet, Felix was alive. I could still feel the faint echo of his presence, like a tether anchoring me to the world I thought I had left behind.

"You've given more than enough, Iris," Eleanor continued, her voice filled with a quiet reverence. "You broke the curse not just with your sacrifice, but with your will. The light of the altar didn't take; it transformed."

"Transformed?" I asked, my voice trembling. "What does that mean?"

She smiled faintly, the corners of her lips turning upward with an emotion I couldn't quite name. "You offered yourself completely to the light," she said. "But the light chose to preserve what matters most. It took the darkness instead—the shadows, the whispers, everything that threatened to consume your world."

Her words settled in my mind, slowly, like pieces of a puzzle clicking together. The altar wasn't just a weapon or a seal—it had been a beacon, a force that drew strength from sacrifice but gave something back in return. It hadn't consumed me. It had cleansed the darkness, obliterating what could never be allowed to exist.

The weight of it all made my legs tremble, and I sank to my knees, the golden glow soft beneath me. "I thought I was going to die," I admitted, my voice barely audible. "I was ready to…"

"And that's why you succeeded," Eleanor said, her voice carrying a quiet strength that wrapped around me like a blanket. "The darkness feeds on fear, doubt, and anger. But you overcame all of it. You let go. And in doing so, you gave the light its power."

I closed my eyes, the tears flowing freely now. The tension I had carried for so long, the pain, the guilt—it began to ease, replaced by a quiet sense of peace. And yet, a part of me still ached, still longed for the world I thought I'd left behind.

"You have more to do," Eleanor said, her voice pulling me back. "Your journey isn't over, Iris. The light chose to keep you because your story isn't finished."

I looked up at her, my chest tightening. "I don't understand. Am I… alive?"

"You are," she said with a nod, her smile softening. "And so is Felix. The two of you have more to fight for, more to protect. The world needs you, Iris."

A surge of warmth spread through my chest, the light around me growing brighter, pulling me upward. Eleanor stepped back, her form glowing more intensely now, blending with the golden expanse around us.

"Wait!" I called out, panic rising in my chest. "What happens now? How do I—?"

"You'll know when the time comes," she interrupted gently, her voice distant now, echoing as though carried on a breeze. "Trust yourself, Iris. You're stronger than you think."

The light engulfed me completely, and I felt weightless again, like I was being drawn toward something brighter, fuller, alive. And then, with a sharp inhale, the world shifted.

The first thing I became aware of was the light. It was soft, gentle, and unthreatening, casting warm tones against my eyelids as I stirred. My body felt heavy, the lingering weight of exhaustion pulling at me, but something about the atmosphere was different. The oppressive darkness that had gripped me was gone. The hum of the altar, the guttural roar of the shadows—it had all vanished, leaving behind an unfamiliar calm.

I opened my eyes slowly, blinking against the muted sunlight filtering in through wooden shutters. The space around me was small and unfamiliar, the walls lined with faded bookshelves and mismatched furniture that looked like it had seen better days. A faint scent of herbs and candle wax hung in the air, soothing and grounding despite the disorientation that clouded my mind.

I wasn't alone.

Jayce sat in a chair beside me, his posture tense yet steady, his dark eyes locked onto me the moment my gaze met his. He looked different than usual, less composed, like he'd been carrying a weight too heavy for even him. His shirt was crumpled, his sleeves rolled up carelessly, and his face was lined with worry—but when I stirred, his expression softened, a flicker of relief breaking through the shadows in his eyes.

"Finally," he murmured, his voice quiet but edged with emotion. "I thought you might never wake up."

I tried to sit up, but my muscles resisted, trembling with the effort. Jayce leaned forward, placing a hand gently on my shoulder to guide me back. "Easy," he said. "You've been out for a while. Don't push yourself."

His words made my heart race, confusion swelling in my chest. The memories came rushing back—the altar's glow, Felix's blood on the stone, the knife in my hand. My breath hitched as I fought to piece everything together, but the harder I tried, the blurrier it became.

"What happened?" I asked, my voice barely above a whisper. "Where am I?"

Jayce hesitated, his gaze lingering on mine before he spoke. "You're safe," he said, his tone measured. "That's what matters. We brought you here after…" His voice trailed off, and he sighed, running a hand through his messy hair. "After everything that happened in Carrow."

Carrow. The name sent a shiver down my spine, and the pieces clicked together in sharp fragments—the darkness swirling around us, the shadows recoiling in the light, the explosion of brilliance that consumed everything. My chest tightened, and I reached for the necklace instinctively, but my hand fell away empty.

"The altar…" I whispered, my voice trembling. "The darkness… it disappeared."

Jayce nodded faintly, his expression hardening for a moment before softening again. "It's gone," he said, "sealed along with Carrow. You did it, Iris."

His words carried a weight that settled heavily on me, but it didn't feel like victory. Something was missing. My throat tightened, panic bubbling up inside me as a name forced its way to the forefront of my thoughts.

"Luna," I said quickly, my voice cracking. "Where's Luna? Is she—"

Jayce's eyes widened briefly, his hand coming to rest on my arm to steady me. "She's okay," he said firmly. "She's recovering. There was chaos at the café when the shadows reached her, but it wasn't fatal. She got hurt—badly—but she's strong. She'll pull through."

Relief swept through me, sharp and overwhelming, and I sagged back against the pillows, my breath shaky. "She's okay," I murmured, almost to myself, letting the words sink in. "She's okay."

Jayce nodded, his grip firm but grounding. "We got to her just in time," he said. "The shadows didn't take her, Iris. She fought them off long enough for us to get her out."

My head swam as the relief settled deeper, though the ache in my chest remained. Luna was safe, but the world around me still felt unfamiliar, broken. The last thing I remembered was the knife in my abdomen, the blinding light, the overwhelming sense of loss—and yet here I was, alive, in a place that felt far removed from Carrow's maze-like prison.

I looked at Jayce again, his presence steady but unshakably distant. "What about Felix?" I asked, my voice trembling.

Jayce paused, his jaw tightening briefly before he sighed. "He's alive too. Hurt, but alive. He'll pull through, just like Luna. You both will."

His words carried a flicker of hope that warmed me despite the lingering unease. I didn't remember Eleanor or the conversation I had with her, but Jayce's reassurance planted a seed of resolve in my chest. Whatever had happened—whatever I had done—it had saved more than just myself. It had saved the people I couldn't bear to lose.

The warm light of the afternoon sun poured through the wooden shutters of the small room, casting soft, golden beams across the walls. The air inside was quiet, peaceful—a stark contrast to the chaos that had consumed us back in Carrow. My heart raced as I walked down the hallway, the faint sound of my footsteps muffled by the creak of the floorboards. Jayce had told me Felix was awake and that he was recovering well. I'd been reluctant to believe it at first, but now, as I reached the door, hope stirred deep in my chest.

I pushed the door open slowly, my breath catching as I saw him sitting upright on the bed. Felix was propped up against a stack of pillows, his bandages clean and neatly wrapped, his color returning to his face. His bright blue eyes met mine the instant I stepped inside, and the smile that spread across his face was enough to make my knees weak.

"Iris," he said softly, his voice steady but carrying the weight of emotions he couldn't quite put into words.

I hurried toward him, my chest tightening with a mixture of relief and joy. "You're okay," I whispered, my voice cracking as I sank into the chair beside him. My trembling hands found his, warm and solid, and I clutched them tightly, unwilling to let go. "You're really okay."

He laughed quietly, the sound light and familiar, like music to my ears. "I told you I'd be fine," he teased, his fingers brushing against mine. "I'm tougher than I look, remember?"

A tear slipped down my cheek, but it wasn't from sadness—it was the overwhelming relief of seeing him like this, alive and smiling. "Don't you dare joke about that," I said, my voice trembling. "You scared me, Felix. I thought I lost you."

His hand tightened around mine, his expression softening. "You'll never lose me," he said gently. "Not to the shadows. Not to anything. I'm always going to be here."

The warmth in his words settled into my chest, grounding me. For the first time since Carrow, I felt a flicker of peace—not just the absence of darkness, but the presence of something good, something worth holding onto.

As we sat in the quiet room, Felix shifted slightly, wincing faintly as he adjusted his position. He glanced at his hands, flexing them slowly, as though testing their strength. A crease formed between his brows, and he looked at me, a hint of confusion flickering across his face.

"Something feels… different," he murmured, his gaze dropping back to his hands. He raised one toward the light streaming through the window, watching as the soft rays illuminated his skin. I followed his gaze, my breath hitching as I noticed it—something subtle yet undeniable. His hands looked the same, but there was a new air about him, something tangible and yet almost imperceptible.

"Felix…" I whispered, my voice trembling. My eyes darted to his, wide with realization. "You're… you're human. Fully human."

His head snapped toward me, his expression shifting rapidly from confusion to disbelief. "What? That's not possible." He raised his other hand, inspecting it as though expecting to feel some residual trace of his immortality—the energy that had sustained him, forcing him through sleepless nights, keeping him alive but never truly whole. But it wasn't there. His skin wasn't as pale anymore. His form wasn't just flesh and bone—it was alive, full, something wholly natural.

I could see it in his expression as understanding dawned, the wonder that overtook him like a storm. His lips parted into the most brilliant smile I'd ever seen, and his laugh escaped before he could contain it—light, carefree, and real.

"I can't believe it," he said, his voice thick with emotion. "I… I never thought—" He stopped, his breath hitching as his smile faltered, giving way to raw disbelief.

Tears prickled at my eyes, and I reached forward, taking his hands again in mine. "This is it, Felix," I said softly, the lump in my throat making it hard to speak. "No more sleepless nights. No more fighting through hunger. You're fully human again."

Felix stared at me, his expression frozen in shock, before his gaze dropped to his lap. "I can eat," he murmured, his voice so soft I barely heard him. "I can sleep. I'm…"

I nodded, my tears spilling over as his joy mirrored my own. "You're free," I whispered, my voice cracking under the weight of the realization. "Carrow didn't just seal the darkness—it gave you your life back."

Felix's arms wrapped around me then, pulling me tightly against him. I buried my face in his shoulder, the warmth of his embrace, the steady rhythm of his breathing, filling every corner of my heart. We stayed like that, tangled in the weight of the moment, the world around us melting away until there was nothing left but the two of us.

When we finally pulled apart, his blue eyes were shining, his smile uncontainable. He reached up, brushing a tear from my cheek. "You did this," he said softly, his voice full of wonder. "Whatever happened in Carrow—it changed everything. It changed me."

I smiled through the tears, my hand resting over his. "No, Felix," I said gently, shaking my head. "You did this. You fought for me, for Luna, for us. You gave everything—and now it's finally yours to have."

"So this is what Eleanor meant," Felix murmured, his voice barely rising above a whisper.

I turned toward him, my brow furrowing in confusion at his sudden statement. "What do you mean?" I asked, disbelief lacing my words as I searched his face.

His eyes met mine, and for a moment, it was as though the entire room filled with light. Hope and happiness radiated from him, softening the sharp lines of his face. "After… that demon pierced me," he began, his voice faltering as he winced, a flicker of pain crossing his expression. He pressed a hand lightly to his abdomen, then took a steadying breath before continuing. "I heard her—Eleanor."

My chest tightened at the mention of her name, and I leaned closer, holding his gaze. "What did she say?" I whispered, almost afraid of his answer.

Felix's lips curved into the faintest smile, his eyes shimmering with something new, something profound. "'You can be happy now,'" he said, his voice soft, reverent. "That's what she told me. But I didn't understand what she meant. Not then." His gaze dropped to his hands, his fingers flexing as though testing their strength. "Now I do."

The weight of his words settled over me, and in that moment, something inside me shifted. This wasn't just a victory against the darkness—it was a second chance. For him. For us. For everything. I watched as Felix's faint smile grew, his whole being alight with the realization of what it meant to truly live. And for the first time, the shadow of Carrow felt like a distant memory.

The sunlight streaming through the window seemed brighter, warmer, as though the universe itself was celebrating the moment with us. Felix leaned back against the pillows, his smile lingering, his joy spilling over into laughter that made my chest feel light. And for the first time in what felt like forever, I felt hope—not just for the future, but for the here and now. Felix was here, fully alive, fully human—and he was mine.

The days passed in a gentle blur, each one blending into the next as Felix and I lingered in the quiet safety of the small house. The weight of what had happened in Carrow still clung to me, but it was lighter now—more a shadow of memory than the crushing burden it had once been. Felix stayed close, his presence grounding me in a way that words couldn't fully capture. Every now and then, I caught him marveling at the little things—how he could feel hunger grow, the pleasant exhaustion that came with finally being able to sleep, the odd joy in tasting food for the first time in centuries. His awe was infectious, and though my own heart was still heavy, I found myself smiling more often than I had in months.

It was Jayce who finally urged us to leave the house. He'd been splitting his time between checking on us and watching over Luna, and though he didn't say much, the lines of worry etched into his face told me everything I needed to know. Luna was still unconscious. Every day that passed without her waking made his voice sharper, his movements more restless. I knew how much she meant to him—and how much she meant to me. I couldn't wait any longer.

When the time came, Felix helped me walk to the room where she rested. My body had grown stronger with rest and care, but the emotional toll still weighed heavily on me. Felix's steady hand at my side reminded me I wasn't alone, and together, we followed Jayce down the narrow hallway toward Luna.

The door was ajar, the soft glow of candlelight spilling out into the hall. Jayce stepped inside first, his broad frame stiff with an anxiety he tried to mask. Felix and I lingered for a moment before following, and my heart clenched the moment I saw her.

Luna lay still on a low cot, her dark hair spilling over the pillow like a halo. Her usually vibrant complexion was pale, her lips colorless, her chest rising and falling in shallow, rhythmic breaths. Her arm was wrapped in clean bandages, a faint bruise visible just above the elbow, and her hands rested loosely at her sides. She looked fragile in a way that made my throat tighten, a stark contrast to the fierce, unyielding Luna I knew.

Jayce was seated beside her, as he had been every day since the battle. His elbows rested on his knees, his hands clasped tightly together as he watched her face like he was willing her to open her eyes. The flickering candlelight danced across his features, highlighting the tension in his jaw and the shadows beneath his eyes.

I stepped closer, my movements slow and careful, as if the smallest sound might disturb her. "How is she?" I asked softly, my voice barely above a whisper.

Jayce didn't look up right away; his gaze was fixed on Luna as he answered. "She's stable," he said, his voice rough with exhaustion. "The healers did what they could. It's up to her now."

Felix placed a reassuring hand on my shoulder, his warmth grounding me as I knelt beside Luna's bed. My fingers brushed lightly against hers, her skin cool to the touch but steady. A lump formed in my throat as I tried to find the words. "She's strong," I said quietly, more to myself than anyone else. "She'll pull through. She always does."

Jayce finally looked at me then, his eyes bloodshot but steady. "She fought like hell," he said, his voice thick with emotion. "Even when the shadows came for her, she didn't give up. She held them off long enough for us to reach her."

His words filled me with both pride and guilt. Luna had always been the one to shoulder the impossible and fight battles no one else could. She had saved us all, in her own way, and now she was the one who needed saving. I tightened my grip on her hand, willing her to wake up, to flash that confident, mischievous smile I missed so much.

Felix knelt beside me, his presence calm and steady. "She's tough," he said, his voice low but sure. "If anyone can come back from this, it's Luna."

I nodded, my tears threatening to spill as I leaned forward, brushing a strand of hair away from her face. "I should have been there for you," I whispered, my voice cracking. "But I'm here now, Luna. And I'm not going anywhere."

Jayce shifted in his chair, his shoulders sagging slightly as he sighed. "None of this was your fault," he said, his voice firm but not unkind. "She wouldn't want you to carry that."

I looked at him, his face worn but filled with the same hope I saw in Felix's eyes. It wasn't over. Luna was still fighting, and I would fight alongside her, no matter how long it took.

Felix reached for my hand, his grip warm and grounding. Together, we stayed by Luna's side, the three of us bound by the shared weight of what we had endured—and the unspoken promise that we would see it through together. As the soft hum of the room settled over us, I whispered a silent prayer to whoever might be listening: for strength, for Luna, for the future we all still had a chance to claim.

The days stretched on, slow and heavy, as we waited. The cabin remained steeped in quiet—too quiet. Every sound seemed magnified: the creak of the floorboards, the murmur of voices drifting through the halls, the steady rhythm of Luna's breathing. It was maddening, that oppressive stillness, like the whole world had frozen, waiting for her to wake. Even the sunlight streaming through the windows felt subdued, casting long shadows across the worn wooden floors.

Jayce rarely left her side, and his determination was an anchor for all of us. Felix and I tried to distract ourselves and keep moving forward, but every thought returned to Luna—to the unshakable question of whether she would pull through.

Felix had grown stronger in those days, his newfound humanity lighting him up in ways I'd never seen before. He laughed more and smiled more, savoring every bite of food and every quiet moment of rest. And yet, even his joy couldn't fully erase the worry that lingered between us.

It was late afternoon when the tension finally broke. The sunlight slanted through the windows, catching motes of dust as it filled the room with a warm, golden glow. Felix and I had just returned from the kitchen, the faint scent of chamomile tea clinging to the air, when we heard it—a sound so soft I almost didn't believe it.

A faint groan.

Jayce shot up from his chair, his broad frame tense and alert as his eyes fixed on Luna. Felix and I froze in the doorway, my heart pounding so loud it drowned out every other sound. Slowly, Jayce leaned over her, his hand hovering just above her arm as he whispered her name.

"Luna?" His voice cracked slightly, barely audible.

Her fingers twitched.

A gasp escaped me, my knees threatening to give out as I stumbled forward. Felix steadied me, his hand gripping my arm tightly as we watched. Luna's eyelids fluttered, her breathing hitching for a brief moment before settling again. And then, finally, her eyes opened—dark and unfocused at first, but undeniably alive.

Jayce let out a shaky breath, his hand covering hers as relief washed over his face. "Luna," he said again, louder this time, his voice trembling. "You're awake."

She blinked slowly, her gaze shifting to him, then to us. Confusion flickered across her features, followed by recognition.

"Jayce?" Her voice was hoarse, barely more than a whisper, but hearing it felt like a miracle.

Jayce nodded, his grip tightening around her hand as he smiled—a real, unrestrained smile. "I'm here," he said, his voice steady now. "We're all here."

I stepped closer, tears spilling down my cheeks as I knelt beside her bed. "Luna," I murmured, my voice breaking. "You scared us."

Her lips twitched upward in the faintest smile, her gaze locking onto mine. "I'd apologize," she rasped, her voice rough but laced with the same defiant spark I'd missed so much, "but I don't think it's my fault this time."

Felix laughed softly beside me, the sound light and full of relief. "You're as stubborn as ever," he said, his blue eyes shining as he leaned against the edge of the bed.

Luna's smile grew, weak but unmistakable, and she shifted slightly, wincing as she tried to sit up. Jayce was quick to support her, his steady hands guiding her carefully. "Easy," he said, his voice gentle but firm. "You've been through hell."

Her expression softened, her gaze lingering on him for a moment longer before shifting back to me and Felix. "What… happened?" she asked, her voice faint.

I hesitated, glancing at Felix before answering. "It's over," I said softly. "Carrow is sealed. The darkness is gone."

Luna's brows furrowed slightly, her gaze distant as she processed my words. Slowly, she nodded, a small exhale escaping her lips. "Good," she said, her voice carrying a weight that made my chest tighten. "It needed to end."

Her fingers curled weakly around Jayce's hand, her grip barely noticeable but grounding. "I guess I owe you all a thank-you," she murmured, her lips curving into a faint smile again. "For not letting me die."

Jayce shook his head, his voice steady and resolute. "You owe us nothing, Luna. You've done enough. More than enough."

Felix knelt beside me, his presence warm and reassuring. "It's not about owing anyone," he said, his voice calm. "You fought for us, Luna. You always do."

Her gaze softened, a flicker of pride breaking through her exhaustion. "Someone has to keep you two alive," she said teasingly, her voice still hoarse but brimming with the warmth we all knew.

The sunlight shifted, casting a soft glow over her face as we sat there, relief washing over us like a wave. The shadows of Carrow felt distant now, its echoes muted by the undeniable hope that filled the room. Luna was awake. She was alive. And for the first time in what felt like forever, the world seemed brighter.

The remnants of winter still lingered in the air, sharp and cool, though the first hints of spring were beginning to show. A faint breeze rustled through the bare branches of the trees, carrying with it the scent of thawing earth and distant rain. The park was quiet, its winding paths dusted with the last traces of snow, and the soft afternoon light filtered through the pale sky, casting everything in a gentle glow.

Felix's hand was warm in mine as we walked, his grip steady and grounding, our fingers laced together like they'd always belonged that way. I glanced down at our intertwined hands, marveling at how something so simple could feel so profoundly right. The mansion loomed in the distance, its stately façade softened by the haze of late afternoon, but neither of us seemed in a hurry to return. The silence between us was easy, punctuated only by the crunch of gravel beneath our boots and the occasional sigh of the wind.

I tugged at the edge of my jacket, pulling it closer as the breeze caught at it. The dark jeans I wore were comfortable but not quite enough to keep the chill out, and Felix noticed, his free hand brushing lightly against my arm as he slowed his pace. "You cold?" he asked, his voice low and filled with quiet concern.

I shook my head, a faint smile tugging at my lips. "Not really," I said. "The breeze is nice."

Felix's blue eyes lingered on me for a moment, soft and searching, before he nodded and turned his gaze back to the trees lining the path. The bare branches arched overhead, their intricate patterns silhouetted against the pale sky. He pointed out small signs of spring as we passed—a patch of snowdrops peeking through the frost, the faint buds forming on the tips of the branches. His joy was infectious, his newfound humanity making even the smallest things seem monumental. Watching him marvel at the ordinary was like seeing the world for the first time through his eyes.

Felix glanced at me, the corners of his mouth lifting into a small, contented smile. "You've been quiet," he said, his voice low, almost teasing. "Thinking about something?"

I shrugged, pulling my scarf a little tighter around my neck as the breeze caught at it. "Just... everything," I admitted. "Luna, Jayce, all of it. It feels like we've finally come out of the other side of something, but I can't quite figure out what to do next."

Felix nodded, his expression thoughtful as his gaze swept across the trees. "That's normal," he said. "After everything we've been through, it's strange to have... peace. You're not used to it."

"I don't know if I ever will be," I said quietly, my breath visible in the cold air. "It still feels fragile, like it could slip away if I'm not careful."

Felix's steps slowed, and he turned to face me, his bright blue eyes steady and warm. "It won't," he said firmly, his voice carrying a quiet certainty that I couldn't help but believe. "Not this time. We've earned this, Iris. And we're not going to lose it."

The weight of his words settled over me, grounding me in a way I hadn't expected. I smiled faintly, brushing a strand of hair from my face as I looked at him. "You're annoyingly good at saying the right thing, you know that?"

Felix chuckled, the sound warm and light, filling the crisp air around us. "One of my many talents," he said, his grin widening as he fell back into step beside me.

Eventually, we came to a small clearing, the remnants of a frozen pond glinting faintly in the sunlight. Felix stopped, his gaze fixed on the way the ice caught the light, a soft smile tugging at his lips. "It's beautiful," he said, more to himself than to me.

I watched him for a moment, the way the light played across his face, the way his expression softened in a way I hadn't seen before. The bruises and bandages were gone now, his strength fully returned, but there was something else about him—something lighter, freer. He looked whole.

"What are you smiling at?" he asked, catching my gaze and tilting his head slightly.

I shook my head, a quiet laugh escaping me. "You," I admitted. "You're… different now. In a good way."

His brows lifted, his lips curving into a lopsided grin. "Different how?"

"You're happy," I said simply, the words spilling out before I could stop them. "I don't think I've ever seen you like this before."

Felix's grin softened, his gaze holding mine. "That makes two of us," he said quietly. He shifted slightly, his hand squeezing mine gently, as though reminding me that he was really here.

"You make it sound like I saved you," I said, my voice barely above a whisper.

"You did," he said, his eyes shining with an emotion that stole the breath from my lungs. "In more ways than you'll ever know."

I looked at him, really looked at him, and for a moment, everything else fell away—the cold, the lingering tension, even the shadows of Carrow. The world narrowed to the space between us, to his warmth and steady presence, to the quiet certainty that we were finally free.

Felix stopped walking, turning fully toward me, his free hand reaching up to brush a stray strand of hair from my face. His touch lingered, gentle and sure, and I felt the world tilt slightly as he leaned in, his blue eyes locking onto mine.

I barely had time to breathe before his lips met mine, soft and warm and filled with a quiet, unspoken promise. The kiss was steady and sure, like the first rays of sunlight breaking through the clouds. For the first time in what felt like forever, everything felt right—no shadows, no whispers, just the two of us, standing together in the light.

When we finally pulled apart, his forehead rested lightly against mine, his breath warm against my skin. I opened my eyes to find him smiling, his blue eyes brighter than I'd ever seen them.

"Together," he said softly, the word carrying the weight of everything we'd endured, everything we'd fought for.

I nodded, my heart full, my voice steady as I replied. "Together."

The stars were beginning to appear, faint pinpricks of light scattered across the darkening sky. Felix laced his fingers through mine again, his grip sure and steady, and we turned back toward the mansion, the world settling into quiet peace around us. There was still so much to figure out, so much ahead of us—but for now, this was enough.

ACKNWOLEDGMENTS

Writing this book — my very first novel — has been one of the most challenging, rewarding, emotional, and surreal experiences of my life. There were days when the words poured out like a flood, and others when I stared at a blinking cursor for hours, wondering what I was doing. But through it all, I kept going — and I didn't do it alone.

To my dad — you're not here to hold this book in your hands, but your spirit has been with me through every word. I often imagined what you might have said, how proud you would've been, and how much you would've teased me about becoming a "real writer." You didn't get to see this dream come to life, but your strength and quiet wisdom gave me the foundation to chase it. You left the shadows behind, and now live in eternal light — but I carry you with me, always.

To Vanity, my best friend — you were the very first person to know I was even writing a book. Before it had a plot, a title, or even a clear direction, you were already cheering me on. Your encouragement in those early, uncertain days meant everything. You read the roughest of drafts without flinching, talked me through the self-doubt, and reminded me that the story was worth telling. I truly don't know if I would have finished without you.

To my husband, Jeremy — thank you for your patience, support, and those very convincing nods when I asked if you read the latest chapter. Even when you were clearly just pretending to read because reading isn't your thing, you never made me feel like this journey was mine alone. You kept me grounded, made me laugh when I wanted to cry, and gave me the space to create when the house was chaos. This book has my name on the cover, but it has your fingerprints all over it.

To my children — my loud, messy, magical toddlers — thank you for teaching me that time is precious and quiet is a myth. Writing this novel in the middle of spilled juice, cartoon theme songs, surprise diaper disasters, and snack negotiations was… let's just say "an experience." You made the process infinitely harder, but also infinitely more meaningful. One day, I hope you'll read this and see how much of my heart — and yours — is woven into it.

To my mom — thank you for being my constant. Your love, your strength, and your quiet belief in me have never wavered. You taught me what resilience looks like, and when I felt like giving up, I thought of you — and kept going. You've been my sounding board, my cheerleader, and my safe space. This book exists in part because you always told me I could do hard things.

To all my favorite people who got to read the earliest, most unpolished versions of this book — thank you for pretending the typos didn't matter, for texting me your favorite lines, and for helping me believe this could actually be something. You saw the rough stone before it was polished, and you treated it like a gem anyway. That kind of support is rare, and I'll never forget it.

Writing this book was a personal mountain, and now that I've reached the summit, I'm looking back with nothing but gratitude — for the people who lifted me up, the chaos that tested me, and the love that carried me through.

And finally, to the younger version of me — the kid who stayed up way too late with a flashlight under the blanket, devouring chapter after chapter, falling in love with stories and dreaming of one day writing her own...

We made it.

You were never silly for dreaming.

ABOUT THE AUTHOR

Veronica Hopkins is a lifelong lover of
stories and a first-time novelist who
finally turned a dream into reality —
often during nap times, late nights, and
moments stolen between the beautiful
chaos of family life. When not writing,
she can usually be found chasing
toddlers, geeking out, or getting lost in
yet another book. This is her debut
novel.